Doris Flies Solo

by

M. W. Arnold

Broken Wings, Book 6

Copyright Notice
This is a work of fiction. Names, characters, places, and incidents are either the product of the author's imagination or are used fictitiously, and any resemblance to actual persons living or dead, business establishments, events, or locales, is entirely coincidental.

Doris Flies Solo

COPYRIGHT © 2024 by M. W. Arnold

All rights reserved. No part of this book may be used or reproduced in any manner whatsoever without written permission of the author or The Wild Rose Press, Inc. except in the case of brief quotations embodied in critical articles or reviews.
Contact Information: info@thewildrosepress.com

Cover Art by *The Wild Rose Press, Inc.*

The Wild Rose Press, Inc.
PO Box 708
Adams Basin, NY 14410-0708
Visit us at www.thewildrosepress.com

Publishing History
First Edition, 2024
Trade Paperback ISBN 978-1-5092-5862-8
Digital ISBN 978-1-5092-5863-5

Broken Wings, Book 6
Published in the United States of America

Dedication

To all those brave women (and men)
who served in the real Air Transport Auxiliary
during World War Two

~

Simply put, thank you.

Chapter One

Sunday 30th April 1944

"I suppose it was inevitable Doris's farewell meal would be fish and chips," Nurse Grace Baxter managed to say. Quite a feat, as she'd just stuffed four fat chips into her mouth and was alternately panting and trying to suck in as much cool air as she could.

The lady of honor raised her head and jabbed a forkful of steaming hot fish at the nurse. "Fish 'n' chips, please get it right," she advised her friend, immediately shoveling in more fish and beaming all around.

"You were expecting something different?" Walter Johnson asked. For once, he sat on the floor between his wife's legs, instead of the other way around, leaning up against the armchair Doris occupied.

Doris lovingly ran her fingers through her husband's hair now, which was once more growing back. She was very happy he'd finally been allowed to remove the bandage he'd worn since being knocked out a few weeks back. For his part, Walter's face screwed up as the hand, quite normally for when she partook of her favorite meal, had been liberally coated in vinegar, most of which was now spread around his sparse follicles. Walter himself wasn't too keen on the condiment, though he put up with it because Doris loved it so.

Realizing what she'd done by the way his ears

twitched on their own accord, Doris picked up a damp tea towel—something she'd taken to keeping around for just these circumstances—and did her best to mop up the mess she'd made.

Ever so patiently, Walter sat stock still as his wife proceeded to make things ten times worse. He raised a silent eyebrow at Betty Palmer, owner of The Old Lockkeepers Cottage where the leaving party was being held. She shrugged her shoulders as if to say, "You should have learned by now." He shrugged back the reply, "I know, but what can you do?"

Doris had discovered a love of British fish 'n' chips, as she insisted upon calling it, nearly the minute she'd stepped off the ship which had dropped her off in Liverpool. The chap who owned the local fish 'n' chip shop made a very good living from the American alone, not taking into account his other customers, and from the amount Doris and her friends consumed, it was as well the meal was off the ration.

"Sorry, love," she told Walter, pecking him on the cheek. "I'll bet you're glad you won't have to put up with this malarky for a couple of weeks?"

Walter nearly twisted his neck out of its socket in his haste to face his American wife, "Don't you dare say that, not even in jest!" he firmly told her, scrambling up onto his knees. He took her least vinegar-coated hand in both of his and brought it to his lips, kissing each finger. "I'm going to miss you more than you can imagine."

Betty paused, a fat, greasy chip hanging off her fork. "We all are."

"Aww…" Doris smiled back.

"Yes," Betty continued, "with you gone, who's going to protect us from Duck?"

Doris immediately grabbed a cushion before thinking twice. Placing it back down, she savagely speared more fish. "If you weren't eating right now…"

"Betty would beat you to death with her cushion," Jane interrupted.

A frown upon her face, Doris stared at both her friends, then down at where her husband was smiling up at her in his best understanding way. "You're in agreement?" she asked.

Somewhat cautiously, Walter nodded. "If it's anything like nearly every other rough-and-tumble around here, I reckon the others would probably take Betty's side and gang up on you. Either that or push me in front of them whenever they go out, so I'm the first one Duck sees."

Doris paused in her consumption of her favorite food and looked around the room. Betty's front parlor was considerably larger than Ruth's just down the riverbank. Still, with all her friends gathered together, there wasn't much space, and the whiff of fish 'n' chips, together with copious amounts of vinegar, was making it more than a little stuffy. It also happened to be one of the hottest Sundays which June 1944 had treated them to.

Glancing down at her beloved husband, she noticed for the first time the small rivulets of sweat running down the back of his neck. "I think we need some fresh air in here," she announced and carefully balanced her food packet on the arm of her seat. Clambering over Walter, being very careful not to catch him on the head, she went and opened both front windows of the cottage. Almost immediately, she caught a breath of fresh air and hungrily took in a full lungful. "Should have done that a while ago."

Her best friend Penny Alsop appeared next to her and draped her good arm around Doris's waist. "Any of us could have done it earlier, but you thought of it," she told her.

The pair stared out the window for a few minutes, enjoying the early evening view over the river and, even more importantly, the chance for fresh air to fill their lungs.

Mary appeared beside the two. "Oh God, yes! Both my stomach and I love you and your obsession with your fish 'n' chips, Doris, but I think we really need to open the windows before we start. It is a little ripe in here."

Doris turned a frown upon her friend, "Afraid that's a new one for this Yank. Ripe? There's no fruit growing around here."

Betty now joined them, leaning out the open window a little before turning back to say, "In your everyday English, Doris my lovely, it pongs in here."

"Stinks," Jane added from across the room.

"It whiffs!" Grace helpfully suggested.

The door to the lounge opened to admit Ruth and her boyfriend, Matt. Both stopped dead in their tracks, their noses screwed up in distaste. "What the hell died in here?" Ruth demanded to know, whilst behind her, Matt was wafting the lounge door to and fro in an attempt to get some air circulating.

"How the hell could you lot not notice how bad it smells in here?" he asked before ducking into the hall to replenish his supply of decent air, reappearing after a few seconds, "and why has no one noticed before?"

Doris made a show of tipping her head back and taking in a very noisy snuffle, presently proclaiming, "I can't smell anything wrong."

Penny squeezed Doris's waist, telling her, "Considering the amount of vinegar you consume, I reckon you've destroyed most of your sense of smell."

"How's the arm today?" Doris asked,

Taking the hint, Penny retook her seat, picking up her supper before replying, "Fine, thank you."

"Would you like it to stay like that?"

"Doris!" Jane exclaimed, before seeing the look upon her face. "Okay, you're only joking, but bearing in mind how many scrapes you lot get into, please don't tempt fate."

Doris threw a salute her superior's way. "Message received and understood, Boss. Sorry, Penny."

Now there was some halfway decent air in the room, Ruth and Matt brought in their suppers and found space on the floor. Jane sat down next to Ruth, the owner and editor of the *Hamble Gazette*, the local newspaper. "Thank heavens you arrived when you did."

"Seriously, none of you'd noticed?" Ruth reiterated, spearing a sliver of moist fish.

All the permanent and semi-permanent residents of the cottage exchanged looks before there was a collective shrug.

"Well, I'd suggest that you all have nasal damage, not just Doris," Ruth told them.

After a few moments' silence, Doris, the architect of the subject, announced, "Ah, well, at least we paid an honorable price."

Walter leaned his head back and his wife automatically leant down to give him the expected kiss. "Don't ever change, love."

Jane tapped the side of her Guinness bottle with her fork. "Sorry to spoil things, everyone, but there's something I need to say to Doris whilst I remember, though you all would do well to listen. Very good, Doris, but you're not fooling anyone," Jane told the American, who'd leant forward, arms resting upon her husband's head. "This is serious."

At hearing these words, Doris relaxed her posture and, along with everyone else in the room, now gave her full attention to Jane. Well, not quite everyone. Unseen, Bobby, Ruth's beloved Cocker Spaniel, had crept into the room and, at that minute, was padding towards Jane's temporarily unguarded supper. Mouth wide open, he was about to snaffle a chip or, if he was particularly lucky, a part of Jane's fish. Ruth happened to notice him in the nick of time.

"Come here," Ruth told the furry felon. "I think you're going to be in enough trouble once we look in your kennel later, don't you? Do you really want to add pinching Jane's food to your list of offenses?"

For his part, Bobby looked with mournful brown eyes at the fish as Ruth pulled him down to lie beside her.

Jane knelt at his side and ruffled his head. "Enough with the eyes. I'm sure Ruth will agree you don't need fattening up."

"Quite true," the lady in question said, making a point of pushing Jane's supper a little farther back on her chair.

"Now," Jane said, straightening back upright, "where was I?"

Mary put her hand in the air. "You were about to tell Doris off before whatever event she gets up to!"

More than one person snorted their Guinness back down their nose, including a mortified Doris, who glanced down at her plate before shrugging her shoulders and tucking back in.

"Very good, and likely to be prophetic," Jane said.

"Hey!" Doris immediately protested, not that anyone actually voiced disagreement with Jane's statement, who waved away the words.

"Right. This Sunday, the last day in April 1944, will be our last full day where Doris graces us with her presence, for the next two weeks. As you all know, and heaven knows why, the powers that be have assigned our dear, calm, polite Doris to ferry a general—sorry, I'm not allowed to disclose whom—around the British Isles. All I can reveal is that this will be an incognito assignment, and the fewer the people which know about it the better."

"I suppose that means I can't write about it in my newspaper," Ruth moaned, before sighing when Jane merely nodded.

"Sorry, Ruth."

"Hey!" Doris suddenly said. "We were going to do an interview, weren't we, Ruth. Well, I guess we'll have to put that off until I come back."

"Interesting," Jane declared, raising an eyebrow. "I know I don't have any authority over you, Ruth, and I don't want to step on anyone's toes, but I'd really appreciate it if you'd let me read the article before you print it."

"I don't have a problem with that," Ruth replied. "Doris?"

Doris shook her head. "Me neither."

"Back onto what I was saying," Jane said. "So, Doris, no matter the provocation, or what mishaps occur—please try and keep them to the minimum—remember that you represent us all. Walter, Matt, you may not want to listen to this. There are still some men, particularly in the military, who do not understand the job we do, especially as women. You are going to be the face of all of us."

In a voice probably more serious than any of them had heard her use, including when saying her vows to Walter earlier in the year, Doris stood up and made eye contact with Jane. "Flight Captain Jane Howell, you have my word that I shall do everything in my power to be nothing but a good example for the Air Transport Auxiliary and, in particular, RAF Hamble."

As a demonstration of her appreciation, Jane brought herself to military attention, "That's all I can ask…plus, keep yourself safe and come back to us in one piece," she added.

"I will," Doris assured her, retaking her seat before bounding back to her feet. "I also promise that I'll have this general singing our praises so much he won't want to let me go."

Walter swiftly got to his feet and wrapped his arms around her. "Don't you dare. If you think I could live without you, Doris Johnson, then you'd be sorely mistaken."

"Quite right!" Mary joined in.

"You put him in his place!" Penny added.

"Hamble wouldn't be the same without you!" Ruth put in.

"It'll be quieter," Jane mumbled, earning herself a glare from everyone else in the room, including Bobby!

Chapter Two

Somehow, Bobby had contrived to have one ear erect, whilst the other was in its usual floppy style. The effect was one so sweet that none of the girls felt it within their hearts to tell him off, in spite of the ample evidence a search of his kennel had provided.

Penny dangled a piece of well-chewed silk which may once have been her lucky bra, whilst Betty tried to make the uppers of her shoe stick down.

"I guess it wasn't such a lucky bra after all," she decided. "What do you think, Bobby? Want it back?" she asked, waving the once very expensive item under Bobby's nose, who took a brief sniff before backing away with a small whine.

Ruth couldn't stop a burst of laughter. "I'm sorry, I'm sorry," she eventually managed to apologize. "We did find it at the back of his kennel under the remains of something furry, or which once was furry and which I don't want to speculate upon, so it must be pretty whiffy by now. I don't understand why he's stored everything here. It's not like he even sleeps in his kennel at night."

Before anyone could warn her against it, Penny had held it up to her face and taken a deep breath. Almost immediately, she dropped it to the floor, nearly ending down on her knees herself. Wafting a hand furiously before her face, she took in great gulps of air, and it was a good minute before she found her voice. All this time, her friends, after taking the precaution of dropping the remains of their previous treasures and nudging them back towards the kennel, simply stood around and laughed.

"You lot were a great help," Penny managed to choke out, glaring at them.

Mary was the first to recover. "Sorry, really! Only, from where we were standing, that *was* extremely funny!"

This only caused everyone else—apart from Walter and Matt, who'd chosen to stay indoors listening to the wireless—to once more collapse into fits of laughter which, after a bit of thought, Penny joined in. Only Bobby seemed above this childish behavior and, bored with his human companions, went off to snuffle beside the rabbit hutches. The rabbits, used to this invasion of their territory, merely turned their furry backs on him and carried on nibbling the grass from under their chicken wire runs.

Once everyone had recovered their control, it was agreed that all which could be done would be to place the recovered items in the rubbish bins. If even Bobby couldn't be bothered with wanting them back, there was little point in trying to wash and recover them. Nevertheless, when it came time for Penny to place her bra into the bin, Mary and Doris had to help her by peeling apart her fingers.

"How come you found it so easy to throw away your wedding veil?" Penny asked Doris.

"Are you kidding? Did you see the state of it? There's no way I'd be smelling that!" Doris told her, laughing.

Jane clapped Penny on the back as they went back

inside. "Seriously, you didn't want to keep that, did you?"

By this time, they were back in the kitchen and Mary was preparing the proverbial cup of tea. "Can I tempt anyone?" she asked.

"Yes, please!" came Matt's voice from the lounge.

Ruth shook her head. "I don't know how he does that. I swear he can hear a kettle being boiled from a mile away."

"But does he know how to boil a kettle and make a decent cuppa himself?" Mary asked, taking the kettle to the kitchen table and pouring its boiling contents into the large teapot.

Ruth took a seat, soon joined by the rest of the girls. "Very much so."

"Handy with his hands and can make a cup of tea. Sounds like a keeper, Ruth!" Doris said, waggling her eyebrows.

"More than you can do."

"My hands are skilled in other ways," she instantly replied, waggling her brows again very suggestively.

With perfect timing, Walter appeared in the doorway in time to hear every word his wife uttered and see her eyebrows dance. Hurrying to her husband's side, she quickly went on tiptoes to kiss his cheek before taking him by the hand and leading him to an empty chair at the table.

"Sorry, love," she told him, as his eyes gradually regained focus. "I keep forgetting. One of these days I'll turn into an English rose." She promptly sat down upon his lap, as was her usual custom, jarring Walter out of wherever he'd gone off to.

He must have heard what she said, though, as he

pulled her closer to him and reprimanded her. "Don't you dare! I've no idea what a beautiful American flower would be, but you're mine and I'd never ask or want you to change one jot."

It was a minute or so before Doris could find her voice. When she did, the first thing she did was to kiss him to within an inch of his life. "I'm going to miss you so much!"

Betty threw a slightly damp tea towel at the pair. "Well, we're not going to miss *you*, if that's how you're going to carry on."

"Hear, hear!" Jane backed her up, with the rest of the room joining in their agreement, including Matt, who now occupied the doorway into the kitchen.

"Aye, pack it in, lad," he told him. "You're going to make me look bad."

"No chance of that," Ruth said, though from the immediate blush which shot up to her ear tips, she hadn't meant to say them out loud. Busying herself with helping Mary with the tea things, she pretended she hadn't said anything, much to everyone's amusement, especially Matt's.

Nevertheless, he got to his feet and took the teapot from Mary's hands. "Allow me," he said in an excruciatingly bad attempt at an upper-class accent, and proceeded to follow his girlfriend around the table, pouring the boiling liquid through the tea-strainer into each cup.

Mary took a seat. "Yes, I can see what you mean, Ruth. He's a keeper all right," she said as the pair got to her seat.

As Ruth and Matt approached Walter and Doris, Doris hopped off her husband's lap and helped him to his feet. "If it's all right with everyone, Walter and I will have an early night."

Despite being married herself, Penny, whose husband was a Mosquito pilot in Bomber Command, could still be a little naïve. She glanced at her wristwatch and began to say, "It's only seven, a bit early for...oh!" she trailed off, her turn to be embarrassed.

"Make sure you're at the ops hut for eight sharp tomorrow morning with all your kit!" Jane shouted after the pair as they rapidly disappeared down the hallway and through the front door.

Once out into what was a balmy April early evening, Doris slowed to a steady dawdle as the pair linked arms and made their slow way along the riverbank. The newly married couple lived with Ruth at the cottage next door to Betty's. "Next door" was being a little generous, although it was the next one down the riverbank towards the local farm where both cottages bartered their chickens and rabbits for extra milk and butter. Riverbank Cottage was slightly smaller than The Old Lockkeepers Cottage and currently the pair's home, though they tended to spend more time around Betty's where most of their group lived. Currently, there were only the three of them in residence at Riverbank, with the arrival of two more being imminent—an old friend, Shirley Tuttle, straight from pilot training, and Penny's little sister, Celia It was likely to feel rather cozy, quite soon.

"I love this part of the country," Doris announced, breaking their companiable silence and resting her head against Walter's shoulder.

Her head moved gently as her husband took in a deep breath. "No arguments here."

Coming to a stop, Doris turned and buried her head

into his chest, worming her nose between the buttons of his white shirt to plant a kiss on his chest. "Let's stay here!" she announced.

Taken aback by this sudden announcement, Walter had to say, "What happened to not making any plans for after the war?"

Doris held up her left hand before Walter's eyes. "I'm not sure having your fingers crossed is complete protection, love," he told her with a small chuckle.

She turned a frown up at her husband, quite an achievement as she was looking at him upside down. "And why not?"

Swiveling her around, Walter relocked his arms around Doris's shoulders and leant down to plant a kiss between her brows. "Why not indeed. Never mind that. What brought on the sudden desire to settle down here? I'd have thought you'd be keen to get back to the States."

She appeared to give this some thought before admitting, "Yes, it would be good to go back for a visit, even though it's only been a relatively short period of time that I've been in England, but here seems far more like home than the USA ever did."

"Ever?" Walter asked, shrewd as always.

Doris shrugged her shoulders. "Oh, all right. Since Donald died, then."

Walter knew all about his wife's first husband and that he'd been killed in the Spanish Civil War, flying for the Nationalist side. "I thought so, and I understand, I really do, but surely some part of you misses it. What about your family?"

"Huh!" Doris snorted, burying her face in his chest so he had to concentrate hard to understand her words. "I didn't hear anything from them after I was disowned, and

I've had nothing from them since I've been over here. Believe me, they would not be a reason to go back."

"Fair enough, but why here?" Walter persisted.

This time, when she leaned back, Doris was able to give her husband the benefit of a full-on pout. "Oh, all right. Contrary to appearances, I like a quiet life—stop right there, Walter Johnson—yes, I like a quiet life, and you'd have to agree this would make a great place to bring up a few kids."

Walter's mouth opened and closed a few times, but nothing issued forth.

"I had a feeling that would shut you up." She grinned.

"Well, yes…sorry, you just took me by surprise. How long have you been thinking about this?" Walter finally managed to ask.

Extricating herself, Doris took Walter's hand and led him once more towards Ruth's cottage, "A while now."

As they opened the gate and hurried up to the front door, Walter was very glad no one was around to hear his "quiet" wife's final words to him as the door closed behind them.

"Come on, we need to get some practice in!"

Chapter Three

"Why's it always me?" Penny whined, taking a firmer grip of the tree trunk she was perched up that Monday morning.

"Aren't you glad we didn't trim those branches back, now?" Betty asked, eliciting much laughter from everyone bar Penny.

If looks could kill, the glare Penny threw their way would be considered a national secret weapon. Penny had been deep in conversation with Doris when they left Betty's a few minutes earlier, leading the way up the path and through the gate. In fact, she was so engrossed she failed to notice everyone else had failed to follow them through the gate. It was only when she heard the gate bang shut, closely followed by a loud and angry *Quack*, that she realized what had happened. Even as Doris made to dart in front of her, Duck side-waddled the American and made for Penny's ankles. She barely made it up the tree with her stockings intact!

"That was a very good test of your arms," Jane helpfully said, though her concern didn't match the twinkle in her eyes.

"Not sure they were quite up to this," Penny replied, wincing. She looked down at where Doris stood at the base of her refuge, Duck now safely gathered in her arms. "Doris, is it safe to come down? As I really need to."

Stroking the head of what everyone except Doris would still describe as a very angry duck—in everyone else's opinion, his normal state of mind—Doris looked up at her friend and, in deference to the obvious pain she was in, told her, "I've got a tight hold. Come on down." As Penny warily, and slowly, made her way back down to the ground, everyone was treated to Doris saying her goodbyes to her favorite feathered fiendish fowl. "Look at my friends," she said, turning to face everyone else, all still safe behind the gate. "They're your friends too. They won't hurt you. If you stop chasing them, you'll get plenty of strokes and a lot of fuss whilst I'm away," she added.

"Not sure I'd go that far," Walter made the mistake of saying a little too loudly.

"Except for that one," Doris immediately retorted, holding Duck up a little so he had a better view of her husband. "That one you can chase as much as your heart wishes."

Walter's face looked decidedly grey when he said to his wife, "And I thought you loved me."

Doris's head went from side to side as she replied, "You, Duck, you, Duck. It's a bit up in the air at this moment."

"Doris!" Jane said loudly, to get her attention. "We need to get to the station or you'll be late picking up your general. It's already a quarter to."

As everyone gaped in disbelief, Doris held Duck up to her face and pecked him on the beak. When she set him down, he gawked up at her, gave a soft *Quack*, and with a wag of his feathered tail waddled down to the River Hamble and jumped in.

"You can all come out now," Doris informed her

friends who, with more than a little wariness, did so.

Betty opened the gate and quite unceremoniously held Mary before her. Everyone else filed out in single file behind them, until they stood next to where Doris was taking a look at Penny's arms, checking she hadn't done any harm in her haste to get up the tree.

Quack! Quack! went Duck, paddling in slow circles beside them.

"He's not going to…I mean…he won't attack us again, will he?" Mary asked, a tremble in her voice and very aware of the firm grip Betty still had upon her and that everyone else was effectively using her as a shield.

"I think you got away with it," Doris informed Penny, "though it may be an idea to see if Grace can pop around tonight."

"I'll see the station doctor after everyone gets off," Penny told her, having seen the pointed look Jane was giving her. At hearing these words, the flight captain nodded her satisfaction.

Doris bent down and held out a hand towards Duck, who promptly swam up to her, investigated the appendage, and upon finding it empty of food, threw her a most indignant *Quack* and paddled off in disgust.

"Hmm. I'd stay away from him for a few days, if I were you," Doris advised them, standing back up. Not giving anyone time to contemplate this thought, she linked arms with Penny and led the way, "Come on! As Jane said, we're going to be late."

****

Though Jane had informed only the pilots, it appeared word of Doris's impending secondment had spread all around the station because, as soon as the group rounded the corner which led towards the ops hut, it seemed everyone who worked on base was lined up to wish her luck. At their head, Jane noticed the likely culprit.

"Mavis, aren't you supposed to be on leave for the rest of the week?" she asked her wee elderly mess manager.

Stood next to her with his arm resting gently upon her shoulder was a bear of a man in army uniform and the cannon badge of the Royal Artillery on his cap. As was usual, he threw a half-salute, half-wave at Jane, before speaking up. "Your pardon, ma'am. My mother knows, but she wanted to say her goodbyes."

Mavis elbowed her son, none too gently, in the ribs—though with the differences in their respective heights, any lower and he'd have been doubled up on the ground. "I'm not dead yet, our Ned." She glowered up at her son before softening up and telling Jane, "Meet my son, Edwin, or as he much prefers, Ned."

Ned, his ears red, shook the hand Jane offered while Mavis clapped her hands upon Doris's shoulders, bringing the American down to her eye level. "As for you, Yank, you behave yourself, or what Jane'll do to you will be the least of your worries."

Blowing on her hand, or what was left of it when released by Mavis's son, Jane told Doris, "Couldn't have put it better myself."

"You already have," Doris muttered, as she absently bent her head to give Mavis a quick hug and an even briefer kiss on the cheek. Hefting her bag—she'd allowed Walter to carry only the lighter of her bags—she strode off through the gathering throng, accepting a handshake here, a slap on the back there, the odd kiss on the cheek or even a simple ruffle of her hair. By the time the group made it to the hut, Doris looked like she'd been pulled through a hedge backwards.

"Well, so long as he's not expecting an immaculately coiffed pilot, this general won't be disappointed, "Walter remarked, earning himself a glare from his wife before she darted into Jane's office to use the wall mirror to put herself into a resemblance of order.

Whilst Doris was otherwise engaged, Penny rapped the side of her cup for attention. "All right, you lot, those of you supposed to be here, listen up. Jane needs to say a few things."

"Thanks, Penny," Jane said, as the chit-chat died down. "Now, as you all know, we've been running under strength for a while, especially since Thelma was…killed," she ended, with difficulty, needing to clear her throat. Once she'd recovered her voice, she added, "and Penny got herself injured again." Penny had to endure some good-natured booing from the direction of Jane's office here. "Yes, thank you, Doris. Hurry up in there, by the way! Where was I? Oh yes. With Penny out of the way for the next two weeks—don't even try to argue—and Doris taken away for that time, it'll mean everyone pulling together and getting on with the job even more so than normal. We're going to have long days, so I hope you all enjoyed that long weekend, as you won't be seeing another for a good while. There's a good chance we'll be working seven days a week soon. I'm sure you've all been keeping an ear to the ground, so you know what's coming, but keep it shut."

Ruth noticed that Jane was looking directly at her, now that she'd paused to make certain everyone was listening. "Yes, yes," she agreed wearily, "I know, but it still goes against my newspaper reporter's instincts, even after this long!"

"And we appreciate it. I appreciate it." Jane made a point of smiling at her friend.

"It definitely looks like we'll have to put off your interview for another few weeks, Doris," Ruth said as Doris finally joined them, wrapping her arms tightly around Walter.

Timing it perfectly, Jane told them, right after everyone in the group had let out a collective sigh, "Well, I can now confirm that could be on the same day Doris is due back. When's that again, Doris?"

"Monday May 15th, Boss," Doris immediately supplied.

"Yes, on that date," Jane continued, "not only will Doris rejoin our little circus…"

"Mystery club," Betty amended, curious to see what Jane would do.

With a small, perhaps reluctant smile, Jane went on, "Mystery club, but we should be joined by Sharon Coates." This news perked everyone's ears up. "So, Betty, Ruth, if one of you is still willing to take her in I—and I'm certain, Shirley—would very much appreciate it."

"As I'm the only one with some room, it'd better be me," Ruth told them.

"Right, well, we'd better meet up around your place soon to discuss it. Okay?" Jane asked.

"Fine by me," Ruth agreed.

Penny coughed and holding up an arm, tapped her wristwatch.

"Good point, thanks, Penny. As I was sure I'd get no end of moans from everyone if you weren't able to see Doris off, everyone flying today go over to the flight line hut and get changed. Meet us at dispersal. Doris's Anson should be all ready to go."

As Doris reached the door, leaving her bags with Walter, who'd finally persuaded her he could manage her two bags without collapsing—his having been knocked out twice in rapid succession had left his wife being, in his and everyone else's opinion, a trifle over-protective—she turned on her heel. "Won't this leave you a taxi short?"

"Don't worry about it," Penny told her. "It's all been taken care of. We've a new one coming in later today, so we'll be back up to strength before the day's out. Now, off you go," Jane instructed, making shooing motions.

****

Doris let out a long, loud whistle of appreciation before turning back to her audience, "Someone's been busy," she began, waving at some of the aircraft maintenance personnel gathered around. "I doubt if she's been this clean since the day she was built."

"No taking up a crate of beer in this one, please," the sergeant in charge said. "You were supposed to have cleaned up after the last time!"

Doris, Mary, and Betty exchanged guilty looks before Mary volunteered, "That must have been the part Doris said she'd clean."

"What did I miss?" Ruth enquired, whilst Walter shot his wife a curious glance.

Penny raised an eyebrow. "You didn't tell him?"

"It was a bit embarrassing, not to mention a total failure," Doris mumbled.

"I wouldn't say that," Jane put in, shaking her head. "That bottle which survived was the best beer I've had in ages—beautifully cold!"

Doris Flies Solo

Ruth and Walter rapidly put two and two together and could only stand there, shaking their heads. "Just how high did you go up?" Ruth asked.

Noticing that both Jane and Penny were paying full attention, Mary diplomatically replied, "A touch too high."

"Have you lot ever noticed how easily we digress from any subject we begin to talk about?" Jane asked.

At least no one disagreed with her.

"Back to this plane. Doris, as you can see, the ground crew have spent a long time getting it spick and span, and I'd like to get her back in much the same condition."

Doris reappeared in the doorway, having hopped on board to stow her baggage. "Clean aircraft, one piece. Got it, Boss." She grinned. Glancing at her watch, she jumped down from the doorway and grabbed hold of her husband. "Um, if everyone would turn their backs for a few seconds, I'd like to kiss my husband goodbye."

Barely able to speak for the grin on her face, as she couldn't believe the words she was about to say, Jane coughed and said out loud, as Doris and Walter wrapped their arms around each other, "You heard the lady, about turn!"

Chapter Four

"Pleased to meet you, General…Kinwen? So sorry," Doris hastened to add. "I'm no good at these strange Scottish names."

If she were expecting to be told off, she instead received a wry smile from the man in question. Taking off his peaked hat, he tucked it under the arm of a beribboned jacket. He must have a good dry-cleaner, she thought, as it appeared as good as new. "It's Welsh, actually, so don't let my mother hear you imply she's of Scottish persuasion, and it's pronounced *Kine-Wen* and spelt *C-e-i-w-e-n*."

"Kinewen," Doris tried it out for measure and was pleased to receive a nod of confirmation from the man. "Please, call me Doris," she replied, reaching for and taking the man's outstretched hand. Then, before she could stop herself, she put into words the first thought which had entered her head as she'd been introduced to the man. "You know, those newsreels don't do you any justice. You don't look anything like yourself in person—there's definitely less of the film star about you."

Next thing she knew, his aide-de-camp, a Major Newton-Baxtor, let out a loud cough, as he shot between the pair and ushered them apart, "That's quite enough of that, young lady," he began, twiddling the end of a rather wispy—compared to Ceiwen's very bushy—moustache with the hook he had instead of a left hand, not noticing Doris's interested expression. "From now on, you shall only talk to the general when addressed.

Shrugging her shoulders, Doris turned her back on the man—quite a simple accomplishment as he was a good half foot smaller than his general, and that man could only have been a few inches over six feet tall—and started back to her Anson, where a team of army privates were loading enough luggage for an expedition up the Amazon, let alone a two-week jaunt around the British Isles. From the look of it, none of them knew how to place things correctly so they wouldn't affect the plane's stability and center of gravity, something she intended to supervise.

Her thoughts were interrupted by an even louder cough from Newton-Baxtor. She turned, ever so slowly, and waited.

"It is customary, young lady, to salute an officer when the conversation is finished." He then stood there, arms behind his back, glancing between Doris and Ceiwen expectantly.

When Doris looked at Ceiwen, she could swear the man's lips were twitching in suppressed laughter. Well, if he thought that was funny… "I expect it is," she began, "only the thing is, I'm not in the Armed Forces, and we don't salute." She then turned back around and strolled towards the Anson to berate the loading crew. Behind her, she heard a short burst of laughter and knew it wasn't the ADC.

As she began to instruct the young men, rapidly persuading them to take out all the baggage except for her own, which, naturally, was stowed correctly, and then follow her directions for loading properly, she could almost sense the ADC's animosity towards her. Still, that was his problem. At last, everything was stowed to her satisfaction, and she let the men escape from her gaze.

Glancing at her wristwatch, she saw it was now approaching midday and they were due to take off for their intermediate stop of RAF East Moor, on the way to their ultimate destination of RAF Turnhouse near Edinburgh in Scotland, in about half an hour. She flipped over the page to see if there was any further information to be found there, only to find there was no page to flip to. This was frustrating, as when the ADC had met her upon landing at RAF Upavon, she'd hoped to be told what her purpose would be and what was expected of her. In no uncertain terms, though, he'd told her she was their pilot, and that was all. If there had been anything else originally on the clipboard he'd handed her with her flight instructions, it was no longer there.

With perfect timing, Ceiwen and his ADC approached her. Doris had to resist the temptation to stick out a leg as the ADC strode right past her to lean in through the open door of the Anson. She saw his head moving left and right and left and right again, before he turned back to face her. Doris couldn't see what he'd hoped to accomplish by the brief inspection.

"Where are the parachutes?"

With great force of will, Doris suppressed the impulse to tell him that there weren't any for passengers—it would have been worth the potential expression such news would bring to the man's face. She leaned past him and showed him that there was one under each seat. Normally, the Anson had a capacity of four passengers, but due to the amount of baggage her VIPs seemed to require, the left-hand seat directly behind the cockpit had been removed. Unless she was much mistaken, in its place was a record player, or as the British still often called it, a gramophone player, not that she'd ever understood if there was any difference, and a tea-chest nearly full to the brim with records.

"If that's coming with us, we'd better make sure those records aren't going to slip out. They're so delicate, they'd be sure to break if they hit the fuselage floor."

She felt someone rest their hand upon her shoulder and only just bit back a sharp retort as she saw it was Ceiwen. It seemed an awfully friendly sort of gesture, she began to think, before she reminded herself she was a civilian as well as a woman.

"I see what you mean, Doris," he added, before turning to his ADC. "Baxtor…" Doris was watching carefully and saw the man wince as Ceiwen failed to use his full surname. She also caught the edges of Ceiwen's mouth go up in amusement; it had been deliberate. "See if you can rustle up some cushions or padding of some kind. It'd be an awfully bad show if some of the general's records were broken."

Doris opened her mouth to comment on the strange way Ceiwen had phrased what he'd just said, only to change her mind. She sometimes had trouble with understanding what her friends said, so for all she knew, what she'd just heard could be quite normal for the British upper classes. She then had to stand and witness Newton-Baxtor approach one of the privates who'd loaded the plane and who'd made the mistake of standing to have a smoke beside the army lorry she'd seen them unloading into the plane. Where his fellows were, she couldn't guess. Either way, when he was still a good twenty yards from him, the ADC began to bellow at the top of his voice. In short order, the private had stamped his out the cigarette and come to attention, saluting smartly as the officer came to stand before him. Even from where she was at dispersal Doris could hear the man yell, though the only words she actually understood were "cushions" and "extra padding" before the poor man threw another salute and ran off in the direction of a hangar, no doubt cursing his luck.

"Likes the sound of his own voice," Doris muttered.

If she believed she'd said the words quietly enough, so no one heard her, she was wrong.

"Very true," Ceiwen agreed, though he kept his gaze upon his returning ADC. "Well done." He looked at his watch. "You did tell them to hurry? We're due to take off in about fifteen minutes. Punctuality is a byword," he ended, not that Doris recognized the phrase. It seemed Ceiwen liked to make up phrases, quotes and the like, as well as his other quirks. She'd have to be on alert, she noted to herself.

A few minutes later, the unfortunate young man the ADC had harangued hustled back bearing an armful of what looked like armchair seats. Doris hoped he wouldn't be around when wherever he'd acquired them from found them missing. Despite their prompt appearance, it still took around five minutes of fussing by the ADC for them to be placed to his satisfaction. When asked, Ceiwen merely glanced in the direction of the boxes before giving a single nod of the head. If they were her records, she'd want them to be secure, which made Ceiwen's nonchalant inspection of them a little strange.

he then surprised her by praising the young man

who'd ferreted out the cushions. "Good job, young man. Go and get a cuppa, then find the rest of your chaps and take yourselves off back to base." Reaching into an inside pocket, he took out a ten-shilling note and handed it to the bemused man. "Make sure you have a few drinks on me this weekend."

"Ten bob? Yes sir, General!" he practically shouted, before treating them to a textbook salute and about-turn before trotting off, undoubtedly towards the NAAFI.

"You, ahem, don't think you were...too generous, sir?" the ADC asked, running his hook inside the collar of his shirt, whilst throwing a glare at the rapidly receding private's back.

"What rot," the general replied, negating any further protests by saying, "Come on, we mustn't keep our pilot waiting," and he clambered up into the Anson with surprising agility for a man nearing seventy years of age.

The exact identity of her passenger had been kept from Doris until the moment she'd come to a halt on the remote hard standing she'd been directed to upon landing at RAF Elmdon, east-southeast of Birmingham, as near to smack in the middle of the country as you could get. At first glance, it appeared to be a strange place to pick up a VIP, the relatively new airfield being primarily used as a training base though, upon reflection, she thought while going through the preflight checks a nondescript airfield was the perfect cover. Who'd think anyone of any importance would ever want to go here? As she glanced over at the empty co-pilot's seat, she couldn't help but let out a sigh of disappointment. It would have been nice if one of her friends could have come along. Ah, well, she'd have to make do with Betty's latest Miss Marple book for company.

Having finished *Death on the Nile*, she'd been looking around for something fresh to help her through what she fully expected to be a very boring assignment, and her eyes had alighted on the latest Miss Marple, *The Moving Finger*. Judging by the position of the bookmark, Betty was only about ten or so pages away from finishing. Nonetheless, acting upon impulse, Doris swapped the dust jacket from the Hercule Poirot novel for the Miss Marple one and, before she could change her mind, had stuffed it—very carefully, as Betty loathed people who damaged books, a sentiment on which all the girls of the Mystery Club agreed—into her suitcase. She'd gladly take the telling-off Betty would give her when she got back, as she'd have finished the book by then.

After checking with the control tower that they were cleared for take-off, she taxied to the end of her designated runway. Turning in her seat as much as the restraints would allow, she raised a thumb at her passengers through the open door leading to the passenger area. Ceiwen reciprocated happily enough. His ADC, on the other hand, already had a hand over his mouth and looked quite green around the gills.

Releasing the brakes, Doris muttered, "Should have brought more sickbags."

Chapter Five

Her last words as she took off proved to be rather prophetic. Barely a half hour after taking off, their aircraft was hit by fierce wind shears causing their Anson to drop violently three times within the space of a few minutes.

"Buckle up back there!" she shouted, as she wrestled with the control wheel, fighting to regain lost altitude.

As she wasn't on a normal ferry or delivery flight, she was flying a good few thousand feet higher than normal, a bit under ten thousand, and had been settling in to enjoy a view she hadn't seen in a while. Thanking her lucky stars she hadn't run into the invisible phenomenon whilst coming in to land, or at her normal flying height of a few thousand feet, Doris wiped her brow and, once back on a level attitude, glanced back through the door at her two passengers. A mistake; very quickly, she wasn't the only one with a grimace on their face.

Just in time, she stopped herself from turning on the autopilot and hoped this pair didn't know the aircraft came so equipped. "Major! You should find some rags stuffed down the side of your seat. I'd use those to mop yourself up as best you can."

"Can't you keep this bloody thing straight?" the man blurted out, as he fumbled around in search of the rags.

Doris got as far as five before she told him, "If you

can predict what the weather's going to be like once we get airborne, you should…"

Ceiwen coughed to get everyone's attention and Doris let her tirade fizzle out. "Now, now, I suggest everyone calm down." He then directly addressed his ADC, who was now in the process of mopping up his mess as well as he could, given his disability. "Major, I did warn you about having a big breakfast before we set out. Perhaps sprinkle some water on yourself. Yes, you'll get wet, but it'll help with the smell."

The major opened and closed his mouth, as if to object to the words, but he wisely decided that not only was Ceiwen used to speaking his mind unworried about what other people thought, he was also right. He forced a smile as Ceiwen passed him a thermos.

"Hot water. Be careful."

Once the general had dealt with the immediate problem, he released his seatbelt and went to stand in the doorway to the cockpit. He placed a hand gently upon Doris's shoulder. "Young lady, perhaps you could be a little more understanding. I do not believe the major has ever flown before, and yes, I know you wouldn't be aware of that, but that shouldn't matter. Do we understand each other?"

Though it was against her nature to put up with people she considered pompous and self-righteous, and she believed the major belonged to both categories, she also realized Ceiwen was correct. Taking a deep breath, she half-turned in her seat and, by ducking down a little, was able to look back at the miserable-looking ADC. "Your general's right, Major. I'm sorry for being rude."

"Thank you, Doris," Ceiwen said, as his ADC didn't look like he was in the mood to say the words himself.

Doris Flies Solo

In all honesty, Doris couldn't blame him. If she were covered in vomit—including carrots, she noticed, though why someone would have carrots for breakfast was beyond her—she wouldn't be in the best of moods either. Checking her watch, she glanced out the windscreen and was gratified she was correct. "Cheer up, Major!" she shouted, Ceiwen having retaken his seat, "We're about twenty-five miles from York. That's about ten minutes. Hitting those wind shears has caused us to lose quite a bit of height, so we should be able to view the towers of York Cathedral very soon."

The major looked up from his ablutions. "I assume you're leading somewhere, Third Officer?"

Doris gritted her teeth again. If he persisted in calling her by her Air Transport Auxiliary rank, then they were going to have words. Probably, she mused, short and sharp ones from her end. This once, and because of the mess he'd gotten himself into, she let it pass. "I am. I'm telling you this because our stopover at RAF East Moor won't be long after. You can get yourself properly cleaned up."

"Excellent," was the mumbled reply.

Before she turned her head back, Doris saw Ceiwen waggle his eyebrows her way. She chose to interpret this as an appreciation for her efforts.

Soon after passing York, having resisted the temptation to circle its cathedral—she'd have to visit as soon as she could, as its magnificent beauty was unlike anything she'd ever seen—Doris began the laborious process of lowering the undercarriage. Nice and clean her Anson might be, but the undercarriage still had to be hand-cranked down. To accomplish this, there was a handle situated beside the pilot's seat, and one hundred and forty-four turns were required…not that anyone counted, merely listening out for a thunk noise to indicate it had locked down and then checked there were green lights on the instrument panel, slightly to the right of the compass before her right knee, to confirm.

From the corner of her eye, Doris could see that her efforts were being closely watched by both men, the ADC still with a disgusted expression upon his face. Doris let out a grunt and stopped to give her arm a quick shake. *Still, if I looked and smelt like he undoubtedly does, I'd probably wear the same expression.* As the airfield came within sight, the undercarriage locked down and she straightened up. Calling up the control tower, she felt a silly surge of satisfaction as she identified herself as *Firecracker* as she asked for and obtained permission to land. The call sign had been given to her by Jane—after much argument, she'd revealed—as she felt it not only suited Doris but would be easy to listen out for. Not strictly in keeping with security, but somehow Jane had got her way. Yet another example of Jane's uncanny ability to get things done. The Air Transport Auxiliary Mystery Club had long ago given up enquiring how.

With her airspeed down to a hundred miles per hour, she lowered the flaps and lined up on the center line of the runway. Either side of her, standing high and proud, were the four-engine Handley Page Halifax bombers of the airfield's resident bomber squadrons. Tail low, Doris brought the Anson down for a feather light landing. As the speed dropped, she was joined by a Jeep which signaled her to follow them, exactly as the tower had advised her to expect. Shortly, she pulled up to a halt next to what a board advertised as 432 Squadron RCAF.

"Cannucks," Doris muttered to herself in surprise, as she went through the shut-down checklist.

"What was that?" Ceiwen asked, appearing in the doorway as she shut the engines down.

Shrugging out of her harness, Doris clambered out of her seat as Ceiwen stepped back and over the covering for the wing spar, then allowed her to pass. Opening the door, Doris took a couple of deep breaths whilst trying not to be too obvious about it, as she'd got a lungful of the odor emanating from the ADC. Ceiwen must be made of stern stuff not to complain about that!

There was a reception committee waiting for them consisting of a young pilot officer, who snapped off such a sharp salute Doris half expected to hear the wind whistle past her ear, and a much older-looking warrant officer who, though standing to attention, appeared to be very amused by the antics of his accompanying officer. Behind him were four airmen in the uniform of the RAF Regiment, men whose job it was to protect the airfield from all manner of trouble, all with Lee-Enfield rifles slung over their left shoulders.

"General Ceiwen," the young officer pronounced perfectly (much to Doris's annoyance), his hand slapping down against his thigh with an audible thump, in contrast to his non-native accent, "I'm Pilot Officer Nail, 432 Squadron, Royal Canadian Air Force. Welcome to RAF East Moor, sir."

Doris stood to the side, stifling a smile, and let Ceiwen past. Once down the steps, he saluted the very nervous young man and then introduced his ADC. "Would you have somewhere the major could clean up? He had a, er, little accident on board."

If the pilot officer felt like smiling, the look of

embarrassment upon the major's face as he carefully made his way down the small ladder, a kitbag in his right hand, forestalled any impulse he may have had to make light of the situation. Rapidly turning a chuckle into a stifled cough, he stepped to one side, fell into step with the major, and told him, "If you'll follow me, sir, I'll show you where you can freshen up and change."

"Fifteen minutes, Baxtor," Ceiwen informed him.

Once the two left, Ceiwen strolled over to where Doris was standing on a small step she used to give cockpit windows a quick polish, whilst ground crew appeared and began the task of topping up the fuel tanks. The handbook said the range of an Anson was around six hundred and sixty miles. Prudence though, meant that the girls of Hamble's ATA always topped up when given the chance; this was no different. The encounters they'd had with the wind shears were still playing on her nerves and she needed some mindless job to help banish the memories.

"Johnson—" the general began.

"Please, General," Doris said, tucking the rag she was using back into a pocket of her flying suit, "if we're going to be stuck together for the next couple of weeks, I'd feel a lot better if you'd simply call me 'Doris.' You already have," she finished by treating him to a wide smile.

"Doris it is," he replied, smiling back.

Resisting the urge to sit down upon her step—civilian or not, the man had been nothing but polite to her, so far—Doris stood at a close-ish approximation of "easy"—or "at ease" as an American would say. "What's on your mind, General?"

"I simply wanted to congratulate you on your flying

skill today," he told her. "That was all."

Feeling herself begin to blush, Doris quickly reminded herself she was a happily married woman and that this man, with his Hollywood star looks and military rank and bearing, if he wasn't berating someone, he was flattering them. Not sure into which category she fell, she ended up stammering a thanks before saying to him, "Now, if you'll excuse me a moment, I'm going to make sure those erks don't splash fuel all over my wings."

Leaving Ceiwen with what was, unmistakably, his bodyguard, Doris went and positioned herself next to the chap operating the fuel bowser. Planting herself firmly in his view, she folded her arms and glared at the one who was holding the nozzle end of the hose, who up until then hadn't actually had a spillage; naturally, he now had one. Doris gave him her best glare and out the side of her mouth told the man next to her, "Make sure you clean up that wing before you go."

She received the usual combination of, "Yes, sir, ma'am, umm, officer…" and was pleased to hear that the confusion her job caused was multi-national.

Satisfied that he'd do her bidding, Doris went and joined Ceiwen whilst they waited for the return of his ADC. Taking advantage of there being merely the two of them—the guard didn't count, though the corporal in charge kept giving her a suspicious look—she came right out and asked, "So, why me? Why was I chosen for this duty, General?"

Her question seemed to unsettle him, for instead of his earlier appearance of being cool and collected, Ceiwen ran a finger around the inside of his collar as if he'd like nothing more than to undo the top button and loosen his tie. Again, rather strange behavior for someone of such high rank. As he shifted from foot to foot, Doris took the opportunity to take a closer look at this man. She knew his reputation, of course. Anyone who'd followed the war news over the last couple of years was well aware of who he was and what he'd done. His part in chasing the Nazis out of North Africa had earned him the personal gratitude of the King and, consequently, a space in the heart of every person in Great Britain. It didn't do him any harm that he was well known for having the best interests of the frontline soldier at the forefront of his mind, not to mention looks very similar to one of Britain's foremost movie stars, complete with moustache.

The appearance looked right, Doris thought, listening to the suspicious part of her mind, yet there was something…something she couldn't put her finger on, nagging away at her. Before she could risk putting her foot in it, the ADC reappeared from around the side of a hangar a hundred or so yards away and broke into a quick trot as soon as he saw them. The same suspicious part of her mind thought he'd noticed how uncomfortable his general appeared. Either way, within half a minute, he was by their side. Doris had to admire him. Though he was a staff officer, he obviously kept himself in trim—he wasn't even breathing hard.

"Can I help you, General?" he asked, not coincidentally placing himself between Doris and his charge.

"Ah, Baxtor!" Ceiwen said, unable to keep the relief from his voice. "Yes, perhaps you can. Doris here was asking why she was chosen for this assignment. If you would enlighten her." Finishing, he nodded at the pair before strolling away, trailed by the bodyguard, who were doing their best not to appear too obviously bored, to go and talk to the same young pilot officer from before, who'd been following the ADC; the man looked petrified at the prospect.

For a few moments, Doris could swear the ADC was muttering under his breath and looking blue murder at Ceiwen for requiring him to explain something to someone he very obviously considered below him in status. Nevertheless, after taking a few steadying breaths, the professional soldier he plainly was kicked in.

"It's quite simple, my dear girl," he began, with a careless wave of a hook, which came very close to clipping Doris around the ear, not that he noticed. "Wherever the general goes there are Movietone and Pathé camera and news crews. They all want their piece of him, and we thought that as we're going to be touring around for the next few weeks, we may as well show the unity between our two countries, and that's where you come in."

Slowly, deliberately, Doris took a couple of steps forward and unclenched her teeth and fists before replying. If the man had said those words to her in her hometown of New York, she wouldn't have done so. "Are you trying to tell me," she stopped for another calming breath, which didn't really work, "that I'm some kind of floozie? Only fit to look good in the background whilst you two prance around for the cameras? I'll have you know I've only run into one hill. One! And that wasn't my fault. I've the piece of paper to prove it."

By the time Doris drew breath, the ADC's expression had settled into a mixture of curiosity and incredulity. It had likely been a long time since anyone had dared use that tone of voice to his face, and it was clear he wasn't sure if he should shout back or consider his reply carefully. In the end, his mouth opened, his face turned puce, but no sound came out. For a few seconds, Doris thought his heart was going to climb up his neck and slap him out of his confusion—that, or he'd have a heart attack.

In the end, he had to physically take a step back, presumably to put some safe distance between them, though for whose benefit was up for auction. By then, he'd got his temper under control and seemed to be regarding her with a certain amount of grudging admiration. She really hoped there was more to their choosing her than what she'd just been told, because if that were it, then she had a good mind to make sure they had nothing but the roughest flights from then on. Her first inclination to leave them in the lurch was only that, an initial thought. Despite how she felt, she'd never backed out of any challenge in her life.

"My apologies, Third Officer," he began. "My words were poorly chosen and," he hastened to add at seeing Doris about to flare up again, "wrong. What I said was the cover story agreed upon by myself and the general's staff."

Doris couldn't help herself, she had to jump in. "Are those people idiots?"

"I'm beginning to think so." The ADC nodded, after making sure Ceiwen was out of hearing range and proving that there was a sense of humor hidden under the suit of armor he projected to the world.

Thinking about that, Doris wondered if the loss of his hand had something to do with his demeanor. She'd have to find a way to ask.

"Ahem," he coughed. "That's by the by. Obviously

they…we…were very wrong to make such an assumption about you, and I apologize, especially for my part. I'm not sure how to reply to the crashed into one hill bit, but as you're obviously still alive, I think we should let that lie."

There followed a Mexican standoff for a minute or so, before Doris finally said, "I'm not going to get anything else out of you, am I?"

The ADC shook his head, at least having the grace to look apologetic. "No, not yet. Don't shoot me"—he held up his arms to show he was getting to know the American—"but if you prove to me you can be trusted, I'll…think about telling you more than you strictly need for this job."

Doris only had time to raise a questioning eyebrow before he heaved his briefcase, which Doris had noticed never left his side, up and onto the wing of the Anson. Flicking it open, he quickly rummaged inside before producing a piece of paper, holding it steady with his hook as he handed it to her.

"What's this?" Doris asked, waving the paper at him, not having troubled to look at it.

He now took a fountain pen out of an inside pocket and also handed this to her before treating her to his own version of an evil grin. "Something I should have got you to sign as soon as I met you. The Official Secrets Act."

Chapter Six

Doris had read plenty of documents in her time, but the Official Secrets Act took the prize for the one coming closest to confusing her. Considering the normal way she and all Air Transport Auxiliary pilots faced flying a new aircraft type, this was saying something.

The Pilot's Notes they read, essentially their bible, could have been written with a child in mind compared to what she'd just been handed. Thinking about it, she absently sucked the end of the expensive-looking fountain pen the ADC lent her, not noticing the frown upon his face as she began to chew the end. That was the whole point of the Pilot's Notes. If they weren't simple, yet concise and containing all they needed to take off, fly, and land whatever type of aircraft they were tasked with, learning to fly it would take longer than the aircraft had taken to be built. The writer of the Official Secrets Act could learn a thing or two from their writers!

After finishing her reading, she signed, thankfully remembering to use her new surname, which she didn't always do, before handing the document back to the ADC. Carefully screwing the lid back on the fountain pen, she handed it to the owner. "Lovely pen," she said by way of passing, only to notice a mixture of sadness and anger flit across the major's face as he somewhat awkwardly took the pen in his right hand.

Brash, loud, outspoken, were all perfectly apt

descriptions of Doris Johnson. Patient, loving, understanding, could also equally apply and, despite their having locked horns since they'd met, Doris's natural curiosity and caring side made a sudden appearance, and before she could clamp her mouth shut, she blurted out, "You were left-handed!"

She got her answer when the ADC rapidly tucked his mutilated arm out of sight, in the pocket of his uniform jacket.

Maybe it was the sight of her face which openly conveyed her regret at the words, though she hadn't moved, or how she didn't cower from the lightning which threatened to erupt from his eyes at her words. Not for the last time, Doris suspected no one had spoken to him so openly in a long time.

Before he could reply, Doris had done some rapid thinking. "I'm sorry, ADC," she began, though immediately recognizing how ridiculous that sounded as soon as the words came out of her mouth. "Sorry, I won't call you that again, but I'm also not going to call you 'Major' or 'sir,' " she told him. She held out her hand and pasted her most honest smile on her face. "I'm Doris—just Doris."

Blindsided by her words, the major held out his good right hand and gripped Doris's, "Marmaduke Newton-Baxtor," he automatically introduced himself, though he immediately fought and lost a war to prevent the flush shooting to the tips of his ears.

Unfortunately for him, not only did Doris have excellent hearing, but Ceiwen was still out of hearing range and all was as quiet as a busy airfield could be. "Marmaduke? Really?"

The ADC shrugged his shoulders. "What can I say?

My parents hated me."

"And what do your friends call you?"

He didn't answer immediately and when he did, he couldn't quite meet her eyes, "Those who are left call me Duke. Though I'm not one. A duke, that is. Know a few, maybe a couple of decent ones amongst them."

Finally, he loosened his grip and Doris shook the life back into her hand. "Quite a grip you've got. You must've been training that hand up! So I can call you 'Duke'?"

After a moment's thought, during most of which Doris was certain he was playing with her, he nodded. Leaning against the fuselage of the Anson, he measured her up before finally asking, "Tell me, Doris, can anyone stay mad with you?"

As the tension between them faded away, Doris went and leant up against the port tailplane. "Not even my wonderful husband."

"Lucky man," Duke told her after a beat.

Doris held up her left hand to briefly flash her ring at him before nodding in agreement. "He knows it. Look," she then said, much more seriously, "I'm really sorry about the…well, the left-handed comment."

It took a few moments, but the man slowly extracted his hand from his pocket, bringing it up before his eyes, turning it this way and that before letting it hang by his side. "Not exactly a pretty piece of ironmongery, is it," he stated.

Now he'd broached the subject, in a way, Doris felt able to ask her question again, albeit phrased much better. "So, Duke, that's going to take some getting used to, I don't mind telling you," she put in, being rewarded by the ghost of a genuine smile. "Duke, what happened?

Did you lose your hand in the war?"

Duke opened his mouth but shut it as he noticed Ceiwen walking their way. When the general was about ten feet from them, he turned and instructed his bodyguard to stay where they were and, turning again, he approached the pair, coming to a stop beside his ADC.

"At ease, at ease," he told Duke, as the man began to straighten up.

"Yes, sir," the ADC replied. "What can I do for you?"

"I think it's about time we set off again, or we'll throw the whole schedule out." He addressed Doris, "That's correct? Doris?" He finished with a smile, the early evening light flashing off a gold tooth.

Doris frowned and went to speak, only to catch Duke vigorously shaking his head behind Ceiwen's back. Rearranging her features, Doris instead nodded and came to stand by the open door of the Anson.

"I don't know what the two of you were talking about, but that's the first genuine smile I've seen on his face since I met him," Ceiwen told Doris, keeping his voice soft and low, whilst patting her on the shoulder and following his ADC up the steps and back into the Anson.

As the ADC passed her, Doris momentarily looked up, told him, "Later," and got a brief nod in acknowledgement.

Taking her seat in the cockpit, Doris hoped her new friend understood her curiosity and that she had no other motive. To say she was happy with Walter would be an understatement. Having lost her first husband, Donald, in the Spanish Civil War—yet another example of humanity's (especially the males of the species) innate stupidity and willingness to kill and maim themselves over issues which could be solved by simply talking—love was the last thing on her mind when she'd decided to come over to England to do her bit for freedom. Yet, as always, it had hit her unexpectedly and harder than ever. She'd always have a very soft spot for her first husband, though she'd never forgive him his, in her opinion, stupidity and gullibility in dumping everything, including her, for a war in a country thousands of miles away, and then getting himself killed.

Walter, despite a certain ability to find trouble, something which she could easily sympathize with, was attentive, caring, and not afraid to show the world how much he loved her. She'd had a little trouble with men in the past when they'd mistaken the attention she paid to them for something else. Was it her fault she gave someone her full attention when she was speaking to them? Or was a naturally caring person? She didn't think the ADC—Duke sounded more like something you'd call a big dog, she thought—was in that category, though she'd make sure to be careful. No, he struck her as someone who hated himself, and she'd bet a great deal it all stemmed from when he lost his hand.

Finishing the preflight checks, she tightened her straps, straightened her flying helmet and, half-turning in her seat, shouted, "Everyone strapped in back there?"

Translating the incoherent replies as in the affirmative, she turned her full attention back to her job. As she pushed the throttles forward and released the brakes, Doris decided that perhaps this trip wouldn't be so boring after all.

****

A short while after Doris judged they'd crossed over into Scotland, she felt a tap on her shoulder, closely followed by Duke's face appearing above her right shoulder.

"Care for some company?" he asked. "The general's asleep," he added with a jerk of his thumb.

She waved him into the co-pilot's seat. "That would explain it."

"Explain what?" he asked, as he clumsily put the spare earphones over his head.

"I thought the engines were sounding a little rough," Doris told him. "Not bad, but I have been keeping an eye out for places to land."

Looking back into the fuselage, Duke let out a laugh, the first one she'd heard him utter. "He does sound a little like a hedgehog in heat."

"Not too sure what that means exactly, but I get it," Doris replied, after a moment's thought.

"Glad you did, as I really didn't want to have to describe it." Duke did have a sense of humor.

Those were the last words he uttered for the next twenty-odd minutes. Doris had decided the man simply wanted a companion who couldn't drone out a pair of Cheetah engines, until she heard a small cough and prepared herself. Which ADC would appear? The one called Duke, whom she was just growing to know before they took off, or would the man be back to the ADC, all business and a decided lack of humor?

"Do you know," he began in a voice which sounded more like he was speaking to himself than to her, "I can't remember the last time someone asked me about how I lost my hand."

"Really?" was all Doris could think of to say.

He turned his head to look at Doris. "Maybe I should have phrased that better," he decided. "I should have said, I can't remember when anyone asked me about it and was actually concerned, as if they wanted to know about…me."

Doris had to stop and think about this for a while before she felt able to reply. When she did, all she could think of to say was, "Well, we've got around another hour until we get to Edinburgh, and by the sound of things, we're not going to be disturbed by your boss. There should be a thermos tucked under your seat, so help yourself to a Bovril if you want. It'll help a bit against the cold."

When she'd called Ceiwen his boss, Doris thought she'd seen a puff of irritation pass before his eyes. At her mention of a hot drink though, whatever had been there swiftly disappeared and his hand disappeared beneath his seat. A moment later, he brought out a rather battered silver-colored thermos flask.

"This has seen better days," he observed, turning it every which way before tucking it between his legs, allowing him to keep a firm hold of it whilst he used his good hand to open the lid.

"Maybe," Doris agreed, briefly checking the compass and then altering their heading a few degrees, "but I've had that ever since I first learned to fly and won't be changing it any time soon." Their course now corrected, Doris turned her attention back to her colleague and didn't quite remember to issue a warning. "Careful!" she hastily half-shouted, eliciting a snort from the sleeping general. "It's either so weak you won't taste a thing or…"

She didn't get any further, and as Duke began to cough heartily enough to wake the dead—though not Ceiwen—Doris quickly unclipped her harness and began to hit the major between the shoulder blades. "Or it's so strong, we tend to use it as deicer," she told him.

After a few minutes, Duke grabbed hold of her hand to stop the beating. "Enough, thank you. I think I'm all right now." Looking at the remains of his drink, he hastened to pour it back into the thermos and placed it, somewhat warily, as if it might explode, back under his seat. "No guesses for which side that was on!" he muttered.

Now back in the pilot's seat, Doris apologized as she strapped herself in again. "Yes, sorry about that. We're used to it by now and can tell by the smell what kind we've got, so we know whether to knock it back or just sip." Knowing the impact the Bovril had upon the unwary, Doris gave him as much time as he needed to recover his breath.

"You know," he eventually said, "we should drop that stuff onto Germany. The buggers would surrender in a matter of days!"

This set them both off laughing again until Doris remembered the bottle of water she kept on the other side of her seat. She handed the bottle to Duke who, after glancing skeptically at her, took a tentative sip when she gave an encouraging nod, taking down half the bottle once he realized it was merely water.

"Thank you," he told her, wiping the back of his mouth with the sleeve of his left arm. "That's much better."

"Now you've recovered your voice, perhaps you'd like to share your story?" Doris prompted, adding a wistful smile of encouragement.

At her words, Duke brought up his left arm and rolled the sleeve back until the hook was fully exposed, including some metallic sheaf which Doris presumed covered his stump. "Pretty sight, isn't it," Duke stated, without a hint of irony.

Doris had led a reasonably sheltered life and even after two years of this war, more or less, the sight before her was one which threatened to set her stomach churning, and she was a little ashamed. She wasn't a fool and knew full well that men, women, and children were being killed at each and every moment, let alone becoming maimed, as this poor man before her bore witness. She wasn't going to say this out loud, though. With a firm and conscious effort, she forced the contents of her stomach to stay in place. Being the pilot, she could hardly pretend to be airsick.

"I've seen worse," she lied, feeling she had no other recourse. She then headed off a response by asking, "Does it work?"

Duke shrugged. "Well enough. I can pick things up and hold them, but my writing with my right hand is abysmal, compared to what it used to be like with my real left hand."

"What happened?" Doris asked once more.

Over the drone of both the Anson's engines and the now thunderous snores of Ceiwen, Duke began to speak. "Silly thing, really. You know all about what happened when the Germans kicked us out of France back in 1940?" She nodded, and he carried on with his story. "There I was, lining up on the beach outside Dunkirk and another Stuka targeted my column. Well, when you're neck deep in water, there's not a lot you can do. You can't run, so you either stood still and prayed, or you blasted away with your rifle or, in my case, revolver, if you had any ammunition left. I expect you can guess what happened next. I was pointing my revolver in the general direction of the dive-bomber when there was this almighty blast, and I was flung into the air. I can still remember the sight. As I went one way, I saw a hand clasped around a revolver going the other and hoped it had more luck than I had in hitting something. My next memory is being pulled up onto the deck of a destroyer, before I passed out again."

"That's...not a nice memory," Doris said, feeling rather inadequate once she'd found her voice.

Duke shrugged his shoulders, rolled the sleeve back down, and then gave her the saddest smile she'd ever seen. "I got off lightly," he said. Before Doris could ask how he could possibly believe that, he elaborated. "There were around a hundred and twenty of us in that line. Only twelve of us survived."

Doris blanched and had to work hard at containing the contents of her stomach once more.

He leaned towards her and then changed his mind, sat back in the seat and held out his hook. Barely thinking about it, Doris took the cold metal in her soft, real hand and squeezed, even though she knew he couldn't feel it. She saw him acknowledge what she did by the way his lips turned up once more.

"I don't suppose you're allowed to go into combat now?" Doris asked.

"It's not for want of trying. I want to get my revenge for all my comrades who died that day," he told her, "but it seems the Army thinks I can do more good with my brain than with a gun these days."

Doris felt the hook let go of her hand. Looking across, she felt there was something which drove this man to appear so cold, and she had to ask, "Was there someone...special?"

The staccato burst of laughter in reply provided half the answer. "There was, until she saw my stump for the first time, and then she couldn't leave me fast enough."

"And since?"

He shook his head. "I've not wanted to take the chance."

Doris glanced back through the door to make sure Ceiwen was still asleep before turning to face him and looking him firmly in the eye. "I think you should. When you're not busy snapping at all and sundry, you're a good-looking man with a lot to give."

Duke waved his hook in the air. "If I give any more away, there won't be much left of me!"

"Oh, very funny!" Doris said, though she didn't add her thought that, by answering as he did, he was only confirming her thoughts. "Want me to go for a barrel-roll?"

The major's hands went automatically to cover his mouth and stomach, though he did ask, "God, no! Can this crate even do that?" he found himself asking, not spotting the twinkle of mischief in Doris's eyes.

"I don't know. Shall we try?" she replied, turning back to her controls, a look of childish glee upon her face.

Chapter Seven

By the time all the arrival formalities had been completed, late afternoon was rolling into early evening and what the major described as typical Scottish weather was threatening to hammer down upon their heads.

"Major?" asked an Army policeman, who looked like nothing more than a brick outhouse in build, and not as handsome, snapping a salute off as he came up to him. "Sergeant Lewis, sir. I'm in charge of your escort up to the castle and for the two weeks of your tour."

Doris's ears prickled. "Did someone say 'castle'?"

It appeared the major had kept most of the good humor she'd seen make an appearance during the last leg of their flight, and he half-smiled whilst answering the sergeant, "Major Newton-Baxtor," as Ceiwen jumped down from the Anson and came over to them. The major introduced, "General Ceiwen, this is the head of our escort, Sergeant Lewis."

"Sergeant," Ceiwen said, after returning the NCO's salute. Turning to his ADC, he told him, "See to the loading of our luggage, will you? I need to have a word with our pilot. Third Officer?"

Curious, Doris followed Ceiwen around to the other side of her aircraft's nose.

"Thank you, Doris," he began, reverting to her first name now they were out of direct hearing of the others. Over his shoulder, Doris could see Duke had reverted to full-on command mode and was engaged in supervising a group of airmen in unloading the Anson and placing the items into the back of a Bedford lorry. This entailed a lot of shouting on Duke's behalf and much running around on everyone else's. Duke appeared most happy.

"Doris," Ceiwen began, lowering his head to minimize even further the risk of his words being overheard, "I wanted to thank you for the flight. It was most enjoyable, and I am so glad you decided not to try a barrel-roll." When he said the last words, not only did Doris go bright red, but Ceiwen appeared to very much enjoy saying them.

"You were, um, awake then?" was all Doris could think to say.

"For the last few minutes of your conversation," he confirmed.

"I wouldn't have really tried it," Doris assured him, before honesty won out "though I have to admit a certain curiosity. I'd like to know if she could do the maneuver."

"Well, do me a favor, and wait until I'm not on board," Ceiwen suggested, smiling.

Doris nodded her head. "Noted, General."

"Good, good," he said. "Now, regarding the major. I also heard what he said about what happened at Dunkirk." Doris waited whilst he formulated what he was going to say. "I've obviously read his file, so I know what happened. But that's black and white. It doesn't say what the chap's like now. I've learned more about what motivates him since you've been around, young lady, than in the two years he's been on my staff."

"Will you talk to him? About…this?" Doris asked.

Shaking his head, he replied, "Not unless he brings it up."

"I suppose it's silly to ask if he'll ever get back to the front line?" Doris ventured.

When he shook his head this time, Doris could tell the man was sympathetic. "Not unless we start losing the war again, no."

"Well, it's probably best to hope that doesn't happen," Doris stated.

"Very true. May I?" he asked, as he offered his arm to Doris. After a brief hesitation, she put her hand through the loop he made. They made their way toward the major and the sergeant, now waiting beside a…

"A Humber Box?" Doris exclaimed. "I've wanted to drive one of these for ages!"

All three men stared between Doris and the car she was staring at. "A what?" Duke asked.

The answer came from a most unexpected source. "It's officially called a Humber Heavy Utility," Ceiwen said as he stepped forward, raising a hand to stroke a round headlight mounted between the high covered bonnet and the mudguards. "It's based upon the civilian Super Snipe, only it's four-wheel drive."

Treating him to a suspicious look for this revelation of an unexpected knowledge of motor cars, Doris stepped up to join him, pulling open one of the rear doors. It unexpectedly hinged at the rear. "I love the suicide doors. Great feature!"

Duke appeared at Ceiwen's side and, leaning in, spoke into his ear words Doris couldn't hear. Whatever he said caused Ceiwen to pull at his collar in either discomfort or embarrassment, she couldn't tell which. Either way, he motioned for Doris to join him, which was when she noticed someone sat in the driver's seat. "Doris, I'm going to ask a favor. As well as being our pilot, would you also take over as our driver for the two weeks we're here?"

The sergeant stepped forward to ask, "Is there something wrong, General?"

Waving away the man's concern, he told him, "Nothing at all, and I'm sure that your choice of driver would do a fine, fine job. Nevertheless, I have my reasons for wanting my pilot to also drive us. During our trips, my ADC and I may have need to discuss certain things which would be covered by the Official Secrets Act, and the Third Officer here has signed that."

"As have we all, sir," the sergeant replied.

"Ah, good point and valid. My choice still stands. No disrespect meant to either you or your man, but I know and trust this young lady. Have him jump out and join the rest of the escort in the lorry."

After a few moments, the driver hauled himself out from behind the driver's seat and made his way over to the lorry. As he passed, Doris would swear there was relief upon his face.

"Well? Is this arrangement agreeable, Third Officer?" Ceiwen finally asked.

****

"I see you drive as well as you fly," Ceiwen declared, once he'd prized his fingers from the back of the passenger seat of the Humber.

"And as fast," muttered the major from where he sat, gripping the sides of his seat.

Doris had already hopped out and stood with her hands upon her hips, her ATA cap threatening to fall off the back of her head, as she turned around and around on the spot. "Wow! A real, honest-to-goodness castle! Don't tell my friend Mary, but this puts her place up north to shame! I can't wait to see it in the light of day! Is this where we'll be staying?" she asked, still turning around and around.

Supporting, though doing their best to appear not to be supporting each other, the two officers shared a look which could only mean they were wondering what they'd got themselves into, asking this American to drive them.

The ADC recovered control before Ceiwen. "Don't get any ideas. If you keep up that kind of driving, I'll make sure you have a nice room to yourself...in the dungeons."

"At least it'll be quiet," Doris replied, without missing a beat.

Ceiwen managed to coax his legs back under his control and took a few steps towards the middle of the courtyard so he could get a view of the gate through which they'd just come; it had been the only time Doris had touched the brakes in the whole journey. "I don't see our escort."

The major joined him, shaking his head, "I think our rebel friend…"

"I'm a Yankee, not a rebel," Doris informed them. "Be careful."

"As I was saying," Duke carried on, with Ceiwen also shaking his head now, "I think our Yankee friend here lost them sometime after she muttered, '*Let's see what this baby can do.*'"

"Wasn't that right after we turned out of the airfield?" Ceiwen asked, though the expression on his face showed he knew the answer already.

Doris appeared between the pair and narrowly avoided clapping both of them on the back. "Well, I can report that she's really cooking with gas, General." She beamed with pleasure.

"I assume that's good?" Ceiwen asked Duke.

"Doris?" Duke asked.

"Very much," she replied, turning to make her way back to the Humber, where she settled in.

She was shortly after joined by Ceiwen, who'd sent the ADC off towards the guard room to await the appearance of their escort and kit. "Doris," he said, clambering into the passenger seat, "I love speed as much as the next person but, if you would keep in mind, whenever we venture out, that we will have an armed escort and you have to allow them to keep up with us. I appreciate you'll find that difficult, but if you can't adhere to that one rule, then I'll have to change my mind and insist that you stay behind."

"Stay behind?" Doris asked, picking up on his tone of voice.

"By which I mean you will be confined to the castle and its grounds unless we are in need of being flown."

"Ah, that wouldn't be nice." She looked towards the gate where the lorry she'd left behind had just appeared.

"So, do we have a deal?" he asked, holding out a hand.

Doris took it without hesitation, noticing it appeared much younger than she'd have expected. Maybe it would be worth asking Ceiwen his skin-care secret? "You've got a deal."

When he didn't let go, Doris looked enquiringly at him, and he informed her, "I believe it would smooth things over with my guard if you apologized for speeding off. Don't you agree?"

As he squeezed her hand with a little more force

than before, Doris thought prudence would dictate agreeing with him. Forcing a smile from between clenched teeth, Doris told him, "I think that would be an excellent idea."

Promptly releasing her hand, Ceiwen clambered back out of the Humber, came around to the driver's side, and offered her his hand once more. A little tentatively this time, Doris took it, though she made sure to release it as soon as was polite.

Just as they were about to set out, they noticed the lorry had been waved through and was on its way towards them, with Duke standing on the driver's step and hanging onto the window frame. No sooner did it pull up next to the Humber than the passenger door was flung open and, before anyone could say anything, Sergeant Lewis was towering over Doris. It was obvious to everyone that if she weren't a woman he'd have been throwing punches at her.

As it was, he chose to vent his ire at her, leaving everyone within earshot—which could have included probably half of Edinburgh city—in no doubt as to how he felt "What the hell did you think you were doing? Do you bloody Yanks have any idea what a guard detail is for? Anything could have happened to the general, and the major," he quickly added, "during the time you decided to play at racing cars!"

"They are both armed," Doris felt compelled to point out, as the sergeant took in a great lungful of air.

This was a mistake, as both officers told her, "I don't know about the major, but I'd be more dangerous throwing my revolver at the enemy rather than shooting the thing," Ceiwen said.

"And I'm not as good with my right hand as I was

when I had my left one." Duke shrugged.

Doris turned her attention back to Sergeant Lewis, who now had his second wind. "Not much help, guys," she muttered under her breath.

Lewis seized upon the officer's words as a hungry dog would a bone. "You see! If I had my way…" he began to rant, only for Ceiwen to hold up a hand, stopping him in mid-flow.

"That will do, Sergeant," he told him. "I've already had words with the Third Officer, and she fully understands the error of her ways. Don't you, Johnson?" he prompted Doris with a slight jerk of his head.

"What? Oh, yes, of course," Doris couldn't help but say, before she recovered and pasted a most penitent expression upon her face. Using the opportunity to take a step back, she still had to look up before she could see the policeman's face, which didn't paint an encouraging picture. Nevertheless she persevered with, "Sergeant, I hope you will accept my apology for my actions. I can assure you, the general has spoken with me, as he said, and I know what I did was very, very wrong and I shall not act in the same fashion again." With no little trepidation, she held up her hand, fully expecting it to get crushed by the man's much bigger ones. She wasn't disappointed.

"Apology accepted, Third Officer Johnson," the man said, before releasing her hand.

Turning his attention back to the lorry, he began to bellow orders at the four men still in the body of the vehicle. At once, one jumped down and ran off to obey the order he'd been given to let Ceiwen's staff know he'd arrived, leaving the other three to unload and begin the job of stowing their gear and belongings.

Doris accompanied the two officers back to the Humber. Opening the tailgate, she heaved her baggage out and asked Duke, "Do you think he believed me?"

All three looked back over at the lorry, only to find themselves caught in the sergeant's gaze.

"As he looks like he wishes he could freeze your heart with one glare, I'd guess no," Ceiwen supplied.

Doris gulped and resolved to try and obey the instructions Ceiwen had given to her. It wouldn't be easy, but going on the way the sergeant looked at her just now, it would be conducive to her continued good health.

Chapter Eight

"Watch where you're going, miss!"

Not quite awake and intent upon searching out some breakfast, Doris had stumbled out into the castle courtyard only to be nearly knocked down by a passing ambulance which had sped from around a hidden corner.

Her savior in khaki released the hold he had upon her shoulders and patted her on the back. "Don't worry, that's only the early morning run from the camp."

"The camp?" she asked, wiping her brow in relief at the near miss.

"Donaldson's School Camp," he began, bending down to pick up his cap from where it had fallen to the ground. "It's a prisoner-of-war camp a little to the west of us. I expect it's someone who's managed to persuade the medical officer he needs a few days in a hospital bed. Still, can't say I blame him. Must be quite a boring life."

Doris only half heard what the young man said. She was staring in the direction the ambulance had disappeared and waiting for her heartbeat to settle down. Being killed by an ambulance in a castle wasn't the way she planned on going. To settle her mind, she forced herself to concentrate upon her surroundings. At a little past seven on a chilly morning, cold enough so she could see her breath before her face, the castle courtyard seemed full of men bustling back and forth, most heading in the direction of a door opposite her. Hedging her bets, she asked, "I don't suppose you know where the mess is?"

Smiling, the lance corporal—now her head was clear, she could see the single stripe upon his arm—pointed towards the same door she'd spotted. "Shall we?"

Nodding, Doris fell into step with the man. Glancing sideways, she noticed his uniform was of the usual quality issued to other ranks in the British Armed Forces; all sizes fitted no one, and as he was on the slight side of short, he really looked like a loosely filled sack of potatoes. Judging by his pimples, he couldn't be that long out of his teens. Realizing she hadn't given him her thanks, she held out a hand, happy to note it was quite steady. "Doris Johnson. Thanks for saving my life."

"Albert Miller." He shook her hand. "My pleasure."

"So, Albert, if you can tell me, what are you all? I've noticed you've all got the same cap badge, so I assume you're all in the same division, regiment, or whatever you Brits call it? Mercury, isn't it? The badge."

Reaching up, Albert tapped a finger to the figure. "If you're referring to this chap, meet Jimmy."

"Jimmy?" Doris echoed as they reached the door.

"Aye, Jimmy."

Doris went up on tiptoes and squinted at the badge. "Are you sure? Still looks a lot like Mercury to me."

"I know, and you are right."

"So why call him Jimmy?" Doris was like a dog with a bone—once she got her teeth into something, she stuck with it.

"Well," Albert said, scratching the back of his neck, "the story I've been told is he's named after a bloke who boxed for the corps in the twenties. Very good, from all

I can gather."

Doris contemplated her reply before saying, "Seems as good an explanation as any to me…and what do you do?"

"Royal Signals. And as for the rest, if I told you, I'd have to kill you," Albert told her, his voice all mock-serious as he waggled his eyebrows at her, totally ruining any effect he was going for.

Waggling hers back, Doris informed him, "That makes two of us."

Albert left one eyebrow where it was. "Well, as I reckon we've both signed the same document, I guess we'd better leave it at that."

"Very sensible. Albert, you're a wise man."

Immediately she finished, her stomach gave a loud growl, reminding her she hadn't eaten the previous evening. She'd spent the time helping with moving everything to where it needed to go, and by the time they'd finished, she'd had just enough energy to find her quarters, which were in what had been the old servants' quarters in the castle's attics, and there to flop down on her bed. She'd been sound asleep before she knew it.

"Er, before we go in, are you sure you're in the right place?" Albert asked, grabbing the handle and causing a queue to rapidly form behind them.

"It's too bloody early to be playing silly buggers! In or out, but make up your mind. Some of us are 'ungry!" someone from near the back of the queue shouted.

"Hold onto your horses!" Albert yelled back before saying to Doris, "Your uniform. Aren't you an…officer?"

Sensing they wouldn't be too popular if the two stayed where they were, Doris stepped to the side, drawing Albert with her. She drew curious glances as the bunch of breakfast-seeking soldiers sped past them.

"I see what you mean," Doris agreed, not needing to know what he was referring to. There was no doubt that her smart not-quite navy-blue uniform looked very out of place amongst the khaki jackets of these men. "Actually, I'm a civilian and as no one's told me otherwise, shall we go inside? I'm starving as well," she finished, holding the door open for her new friend.

****

Not unnaturally, where Doris and Albert chose to sit down became a magnet for every squaddie who fancied himself as a ladies' man, much to the amusement of the lady in question. Albert looked a little over-awed by it all and nearly managed to slop his tea over the tabletop once they'd collected their porridge and hot drink from the servery. Fortunately, he saw the funny side when she asked if he was always so clumsy.

"Only in the presence of beautiful women," he stammered, managing a grin.

Doris got to her feet and stuck her left hand under his nose and then waved it around so everyone else who had now congregated around the table could see, "Beautiful, thank you, but also very, very happily married. Are we quite clear, gentlemen?" she asked, raising her voice, so everyone in the room could hear.

Glancing around the room before she sat back down, she noticed a small table, in the far corner from her, which seemed to be composed entirely by Auxiliary Territorial Service girls, or ATS for short. More than one of the six at that table gave her a thumbs-up sign, which she acknowledged with a nod before taking her seat. From the many attentive looks she was getting, none quite veering over into a leer, she wasn't certain her message had gotten across. Still, she was sure she could handle anything that came her way.

She decided to continue the conversation she'd been having with Albert, even though her friend had picked up on the tension radiating from her.

"I know you can't tell me everything, but I've got to ask, what's a Yank doing way out here? I see the wings on your jacket. Are you a pilot?"

"Blimey! Things must be bad if we need women to fly for us!"

"Shut your mouth, Mike!" Albert surprised her by snapping. The man in question happened to be a bruiser of a bloke, at least six and a half feet tall and seemingly as wide. His face looked like it had repeatedly run into a brick wall, so crisscrossed with scars it was, whilst his nose was a squashed, misshapen stub of a thing.

"'Ere, no need for that, Albert," the man said. "The lady knows I was only joking."

The look Doris was getting from him sent a shiver down her spine, and if her senses weren't already telling her to steer well clear of this man, she'd have been worried. Vowing to listen to her senses, she was about to give him a piece of her mind when Sergeant Lewis appeared in their midst.

"Put your eyes back in your head, Garner. You wouldn't know a lady if you saw one." With no further preamble, he leant down so his head was at Doris's level and, keeping his voice as low as possible—every other man at the table was doing a poor job of pretending not to try and listen in to what was being said—told her, "We've been looking for you everywhere, Third Officer Johnson. Come with me, now," he finished and stood glaring down at her.

Deciding that to go with him now would complete any debt of apology she owed him for yesterday, Doris picked up her cap, donned it, and pushed back her chair. "Nice to meet you, Albert," she told her friend. Looking around the table, she quickly found the one who looked like he was chewing a bee. "Gentlemen," she finished before following the policeman out of the room.

Acutely aware of the eyes of the mess following her as she went, she wondered what stories would soon be going around about this strange Yank in their midst. No doubt by the time she next made an appearance, she'd either have been unmasked as a Nazi spy, worked for MI5 or MI6, or some other wildly implausible scenario. She was quite looking forward to finding out the details.

Sergeant Lewis didn't slow up until he came to a stop beside the same Humber and lorry they'd all arrived in the previous day. Waiting for them was Ceiwen, looking relaxed and more out of uniform, taking into account the rumpled grey jumper he was wearing and the cap on his head instead of the more usual officer's hat he'd worn the day before. Duke stood next to him, looking much the same, other than he'd swapped his full ADC jacket for an army battledress blouse and he'd kept his normal hat. Whereas Ceiwen appeared more than a little relaxed, Duke looked on edge.

Indeed, it was Duke who spoke first, as soon as the sergeant had prudently ushered the guard detail to the other side of the lorry, nominally out of earshot.

"Where were you this morning, Doris? We were waiting for you to appear in the officer's mess."

At least they were still on first-name terms. She did her best not to sound confrontational. "No one mentioned I should dine there last night, nor breakfast there this morning, not that I know where it is anyway."

Looking very much like he suspected he knew the answer already, Duke asked, "So where did the sergeant run you to ground?"

Doris jerked a thumb over her shoulder in the vague direction she'd come from as she replied, "The Other Ranks' Mess."

As Duke's eyes went wide, Ceiwen let out a loud guffaw of laughter. "Oh, I'd like to have observed that!"

"Well, your sergeant interrupted, just as the conversation was getting interesting, so you didn't miss much," Doris replied.

Duke held up his left arm between the pair and tapped his wristwatch. "We need to be leaving or we'll be late. Doris, if you'll take your seat?"

As she went to clamber into the Humber, Ceiwen waited for Duke to settle into the back seat before laying a hand on her shoulder. "Remember what we discussed yesterday? Must I remind you?"

Though there was no smile on his face, there was still that hint of amusement behind Ceiwen's eyes, almost as if he thought of everything as part of a big game. The more she thought about these times, the more she was sure something more was going on than was out in the open, and she'd have to get to the bottom of it. The only questions were "how" and "when."

Nevertheless, she nodded and told him, "No need, General. I'll play nice."

Duke looked as if he might say something before closing his mouth and looking around, as if for something with which to tie himself to the seat.

Noticing, Doris turned her head and smiled. "Sorry,

if you're looking for something to make sure you won't bounce out. You'll just have to trust me."

Demonstrating his sense of humor was still present, Duke held up the arm with the hook. "I'd appreciate it. I don't have that many more body parts I can spare."

Ceiwen clapped him hard upon the shoulder. "Well, well, I do believe there's hope for you yet, Major."

Chapter Nine

Though she'd signed the Official Secrets Act, Doris was still no clearer on what it was Ceiwen was in Scotland to do. It had seemed far away to her friends when they'd discussed this secondment before she'd left. Yet the trip up to Scotland had seemed like a mere afternoon jaunt to Doris, compared to the long distances that were the norm if you wanted to go anywhere in her native United States. Rarely had she ever driven anywhere over three hours away from New York, preferring to either fly or take the train., as being cooped up in an automobile for any longer than that was usually enough to put her into a rather bad mood.

Perhaps it was the spectacular scenery which prevented the boredom and the bad mood from occurring. Or maybe it was the snippets of information with which Duke had peppered their journey. When they passed the sign for BannockBurn, he'd begun a very eloquent description of what he said was a famous battle between the Scots and the English way back in 1314. When he'd mentioned the Scots' leader was called, Robert the Bruce, she'd nearly swerved off the road and, for once, it was Ceiwen who asked her to concentrate on the road. Until then the general had been content to sit quietly beside Duke. Doris made a mental note to visit the site of the battle if she had the chance.

They were approaching the city of Stirling now, and

she was enjoying the scenery. Although the general didn't ask his ADC to discontinue his commentary, Duke had chosen to be silent since their near crash. As most of her deliveries were to airfields around England, the scenery didn't change much, at least in her opinion. New York was an urban sprawl, punctured by looming concrete-and-glass mountains, and there wasn't anything similar in England that she'd seen. Now, she was beginning to see hills larger than most she'd come across lately, and she was enjoying them immensely. Hopefully, she'd get the chance to take her Anson over them soon! If only she could have had a camera handy. Mind you, if she had and she'd whipped it out anywhere near the sergeant or his men, she had no doubt it would be taken from her in an instant.

She slowed a little as they came into the city. Duke perked up again and leant over the back of her seat to direct her towards Stirling Castle. It was as well he was reading from a list in his hand, as there were no signposts around. This still slightly amused Doris. At the height of Hitler's power, just when there was a distinct probability the country could be invaded, the order to remove all the country's signposts had gone out. Even now, when the tide of the war had turned and there no longer seemed even a possibility of invasion, they hadn't gone back up. Knowing the British, she thought they'd probably all been burned for firewood.

Soon, she found herself driving up a busy street, busier than she would have expected at just past ten in the morning. It was obvious that, like Edinburgh, Stirling was untouched by the devastation wrought upon much of England's cities and towns. She wasn't sure she'd ever get over the first time she saw bomb damage upon disembarking at Liverpool docks and during her time looking around that city before catching a train south to the beginning of her adventures with the Air Transport Auxiliary.

Pulling up to let a couple of little old ladies cross the street, their wicker baskets full of whatever the ration was able to provide, yet with the reasonable smiles of thanks-for-stopping of those whom the war had left relatively untouched, she let her mind turn to her first visit to London. She'd wondered how anyone could have lived through the bombing the place had suffered, and here she was, on the same small island, and apart from the military striding up and down the street wearing different uniforms, things had probably changed little in a few hundred years.

She continued driving and before long was parking outside the impressive walls of Stirling Castle. Feeling a little conspicuous in her ATA uniform, Doris decided that as part of her duties she may as well open the doors for her passengers. The good thing about suicide doors was that you didn't need to move much to open them. So she hopped out and pulled the back seat's door open as she walked past. Ceiwen climbed out of the back of the Humber, nodded to Doris in thanks, and she promptly shut the door on Duke's leg.

"Oh, hell! Sorry about that," she said, hurrying to pull the door wider and allow Duke to actually get out. "I was expecting you to wait for me to open the other door," Doris explained as he bent down to rub his leg.

"Are you all right, Baxtor?" Ceiwen asked, bending down and clapping the man upon the back, a look of concern upon his face.

Doris joined them, though she did manage to stop

herself from also rubbing the poor man's leg.

Duke looked up from under a pain-furrowed brow. "I thought I'd mentioned I was a little short on limbs?"

"I really, really am sorry, Duke," Doris muttered, getting to her feet and taking a few steps backwards to allow the man to stand up and flex his leg.

"I'll live," Duke shortly told her, reaching back into the car to retrieve his briefcase. "Shall we go, sir?" He addressed Ceiwen. "They'll be waiting for us and," he added with a pointed glance in Doris's direction, "the walk will do my leg good."

Not really knowing why, Doris put up her hand. "What should I do?"

"Here's where, if you'd joined us for breakfast, as you should have, you'd have known," Duke told her, wincing a little as he tried to stamp some life back into his leg.

Taking advantage of not being in the military, Doris retorted, "If you'd have told me last night where I was supposed to have breakfast, I wouldn't have to ask!"

"Enough, you two," Ceiwen told them. "Doris, please join us. It took a bit of persuasion…"

"A bit? More like being browbeaten," Duke muttered behind him, though not without a smile upon his face.

"Yes, well, never mind. You're covered by the Official Secrets Act and, more to the point, I trust you. Now, shall we?" Ceiwen turned to address Sergeant Lewis. "Sergeant, if you'd detail two men to guard our vehicles? Everyone else, follow me."

After going through a number of security checks, none of which seemed to know what the ATA was and required an explanation from both Doris and Ceiwen, really annoying her, they found themselves in a large, rectangular room deep inside the castle. From its size, Doris guessed it could have been a dining hall, which was soon confirmed by Duke, who was turning out to be a font of knowledge and insisted it was more correctly called the Great Hall. Their escort had been instructed to wait outside the room, which currently was outfitted with row upon row of desks, most of which had military radio sets upon them and were manned by army men of various ranks. Peering closely, once she'd torn her eyes away from the ornate wooden-beamed ceiling and the high-set windows, it was plain to Doris from the same cap badge adorning their headgear, that these men were from the same branch of the army as her new friend Albert.

Tapping Duke upon the shoulder, she asked, "Signals?"

"That's right," Duke had time to confirm before he knocked upon the only other door in the room, immediately pushing it open.

Not a hundred percent certain but inclined to follow until told otherwise, Doris followed the pair into the room, just making it before Duke shut the door behind her. It was obvious that this wasn't an original room, as the walls on two sides were the same stone as the rest of the dining hall, with the remaining two being obviously temporary wooden structures. Already on his feet behind a small desk was a lieutenant, the same cap badge upon his hat, which hung on a nail behind the door.

"General Ceiwen, I assume," the junior officer said, snapping to attention. "I was informed you'd be coming along today. Please, take a seat," he invited, motioning to the two chairs before his desk.

"Lieutenant, good to meet you. Quite the spectacular

office you have here," Ceiwen said, taking one seat whilst Doris and Duke looked at each other, having a silent discussion as to who should take the remaining one.

"Duke?" Doris said, forgetting she should address the major by his military rank.

"Doris, please?" he replied, pulling out the chair and slightly forcing her hand.

"Doris? Duke?" the lieutenant said, raising an eyebrow.

"It does sound a little like a comedy double act," Ceiwen blurted out, earning himself a look from the pair before Doris allowed herself to laugh.

"I hadn't thought of it but you're right…sir," she remembered this time, taking the seat with a nod of thanks.

"Forgive me for saying, sir, but the…young lady?" the lieutenant asked.

Ceiwen peered at a name block on the desk. "I'm going to ask a favor of you, Halifax." He took a document from his inside pocket and shoved it in front of the man. "Read that, please."

It only took a minute for the young man to finish. Then he pushed it back to Ceiwen, who folded it and placed it back from whence it came. "And what can I do for you?"

"Whilst we 'show our faces' around the room, I'd like you to call every unit on that list and make them aware of who this young lady is. Please tell them that when she is with either myself or my ADC—or both of us, for that matter—she is to be accorded the same respect as the two of us. That's not to say she should be allowed to ask questions of the men, nor to wander off."

He added these latter two whilst looking at Doris, so she understood she wasn't to disobey or disrespect his orders. Doris nodded, keeping her face as serious as she could.

If he thought the order a strange one, Halifax had the good sense not to say so out loud. "Very good, sir," he said, obviously doing his best to portray professionalism. "Is there anything else I can do for you?"

Standing up, Ceiwen shook his head. "I don't think so. I'll take a turn around the room, speak to some of your chaps, make sure they know how important what they're doing is for what's to come. Scribble down each name on that list whilst we wait, then destroy it once you've finished," the general told him. "We'll wait whilst you do so." After a minute or two, Halifax pushed the letter back a final time. Ceiwen held out his hand. "By your leave?"

"If you'd let me know when you're leaving, sir, that's all I ask."

After handshakes had been exchanged, the three exited the office, with Doris closing the door behind her. Quickly, she tapped Duke on the shoulder. "How's the leg?"

"Sore, but I've had worse." He smiled, actually waving his hook in the air. Whilst Duke went to speak to some men at the far side of the room, Ceiwen gently took hold of Doris's arm. "Seriously," he leant in to whisper, so only she could hear, "I don't know what you've done with him, but he's so much more relaxed since you came along."

"Only too glad to help," Doris replied.

Hanging close behind him, Doris listened in as Ceiwen moved from man to man, telling each a variation on the same thing: "Keep up the good work; it may not seem it, but you're playing a vital role; excellent job, soldier!"

Having met up somewhere around the middle of the room with Doris still no clearer on what was going on, the two prepared to follow Ceiwen out of the office. Halifax chose that moment to come out of his office and, seeing the three, made his way quickly over before coming to attention before Ceiwen.

"Everything to your satisfaction, sir?" he asked.

Very eagerly, maybe too much so, Doris mused, Ceiwen nodded. "Absolutely!" He'd opened his mouth, though what was about to come out was pre-empted by the major coughing and raising an eyebrow.

"Sir..."

"Ah, quite right. Thank you, Major." He turned his attention back to the lieutenant. "How are you getting along with those phone calls?"

"About a third of the way through, sir. I should have the rest finished by the end of the day," he added.

"Excellent, excellent," Ceiwen gushed once more, shaking the man's hand and then turning to make his way towards the exit.

Slightly caught off guard, Doris and Duke hurried to catch him up. Picking up their escort, the group made their way back to where they'd left their transport.

"Sergeant," Duke turned and addressed the escort commander, "I believe it's time for some coffee. I take it you brought along the good stuff?"

The mention of the magic word "coffee" instantly gained Doris's attention, as it had been a week since she'd run out of hers at home, and the chance to have a cup was just what she needed. "Did someone say coffee?

You do mean real coffee? Please, don't tease me!"

Instead of saying anything, Sergeant Lewis went to the cab of the lorry, opened the door, and reached up inside. Turning back to her, he proudly held up what was unmistakably a bag of coffee.

"Yes!" Doris crowed, punching the air and, completely on impulse, ran up to the man and kissed him on the cheek. "I am so pleased I made peace with you!"

"You did?" he replied, completely straight-faced, causing Doris's expression to fall before Lewis broke into a grin, unable to tease her any longer. "Come on, give us a hand with the water, and answer me one question and we will be okay."

"Anything," Doris declared, going around to the back of the lorry and accepting a water container.

Holding the precious coffee before Doris's nose, he asked, "Before I came into the mess this morning, what did you tell those lads about yourself? Also, did you say anything about the mission?"

Doris was pleased to be able to put his mind at rest. "Only that I was a pilot, and I didn't even tell anyone that, they deduced that much from my uniform," she told him. "As for anything about the mission? I couldn't have, even if I'd wanted to. I still don't know what this is all about!"

Lewis frowned. "But you've signed the Official Secrets Act?"

"So I have," she agreed, with a wry chuckle. "Doesn't mean I know anything about this all." She turned to address Ceiwen, who along with Duke had joined them. "What do you say, General? Care to brief me? I presume these chaps know what this is all about?"

Ceiwen exchanged looks with Duke, who after a few

seconds began, "Sergeant, if you and your men would start boiling the water, I'll take care of the briefing. Follow me, please, Doris."

Safely ensconced in the back of the Humber, Duke told her, "Right, yes, you've signed the act, but I still need to warn you that what I'm about to tell you goes no further. You will not discuss with anyone, including your husband and your friends. I don't care how close you are. They do not need to know. Understood?" Doris nodded, knowing and treating this as the serious matter it was. "Good. We are doing a tour of what is known as the Fourth Army. This is a virtually entirely fictitious outfit, though some of the units are genuine. The men you saw in the castle today? They're all part of a deception plan called Operation Fortitude North, to convince the Germans that the upcoming invasion will be elsewhere than where it should logically fall."

"You mean, France? And shouldn't Ceiwen be telling me this?"

"That's what an ADC does—takes care of the briefings, amongst many other things."

"Okay," Doris said, though she couldn't help but take a look outside in the direction of Ceiwen before returning her attention to Duke.

Duke nodded. "The general is principally responsible for the sending out and receiving of wireless traffic from various units. The Germans will intercept the messages and hopefully put two and two together and come up with four, but only the kind of four we want them to. That's all you need to know. I could tell you more, but the least is always the best, plus, I couldn't tell you everything even if I wanted to. Even I know only what I need to do my job."

"And Ceiwen?" Doris needed to ask.

"Ah. Along with your General Patton, Ceiwen is the one man the Germans admit to being afraid of, so we're allowing him to be seen up and around here. The Fourth Army is based at Edinburgh Castle. Hence we'll be going back there most nights, but the more he's seen out and about amongst units which we've let the Germans believe are based up here, we're hoping to convince them that the invasion will be anywhere but France."

"You mean, Norway? I know my geography, Duke, so don't look at me like that," she told the major.

"Like…you said," he admitted. "There's enough real units up here that the Germans have come up against before and which they have respect for, so that will also reinforce their belief that he's going to be in charge of our main invasion force. You're a very intelligent woman and I'm sure I don't need to tell you a deception story must be believable, verifiable, executable, and consistent."

The major stopped talking and sat back, watching the various emotions flit across the American's face.

Finally, she let out a long, low whistle. "That's a hell of a ruse you're hoping to pull off!"

More serious than she'd yet seen him, Duke nodded. "If we succeed, we could save thousands of our troops' lives."

Without hesitation, Doris held out a hand, her face just as determined. "Then let me know if there's anything I can do to help. Anything!"

Chapter Ten

"If I buy you a cup of the best coffee I can find, will you please stop moaning?" Exasperated, Duke toyed with the idea of opening the window but quickly decided against it, as Doris kept speeding up and he had to constantly tell her to slow down so they didn't lose their escort.

She was now half-turned around in the front seat as she complained once again. "It's going to be a long time until I can get that taste out of my mouth!"

"I know, Doris," Duke repeated, finding he had depths of patience he hadn't previously been aware of.

"You had my hopes up, you know. Real coffee, you said. Ha! Bloody instant in a real coffee bag. That's just being mean," she added, before having to apply both hands to the steering wheel to avoid knocking four innocent Lumber Jills off their bicycles into a ditch. She waved a blasé "Sorry!" out the window as they sped around the corner.

Duke peered out the rear window and was witness to the girls treating their pursuing escort to a wide range of gestures, none of them suitable to innocent ears or eyes.

"As I've tried to tell you, a few times now," he muttered, not quite under his breath, "I hadn't opened that bag, so I didn't know I'd been had. I bought that bag—for an extortionate amount, I'll have you know—

specifically because I knew you were American and I wanted to be able to provide you at least one of the comforts of home. So, please, once again, accept it was a mistake."

This time, Doris didn't immediately reply, though the word "bagel" was heard but didn't make it into what she said. "Aw, hell!" she eventually cried, nearly sending her passengers' nerves into overdrive by throwing both hands off the steering wheel as she spoke. "I'm sorry. If you'd told me that bit about buying it especially for me, I wouldn't have been such a pain in the ass."

"Really?" Ceiwen asked this time.

With her head half over her shoulder again, Doris could only shake her head. "Maybe not. Look, if you want to change drivers, I'll understand."

Becoming aware that Doris had slowed right down and the faces of their escort, which had once again caught them up, appeared to be showing less sign of stress or desire to murder the resident American, Duke risked leaning forward, his elbows on the rear of the front seat. "That's at least twice you've offered to be replaced. We can, if you really want. It's not a duty. You do know that."

"The major's right," Ceiwen, put in, putting down a copy of the *Daily Record* he'd had his nose in since they'd set off from Stirling. "We asked if you'd drive us, as we quickly came to realize you're a woman of action, and I suspect you get bored easily. I don't think it would have been good for the health of Edinburgh if you were left to find your own amusement when we didn't need your piloting services though, if you really wish, we can replace you."

Displaying that the two were correct in their

assessment of her character, Doris swiftly replied, "No way! I mean, no thanks. I'm quite happy driving. So," she said turning her full attention onto the road, the same one they'd taken that morning, "are we off anywhere else today?"

As seemed to be usual, Ceiwen let his ADC answer for him.

"We're off to Linlithgow Palace…"

He didn't manage to get any further before Doris interrupted him, jerking the wheel hard to the right, only managing to keep them on the road with difficulty. "A palace? Really? Like Buckingham Palace in London?"

"Eyes on the road, and please calm down," Duke requested.

"Right, right," Doris muttered, swearing under her breath as she wiped an arm across her brow. "Bloody roads are so narrow up here!"

"I'll have you know that this is most certainly not narrow, Doris," the major told her. "In fact, you may not have noticed, but this is the main road between Edinburgh and Stirling."

"Really? I thought you were taking me by the scenic route!" Doris replied, managing to keep her attention on the road with some difficulty.

"Er, no, nothing like that. Anyway, as I was saying. We've only one more stop today."

"This *palace*!" In interrupting Duke, she managed to make every letter sound like it was a capital, such was her excitement at going to a palace.

Ceiwen laid a hand upon his ADC's shoulder. "Suppose we don't spoil the surprise?" he suggested.

If Doris could have seen the slight smirk upon Duke's face, she'd probably have been more suspicious of what was to come.

About fifty minutes later they arrived at the town of Linlithgow and Duke directed Doris to take a left, over the railway tracks, and soon they were passing a loch on their left, the late mid-afternoon sun reflecting gloriously off its surface. Even nature's beauty paled into insignificance as they passed what still advertised itself as St. Michael's Parish Church on their right, before going through what Duke described as "the Fore Entrance," which looked like a mini-medieval castle to Doris. The next thing she saw was a magnificent stone building, obviously much older than Buckingham Palace, yet despite its location away from the main towns and cities it seemed eerily quiet.

As she looked around, their two vehicles at first appeared to be the only ones around. It wasn't until she stared harder at her surroundings that she began to make out various military lorrys and cars amongst the trees, all very well camouflaged. Opening her door and climbing out, she opened the rear one whilst continuing to look around. That was when she saw two soldiers appear from the side of the impressive entrance they'd just come through. Unlike the ones she'd been around lately, this pair were in full battledress, each toting a Sten gun. Neither appeared to be about to open fire on them, though. Meanwhile, from a smaller version of the entrance they'd driven through, this one built into the palace itself, a uniformed man hurried towards them, arriving as Ceiwen and his ADC were stretching out the kinks in their backs.

"General Ceiwen, sir! Captain McSwain, at your service. Glad you didn't have any problems in finding us," the man said, snapping off a salute which was promptly returned.

The formalities over, Ceiwen and Duke exchanged hearty handshakes with the captain before a slightly less sure hand was offered to Doris, her Air Transport Auxiliary uniform once more proving a curiosity. With that explained, Ceiwen turned his attention to the captain's original question.

"None at all," he assured him. "In fact, if the major here ever gives up the Army, he could make a very decent living as a tour guide."

"I'll second that," Doris agreed, "though I'd like to see how he does without his direction notes," she added, smirking as Duke quickly reached back inside the rear of the car to stuff those notes back into his briefcase.

With his briefcase now safely clutched in his hand, Duke asked, "I take it Lieutenant Halifax warned you we were on the way?"

With a gesture of his own, McSwain led them through the archway. "I wouldn't put it like that, sir. After all, the general did instruct him to call up all the units."

There was something about the quietness of the place that bothered Doris, and whilst the men made what sounded like small talk to her ears, she cranked back her head and opened her ears. There was that quietness again, only the further they walked, the less quiet it got. Doris shook her head. She wasn't making much sense, even to herself, and it was becoming difficult to filter out the men's voices. If anything, they were getting louder and, strangely, taking on an echoey resonance. Where was the birdsong? This far away from so-called civilization, she should be able to hear birds!

It wasn't until she came into the courtyard beyond

the entrance that all became clear. As her head was still canted up towards the sky, she instantly saw there were no roofs. She turned on the spot to check—no, none to be seen anywhere. Lowering her gaze, she also found the source of the extra voices she'd been hearing. Before her, and tucked into virtually every nook and cranny she could see, was what could only be described as a tent city.

Only when Duke called out to her, "You joining us, Doris?" did it occur to her that she'd come to a halt, her mouth open at the sight before her.

Lurching forward, she immediately had to dodge the guy-ropes securing a towering radio mast, the top of which appeared to only just poke above where the roof of the building which surrounded the compound would have been.

"What the hell's this place?" Doris couldn't help but blurt out.

Captain McSwain held open the flap to a large green tent set against the wall. "Welcome to the ruins of Linlithgow Palace, Third Officer," he declared, cordially, and at least proving he had a good memory.

"A ruin?" Doris echoed. "This whole thing is a ruin?"

"The perfect cover for a secret radio transmitting establishment, wouldn't you agree?" Duke asked.

"Absolutely," she agreed, turning to take in the strange site once more before joining the others in the tent. "Don't you have problems from the locals? I mean, this place looks like it's been empty for…years, and then, all of a sudden, there's all these soldiers turning up for who knows what reason?"

McSwain looked momentarily uncertain, swiftly

exchanging looks with both Ceiwen and the major before obviously deciding that, as this strange American woman had been allowed into his tent, she must be in-the-know. So he told her, "We do have guards posted, as I'm sure you've seen. However, like most of the citizens of this country, we trust our military, and as for surreptitious investigations…"

"Listening in at the pubs?" Doris suggesting, earning herself a raised eyebrow.

"Well, yes," McSwain admitted, before swiftly completing his explanation, "…we've ascertained that they think we're just conducting exercises. We've not come across anything of concern, General," he finished, directing the comment at the senior officer.

"Good to know," Duke quickly replied, then asked, "How are things going?" Duke asked as soon as they'd all taken seats or, in Doris's case, an upturned tea chest.

McSwain's eyebrows lifted as he turned his attention to the major to answer, though Doris had the distinct impression he would have been happier addressing Ceiwen. "Fine, fine. The chaps are doing a good job following the script."

"You've everything you need, Captain? Cooks receiving enough food to keep the men happy?"

McSwain gave them a wry smile, "You know Army rations. They're well fed, though you could hardly describe the quality as haute cuisine, nor is it a very variable menu. Still, when's it ever, and at least it's not as bad as in the desert. Remember the trouble we had, eh, General? Usually enough to eat, so long as you didn't mind a side order of sand!"

As soon as he'd stopped talking, the captain let out a small chuckle. He stopped as soon as he realized

Ceiwen hadn't joined in with what, to Doris, sounded like the end of a shared memory or joke. Turning to look at him, she saw Ceiwen had gone white as a sheet.

Chapter Eleven

The atmosphere in the Humber as they left Linlithgow Palace was strange, to say the least.

After what was looking more and more like something private between Captain McSwain and Ceiwen had gone down with all the grace of a beehive in a locked room, Duke had jumped to his feet and, with the minimum of pleasantries, ushered Ceiwen from the tent, barely pausing to make certain Doris followed them out. The poor captain, who Doris was certain hadn't done anything untoward, was left to scratch his head in bemusement at their exit. Not even pausing to make sure their escort, left by the entrance to the ruined yet still magnificent palace, took up their place in their wake, Duke had hustled Ceiwen into the back seat, took his own next to him and then told Doris to get them back to Edinburgh.

"Anyone care to tell me what just happened?" Doris asked, her hands rigid on the steering wheel.

"Not yet," Duke mumbled, causing Doris to do her half turn. When she saw Ceiwen was still white and now sitting rigidly staring ahead, she didn't ask any further questions but concentrated upon her driving.

It was hard for Doris to make certain their escort didn't lose them, though it was obvious Duke wanted her to get them back to headquarters as soon as possible. She knew she'd be in trouble if they made it back on their own. At least there was one thing to be said for wartime roads—most of the traffic was military, and this far north, there wasn't that much of it. Paradoxically, if there really had been an invasion force gathering, their journey would have been much more taxing. This likely explained the drastic increase in road traffic in and around the area where she now lived, on the south coast. Something was certainly building down there, and Southampton was bang in the middle of it all.

Arriving at the entrance to Edinburgh Castle, Duke was nearly hanging out the window, waving his pass towards the guards. Nevertheless, they made Doris stop and insisted upon inspecting everyone's passes and paperwork before waving them through.

"Orders of the general, sir," the corporal instructed them, saluting the man in question, who managed to return the salute and nod in acknowledgement.

When Duke muttered something under his breath as they raised the barrier, Doris had to defend the man. "Don't blame him for following orders," she stated, before stomping on the accelerator, deciding a little jerk for the pair would be par for the course, as she thought one of them was behaving like a jerk. No sooner had she brought the Humber to a stop, their escort pulling up close behind, than Duke flung open his door and was actually dragging Ceiwen by an arm into the same building which housed Doris's room.

She opened her mouth to ask him what the hell he thought he was doing, only by the time she opened her mouth he'd already disappeared up the stairs. Hastily looking around, she was relieved to find no one had witnessed the show. Ceiwen hadn't appeared to be objecting. Nevertheless, she was certain that if another officer, especially one of higher rank than Duke's, had witnessed what occurred, there would have been a high price to pay.

Hurriedly locking the Humber and pocketing the keys—she'd made certain to bring with her only ATA uniform trousers rather than skirts, which had no pockets—she started to follow them up the stairs, their heavy footsteps echoing on the wooden steps. At least she knew where they were heading, as this entrance led up only to the servant's quarters she was sleeping in. She was yet to discover how the servants went about their duties around the castle and assumed there must be other exits she had yet to discover. Putting her Miss Marple hat back on the peg, she'd do some exploring as and when she could, but first, she needed to catch up with her companions... but a few seconds later, she hastily unlocked the Humber and grabbed Duke's briefcase from the back seat. Then she was ready to relock the vehicle and pound up the stairs in the men's wake.

Her hand was about to push the half-closed door fully open when a high-pitched meow prickled her ears. Momentarily torn between her need to get to the bottom of whatever was going on with Ceiwen and his (hopefully temporarily) deranged ADC, she hesitated, leaning her head back and holding her breath. After a moment, it came again. Stepping back down, she leant her head to one side and then the other, trying to zero in on the faint noise.

There it was again! This time, as she knew what she was waiting for, she began a search through the gap between her building and its neighbor, carefully stepping over bags of rubbish which seemed to have been merely flung in the direction of the bins. Her foot was hovering over one small, black bag when the noise came again and this time, the bag also moved. Doris's free hand flew to her mouth and dropping to her knees, she let the briefcase rest on the ground as she unhesitatingly began untying the knot at the top of the bag.

Peering inside, she was presented with the sight of a scruffy grey tabby cat staring up at her. Sensing hope, the cat looked up at her, sat down, held up one of its front paws and let out a full-throated "Meow!" before flopping down.

Reaching inside, Doris gently wormed her hands under its pathetically thin body and, to her relief, the cat allowed itself to be picked up. Kicking the bag disgustedly to one side, she held him under the tummy with one hand whilst she ran her free one over the rest of its body, giving it a quick check for any noticeable injuries. With nothing obviously wrong, apart from being hungry and dirty, she tucked it inside her jacket, not caring for the dirt which would rub off, and picked up the briefcase.

"Come on, Scruff," she told it, "let's get you indoors. Casting a scornful eye at the plastic bag, she looked up at the sky and, with a tight hold on the cat, shouted at the top of her lungs, "If I find out who threw out this cat, I'll castrate the bugger!"

Just above her, a window was flung open. "What's this racket?" a man in cook's white asked, looking down into the alley.

"You know anything about this cat?" Doris yelled back, allowing the cat's head to show.

Confronted with a fierce American, the head hastily withdrew, shaking vigorously.

Still muttering threats to the world at large, Doris

hurried back into the building—with one hand under the bulge of her jacket—as quickly much as she could without disturbing the cat, which was making very cute purring noises against her breastbone. Halfway up the flight of stairs, she stopped, hearing the voice of Duke half-shouting at Ceiwen. Slowing her pace, so as not to make a commotion, she strode upstairs and came upon the sight of Duke gripping Ceiwen by the shoulders and shaking him!

"What the hell do you think you're doing?" he hissed, getting no sound in reply.

Planting herself, possibly a little foolishly, at the top of the stairs so as to prevent either man from escaping, Doris glared at the pair. "I don't know—though I have my suspicions—what's going on, but someone had better tell me, reeeaal soooon!" She let a Hollywood American accent extend as much as possible without sounding ridiculous.

It at least stopped Duke from shaking Ceiwen, she noted with a satisfied nod. What happened next took her by surprise and, taking in the number of surprises she'd been through already that day, that was saying something. Scruff, as she was already beginning to think of the cat she'd rescued, woke up, poked his head out of her jacket, and sneezed. Almost immediately, Ceiwen began violently sneezing, causing Duke to jump backwards out of the firing line. Scruff merely tucked his—she was assuming it was a he until she had the chance to check—head back down and a moment later was back asleep.

Released from Duke's grip, Ceiwen staggered back, waving his hands in front of his face and continuing to sneeze. Strangely, as if there hadn't been enough of that going around today, Duke had backed away as well. In fact, he was about as far from Doris and her little friend as was possible whilst still being on the same landing. Looking at Ceiwen, who was continuing to sneeze, she could see no other symptoms whatsoever, no runny or red eyes, nothing. If she didn't know better, she'd say here was a man pretending to have a violent allergic reaction to a cat!

Trusting her eyes, she ignored Ceiwen and approached Duke, who promptly tried to back farther away, only he already had his back against a wall. Instead, he put his hands over his face and appeared to be doing his best to simply not breath.

Taking pity upon the man, Doris put some distance between them. Finding herself next to Ceiwen, she openly stared at him before taking a deep breath and acting upon the feeling she'd had virtually since she'd first met the man, reinforced by a lot of little things which had since occurred.

"General Ceiwen, if that's who you are, I apologize. If I'm right though…please stop pretending to be allergic to the cat."

Only a little to her surprise, Ceiwen stopped sneezing immediately, took in Duke's and then Doris's expression, before whipping off his hat and slumping back against the rails.

"Duke, care to tell me what's going on?" Doris immediately asked.

From behind his hand and between sneezes, Duke managed to get out, "Get that, that thing away from me!"

Doris put the briefcase on the floor and placed a hand around the cat's ears, not that the still-snoozing creature seemed to notice he was the center of attention.

"Come on! It's not that bad. Your eyes aren't even running!" Doris told him, before turning her attention back to Ceiwen, who looked as miserable as could be. "As for you, judging by what just happened and what I've noticed since we met, I don't think you're the real general." She turned her best don't-mess-with-me stare upon the pair, daring either to contradict her.

Finally, Duke sighed from behind his hands. "Do you know where my room is?" Doris shook her head. "Down this corridor, third on the right. Meet us"—he shot a barbed look at Ceiwen—"there in five minutes. Oh, and lose the cat." Without another word, he grabbed Ceiwen by the arm, snatched his briefcase up, and strode back towards the stairs.

Once they'd both gone, Doris shook her head and looked down at her find. "Come on, you, let's get you back to my room."

After nearly dropping the cat whilst she was juggling to get her room key out of the opposite pocket—why, she pondered, is that always the case?—Doris kicked open her door and managed to make it to her bed before Scruff finally tumbled out. Unbuttoning her jacket, Doris did a quick bit of damage inspection and, apart from a few lines of dirt, nothing sprang out at her.

As for Scruff himself? The cat was sitting down, both striking hazel eyes staring up at this strange woman. Aware she needed to be upstairs in a few moments, she reached out a hand, slowly, slowly, until her fingers were directly under his nose. To her delight, Scruff leant forward a little and began to sniff her fingers before he got to his feet and rubbed the side of his head against her hand.

Delighted, Doris bobbed her head down, kissed the

top of his head and immediately recoiled, wafting a hand vigorously beneath her nose.

"Wow! Do you need a bath?" The cat let out a plaintive yowl, which Doris chose to take as meaning he agreed. Looking around, though she didn't know why, as she was very much alone, she lifted him up by the tail and tummy; definitely of the male persuasion and, by the look of it, a full tomcat! Straightening up, she redid her jacket buttons and turned to put a hand on the door handle. A smile upon her face, she told the cat, who'd already made himself comfortable by settling down in the middle of her bed, "Well, young man. When I get back, we'll give you that bath, but I'll pick up something for you to eat as well, so it'll be worth your while. In the meantime," she threw a glance at the ceiling, "I've got a bit of a mystery to get to the bottom of."

Chapter Twelve

"Enter," Duke called, as Doris raised her fist to knock. "I saw a shadow under the door and made the assumption it was you," he explained to her frowning face.

"And if it hadn't been me?" Doris asked, closing the door behind her.

He shrugged. "Then I'd have told them to go away." He sneezed once more.

"Scruff's in my room."

Sneezing again before taking out a handkerchief and blowing his nose, he eyed her suspiciously before deciding, "You're probably covered in cat hair."

Doris didn't even bother to look down at herself. "Very likely." Looking around, Duke's room wasn't any different from hers—a single bed placed under the window, a basic wardrobe in one corner with a desk and chair completing the furniture. She wondered if you had to be of a certain rank to get some decent accommodation. This reminded her of her purpose in being there.

She leant against the wardrobe, which gave an ominous creak, so instead she settled herself down on the bed next to Duke, who promptly shuffled as far away from her as he could. This reminded Doris about her cat-hair-covered clothes and she hastily got to her feet, brushed the blankets down, and went to stand beside the very bemused-looking general. "Who's going to start?" she asked.

"I'll leave it to you, Duke," Ceiwen said, in a very distinctly cockney accent that had Doris whipping her head around.

Before she could say anything, Duke stood up, made as if to pace but immediately thought better of the idea—in such a small room it would have brought him into range of Doris's cat hair once more. Nodding at the senior officer, who all at once didn't look very officerish, he said, "Doris, I'd like you to meet Rob Barnes, amateur impressionist."

Automatically, Doris held out her hand, hearing herself say in a rather dazed voice, "Pleased to meet you," before she recovered her wits. Jumping to her feet, she exclaimed, "I knew something was up!" and leant down to run a finger along one of this Rob's eyebrows. "I knew it! Makeup!"

Rob deflated even more and let himself flop forward so his elbows were on his knees and his head in his hands. "I thought I was doing well," he muttered.

Duke opened his mouth once, twice, before finally settling upon what to say. "You were. So what happened?"

Though dying to join in the conversation, Doris kept quiet, knowing she'd learn more with silence, no matter that the urge to jump in was almost physically hurting her.

"There's something I didn't mention before, you know, when you were interviewing me," Rob began, his head still in his hands, so his words came out muffled and a little hard to understand. "In my defense, you didn't ask," he finished, looking up, a slight look of defiance on his face.

Doris shot an eyebrow Duke's way, her curiosity piqued.

With a little of what she'd come to think of as a senior officer's pomposity—she'd run into enough—Rob thrust out his chin, "I'm also known amongst my friends as a bit of a memory man."

"A what?" Duke asked, before slapping his forehead in realization. "You've seen—what's his name—before?"

"McSwain," Doris helpfully chipped in.

"Him! That man!" Duke said, waving a finger in Doris's direction. "You've seen him before?"

Rob nodded. "He was third row from the front, second seat on the right, in the last show I did at the Crown and Anchor in the east end of London, the day before I joined up."

"Guess you do have a good memory," Doris told him, shaking her head in amazement. "You didn't just make that all up?" she had to ask.

Shaking his head, Rob smiled for the first time since he'd been ushered out of the ruin. "Afraid not. Once something goes in here," he prodded the side of his head, "it stays in."

"I bet you're great at quizzes!" Doris asked, warming to her subject.

Duke broke into their discussion by coughing loudly. "Can we please stay on subject? Thank you," he said, after the other two turned sheepish looks upon him. "So, you'd seen McSwain before. Why would that put you off your game? No disrespect, but he couldn't have recognized you. With the makeup, new haircut, and uniform, you can't have looked anything like you'd have been that night."

Rob shook his head. "True, but he had Ceiwen next to him, and from the way the two were laughing and joking, he knew him well. There's no way I could have carried it off with that! You know I've only seen him on film, which together with what you and the others in the know have been able to tell me wasn't enough. I couldn't have pretended to be Ceiwen that well. It's not as if I can talk to the man," he finished.

This immediately piqued Doris's curiosity once more, though, truth be told, everything which was being said only served to reinforce her suspicions. She was unable to keep quiet any longer. "Oh, would the girls love this! They're going to kill me when I get back."

"What are you talking about?" Duke asked, trying and failing to not let his annoyance with the situation show.

"I said that out loud? Sorry," Doris muttered, before saying, "My girlfriends in the ATA. We, well, we kind of get mixed up in adventures all the time…not," she hastened to add, "that we go looking for them. It's more that they keep finding us."

Rob appraised her with interest. "So, you're kind of flying Hercule Poirots?"

She had to put him right, "More like, Miss Marples, only younger and better-looking."

"I'll say," Rob immediately came back with.

"Down, boy," Doris scolded, holding up her ring finger. "Happily married, remember?"

A shoe banged down on the small table causing both to look up at Duke, who stood hopping on one leg—the floor, presumably, being too cold to put his foot down on. "When you've quite finished?" he said from between clenched teeth, putting his shoe back on.

"Sorry," they both told him at the same time.

"As we were discussing…"

"Yes, we were!" Doris interrupted him. "As I was getting along to. So Ceiwen, the real general, is ill? Out of the country? Something else?"

Both men looked at each other before Duke slumped down, appearing as if the world's troubles were upon his shoulders.

"You'll have to tell her," Rob said into the silence. "She's probably guessed anyway and is being…" He glanced over at Doris. "Polite?"

"Something like that," Doris agreed, fixing her attention on Duke.

Instead of answering straight away, Duke went to the wardrobe and took down a small case from its top. Turning back, he placed it on the just abused table and, flicking the two catches, flipped it open. There was a clinking of glass and he turned around with a small bottle of whisky and two glasses. Setting them down, he poured a shot into each before asking, "Hand me that mug, please, Rob." Accepting the mug that had been residing on the floor at the head of the bed, Duke opened the window, carelessly flung out whatever it contained—there was no commotion from beneath the window, so he didn't hit anyone—before pouring some of the life-giving nectar in as a replacement. "Take one." He indicated the glasses whilst holding onto the mug. "I think we could all do with it."

As one, the three drank up and promptly proceeded to cough their hearts out.

Doris picked up the bottle and peered suspiciously at it. "Real smooth," she declared, putting it back on the table.

"Don't be fooled by the label," Duke advised, too late. "It may say Johnnie Walker, but it last had a decent brand in it when I bought that bottle about three years ago."

Doris's voice sounded like it had been rubbed with sandpaper. "Thanks for the warning." A pause for another cough. "Now, the real general… I take it he is dead?"

Though it was unlikely anyone was listening, Duke hastily closed the window and then opened the door, poked his head out, and then locked it before replying, "He was knocked over by an ambulance coming out of a casino in London," Duke began, his head down before he looked up. "I was with him, only a few steps behind. There was nothing I could do. You know the silliest part? He wasn't even drunk! The silly bugger decided to stoop down and tie his shoelace, in the middle of the road, just as the all-clear siren sounded. He didn't stand a chance. The ambulance came tearing around the corner and took his head clean off!"

"That brings me to my next question," Doris stated.

"Which is?" Rob asked.

"How his death was kept from the papers."

Duke nodded, refilling their glasses and taking a tentative sip, accompanied by a shudder. "Let's put it this way. I was able to convince the policeman who turned up that he never saw anything."

"How on earth did you do that?" Doris asked, taking the smallest of sips.

With a shrug, Duke told her, "I may have threatened to throw him in the Tower of London."

"And he believed you?"

"He was only a young lad..."

"Wasn't there any trouble from the other witnesses? The ambulance people, for example?" Doris wanted to know,

"That's where we got lucky...relatively," he hastened to add, as Doris opened her mouth. "Like I said, there'd just sounded the all-clear, so there weren't that many people about, and the ambulance crew were both ex-army from the first go-around and readily agreed that nothing had happened and they'd not say a word."

"And you believed them?" Doris felt compelled to ask.

"As much as I believe anything anyone says these days." Duke nodded. "It helped that he wasn't in uniform and I was able to stand over the body and stop the policeman from getting to his ID."

"Hold on," Doris butted in. "What happened to his body?"

Duke looked away before replying, "You're probably not going to like this, but as you know, in wartime we sometimes have to do things which we wouldn't normally contemplate."

Doris finished her drink, trying not to grimace too badly before waving him to continue.

"We put him in the back of the ambulance, after taking all identifying papers and objects off him, and they took him to where they'd been called out to. A V1 had come down on a church hall." There was a defiant expression upon his face as he looked Doris in the eyes and finished, "What's another body?"

Getting up from the bed, Doris walked to the window, flung it open and leant out, taking in some deep breaths before she felt able to turn back around. Duke's face radiated defiance, almost daring her to call him out on the decision. It was a few moments before she could get her thoughts in order. "You're right. I don't like it."

Emptying the last of the bottle into their glasses, Duke knocked his back in one, visibly ignoring the effects. "I didn't expect you to. I'm not totally heartless, despite what I've just said and what you may think. I made certain his body was separated from the other casualties and eventually delivered to his wife for burial but,, she can't give him the burial she wants, at least not until after the war's been won. She understands but doesn't like it. She and her family are sworn to secrecy. Hell, even the Prime Minister doesn't know about this! The last thing we need is the Germans finding out."

Doris directed her next question at Rob. "So where did they find you?"

"You'd be surprised who MI5 keep an eye on," Rob cryptically replied.

"Which means?" Doris asked, when he didn't elaborate.

"It means they pulled me out of the nick."

"Why were you in prison?" Doris asked after a few seconds, not expecting that answer.

"Tell the truth, Barnes," Duke told him, receiving a raised eyebrow from Doris at his tone of voice.

"Yes, sir," Rob said, throwing a terrible salute the major's way before telling Doris, "I'm a conscientious objector who didn't want to do any kind of war work."

This puzzled Doris. "What do you call this, then?"

Rob snorted, not a nice sound. "Shall we say MI5 can also be very…persuasive."

Doris raised both eyebrows and shot them in Duke's direction, who held up both hands.

"I swear, not a hair on his head was hurt!"

Rob nodded. "He's right, they never harmed me; threatened to, but never actually did."

"So how did they persuade you?" Doris had to know the truth.

It took a little while for Rob to tell her. "I've some relations who're interned on the Isle of Man; that's all I'm going to say, so Doris, please don't ask any more."

Doris walked to the door where, with her back to the room, she asked, "Assuming we're still going somewhere tomorrow, what time shall I meet you, sir?"

This last was directed at the room at large, though it was Duke who replied. "Breakfast in the officer's mess at seven!"

Doris had already let the door bang shut behind her.

Chapter Thirteen

After a hurried and rather tense breakfast the next morning of bacon, toast, and tea strong enough the spoon could stand up in the cup, the trio silently made their way to the Humber. Duke asked Doris to get them back to Linlithgow Palace as fast as she could—without losing their escort.

Once away from the relative confines of Edinburgh, Doris, who'd been fussing behind the wheel due to the continued silence, briefly stamped her foot on the brake, jerking her passengers forward almost out of their seats.

"What the hell?" Ceiwen yelled, slipping back into his real voice from the shock.

"As we all seemed to be either stewing or sulking over breakfast, I thought I'd get your attention." Without looking around for once, Doris proceeded, "As you're here and in uniform, I assume we're continuing with this ruse. Further, I assume, we're going to this palace to have a, shall we say, private word with McSwain. How am I doing so far?"

After a moment or two, Duke spoke, "Two for two, Miss Marple. Go on."

As that was as far as Doris had deduced, she said so. "That's it. Excuse me for asking, Rob, but you're going to be all right with carrying on?"

When he spoke this time, he was back to using his general's voice. "I am, Third Officer Johnson, thank you."

"Well, all's fine and dandy then, all actors together! Onward to Linlithgow Palace!" Doris declared, coaxing the Humber back to a sedate thirty-five miles an hour, the lorry close behind, and ignored all attempts by Duke to engage her in conversation until they reached their destination.

As soon as they pulled up outside the ruin, Duke hopped out of the Humber and, pausing only to instruct the guard to stay with Ceiwen, sprinted into the Palace and out of sight. Barely five minutes later he reappeared, this time with a frowning Captain McSwain close behind.

"I want you and your men to make yourselves scarce for five minutes, Sergeant," he instructed Lewis.

"Scarce, sir?" he asked, gawping at him from beneath a forehead the size of a block of flats.

"We want some privacy," Duke tried, still failing to consider that he may need to use smaller words. The man, Doris thought, was undoubtedly good at his job, but he was never going to finish *the Times*. "Sir?" Sergeant Lewis merely said again.

She could see Duke resisting the urge to groan. Finally, after obvious thought, he got it right, "Deploy your men, Sergeant. I want a cordon around us at a distance of about twenty yards and I want no one and nothing to get through until I say otherwise. Clear?"

"Clear, sir!" Lewis immediately said, snapping a quick salute before, in the time-honored fashion of non-commissioned officers everywhere, beginning to shout orders at and above his men. In a surprisingly short period of time, they were all either hunkered down behind trees or lying on the ground, with all their rifles out and pointed everywhere other than towards the group of four in the center of their cordon.

No sooner were they alone than McSwain began talking. At least he had the sense to keep his voice low. Doris suspected that if he'd shouted what he said, Duke might have pulled his revolver on him. Whether he would have shot him was another question, one she didn't like to dwell on. Glancing at his waist, she was relieved to find his hand wasn't anywhere near his holster.

"Do you want me to take a walk?" Doris asked.

Duke shook his head and joined Ceiwen in the back of the Humber. McSwain began to come to attention before changing his mind and, after a moment or two, nodded at Ceiwen. Apparently, Duke had been waiting for this and, with one last glance around to make certain no one could hear them, told them, "Everyone in the car, please."

Once Doris and McSwain were in the front, Duke got straight to the point. "Captain, you obviously know this isn't the real General Ceiwen."

The professional he was, the captain didn't speak, instead giving a single nod of the head and waiting for the major to continue, not that the man appeared to be thrown off by this.

The major cleared his throat before turning on McSwain one of the most intense stares Doris had seen since Betty had last accused her of swiping the Miss Marple book she was reading. She was quite impressed, though she decided his confidence didn't need boosting, so she resolved to keep the thought to herself.

"Right. Captain, after I tell you what's going on, you'll have two minutes to convince me you're a man of your word or you'll find yourself posted down to the Falkland Islands…and you'll get there by a single-man rowboat. Not even Churchill knows what I'm about to say."

If the man thought the major may have been laying things on a little thick, what he said about Churchill was enough to convince McSwain of the truth behind his words. It probably didn't help him, that he was being scrutinized by every other occupant of the vehicle.

Doris, for one, couldn't wait to see his reaction. He put her in mind of Scruff's face when she'd had to shut the door of her room on him that morning. The cat, now looking less like what he'd been—something which someone had thrown out—and more like the handsome tabby she believed he'd morph into, had canted his head to one side, frowned at her, and then sat down to face the door. She'd barely had the time to pop back to her room, place a newspaper she'd taken from a table for him to, hopefully, use as a toilet—she'd found no little piles when she'd got up, so presumed he'd had his legs crossed since she'd found him—and left a little pile of cut up sausage for him to eat before she'd had to run off to meet her colleagues. Sighing, Doris forced her mind back to the present. She'd spend the evening getting to know her new friend.

Duke proceeded to give an edited version of the previous night's tale, leaving out some of the more gruesome details and unwholesome methods he'd employed. By the time he'd finished, McSwain, if not sweating, was looking rather nervous, and his eyes kept fixing themselves upon the false general.

Not able to help herself, Doris kept an eye on her watch as soon as Duke had finished speaking. She was about to raise an eyebrow when time was up when McSwain cleared his throat.

"You understand that this has all come as a bit of a shock," he began. "Ceiwen and I grew to know each other well in Africa, and I was rather fond of the old boy. They don't make many like him," he added, jutting out his chin so the others knew he meant every word. He let out a deep sigh. "Well, I suppose he can't have suffered, and this is vital for what's about to happen." He held out his hand towards Duke who—and Doris was certain the action was deliberate, meant to intimidate - shook it with his hook. Blanching a little, McSwain let go as soon as was politely allowed and went to rub his hand upon his trousers, only for Doris's glare to forestall him.

Duke was out and opening the door for the captain before Doris could even think about moving. "Come, let me walk you back, Captain."

If anything, McSwain went a little paler and shook his head. "That's quite all right, Major. I know the way."

Wondering if McSwain had seen the same steely expression in Duke's face as she'd done, Doris waited until the two were out of view before leaning back around the Humber's bench seat. "So, General, I think it's best for all of us if I address you like this, don't you?" Not giving Rob/Ceiwen time to reply, she continued, "As I was about to say, do you think Duke wanted to put the heebie-jeebies on our friend?"

When he didn't answer straight away, merely sitting there with a frown upon his face, Doris rightly guessed, "It means Duke wants to frighten him."

"Ah!" he answered with a shake of his head. "We really do speak a different language at times, eh? But, to answer you, yes, I think that's exactly what he wants to do." He tried and failed to suppress a shudder. "I don't envy the poor chap."

Doris quickly checked that Duke wasn't in view. "What *did* he say, or do, to convince you to play this part?"

Her answer was another, deeper, longer shudder, and it took him a good thirty seconds to find his voice. "Nothing physical, I can assure you of that," he told Doris, knowing it would be what she'd want to know. "Cross my heart and hope to die."

"What was it, then?" Doris was nothing if not persistent.

"Can we just say he made me see I could be of service to my country?"

When he didn't elaborate, Doris prompted, "And?"

Another sigh. "And, I had no wish to break rocks for the rest of my life."

Doris turned fully back around, slumped into her seat, and whistled. "And he seems such a nice man."

With the man in question still not in sight, Ceiwen said, "I'm sure he is. War has a way of making people do things they'd never dream of, though, doesn't it?"

Thinking that, at this moment, she'd like nothing better than to curl up with her dear Walter, Doris shook her head and muttered, "It sure does."

Chapter Fourteen

After Duke returned from scaring the living daylights out of the unfortunate captain, or so Doris presumed, he suggested the three of them should cancel the other visit they had lined up for that day and spend the rest of the day either back at Edinburgh Castle or, if they wished, taking a walk around the city. Now that the truth was out about Ceiwen, it looked like Duke was more obviously taking the lead when it was only the three of them.

As it turned out, no matter how tempting it was to look around her first Scottish city—Stirling didn't count, as she'd never had the opportunity to investigate in the short time she'd been there—by the time they got back, both Doris and Rob declined that offer. Rob—Ceiwen, her brain hastily reminded her, because thinking of him as anyone else could get them all into deep trouble, up to and including at the cost of their lives—didn't give a reason. For her part, Doris didn't feel like doing anything other than lying down and reading some more of her book. Scruff had other ideas though, and all thoughts of picking up and starting once more on *The Moving Finger* were banished from her mind as the tabby made a break for freedom as soon as she cracked open her door.

Bending down, one foot hard behind the door to stop it from opening further, she placed both hands under his skinny, furry body and scooped him into her chest. To her relief, he didn't struggle too much, nor lash out. She'd seen his claws and didn't like to think what damage they could cause. She suspected he was the unwanted pet of someone who worked in the castle, so his claws weren't overlong, but they were still longer and sharper than she'd care to get acquainted with.

"Shh," she cooed, hugging him close to her breast and backheeling the door closed. "I don't blame you for wanting out, but someone here's got it in for you, so you're staying in my room until we finish here, and then you get to come back down south with me!" Doris held him up before her and was presented with a pair of beautiful but malevolent eyes surrounded by an extremely grumpy-looking furry face. Both ears and whiskers were fully forward, yet he kept all four paws hanging loosely, with no attempt at trying to swipe at her nose.

He let out a plaintive "Meow," wriggled his nose, and turned his head towards where Doris had laid some newspaper down. Frowning at first, Doris tucked him under one arm and made towards the corner, only to come up short as a pungent aroma hit her nose like a sledgehammer! She hurried to open the window a crack and, still with Scruff hanging from an arm, wafted like crazy in an attempt to shoo the smell out of the room.

"Phew! You needed that," she said, getting another "Meow" of agreement from Scruff, who wriggled out of her grasp and, using her hip, leaped onto the windowsill. Sticking his nose into the small gap Doris had opened, he snuffled and then scrabbled with his paws trying to widen the gap. Doris let him try, though the attempt only lasted a few seconds as he quickly realized the window was too heavy for him to move. Nevertheless, she was extremely impressed with him. "You're a smart one, aren't you," she told him, adding, "I can see I'll have to keep an eye on you."

Under Scruff's watchful gaze, Doris cleared up his poo, all very neatly piled smack-bang in the center of the paper. He wriggled his bottom as she edged the door open but decided against making a move. When Doris came back up from having deposited the offering in the outside bins, she barely opened the door an inch, just wide enough so she could peek through with one eye. A little to her surprise, Scruff had stayed on the windowsill. Obviously he knew her well enough already to know she wouldn't make the same mistake. Doris's admiration for the cat went up another notch.

"Good boy!" She fussed him around the ears, which he obviously loved as he leant into her touch and nearly fell off the sill. Laughing, she pushed him back, laid down some fresh newspaper, and then tried calling him over. "Scruff! Down here…" She showed him a bottle of milk she'd persuaded a cook she'd run into downstairs to let her have, and poured some into a saucer and placed it beside the paper. Nothing does a disdainful expression as well as a cat and Doris immediately recognized the one she was being shot. Picking up the saucer, she brought it to him and put it down beside him. The expression softened only a little.

"Hmm. If it's not the milk, why the grumpy face, Scruff?" she asked, not expecting any reply, though when he sneezed in her direction immediately he heard the name she used for him, it was like a lightbulb came on in her mind. "I am so sorry," she told him, pouncing to clutch the surprised feline to her chest. "I quite agree. Who would like to be called Scruff! Especially a handsome boy like you. Hmm, let me think."

Walking back and forth across the limited space in her room, she eventually came to a stop before her slightly open window. As she was fortunate enough to be in a room located on the outside castle wall, she had a wonderful view of the city of Edinburgh spread out below her. Not for the first time, she marveled at viewing a major city which had escaped the terror of aerial bombing. The people who lived below no doubt worried daily about receiving the same treatment as London, Coventry, Liverpool, and other cities had received, though most would believe that with each passing day bringing little other than continued Allied victories the chances lessened. Each likely also didn't care to share such thoughts out loud, fate not being something anyone cared to risk in wartime.

The unmistakable cacophony of vehicles invaded her thoughts, though as she was on the point of yelling at them to be quiet, no matter how pointless the action would have been, a long derelict memory of New York and its fleets of bright yellow taxis invaded her mind.

"That's it!" she announced in delight and kissed the top of the cat's head. "Taxi. I'll call you Taxi!"

The tabby cocked his head to one side, giving all the appearance of thinking the suggestion over. Next thing Doris knew, he launched his head at hers and the pair shared a surprisingly forceful headbutt, before he settled down in her arms with what could only be a contented purr thrumming through Doris's chest.

"Well, I'll take that as a yes," she told the newly rechristened cat. "Can you imagine the fun we can have with your new name?" Lying down upon her bed, the cat named Taxi allowed Doris to clutch him to her chest as she stretched out. Still in uniform, Doris could feel herself succumbing to the land of nod, idly musing that she hadn't felt tired, so it must be something in the purr. Just before she finally nodded off, she wondered how he'd get along with Bobby and Duck.

****

A singularly pungent odor prodded Doris from her slumber. Sitting bolt upright, she felt her eyes open wide as if needles pierced her scalp. A startled sounding "meow" reverberated loudly in her left ear, and Taxi sprang off her shoulder to land at the bottom of the bed. Rubbing her head, Doris realized her new friend must have curled up on her pillow and been wrapped around her head, with the needles being where his claws had stuck in at her sudden movement. Looking at her palm, she was happy to see no evidence of blood and began to smile before the smell reminded her why she'd woken up.

"Taxi?" she said, raising her voice slightly at the tabby who was happily turning around and around, prior to settling in once more. He deigned to open one eyelid in reluctant acknowledgment of ownership of the smell, and promptly fell fast asleep.

Grumbling to herself, Doris glanced at her watch before swinging her legs off the bed. To her astonishment, it was half past four! Her stomach groused to be noticed. After quickly rubbing the sleep from her eyes, she busied herself with tidying up Taxi's further donation, grateful once more that he knew what the sheets of newspaper were for.

"You be a good boy and stay there," she unnecessarily instructed her comatose cat, not even getting a grunt or purr of acknowledgement this time.

As she hurried out the front door of her accommodation building, the bundle of newspaper held gingerly at arm's length, she bumped right into a khaki uniform she hadn't noticed standing at the bottom of the steps. A pair of strong hands prevented her from stumbling backwards and falling to the ground.

"Steady there," a familiar male voice advised her.

Throwing out her own hands, Doris gripped the rough cloth surrounding the arms which had saved her, finding herself in the firm grip of "Albert!"

"Guilty as charged," he replied, keeping his grip upon her waist until he was certain she was steady once more. "If you're all right, could you let go, please? I think I've lost some hair from my arms." He grinned, nodding at where Doris's hands were still tightly gripping his battle-blouse.

"Sorry," she apologized, "and, thanks."

Instead of replying, Albert was sniffing the air.

With mounting dismay, Doris looked at the package she still held and reluctantly turned that hand palm upwards. As she'd dreaded, in trying to avoid falling, she'd let her hand tighten on the package and her fingers had gone right through the newspaper and onto his sleeve. She held up her hand, only for Albert to automatically recoil.

"What the hell is that?"

She had been about to ask what he was doing there, but the ripeness in the air overrode her curiosity, and not really sure how to explain, Doris stumbled over an explanation until she finally settled upon saying, "I have a cat. Some swine threw him out in the garbage, and I rescued him."

Albert pointed at the remains in her hand. "That's

not…him…it…is it?" His face had a horrified expression at the prospect.

Doris could at least smile at what he'd said. She shook her head. "No, well, it's a part of him. It's his," she searched for the right word, "toilet, you could say. Poo," she added upon seeing his confusion. With her poo-free hand, she pointed at his sleeve. "I'm sorry, but I think I've got some onto your sleeve."

To hit credit, Albert barely glanced at the stain. "Don't worry, it'll clean off easily enough. I've had worse!" he added, upon seeing her disbelieving face. "So, you've got a cat. Are you going to keep him?"

"Come on," was Doris's only reply. "I need to get rid of this in the bins and clean up. There's a tap underneath a window by the kitchens. So, what were you doing? Apart from saving damsels in distress, that is?"

He had a wonky smile when he replied, "Don't get me wrong, saving you is a pleasure, but I seriously doubt you'd ever be in any kind of distress you couldn't handle."

As they made their short way to the alley which the kitchens backed onto, Doris pondered if she was being flirted with. She knew she was pretty, though not in either Mary or Penny's class as far as looks went, so it wasn't beyond the realm of possibility. Recalling that Albert had been next to her when she'd displayed her wedding ring in the Other Ranks Mess the other day, she decided to give him the benefit of the doubt and not say anything.

Once the remains of the newspaper had been disposed of, Doris knocked on the kitchen window until she got the attention of an ATS girl and persuaded her, as soon as she'd explained where the mess on both her hands and the soldier's jacket actually came from, to allow them in to use the sink and clean themselves up.

"You don't know of anyone who's thrown a cat out, do you?" she asked as she scrubbed her hands clean.

The fresh-faced girl, likewise dressed in an ill-fitting uniform as was Albert, shook her head, after a few moments' thought, and replied, "No, but if I do, they may have an accident with a sharp knife!"

Doris clapped her on the shoulder with a not-quite dry hand. "That's my girl! Well, I guess I'd better get going," she said. "I've a hungry moggy to scrounge some food up for."

As she'd hoped, the girl grabbed her forearm. "Well, we can't have the little chap... It is a chap?" Doris nodded. "Can't have him going hungry. I take it you're planning on taking him back with you when you leave?" Another nod. "Stay there," she told them and disappeared out of sight barely long enough for the two to exchange glances. "Here! Take that and come and find me when you need more. I'm a cat girl and would love to meet him."

With a slightly soggy newspaper-wrapped package in her left hand, for a different reason, as Doris stated with a laugh, Doris held out her right one and shook the girl's hand. "Doris Winter, pleased to meet you."

"Rachel Carter, pleased to meet you."

"And I'm Albert Miller," Doris's companion contributed, with a smile toward the girl.

Rachel though, barely seemed to acknowledge him, instead telling Doris, "You're the first Yank I've met! I love your accent!"

Blushing a little, Doris smiled. "Well, apart from my friends and my husband, you're the first one who's told me that. Anyway, I must be going. I don't want to leave Taxi alone any longer."

"Taxi?" both Rachel and Albert said at the same time, mirroring eyebrows shooting for the stars.

"That's his name, and he and I both like it. It's fun!" Doris stated defensively.

Rachel quickly assured her, "I didn't mean anything by it. Just surprised. Yes, it is fun!"

"I knew you were a little weird," Albert simply said.

Once outside, Albert enquired, "What did she give you?"

Carefully, not wishing to drop anything, Doris unwrapped a corner of the package. Both whistled appreciatively.

"That's about a quarter of a salmon!" Albert commented, shaking his head in disbelief. "Where the hell did she get that?"

"Something tells me the officer's mess will be a little short tonight," Doris guessed, glancing over her shoulder, and seeing Rachel standing in the doorway. Once the girl saw her looking back, she waved enthusiastically. Doris did the same, as Albert was still shaking his head.

When they reached Doris's accommodation block, Albert looked at his wristwatch. "Mess'll be open. You coming? I could wait until you've fed…Taxi."

Doris shook her head straight away. "Thanks for the offer, but I can't. I've been told I must eat in the Officer's Mess, and…" She ended with a grin, holding up the illicit package.

Chapter Fifteen

As she hurried back up the stairs, Doris was acutely aware of a loud, plaintive *meow* echoing down the staircase. Speeding up her pace, Doris had her room key in hand and on its way to the keyhole when a glint of something metallic caught her eye. Approximately a foot to the left of her door was an alcove where a broom, mop, and bucket stood.

"Quiet a few seconds longer, Taxi," she implored. Going down on one knee, she reached out a hand and came up grasping her discovery. Opening her hand, she immediately recognized what she'd found. Trusting Taxi not to break through her door, she half-jumped down the stairs and rushed outside. Turning every which way, she wasn't too surprised to find she was on her own. Albert was nowhere in sight.

Wasting no more time, she hurried back to her room and, after a quick battle to keep her somewhat stir-crazy cat inside, made it into her room and shut the door behind her. With one hand holding the salmon high above her head and hoping Taxi wouldn't decide to climb up her legs and body to get to it, she used the other to slip her find into her trouser pocket and lock the door.

Once secured, she now turned her full attention to fending off her obviously hungry cat.

"Well, I'm not overly fond of salmon, my friend," she told him as she hastily cut a quarter of the salmon onto a plate she'd "borrowed" from the mess. She began to cut it up but soon gave that up as an exercise in futility, as Taxi had now leaped up onto the small table and was nudging her knife out of the way with his nose. Taking the hint, she stepped back and became aware of what could only be a very contented purr coming from her new friend.

"Now, what shall I do with the rest of this?" she muttered to herself. Glancing at the window, she shook her head. It wasn't cold enough to leave it on the window ledge. Besides, some bird would come along and take it away, and she hoped she'd get another two or three meals out of her slightly ill-gotten gains. "There's got to be something I can seal this up in. Not sure I could sleep in a room which stinks of fish. No offense, Taxi," she added, ruffling his head as he looked up at her before going back to munching his tea.

There was a knock on the door, closely followed by a loud sneeze. Smiling to herself, she called out, "Coming, Duke!" Checking that Taxi was too engrossed to make another escape attempt, Doris unlocked the door and ushered her visitor quickly through, ignoring the handkerchief he held over his nose.

"Don't take it personally, Taxi," Doris called over her shoulder as she automatically locked the door once more. "He's not normal."

"Is there a reason you've locked the door?" Duke asked, as he backed into the corner next to her wardrobe, farthest away from a still happily munching Taxi.

Doris had opened her mouth to reply when something atop the wardrobe caught her eye. "Hold that thought," she advised. Coming towards him, she went up on tiptoe, felt around with her free hand and came away with a rather dusty cardboard box. Placing it on her bed, she warily opened it up, only to find it empty of anything, except more dust. She handed it to Duke and asked, "Can you give that a quick wipe down, please?" She pointed at her jug of water and towel.

Perhaps it was that the major was getting used to the American's strange ways, but he didn't waste breath questioning her reason. Instead, he swiftly did as she asked, returning the now reasonably clean box to her.

"Thanks," she said, and placed the remains of the salmon, once more wrapped in its newspaper, into the box and replaced the lid. Frowning, she went and gave her hands a quick wash, dried them, and then her head snapped up. Pulling her suitcase from beneath her bed, she flipped it open and rummaged in the corners before she emerged with what she'd been hoping to find.

"Do you often carry lengths of string with you?" Duke asked.

Taxi looked towards the man, burped in a very self-satisfied manner, and immediately sat back on his haunches and began a round of ablutions.

This was very much to Duke's relief. "For a second, I thought he was going to jump at me."

"He probably considered it, then decided a wash would be a better use of his time," Doris told him. "Come here, I need to borrow a finger."

Obviously distracted by the idea of being pounced on by such a wee furry beast, Duke made his way to her, keeping as physically far away from the cat as he was able. "So long as you give it back. I don't have that many to spare," he muttered, correctly laying a finger where Doris was tying a knot. He didn't notice the surprised look upon her face from the joke he'd just made at his own expense. As Doris went up on her toes to place the box back in place, Duke asked, "Do I want to know where you got some salmon from?"

"Not unless you want me to lie to you," Doris replied, sitting down on her bed. Taxi immediately jumped into her lap.

"You've still got your furry friend," he remarked, punctuating the comment with a sneeze.

"Obviously," Doris said, scratching Taxi between the ears. "You're not going anywhere until we fly out of here, are you, Taxi."

Duke's eyebrows shot up, "Taxi! You've named it…Taxi?"

"Cab would be too weird," she replied, not having any effect upon his eyebrows. "Well, he's certainly not a Scruff anymore," she added.

Duke took a little time to reply, thinking Doris's words over and wiping his nose. "I don't suppose this new name would have anything to do with your friend's face when you open the door and shout his name?"

Her wide grin was all the answer he needed.

"So, what can I do for you?" Doris eventually deemed to ask.

"Hold on," he asked, going to the door and then asking, "Could you open it, a little? I won't let…Taxi…escape. I promise."

Keeping a firm hold of her cat, whose eyelids were drooping due to a combination of the large meal he'd just consumed and the scratching which he was still enjoying, Doris passed him the door key. As Duke unlocked and opened it, leaving the key in the lock, he stood sideways to a gap no more than a couple of inches wide. Doris nodded in satisfaction. Taxi began snoring.

Tearing his nose from the gap of cat-free air he was letting into the room, Duke said, "Ceiwen and I would like to know if you'd join us for dinner?"

"The mess isn't having Taxi's salmon back," Doris immediately informed him.

Duke let out a small chuckle and shook his head. "We're not going to the mess. After what's happened over the last couple of days, I feel we need a clear-the-air meal, and I've called in a few favors." Now it was Doris's turn to raise her eyebrows. "We're going to a place I know, the Young Chevalier, in the center of the city."

Doris frowned, her mind and eyes searching for any ulterior motives her friend might have. Since the revelation of how Rob became involved, her suspicions that the major could have something to do with the secret services were in danger of running out of control. She glanced down at her now-fast-asleep furry companion, ruffling him under the chin. "No ulterior motives?" she finally enquired.

If anything, Duke answered too quickly. "Absolutely not."

Casting a glance at her garb, her normal navy-blue ATA uniform and trousers, Doris said, "I'm hardly dressed for a night out, and this sounds like a rather high-class place. Are you sure they'll let me in?"

Believing he'd won her over, Duke forgot where he was and turned back around. With his back to the gap in the door, he opened his mouth to speak and in doing so, immediately sneezed.

"You'll have to get used to him a little," Doris advised him. "He'll be coming back down south with us when we fly back."

"Over my dead...achoo! Achoo! Achoo!" He let out an explosive series of sneezes and when he finished, looked distinctly sorry for himself.

Doris shrugged, impervious to his discomfort. "It's non-negotiable so, if I were you, I'd perhaps see about working something out. Perhaps you could wear a gas mask?"

"May have to," he muttered, blowing his nose. Putting away his handkerchief, Duke informed her, "Don't worry about standards of dress. I'm sure you've discovered things are a lot more relaxed than pre-war."

"Well, I don't know much about that, not having been over here before the war started, but I'll take your word for it." She got to her feet. "Now, give me ten minutes to have a wash and get this one settled in for the evening."

"We'll meet you downstairs," Duke told her and, with a small nod, dashed out of the room, slamming the door shut behind him.

"Guess I'd better spruce myself up, eh, Taxi," she told her still sleeping cat.

****

"Your furry companion all tucked up for the evening?" Ceiwen asked, as Doris appeared at the entrance to their accommodation.

Doris nodded. "Fresh newspaper and water are down, but he's fast asleep on my bed. He'll be fine," she answered. "Right. How are we getting to this Chevalier place?"

"Mark one feet, Doris," Duke told her. "It's only about fifteen minutes from the castle entrance. Shall we?" He invited her to walk between the pair.

"Nice evening to build up an appetite," Doris

remarked as they passed through the castle. A thought struck her. "I assume this is a good place to eat? If you understand what I mean."

By her side Duke, who appeared to be in a good mood, chuckled. "If you mean, is it better fare than what we'd get in the mess, I'd say that's a given. Especially as your cat seems to have tonight's main course."

"Have I missed something?"

"Only, my dear general," Duke began to inform him, not troubling to keep his voice down—not that anyone else was close enough to overhear them—that it may say salmon on the mess menu for tonight, but they'd have to fight Taxi off to get their hands on it."

"Now I know I'm missing something else," Ceiwen said, taking off his general's hat to scratch the top of his head. "Who's Taxi?"

"My cat," Doris informed him.

"Do I want to know?" he addressed Duke, who shook his head.

"Not unless you want to end up as confused as me."

Everyone walked in in semi-companionable silence along the deliberately darkened streets until they came to a halt before a large building which may have once been someone's pride and joy townhouse. The black-and-white face, all exposed beams of wood and tiny windows, reminded Doris of similar places she'd passed on her many travels around the United Kingdom, all of which had always struck her as being both very old, quite possible much older than her entire native country of the USA, yet proud and imposing. The latter was likely the original owner's idea here when it was built. Craning her neck, she looked up and saw, only about five or six feet above her head, a wooden overhang. Stepping back, after making certain there was no traffic likely to hit her, she could see the structure was an extension from a room. Held up by more beams, she assumed, it would have been even more impressive if not for the blackout.

"Remind me to come back in the daylight," she said aloud. "This pub looks wonderful!"

"It is," Duke agreed, "and it's much more than a pub."

"How do you know this place, Duke?" Ceiwen asked, as Doris rejoined them.

Duke held open the entrance door for the pair. "I attended university here."

As soon as she'd entered the reception area, Doris couldn't help but let out a long, loud whistle. "Holy cow! What a joint!"

Ceiwen nudged her gently in the ribs. "You're going all American on us. What's next? Jiminy Cricket?"

Doris elbowed him back, a little harder than he'd done to her. "Don't take the micky out of the afflicted." All the same, she quickly brushed her hands down the front of her uniform and straightened the seams on her trousers, though neither were in need of any attention.

Duke offered her the crook of his arm—which, after a moment's hesitation, she took. "Come on, we've reservations and I'm hungry."

It was as well Duke had her arm, as Doris allowed herself to become distracted by a huge stone fireplace set into a wall. There, even though it was a mild May evening, a conflagration a dragon would be proud of belched forth flames. Above was a most impressive set of deer antlers. Doris let another whistle out, waking up an elder gentleman who had been peaceably sleeping in a brown leather wingback chair.

"What the devil?" he exclaimed and began to wave his weather-beaten walking stick around.

As the man was now wide awake, he appeared intent upon making a fuss, so Ceiwen detached himself and went over, shooing his companions on their way "I'll find you in a minute. I'll get this chap a drink. That should quieten him down."

At the mention of the word *drink*, the old man did indeed quieten down, and Doris and Duke both watched him willingly follow Ceiwen in the direction of a bar.

"Hmm, he does have more than one use," Duke mused.

Doris tutted. "Don't be unfair. You know you've put him in a very difficult situation."

The pair came to a stop at the entrance to the dining room. Their view of the room was blocked by a rather wide, obviously well-fed couple, in full evening dress and suit, who were conversing with the hostess, who had her back to them.

"You're right," he said. "Obviously, you're right and…I'll try…I'll try to treat him better."

That's all I ask, thank you," Doris told him.

Her head was turned, watching as Ceiwen escorted the man she'd disturbed back to his seat. In his hand, he clutched a large tumbler of what she assumed was whisky. Consequently, when he took a few steps forward, her hand slipped from where it had been lightly resting upon his stump, above the hook.

"Duke? Duke?" she repeated when the major didn't answer. He was staring open-mouthed at the pretty redhead hostess.

"Morag?"

Ceiwen chose that moment to re-join them. "Sorry.

Who's Morag?"

Turning his back upon the woman, whose expression matched his own, Duke told them, "This is my ex-fiancée, Morag Blessed."

Chapter Sixteen

Dinner plans were, unsurprisingly thrown into disarray, with both Doris and Ceiwen in agreement that Duke had a lot to talk over with his ex-fiancée. Yes, they tried to carry on with their plans, only Duke had been so distracted by the unexpected encounter that he tried to pick up his wine glass with his hook, ending up with both a smashed glass and an embarrassed major. The latter was far worse to observe for Doris as, apart from the other day, she'd never witnessed the man losing control of himself and his surroundings. When the minor incident occurred, she glanced over towards where this Morag stood, to find her full attention upon them. Though she couldn't be sure, Doris believed the expression upon Morag's face was utterly sympathetic. Not wasting any more time, she told Duke that she and Ceiwen were going back to the castle and he should talk to Morag.

To his credit, Duke gave them a simple nod, pulled out his wallet and laid a few pound notes on the table to cover the cost of the wine and the broken glass, and was over by Morag's side before either of his companions had a chance to even say goodbye. As they left the hostelry, they were witnesses to Duke and Morag disappearing towards the kitchen. Neither stayed around to find out what happened with them or with the dining room.

If there was one good thing to come from the evening, it was the pair of them, through a fortunate wrong turning, discovering a fish and chip shop. Doris was delighted to find that Ceiwen loved the delicacy as much as she did, though the proprietor looked aghast when Ceiwen requested some mushy peas.

What was unexpected was that Duke didn't appear at breakfast the next morning, nor at their transport for the day's visits. As only Duke had their itinerary, and a visit to his room had proved fruitless and discreet enquiries failed to pin him down, and as, apparently, even his guard weren't informed where they were going until the day of the visit, it fell to Ceiwen to make up an excuse to cancel things. Though she didn't think he'd win any prizes for acting, at least he wore the rank, so when he said he had a bad cough and intended to spend the day in his quarters, his word was believed.

With an unexpected day off, Doris spent most of it, meals apart, catching up on washing her clothes—not an easy thing to do in a castle full of men in the peak of fitness and seemingly turned on by the sight of a pair of stockings, even those being wrung out to dry. With this done, which took up most of a normal working day, she spent the rest of the evening getting to know Taxi a little better. Importantly, he knew exactly what the newspaper was for and there had been no *accidents*. Unexpectedly, Ceiwen had knocked on her door around six in the evening with some cut-up ham for Taxi and some ham and cheese sandwiches for Doris.

"I didn't see you in the mess, so thought you may be hungry," he'd explained. "Plus, I love cats and would love to get to know this little chap," he added, absently reaching down to scratch Taxi behind the ears.

Doris Flies Solo

Not quite knowing what to expect, Doris had been prepared to rescue the man, in case Taxi went for him. Happily, Taxi allowed the man to scratch him and then, at a gesture from Doris, Ceiwen took the lone wooden seat in the room and Taxi jumped onto his lap. Taking the hint, Ceiwen proceeded to hand feed a now loudly purring Taxi the ham he'd brought.

The two sat in companiable quiet with the only sound being that of Taxi munching his way through his food. He did take a nibble on one of Ceiwen's fingers, twice, and they also heard the occasional shout emanating from elsewhere in the castle. The former, the fake general took with good humor, and the latter Doris ignored, shouting being the army's normal method of communicating. Once the food had disappeared, Taxi further surprised them both by settling in on Ceiwen's lap and, within a minute, was fast asleep.

"If only I could bottle that ability," Ceiwen mused, with a shake of his head.

"It would be very useful," Doris agreed, licking her fingers after finishing off her last sandwich. "That was delicious!" she told him. "The officer's mess, I presume."

Ceiwen nodded. "It seems they had been planning on serving salmon from the previous day, only as the salmon went missing…"

He let the sentence go unfinished, though his eyes went to where the salmon had been, Doris having been unable to resist letting the cat finish it off the previous night. Seeing as she'd come in smelling of fish 'n' chips, it was the least she could do, she felt. It was either that or succumb to being washed by Taxi to within an inch of her life, and as his tongue had the texture of rough sandpaper, it hadn't really been a choice at all.

"Duke told you, then?"

"He may have let the cat out of the bag, yes," he replied, scratching Taxi on the top of the head.

Doris shuffled on the bed until her back was against the wall, and tucked her legs underneath her bottom. "I don't suppose you know what's happened to him? Duke, I mean."

Ceiwen shook his head. "Not a clue. I've done some discreet enquiries, but no one, including the guard room staff, has seen him. That took a bit of flannel, I'll tell you. I think we both suspect he's with this Morag."

"Do you think he'll turn up tomorrow? You know him better than me," Doris asked.

After a moment, Ceiwen shrugged. "Barely. "I hope so. I'm not sure how long I can keep this sick act up."

Doris cast her eyes up at her window as a bird flitted by. "Me too. You're not that good an actor," she told him, smiling.

"Well, I was going to try and get you to call me Rob, seeing as we're on our own, but…"

"The truth hurts?" Doris got in quickly, raising an eyebrow, which got a soft chuckle and the beginning of a purr from Taxi. "See, Taxi agrees!"

"Probably," Ceiwen replied, smiling down at the contented cat. "And?"

"And…we've already discussed this. I'd like to, you seem a good lad, for a limey," she added, "but I don't want to risk slipping up at any time."

A sharp rap on the door interrupted further conversation, and it was flung open, not giving Doris a chance to utter a word, to reveal a slightly less than perfectly attired Major Marmaduke Newton-Baxtor.

"Door!" Doris yelled, recovering quickly, but not quickly enough.

Before anyone could react, Taxi's ears pricked up, his eyes snapped open, and he launched himself from Ceiwen's lap, landing with four feet together on Duke's left shoulder. This caused the man to violently sneeze, which triggered Taxi to dig his claws in and launch himself through the still open door.

By the time Doris had struggled off the bed—the springs hardly worth being called as such, since when she was on it the mattress nearly reached the floor—and pulled Duke inside so she could stand outside her room, there was no sign of the cat. Without another thought in her head, she padded downstairs as quickly as she could, to find the door to the side of the building was open. It was with a heavy heart and far from great expectation, that she stood outside and, without consideration to how it sounded or how she looked, she shouted at the top of her voice, "Taxi! Taxi!"

Naturally, no sooner did she pause for breath than a squad of soldiers marched past, all openly staring at the strange semi-uniformed woman yelling for a taxi. The man bringing up the rear had to tell her, "You won't find one here, luv!" before chortling to himself.

Doris was about to run after the unsuspecting man and teach him a few manners, when she felt a pair of arms grab each of hers.

"Oh, no, you don't," Duke told her, tightening his grip.

Still annoyed with the man, Doris went to elbow him in the stomach, only he seemed prepared for this trick and quickly released his hold and took a hasty couple of steps back. She wasn't going to let him off, though, and she was right on his toes and took a surprisingly forceful grip upon his neck before he could stop her. She twisted his head to the left and then the right before he managed to force himself free.

"What the hell was that?" he asked, holding out his hands before him, just in case the American came at him again.

Before replying, Doris shouted out her cat's name once more and then sank onto the steps. Planting her elbows on her knees, she rested her head on her hands, her face a picture of misery. She glanced up. "I was checking you for lipstick."

Slightly hesitant, he came and sat down beside her. At the same time, Ceiwen sat down on her other side, squeezing her shoulder in support as he did so. "No sign of him?" he asked.

Doris shook her head. "Where've you been?" she asked Duke. "We've been sitting around like a couple of dead hoofers all day!"

"Dead hoofers?" Duke couldn't help but ask.

She couldn't keep a slight smile from her face as she answered, "It means you're a very bad dancer, that no one wants anything to do with."

"I like that!" Ceiwen announced. "Dead hoofers. I'll have to remember that."

Duke ignored this. "I owe you two an apology," he began, but was interrupted by Doris, who wasn't feeling too gracious towards him.

"You think? I know you didn't like Taxi, but you could have thought before barging into my room!"

Taking his hat off, Duke ran his fingers through his hair. "Believe it or not, that wasn't deliberate."

Opening and closing her mouth, Doris eventually

and very reluctantly nodded, "I suppose. Doesn't change things though, Taxi still ran off."

"For which I really am truly sorry," Duke informed her and waited until she looked at his face and gave a slight nod. "As to where I've been. Well, you've both probably surmised I've been with Morag."

"You dog!" Ceiwen blurted out, before placing a hand over his mouth and mumbling, "Sorry, sorry. I don't know where that came from."

Ignoring the unexpected outburst, Doris pressed Duke for more of an explanation, but no matter how she phrased her questions, he would only say, "We began to talk and wound up in her attic room, only talking, until I left there an hour ago."

"Only talking?"

Duke canted his head so he could look her firmly in the eye. "Only talking." After a few minutes' silence, Doris gave him a genuine smile—well, perhaps more of a smilette, but it was the thought which counted. "I suppose we should just…watch this space for further announcements."

"And I really am very sorry, to you both," he told the pair, getting back to his feet and holding out a hand for Doris, "for wasting your day. Can I ask, was I missed?"

It was Ceiwen who replied, "Don't worry, we covered for you."

"You did?" Duke said, unable to keep a note of incredulity from his voice. "How?"

"I acted ill!" Ceiwen announced proudly.

Doris added, "Badly, but it seemed to work," she added, to forego the protest she was certain Ceiwen was about to present.

With everyone now on their feet, Duke cleared his throat. "Shall we say, normal time tomorrow morning?"

"Suit's me," Ceiwen told him.

"And me," Doris added before turning back towards her billet. "I'll see you both tomorrow."

"What are you doing now?" Duke found himself asking as she was about to enter the building.

Doris waggled a foot. "Put on some shoes and go look for Taxi."

Chapter Seventeen

If Doris and Ceiwen had been hoping to find out the next day more details on what exactly Duke and Morag had spoken about, they were sorely disappointed. Duke was polite when spoken to, but apart from briefing both them and their escort as to where they were going and, in the case of his two companions, what to expect, he barely uttered a word the entire day. The same occurred over the following two days, and as soon as they arrived back at Edinburgh Castle, he simply wished them both a good night, dismissed the escort, and disappeared through the gates.

And each night, Doris was up until the early hours trying to find Taxi, with no luck. This didn't do anything to improve her mood.

In fact, it wasn't until they all met up next to the Humber and the escort's lorry on the morning of the 7th May that things began to become interesting once more. The units they'd visited since the incident with Morag—and Doris had mentioned to Duke on more than one occasion that he still owed them a decent meal—had merely been more units which were responsible for the sending of fake radio traffic.

It was an early start that morning, with Duke having to rush about to make sure everyone was at the vehicles for the crack of dawn. Once everyone was present, though Doris found herself fighting to keep her eyes open, he clambered up onto the lorry, hanging from the open door to deliver his briefing.

"Sorry for the early morning, but we've a bit of a drive this morning, as we have to be back here for around midafternoon." He stopped to glance over at Doris, whose eyes were drooping once more, and addressed his next statement directly to her. "Doris," he barked, which had the wished-for effect of causing her eyes to snap open. "When we get back, we're going to need you to drive into Turnhouse and give your Anson a onceover. Make sure she's fueled and ready to go, as we'll be flying to Northern Ireland tomorrow morning."

At the mention of the word "flying," Doris became fully awake and answered him clearly, so he knew she'd heard each word he'd said, "Understood, sir." She still didn't salute him, though, and took some pleasure in noting the look of displeasure upon his face and surprise on the other ranks present.

Once he'd rearranged his facial expression into something more his norm, Duke carried on as if nothing had occurred. "As I was saying, we need to make this early start as we're driving up to RAF Peterhead. That's about seventy-odd miles north-northeast of here. Drivers, you all know what the roads are like these days, and I expect the ones we're going to be using will be in an even worse state than you may be used to, so be careful, as I don't want to have to stop and try to change a tire on either of these wagons. We've a schedule to keep to, plus there are going to be cameras. Pathé are going to be covering Ceiwen's visit, and the last thing I want them concentrating on would be a bunch of oil-and-grease-smeared squaddies. So drive carefully and watch out for potholes. Once we arrive, smarten yourselves up before you disembark. Keep this in mind if you see a camera pointing your way—your sole purpose is to protect Ceiwen. Nothing...I repeat, *nothing* else matters. If I catch any one of you waving at Granny, I'll have you up on a charge so quick your feet won't touch the floor! Do we understand each other?"

There was a loud chorus of "Yes, sir!" and then they were dismissed.

As Doris watched everyone gather up their kit and board the lorry, she remembered her own job and went to open the door for Ceiwen, just as the man went to pull it open himself.

"Perfect timing, Doris, thank you," he told her, clambering into the back seat as Duke joined him from the other side.

Once she was behind the wheel, Doris turned and with mischief dancing in her eyes asked, "So I shouldn't have bothered bringing the makeup then, Major?"

Whilst Ceiwen chuckled, Doris only heard a grunt from Duke as she settled down to what she hoped would be a pleasant drive. As was typical for these times, most of the traffic they met was military in nature and their escort had to flash their lights at her only twice to get her to slow down. You couldn't call the silence which reigned in the car companiable, though at least the atmosphere seemed a little better than the previous days. Doris tried to get Duke to describe anywhere of interest they happened to pass, but with a singular lack of success. Ceiwen could only shrug his shoulders in empathy, so Doris settled in and was monosyllabic in replying whenever Duke spoke to give her directions.

Nearly two hours later, they pulled up at the gates of RAF Peterhead. "Windswept and totally uninteresting,"

Doris muttered as they were let through the gates. Following a Jeep which contained the Station Commander and his driver, the small convoy wound its way around a perimeter track until they pulled up outside a hut upon which a sign declared they'd arrived at "19 Squadron." Already parked was a small blue van which informed all it was the property of Pathé, whilst next to it was a somewhat battered Morris Oxford Six. A mudguard and headlamp were missing, yet its candy-apple-red body shone as if new.

"Pull up here," Duke instructed, tapping Doris on the shoulder, and pointing to a spot just in front of the Morris. Their escort slipped into a place a few feet in front of them, and even as Doris hopped out to perform her chauffeur duties for Ceiwen, she noticed the escort were already forming up much quicker than usual.

As he got out, Ceiwen leaned down to quickly whisper in her ear, "Best foot forward, Doris, the cameras are rolling."

Once the door had shut, Doris waited for Duke to join them, and whilst Duke performed his ADC duties, making sure Ceiwen's tie and hat were straight, Doris had time to glance around. Sure enough, there was a suited man behind a large tripod upon which was mounted a cine-camera, and it was currently pointed at their escort. Doris snorted with amusement because even as she watched it was clear that Sergeant Lewis was trying to mug to the cameras. His voice when he shouted out orders was even louder than normal, and she noticed that he kept his right side facing the lens. One of his men must have noticed too, as he was struggling to keep a straight face. For his sake, she hoped the sergeant didn't see him.

Duke tapped her on the shoulder. "Fall in just behind us, please, Doris."

In short order, the three of them walked towards the hut, where the Station Commander was waiting. Doris saw that he'd been joined by what she suspected to be everyone on the squadron who wasn't engaged on any urgent job. Not normally someone to be intimidated by crowds, she unexpectedly felt a cold sweat break out between her shoulder blades, and she swallowed, hard. Keeping her eyes straight ahead, coincidentally between the small gap of her two companions, she swiveled her eyes and saw that the camera was now focused upon them. Perhaps that was the cause. Well, so long as they didn't want her to say anything, she thought, as her mouth was unnaturally dry.

After a short speech of welcome from the Wing Commander—she immediately forgot his name—Ceiwen stepped up to say a few words. These turned out to be much the same as he'd said when they'd been at the army signals units, though with a few embellishments and compliments on what he'd seen of the airfield so far. At this, Doris couldn't stop herself from looking around. From what she could see, a dog would find it hard to locate a convenient tree for its needs, the place was so open. With perfect timing, a gust of wind shot around them, and she was extremely glad to be wearing trousers. The cameras would have had a great piece of footage otherwise!

Once the speeches were over, the anonymous Wing Commander came over, and next thing she knew, they were being invited to follow the man for a walk towards one of the squadron aircraft. Stood beside it was an RAF corporal and two airmen, none of whom appeared to be overly enthusiastic at being interrupted from the maintenance they'd been in the middle of. The engine covers were off, as were a couple of panels from the rear fuselage. Nevertheless, all three came to smart attention as Ceiwen was introduced to them.

Doris took the opportunity to give the North American Mustang they were working on a look over. She'd flown many different types of planes by now but hadn't been lucky enough to be assigned one of these superb fighters. From what she could tell, there was a split of opinions as to which was the best, the Spitfire or the Mustang. All Doris could think of when that thought entered her head was that this aircraft had the cleanest lines she'd ever seen and if circumstances could have allowed it, she'd have begged to be allowed to take it up for a spin. As it was, she was in the middle of stroking the leading edge of one of its wings when one of the airmen, taking advantage of not being talked to, turned his head to tell her, "Oi! Hands off, miss!"

Turning, she allowed the young man, who couldn't have been much over eighteen, to have a clear view of the wings she proudly wore upon her chest. She noted the confusion upon his face and was considering what she should say when Duke stepped in for her.

"It's fine, young man. Third Officer Johnson has probably flown more hours than anyone else on this station. She knows her way around an aircraft." He then nodded at Doris, assuming he'd saved her some trouble, before turning his attention back to his duties.

If he'd really known Doris, Duke would have noticed the way she was viciously twanging the rubber band around her wrist and been aware she was annoyed with him. She thought she'd made it perfectly clear that she could take care of herself. Where did he think they were? Back in 1902?

The rubber band broke, and Doris glared at Duke's back. She'd have to get a replacement as soon as possible, certainly before tomorrow's flight.

She was about to open her mouth when she noticed the camera crew had caught them up, and was rather surprised to find the camera now mounted upon a tripod on top of the van! Remembering her promise to Jane that she'd be on her best behavior, she reluctantly tore herself away from the sleek plane and retook her place behind Ceiwen and Duke.

With the all-seeing eye of the camera following them, they had just bid the three mechanics goodbye when a huge gust of wind blew over them and everyone made a grab for their various hats. Where they were was quite close to the perimeter fence, around fifty feet or so, in Doris's opinion, and a movement by it caught her eye. Something was flapping in the wind's grip, and she involuntarily took a step or two towards it, only to find her progress halted by Duke's sudden firm grip upon her shoulder. She was about to object when she noticed he was silently and minutely shaking his head.

The movement had also caught the eye of the Pathé crew, and the camera had already swiveled around. It was now pointing towards what she could see to be a loose sheet of camouflage netting. Clearly visible was a row of what Doris recognized as American half-tracks, a kind of lorry which had wheels at the front and tracks at the rear, designed to make it easier to drive off the road, though these ones appeared to be staked down, as if they might blow away. As she looked, that was indeed what one of them seemed to be trying to do. Two men made a grab for some ropes and were just in time to prevent it from blowing away in the wind. The strange sight made her glance around the airfield, and in the distance, she focused upon what, at first glance, appeared to be more Mustangs, but these appeared to be tied down too, and Doris's mind quickly put the pieces together.

"These are all inflatable what, decoys?"

Duke nodded, his attention still focused upon the camera crew who also seemed to notice these dummy aircraft and had swiveled the camera to point at them as well.

"Shouldn't we stop that?" Doris pointed at the camera.

"Give them a minute," Duke leant in to tell her.

"But…" Doris began to automatically say, before a light bulb came on. "Oh!"

Not quite a minute later, Doris caught Duke nodding at Sergeant Lewis, who immediately pointed at two of his men and ordered, "You two! With me, now!" and the three rushed up to the Pathé van. Once they'd reached the van, Lewis banged a spade-sized fist upon the side, causing the whole vehicle to shake and instantly getting the attention of the two men standing atop. "Stop filming, now!" he shouted and the men, obviously not being stupid, stepped away from the camera. "Get down!"

"If you please, gentlemen," Duke added, his voice not quite as loud or as full of threat as the sergeant's but with that touch of quiet authority which made the two men clamber down from their perch a little quicker than they'd been doing.

Following the major, with Ceiwen close to her shoulder and a slightly bemused station commander close behind, Doris went over to the worried-looking camera crew. Once there, Duke took control and Doris was treated to the sight of the man conducting an impromptu interrogation; it was a rather unnerving sight.

"Gentlemen," he began, striding up to the one who'd been behind the camera, "I assume you know you just saw and filmed some things which you shouldn't have." He didn't wait for an answer. "Because of that, I need to take possession of the film you just took."

"But…" began the one wearing a bowler hat, presumably the one in charge, only to find himself cut short.

"But nothing," Duke told him with a smile a crocodile would be proud of. "It's quite simple. Because of that…incident," he flapped a hand in the direction of the camouflaged half-tracks, where a bunch of airmen were now busily securing the nets once more, "I shall need to review your footage and, if need be, do some editing. Once I'm satisfied, the film shall be returned to you."

Once he was sure he wouldn't be cut off again, Mr. Bowler Hat cleared his throat and said, "You invited us, Major. You do remember that?"

Duke inclined his head. "I know that. You, though, must realize that you weren't meant to see…any of…that," he added, waving a hand in the direction of the decoys.

Whilst his cameraman quickly nodded his head in agreement, his boss took a few more seconds before he let out a sigh and then with obvious reluctance in his voice said, "Brian, get the camera down and box up the film for the major." He then asked Duke, "When do we get the film back?"

Doris was fairly certain Duke winked at her as he turned his head away from the man, as if to give himself some thinking time. "A couple of days. Where are you staying?"

It was Brian who answered, "We're bedding down in a hotel called the Young Chevalier. Do you know it?"

As she was watching him, Doris noticed Duke having to quickly keep a smile from appearing. "I can find it. Once I'm finished, I'll give the reception a phone call and arrange to come down. In the meantime, it goes without saying, you're not to utter a word about what you've seen here. Agreed?" He held out a hand, letting a small smile of sympathy show, though his eyes were as hard as flint in warning, too.

After a slight hesitation, Mr. Bowler Hat shook it. "Agreed…not that I've much choice."

Duke ignored the jibe as Brian handed him a can of film.

"Would you like me to take ahold of that, Major?" Doris asked.

Without hesitation, Duke handed her the film, thanked the disgruntled Pathé men, and then led the way, Sergeant Lewis and his two men striding along with them, back to where Ceiwen seemed to be doing a good job in pacifying the station commander and the rest of the station staff in attendance. Perhaps, Doris mused, she'd have to reevaluate her opinion of the man's acting skills.

"There you are, Major," Ceiwen said as they joined him, returning the ADC's salute. "I think it's about time we were off, don't you?"

Duke made a show of looking at his watch before opening his briefcase, rummaging around for a few seconds, and then closing it once more, before saying, "As you wish, General." He turned and saluted the wing commander. "Sir, thank you for your hospitality."

The way the visit had gone must have flustered the poor man, as he was only able to utter incoherent sounds in reply.

Once the three were back inside the Humber, Duke asked Doris, "When we get to the bend before the guard room, slow down to a crawl, please."

"Why should…" Doris began to say, only to notice Duke had raised an eyebrow once more, so she turned to concentrate on her driving.

As they approached the spot Duke had mentioned, Doris slowed right down and looked out and around her. Because of this, she caught a glimpse of a man in khaki as he rushed out from behind a building and sprinted up to the lorry behind her, where the passenger's side door opened and the man was hauled up into the cab. Doris didn't need Duke tapping her on the shoulder to speed up again. "Clever so and so," she muttered, as she caught the station commander's Jeep back up.

Doris waited until she'd set course for Edinburgh before saying, "That was all a setup for the cameras, wasn't it?"

Chapter Eighteen

Blearily, Doris rubbed the sleep from her eyes and sipped her second cup of what the officer's mess called coffee. She would have laughed if it weren't so awful. Instead she pulled a face she didn't bother to hide, it being only just past six in the morning, with precious few other people around in the dining room. Looking down at the steaming pile of eggs (probably dried) and strips of bacon before her, she picked up her fork and forced a few forkfuls of the eggs down before placing the bacon into a napkin and pushing her chair back.

"Finished, ma'am?" a steward asked, appearing behind her as if he'd been there all the time.

"All finished," she told him, clapping the man on the shoulder, causing him to jump slightly at the unexpected contact.

As she started to turn away, he told her, "Good luck. We hope you find Taxi."

Turning back and ignoring the grease now soaking into her fingers from the bacon, she regarded the young chap a little suspiciously before deciding he was in earnest. "You know about him?"

He nodded, as he picked up her empty plate. "All the staff have heard you calling for him." He shook his head before telling her, "We're all looking out for him too."

"I found him in a bag, out the rear," she told him, adding, "Some bastard had thrown him out in the trash...rubbish," she amended. "I don't suppose you have any idea who that was?"

By the looks of the man, if he could have held up her plate as a shield without making a mess on the floor, he would have. Deliberately, she took a calming breath. It was unfair of her to take out her anger and frustration on him, as obviously he hadn't been responsible for Taxi's predicament.

"I'm sorry..." She held out her hand, hoping he'd supply his name.

"Snodgrass, ma'am." He shook her hand, allowing a small smile to grace his lips.

"I'm Doris. Enough of this 'ma'am' nonsense, and I can't call you by your surname."

Glancing around to make sure no one was around to overhear, Snodgrass said, "Percy."

Doris shook his hand again. "Very pleased to meet you, Percy, and..." she surprised him by going up on tiptoes and quickly pecking him on the cheek, "thank you very much for looking out for Taxi. Pass on my thanks to your mates too, please."

Walking towards the exit, Doris put her hand on the door, about to push it open, when Percy raised his voice to call, "Best of luck, Doris!"

Rather than leaving, Doris glanced around the dining room and noticed a very young officer, a lieutenant, she thought, glaring between the two of them. "You have a problem?" she announced, striding over towards where the man now had his knife and fork poised in midair. When she arrived before him, Doris planted her balled fists before him on the table. "I gave him permission to call me by my first name. If you've a problem with that, I suggest you take it up with me. If I hear you creating trouble for my friend, believe me, you'd prefer to face Hitler rather than get on my bad side."

At being presented with a visibly angry American, in a uniform he obviously didn't recognize, the man barely managed to stammer out, "I don't doubt that."

"Good." Doris nodded her head at him before standing straight and smiling the sweetest smile she could muster. "Have a nice day," she told him, before finally leaving, throwing a friendly wave Percy's way.

Very shortly, her voice could be heard yelling out, "Taxi!" at the top of her voice.

Pushing aside his plate, all appetite gone, the lieutenant got to his feet, only to find the steward in question before him.

"Finished, sir?"

For a second or two, it looked like he might say something to him, only for Doris's voice to ring out again, and he rapidly changed his mind rapidly. "Yes. Yes, thank you, Snodgrass." Picking up his hat, he jammed it on his head, peered in the direction of the windows as Doris shouted again, before nodding at the steward. "I don't know who that is, but she's a little…scary!"

"I think she's wonderful, sir," Percy told him, as he began to clear the table.

****

"Not keeping you awake, are we?" Ceiwen asked and nudged her in the ribs. Duke was busy trying to persuade one of their escorts that Doris flew better than she drove—quite true, but everyone had better not make any cracks about women pilots, or they'd find out exactly how good a pilot she was.

Finishing off her yawn, and as they were the other side of the lorry, Doris stuck her tongue out at him. "In case you're deaf, I've been out looking for Taxi."

The man at least had the grace to look contrite. "I know, and I'm sorry." He looked around and then, as seemed to be a habit for the English, stated the obvious, "Still no sign?"

"Thank heavens for small mercies," she muttered under her breath as Duke appeared in their midst.

"All sorted!" he declared. "Lewis wasn't happy about not being able to take his full body of men."

As Sergeant Lewis joined them, Doris suggested, "We could probably squeeze one more person in."

Lewis's head immediately snapped up. "We could? I'd feel so much better."

"So long as they knew they wouldn't have a parachute. We only carry enough for two crew and the four passengers," Doris informed him, working hard at keeping her smirk from showing. When it looked like Lewis might collapse from trying to figure a way around the issue, she took pity on him. "Look, Sergeant, what I said is true. We don't carry parachutes for more than six, and though I'm certain we could borrow one from somewhere at Turnhouse, we still couldn't carry more bodies than the Anson's fitted out for. You'll have to do with yourself and the other two you've chosen."

"There are times..." the man muttered to himself, as he turned back towards where his men were waiting for him at the rear of the lorry.

"I do wish you wouldn't do...that," Duke told her, with a shake of his head.

"Shall we make a move? It's nearly half six and I thought you wanted to be in the air for half seven?" Doris asked, not troubling to reply.

On the approach to the airfield, Doris broke the silence. "I must ask. Why are we going over to Belfast? For my part, it'll be nice to see another part of the country, only I don't see what this has to do with all this deception stuff."

Not answering immediately, Doris heard Duke open his briefcase and take out some papers. There followed the sounds of them being shuffled before they were returned to the case, which was shut up once again. Doris was beginning to think of the briefcase as more of a comfort thing than anything else. So far as she could tell, anything he needed to know was tucked away inside his head. Musing to herself whilst she waited for him to speak, the idea occurred to her that perhaps she should suggest they visit Las Vegas when the war was over. She'd bet anything that he'd make a damn good card-counter.

It wasn't until they were within a mile of Turnhouse that Duke spoke again. "As I've already said, I can't tell you everything. Only a few people do know all. What I can tell you is that we suspect Belfast to be a hive of activity for Nazi spies, or at least it's easy enough for them to cross the border and find their way to Belfast from Eire. The idea is for Ceiwen here to be seen inspecting the troops of the American Fifteenth Corps."

"These are real men?" Doris interrupted.

"As real as you and me," Duke assured her. "Some things have to be real, as we can't assume that everything we want to get back to the Germans is completely under our control, hence this visit. There's going to be a very public inspection and march past of these men, which would be enough on its own to pique the interest of any enemy agents. Put Ceiwen into the mix, and with Hitler's and the German' fixation on the man, it'll be like attracting bees to honey. They won't be able to resist it!"

"You hope," Ceiwen added.

Duke shrugged. "True, but the odds are good."

"So all this for a roll of the dice," Doris said.

It took a second for Duke to translate the analogy, and when he did, he could only shrug, adding for Doris's benefit as she couldn't see the gesture, "As you say. The press will be there too."

A short while later, as they came up to Doris's Anson, Duke tapped Doris on the shoulder, "You're sure everything is, er, top-notch with your aircraft?"

Doris had time only to nod before Ceiwen asked, "Are you feeling all right?" as Duke slumped back into the seat. "You appear a little pale."

Doris quickly glanced over her shoulder. "He's right. You are definitely off-color."

After a few moments Duke reluctantly, so it appeared from his tone of voice, told them, "I'm remembering Doris's flying from coming up here."

"Hey! You know that wasn't my fault," Doris protested. "No one could have known that windshear was coming." Bringing the Humber to a stop, Doris turned fully around and fixed the major with a calculating look. "That's not it. You're worried I'm still hacked off with you for letting Taxi out and that I intend getting my own back!"

Duke nodded and swallowed. "Okay, you've got me. Oh, and to preempt you, I'll cut back on the sarcasm."

"Good boy." She smiled and hopped out to open the rear door, in keeping with her role as chauffeur.

She took a minute to think things over. "Well, it hadn't entered my head, but you have my word I won't try anything. I still haven't forgiven you, so take this as being more for everyone else's sake than yours."

Duke held out his hand. "I'll take that, and again, I am sorry."

"If you're really sorry, then you can come out and help me look for him when we get back later."

"Deal," he replied immediately. Only then did Doris take his hand.

****

Take-off was uneventful, if you didn't count one of the privates in the main cabin screaming at the top of his lungs until Doris was able to level off. Turning around as far as she could, Doris looked back into the cabin and was greeted with a real smile from one private, who looked like he was having the time of his life, staring at everything, his eyes out on stalks, and an obviously fake one from the other who'd been screaming during take-off. She wondered why Sergeant Lewis hadn't said anything—the man's hands were gripping the edge of his seat as if his life depended upon it.

Waving to attract his attention, she mimed taking her hands away from the seat and added a smile. Now was not the time to toy with the poor man's mind. After the third time she made the motions, he somewhat gingerly removed first one hand and then the other. Giving him a thumbs-up, she then mimed her advice he should take a drink of water from his canteen, holding up her thumb and forefinger close together so he'd know to only take a sip.

Thankful that the man seemed to understand her sign language—otherwise it would undoubtedly have been down to her to at least help clean up—she turned back and hovered her hand over the undercarriage retraction lever.

Next to her in the co-pilot's seat, Ceiwen saw the movement. "Thinking about leaving the gear down?"

"It does seem like a bit too much effort to crank it up for just over an hour's flight," Doris agreed.

Fate, though, must have been listening, as no sooner were the words out of her mouth than a tremendous gust of wind hit them square on the nose and the Anson, already at near enough full load, began to struggle to maintain forward momentum. Doris adjusted throttles to compensate and then, throwing a wry smile Ceiwen's way, began to crank up the undercarriage.

After a few minutes, he asked, "Would you like me to take over?"

Thankful they were the only two with flying helmets on and none of the escort had thought it strange for a general to sit up front with the pilot, Doris told him, "Thank you, but that would look a little weird."

Showing he was "in character," Ceiwen promptly took off his flying helmet, put his officer hat on, tipped it over his eyes and settled back in his seat. Within a minute, he was happily snoring away, leaving a sweating Doris to slightly regret her comment and more than a little envious of the magical ability to fall asleep so quickly, especially in such a noisy environment.

Soon, with the undercarriage retracted, or as much as it was possible to be in an Anson, Doris shook the ache out of her arms and unscrewed the top from her thermos flask. Not bothering with pouring into a cup, she took a hefty swig of what turned out to be strong tea. Wincing and wishing, not for the first time, for a decent cup of coffee, she checked her instruments and that they were still on course.

A thought struck her that made her forget her still-aching body. As they were going to visit an American unit, perhaps she could persuade them to part with some real coffee!

Chapter Nineteen

Naturally, since she'd gone to the trouble of cranking up the undercarriage, the wind direction changed, and they ended up arriving at their destination, RAF Nutts Corner, just a little short of ten miles northwest of Belfast, around fifteen minutes early. Doris had asked Duke during the flight about the choice of airfield and was told it was one of the trans-Atlantic reception centers for the arrival of American B17 Flying Fortresses and B24 Liberator heavy bombers. She was looking forward to seeing what was there—and if there was the chance of obtaining some coffee, she was quite prepared to turn on the charm. Checking her flight bag before lining up for landing, she made certain she'd remembered to pack her hairbrush. When on delivery flights, she wasn't normally too bothered how she looked but, with something as important as real coffee on the agenda, she was prepared to spruce herself up a little.

Once they were down and the Anson had been secured, Doris walked over to join the rest of her, well, "crew," for want of a better description.

"Well, this is…flat," she declared, after looking around her.

Flat but busy would have been a more apt description, though Doris didn't trouble to correct herself, as she was too busy looking around. RAF Nutts Corner was, no arguing, the most strangely named base she'd ever visited, but, the name apart, it was little different. Scattered around in seemingly random locations were multiple B17s and B24s, with a smattering of various aircraft making up the numbers. She felt a tap on her shoulder.

"Come along, Doris, best not to keep the general waiting," Duke told her, pointing to where a Humber, closely followed by two Jeeps, was bearing down upon them.

About to point out that Ceiwen was beside them, Doris realized the arriving officer must be someone else. "I assume this is the person in charge of this Corps thing we're over for?"

"Well put," Ceiwen leaned over to tell her, not troubling to keep a small grin off his face.

Glancing out of the corner of her eye, Doris could see Duke's mouth also twitching, only he had more control than their general. By the time he replied, there wasn't a hint of amusement in his voice, not that he was angry with her, either. "He's called," there was a slight pause whilst he held up a document in his hook, "Major General Wade Haislip. Do you know him?"

Turning her head as they came to a stop, Doris turned a shrewd eye upon the major, "Are you teasing me? There's a few more of us than you limeys, so, unlike you, we're not on first-name terms with each other."

Further banter was cut off by the vehicles coming to a stop before them. An American military policeman approached them, momentary confusion showing on his face whilst he worked out which was the highest ranking of them before he stood to attention and saluted Ceiwen.

"General," he began, "I've been instructed to give you General Haislip's greetings and to escort you, along with your staff," he hastily added, having noted the way Sergeant Lewis had bristled, "to his headquarters. Your men can get into my Jeep and the one behind, sir, and you and your staff have use of the Humber."

After an argument between Doris and the American private behind the wheel, Doris found herself in the back of the Humber next to Ceiwen.

"I don't think I've seen you lose an argument before," the general said, causing Duke to turn around to observe.

Doris was the only one to notice the waggle of eyebrows the driver shot up at the rearview mirror. "Who said I lost an argument?"

Duke, who was obviously used to treating other ranks as if they weren't there, asked her, "What was with all that hand-waving and raised voices, then?"

"We were setting a price," Doris told him.

"What for…" he began to ask, before changing his mind. "You were doing a deal for some coffee, weren't you."

"Sure was, mac," the driver told him. "Remind me not to play poker with you, Doris," he threw over his shoulder before honking the horn and yelling out the open window at a cyclist he'd just driven off the perimeter track. "Wrong side of the road, pal!"

Ceiwen turned to look back at the debris they'd left behind. "Shouldn't we go back and see if they're all right?"

The driver at least didn't call Ceiwen anything other than, "Sir. He'll be fine. I knocked him over yesterday. He just can't get used to riding on the wrong side!"

"That's all right, then, I suppose," Ceiwen muttered, though he shook his head in bemusement.

"We'd all appreciate it if you didn't knock anyone else over. At least whilst we're in the car," Duke told their driver.

It may have been May, but Northern Ireland decided to be kind to them and held off from raining. Indeed, their driver, who'd since told them to call him Ed, informed them that it was nice to be somewhere where it never rained.

"Where're you from, Ed?" Doris asked, suspicion tinting her question.

"Seattle," he replied, adding, "That's in Washington State."

Doris settled back, a smug expression on her face.

"What's so funny?" Duke eventually had to ask.

"Seattle's rather famous for its weather," she supplied. "Right, Ed?"

"You got it," Ed replied, and edged a little farther towards the left-hand side of the road, ignoring the snort of laughter from Doris.

When Duke didn't appear to be any wiser, Doris enlightened him, "It rains a lot in Seattle."

Ed nodded. "A lot!"

Puzzled, Duke then asked Ed, "Exactly how long have you been over here, Private?"

"Five days," he replied.

Duke's face mimicked that of Doris. "Ah. Welcome to Great Britain. I hope you'll feel…at home."

Ed must have missed the irony in Duke's voice, as he merely grinned at what he thought was a friendly sentiment.

Soon enough, they pulled into the American base camp and stopped outside the guardroom.

"Looks like the boss is waiting for you guys," Ed

observed, before rushing to open the rear doors of the Humber.

Sure enough, at the bottom of a set of steps leading up to a low wooden hut-type building, was a stout, imposing man with the two silver stars of a major general of the United States Army on his shoulders. Ignoring two officers of lower rank who were fussing away behind him, Major General Wade Haislip half-pulled Ceiwen out of the car, giving him a slap on the back and a hearty handshake. "General Ceiwen, very pleased to meet you!"

"General." Ceiwen nodded, once he'd managed to extract his hand. "It's good to meet you too." He brought his hand down upon Duke's shoulder. "Let me introduce you to my aide, Major Newton-Baxtor."

Doris was getting used to the sight of people holding out their right hands to shake Duke's, only to hesitate at noticing the hook on his left. To his credit, Haislip barely turned a hair. "Major, welcome to Belfast. Now," he began, as he noticed Doris standing slightly behind the major, "just who do we have here? Is this little lady part of your escort?"

Rather bravely, seeing as his American counterpart was a genuine general, Ceiwen barked out a peal of laughter and playfully punched his shoulder. "You're closer than you think! I'd like you to meet Third Officer Doris Johnson, of the Air Transport Auxiliary."

Allowing a little of the drawl in her voice she'd got used to toning down, Doris took the initiative and shook Haislip's hand. "Pleased to meet you, General."

The homespun voice coming out of what he'd presumed to be a British uniform obviously took the man by surprise and, going on the looks his two junior officers were exchanging, he wasn't the only one.

"You're a Yank!" he managed to say, and then he just stood there shaking his head.

When no one else seemed to be in a hurry to fill the silence, Doris stepped into the void with, "By birth. Brit by adoption."

No immediate reply came, but eventually the man managed to say, "Well, it's not often I'm tongue-tied." Behind him, the braver of his junior officers smiled and shook his head at this remark. This was short-lived though, as the major general immediately took Doris by the hand, not noticing the way she tensed. Duke did and appeared to brace himself to intervene in case Doris did something silly. The older man threaded her hand through his arm and patted it genially, saying, "Come, it's getting towards noon, and we can't keep the cook waiting. Do you like steak, my dear?" he asked, beginning to walk down the road.

****

Doris managed to have a private word with Duke on the way out of the officer's mess. The steak had been thick, juicy, and utterly delicious, easily the best she'd had since leaving America, and she'd devoured each and every bite, much to the satisfaction of Ceiwen—who'd been trying to convince her to call him "Ham" with no success. Wonderful meal or not, something had been bothering Doris ever since they'd arrived on the base, and to put her mind to rest, she'd decided to be direct. As Duke laid his spoon aside after finishing off his dish of vanilla ice cream, she got to her feet and whispered in his ear.

Once they were outside the dining room, Doris scanned the corridor and, as soon as she was satisfied there was no one in earshot, asked, "How much does

General Haislip know?" Then half-answered her own question, "You don't want me to say or do anything around him that could reveal anything about the...operation."

Duke smiled in appreciation. "Good thinking," he told her, then proceeded to clear things up for her. "Knowing you as I do, you're probably thinking this officer doesn't know anything about the deception plan." Doris provided another nod. "You're quite correct. I won't go into details, but this is one of the real units, and so it's being treated as such."

"So," Doris replied, after letting a steward carrying a tottering pile of crockery stagger past, "lips shut and treat him with the deference his rank demands."

Duke observed Doris with his head canted over to one side, a curious expression on his face. "I do believe there's hope for you yet."

Doris immediately punched him, not too lightly, on the upper arm. "You're not forgiven yet, so don't get cheeky."

Shaking some feeling back into his dead arm, Duke took a step back. "Serves me right," he muttered. After a moment, he asked, "Do me a favor, please. Pop into the kitchen and get Sergeant Lewis and his men, and meet us at the cars? We'll be out there in a few minutes."

"You know he won't be happy with that, Duke. We'll meet you at the entrance to this place."

"There you two are!"

Turning their heads, Doris and Duke saw the speaker was one of Haislip's entourage.

"Can we help, Captain?" Duke asked.

"Your general's about to make a speech, and he's asked for you both to retake your seats," he told them.

Left with little choice but to follow, Doris told Duke, "I'll slip out as soon as he's finished."

Hurrying back to their seats, they'd no sooner sat back down than Ceiwen began reading from a page. Beside her, Doris could see Duke's lips moving along to the words issuing from Ceiwen's mouth. For the most part, the best which could be said about the speech was that it seemed to have been designed to be short and to the point: Welcome to the United Kingdom; we hope you're settling in well with the locals; making friends, that sort of thing. Certainly it was nothing she hadn't heard on any number of newsreels, and Doris found her eyelids were beginning to droop, the combination of steak and ice cream not helping matters. From the looks of their American hosts, she wasn't the only one.

It wasn't until Ceiwen started to say, "After reading reports about you and your men's conduct on the various exercises you've undertaken, I can only say that when you go into battle, I am positive that you shall perform as well as any Guardsman, and, being a member of that elite band of soldiers, I can offer you no higher praise. Gentlemen," he began to wind up his speech, and took up his wine glass, "I salute you and wish you all a soldier's good fortune."

At hearing these words, each and every man in the dining hall scrambled to push their chairs back and, very quickly, they were all on their feet, glasses raised in salute. With the dinner having ended on a high note, Ceiwen was persuaded to take up position at the open double doors to the mess, where he proceeded to shake hands with every one of the officers who'd been present. Doris took the opportunity to slip out and find the kitchens, where their sergeant and his men were now waiting for them, having finished up what she was told by them to have been the best steak they'd ever had. A little embarrassed at her own people being able to fly over food which the war-weary British hadn't seen for so many years, she willingly led them out and to the entrance of the officer's mess.

"Where are we going to now?" Doris asked Duke when he appeared.

Glancing at the watch strapped just above his hook, Duke said, "In about an hour's time, there's going to be a march past of the cathedral by a company of General Haislip's men."

Doris leant in slightly. "And that's where the cameras will be? And where you expect you-know-who to turn up?"

"Exactly," he had just enough time to say, before there came the thunderous sound of running army boots and what had to be the full contents of the officer's mess ran past them, only to form up on the grass outside. Close behind came both generals, who seemed to be locked in amiable conversation—Doris's opinion of Rob's acting ability went up another notch. As soon as both stepped outside, someone shouted, "Three cheers for General Ceiwen! Hip, hip, hurrah!" No one noticed the person pronounced the name as *Kiwin*.

Once the three were safely ensconced in the Humber, Doris leaned in close to Ceiwen and whispered, "Don't get overconfident."

To his credit, Ceiwen blushed and gave her a smile of understanding.

The parade itself was a little bit of a let-down, as it took only a few minutes, though Ceiwen appeared to thoroughly enjoy himself. Stood at attention, performing a perfect salute next to his American counterpart, he really looked the part of a fine, upstanding, British Army officer. Doris wondered what the happy-looking American would say if he knew he was actually standing next to a second-rate magician, albeit a good person, even if he'd been coerced into helping with the mission. From her position a little behind and to the left of the saluting dais, Doris shook her head. Would she have some tales to tell when she got back to Walter and her girlfriends! Mind you, she'd have to censor what she said…

Directly in front of the dais, on the opposite side of Donegall Street, Doris watched as the Pathé film crew shot the event. The backdrop of St. Anne's, still incomplete, must make for an interesting sight and Doris would have liked to investigate it, but she knew there wouldn't be the time. Trying not to look like she was up to anything, Doris peered around at the small crowd of civilians who'd turned up to watch, but she totally failed to spot any Nazi spies.

Once the parade had passed uneventfully, Sergeant Lewis, obviously pleased to have something to do, led his men back to their transport.

As Doris stood by, watching, General Haislip shook hands with Duke and then Ceiwen, finishing, much to her surprise, with herself.

"Doris, my fellow American, it's been a pleasure meeting you. Now, before you leave, I've a little present for you. Private Miller!" he shouted. Momentarily, the driver who'd brought them from the airfield appeared at his side. "You have them?"

"Yes, sir," came the reply, as he handed a couple of paper sacks to him before stepping away.

"Here," Haislip said, gesturing for Doris to hold out her hands. "I found out Miller here did a deal with you. Please accept these with my compliments, no charge."

With both her hands full, she couldn't shake the man by the hand. Instead, she looked into the sacks and broke out into a wide grin. Looking up, she bobbed her head. "Gratefully received, General, thank you."

It wasn't until they were stowing everything away in the Anson in preparation for take-off that Duke was able to ask Doris what she'd been presented with.

"Take a look," she invited him, and after taking a look, he handed the sacks back to Doris, who stowed them safely away.

"Two large tins of coffee. I should have known," he added, shaking his head, "and you didn't end up having to pay for it, either. A pretty perfect day, I would say."

"Oh, I wouldn't say that," Doris replied, as she helped one of Lewis's men fasten his seat belt. "I never managed to get a pint of real Irish Guinness."

Chapter Twenty

Because of strong head winds, which Doris had to fight the whole way back to Edinburgh, they were around thirty-five minutes late in landing, and no one was in a good mood. To his credit, the same private who felt ill on the way to Belfast had managed to hold his stomach in check until he was out the door. Stepping over the mess whilst holding her breath, she shot a look of sympathy towards the poor chap. Perhaps he'd appreciate it once Sergeant Lewis had finished berating him. Mind you, judging by the way the man took to his heels in search of the bucket of water and brush he'd been ordered to find, she doubted it.

Turning around, the sergeant actually blushed a little to find he was shoulder to nose with Doris, who wasn't bothering to hide her disapproval of what she'd witnessed. At least he had the integrity to apologize for his language. "Sorry about that, Mrs. Johnson." Doris raised an eyebrow at the choice of salutation, it still being new enough for her to sometimes wonder who was being talked about, expecting to still be called by her previous surname, Winter. He then spoiled the apology by immediately turning his attention back to his remaining man and reminding him that they were still on duty and to have his Sten gun at the ready.

Everyone else, including the rest of their escort, who Doris hoped hadn't been waiting around on the airfield all day, milled around drinking tea whilst Doris performed her post-flight checks before turning her Anson over to Visiting Flight's care.

Ceiwen and Duke came up just as she was shutting the cabin door.

"All done?" Duke asked.

Doris finished trying to shake the cramp out of her hands before answering, "All done." She looked back wistfully at her faithful taxi as they made their way over to where their Humber and lorry sat waiting for them on the edge of the dispersal.

Ceiwen must have sensed she was feeling a little melancholy, as he hung back a little and offered her his arm, which she took after allowing a sigh to escape. "Penny for them?" he asked.

"Hmm? Sorry, what did you say?"

"Your thoughts, what are you thinking? It looks like something's troubling you," he clarified.

She gave his arm a reassuring squeeze before saying, "Not really. It's silly, but even though it's only been a few days, I miss flying."

"Cheer up," Ceiwen replied. "You've only got to put up with us for another week!"

"Amen to that," Duke muttered, as he walked past, hopping over the leg Doris stuck out. "Care to let us in?" he asked, now waiting by the rear door of the Humber.

With a smirk on her face, Duke allowed Ceiwen to lead her around to the other side where she stood to attention and opened the door.

"Your transport, sir!" she barked out as he took his seat. As she marched, rather smartly, around to where Duke was waiting, she noticed the same member of their escort who'd just been sick giving her the thumbs-up. So far as he was concerned, he was witnessing a person of lesser rank acting up to the bigwigs. Well, the chap wasn't to know that she was merely playing along. Still, if it helped improve his morale… "Your chariot, my lord," she decided to say, knowing he couldn't tell her off as, technically, she was right to address him as such. As he lowered himself past her, she lowered her voice so only he would hear, "Don't get used to this," before slamming the door so quickly he was inadvertently in danger of losing his other hand. Noticing what she'd come so close to doing, she pulled the door back open and told him, "Sorry," before closing it once more.

Once they'd begun the short trip back to Edinburgh castle, Duke leant forward and tapped Doris on the shoulder before settling back. "By the time we get back, we'll have missed the main seating for tea, and I don't know about you two, but I'd rather not risk whatever we'll get for leftovers. Care to come down to the Chevalier? I promise we'll eat this time," he hastened to add.

"Will Morag be there?" Doris couldn't resist asking.

****

After another fruitless hour spent calling out Taxi's name—word seemed to have got around, as none of the sections of men who happened to walk past her dared to crack any bad jokes. Indeed, more than a few promised her they'd keep an eye out for the cat too—Doris was sat next to Ceiwen in the restaurant at The Young Chevalier once more.

Ceiwen's stomach let out a very audible grumble. As Doris was about to say she was hungry too, her stomach decided to come out in sympathy. From the looks they were getting from the next table, their unorthodox complaints had been heard. Believing there was little else she could do and too tired to bother herself with an apology, she merely shrugged her shoulders at their neighbors, a couple of captains in the Army and what were either their wives or girlfriends, or a mixture of both. When they nodded and turned back to their interrupted conversation, Doris felt a jab of sympathy for them. Undoubtedly, they'd have liked to have put her and her companion in their places, only with one of them wearing the uniform of a general, there was little they could do.

"That uniform does have its uses," Doris told Ceiwen, keeping her voice down.

Without looking, he brushed some imaginary dust from the left breast of his jacket. "I am getting quite attached to it," he admitted.

"Don't," Duke advised, appearing at his shoulder.

"Did you find her?" Doris asked.

By way of a reply, Duke raised his left arm and waved his hook towards where Morag stood behind her dais. She'd obviously been watching him, as when she saw him raise his arm, she'd begun to raise hers too, only to lower it quickly when she saw it was the one with the missing hand. Quickly she looked up to see if Duke had seen. Fortunately, he'd already sat down and, as he was side on to where Morag stood, with Doris in between, she was pretty certain he hadn't seen. Frowning, Doris resolved to have a serious conversation with the redhead before the evening finished. Despite her occasional run-ins with him, she wanted this woman to be reminded what a brave, honest, and true man Duke was.

As it was now approaching half seven in the evening, the early evening crowd were just coming in and the restaurant was filling up. Perhaps, if the people milling around were to be believed, this restaurant had managed to maintain the reputation for excellence which Duke insisted it had acquired whilst he'd been here in pre-war days.

Placing her hands over her stomach, in case it decided to betray her once more, Doris turned to Duke and asked something she'd been meaning to ever since they'd arrived in Scotland. "Do you think haggis will be on the menu? All this says," she complained whilst waving the menu on the table before his nose, "is *Special of the Day*, against main course."

"I'm not sure how much you eat out…" Duke began, before being interrupted by Doris.

"Not as much as I'd like. Too busy during the day and too tired to go out on most of my days off," she explained. "My idea of a treat is fish 'n' chips and a pint of Guinness with my husband and friends."

"Sorry to hear," Duke managed to say, before Doris interrupted once more.

"Don't be! It's my favorite food now. Anyway, you were saying?" she finished, planting her elbows on the table and cradling her chin.

Slightly flummoxed, Duke recovered, after a slight stuttering start, to give her his explanation. "When you see that written, it usually means they'll be providing what they can."

"Oh! So, there's a possibility we will have haggis?"

Ceiwen took a sip from his wine glass before asking, "Why the fascination with haggis? I've tried it once…and that was enough for me," he ended with a shudder.

Doris regarded him for half a minute, frowning.

"Well, I suppose not everything is to everyone's taste, though you've got to admit, you have to try something which has longer legs on one side than the other!"

Duke managed to spit his wine back into his glass rather than all over himself and turned an incredulous look upon the American.

"What?" Doris asked, taking a long pull from her pint of Guinness and, when her companions merely stared back at her, repeated, "What?"

"Would you care to take this one?" Duke asked Ceiwen.

"I'd love to!" he replied, grinning.

By now, Doris was suspicious. "What's going on?"

Instead of answering straight away, Ceiwen asked, "What exactly, do you know about the haggis?"

Doris shrugged, "Only what my friends told me the night before we left."

"Which was?"

"That it's a strange wire-haired creature which has longer legs on one side of its body than the other, so it can run around the hills and mountains without falling."

"And who, um, told you that?" Ceiwen asked. By now, he was struggling to control a burst of laughter—Doris recognized the symptoms.

Her guard now up in response to the strange line of questioning, Doris took a fortifying drink and told him, "Two of my best friends, Penny and Jane."

"They weren't, by any chance, laughing when they told you about this animal?" Duke couldn't stop himself from enquiring.

"We'd had a few drinks," she told them, after she'd thought about it for a short while. "You're telling me it's not true? That they don't exist?"

To his credit, Ceiwen had pulled himself together and instead of laughing, gave her what was unmistakably a sympathetic look. "You didn't think it was a strange-sounding animal?"

"In my defense, we've got some pretty weird creatures in the States," Doris said.

"Any have legs longer on one side than the other?" Ceiwen had to ask.

"Well…no," Doris admitted, slumping back in her seat.

Conversation was decidedly lacking for the next few minutes as both men, by now quite familiar with Doris's temper, appeared to be mulling things over. When she eventually broke the silence, coincidentally right as the waiter appeared, her words almost sent the man running for the police.

"I'm going to kill them…slowly."

Fortunately, Ceiwen put on his "general" persona. "Ignore her, my man," he advised their waiter, who had to be seventy, if he was a day. "What's on the menu today?"

Obviously placated by the high-ranking gentleman he believed he was addressing, the waiter informed them that today's menu was braised lamb and roasted vegetables. As this was the only item offered, they all nodded in acceptance, though Doris had to be prodded out of whatever she was brooding upon first.

Deciding she may as well find out the lay of the land between Duke and his lady whilst they waited, Doris with her customary tact asked, "Are things still going well between you and Morag?"

As if they were in the eye of a hurricane, perfect silence swallowed the room as she spoke, causing all eyes to automatically zero in on the three of them.

Unfortunately, this included the lady in question. Doris and her friends held their breath, but instead of the tears Doris expected, Morag's face rapidly matched her hair and she promptly stormed over to the table.

A single palm slammed down before Doris, making her pint of Guinness bounce. Leaning down so she could look into Doris's eyes, she fairly roared, "What gives this Yank the right to neb around in my business?"

Chapter Twenty-One

It appeared to Doris that despite being thrown into the service business and possibly renewing her relationship with Duke, that if you annoyed Morag (even inadvertently) she came out with all guns blazing! She had to be approaching six feet tall, and with her red locks flowing around her shoulders, she bore a strong resemblance to what Doris thought a highland warrior maiden must have looked like. All it would have taken to complete the illusion was a brandished broad sword.

Never one to back down, Doris pushed her chair back and drew herself up to her full height to look her opponent full in the bosom. "You're Morag, right?" she began, holding out a hand and beaming as she clutched the hand which hadn't crashed down on the table, and shaking it with all her strength. Morag did her best to crush her fingers, but Doris refused to give her the satisfaction of seeing she'd hurt her. Fair's fair, as she'd obviously upset the woman. "Pleased to meet you."

All around, everyone who'd been staring at the table as Morag approached let out a collective sigh of disappointment—there wasn't going to be a fight, there wasn't even going to be an argument. They could all sense it. Turning back to either having a drink or ordering their meals, waiters having appeared at the sound of Morag's voice in an effort to turn other patrons' attention away, normality swiftly resumed. This was helped by the appearance of a man with slicked-back hair and wearing a full dining suit and a face somewhere between thunder and one of placation. He rushed over and stood next to Morag, who now had a slightly flummoxed expression on her face. She didn't know it, but this was quite common when people first met Doris.

"Gentlemen, ladies, I am the manager. What seems to be the problem?"

His voice reminded Doris of one of the announcers on BBC radio, the ones who spoke as if they had a plum in their mouth. Acting quickly, as despite the accusation—she also had no idea what a *neb* was, so she wasn't sure if she'd been insulted or not—she certainly had no desire to be the cause of Morag losing her job.

"No problem," Doris managed to say, just beating Duke to speaking. Thinking quickly, Doris quickly brought the subject around to the one thing men never felt able to talk about. "I accidently said out loud what I was thinking, and my voice must have been way too loud." Doris knew she was on dodgy ground, her explanation so far being far from concise, so she hurried to her point. "I was wondering where I could buy some things to help with Aunt Flo"—immediately Ceiwen had to stifle a cough, as did the manager, though a little to her surprise, Duke merely appeared baffled—"and wondered if Morag, being local, could help. Still," she hastened to add, "what came out of my mouth was entirely different. I was paying attention to Duke when I spoke and knew of his relationship with Morag." Doris now addressed Morag directly. "Morag, I'm very sorry if I upset you, but," she said as she got to her feet, "as you're here, let's go outside so we can discuss it."

Morag was undoubtedly as confused as everyone

else now was, which was probably why she allowed Doris to take her by the arm and lead her away. Once they were outside, the first gust of wind must have cleared her head, as the Scotswoman jerked her arm from Doris's grasp.

Planting her fists upon her hips, Morag lowered her head until she was nose to nose with Doris, and demanded, "Care to tell me who the hell you are and what gives you the right to poke your nose into my business?"

Ignoring the impulse to take a step back, Doris glanced sideways. "Duke. Would you mind giving us a bit of privacy, please? We won't be long."

Morag hadn't seen the man following them out of the hotel, so was forced to take a step back so she could see for herself. Her gaze whipped back and forth between Doris and Duke before she came to a decision. "Yes, wait inside for us, please."

Somewhat reluctantly, as was obvious from the way he dragged his feet, Duke turned around, opened the door and stepped inside. He didn't go any farther than the reception area.

Now that she didn't have the other, much taller woman in her face, Doris took to the offensive. "Come," she patted the wooden bench she'd sat upon, "sit down. Your feet must ache, with you being on them all evening."

Morag's mouth opened and closed a few times, as if she were reading something into Doris's words which wasn't there.

Doris read her mind. Smiling, she told her, "I mean no harm, honest! Please, sit down?"

Doing so, Morag sat as far away as the limited space

on the bench allowed. "Who are you? And what do you want?" This time, there was no banging of fists, no raised voices, merely curiosity.

Doris held out a hand which, tentatively, Morag shook, very briefly, before releasing. Encouraged, Doris told her, "Doris Johnson. Yank pilot in the Air Transport Auxiliary and new friend of Duke's. I believe you're Morag Blessed. Duke's told me all about you," she said, leaning in closer and opening her eyes a little, hoping the woman would pick up on the gesture and she wouldn't have need to embarrass her by recounting the tale she'd heard.

From the way Morag gulped, even allowing for the poor light, and the way she'd recoiled a little, Doris could see she believed her. The reaction also confirmed, as she'd allowed a part of her mind to give the benefit of the doubt to the woman, that Duke's story was true. Doris resolved not to judge her too quickly on that, nor on the reaction she'd seen earlier that night, until she'd got to know her better. She hoped things could be resolved between the redhead and Duke, as there was something about her she liked, though she couldn't put her finger on it. If it came down to her gut, in this case, she really hoped she was right in following the path she was about to go down; and that Duke wouldn't put her before a firing squad for interfering. She had little doubt he had the power and means to do just that.

"Look, you heard right, in the restaurant," she began. "I only asked Duke that because I've got to know him over the last couple of weeks—"

"Couple of weeks. Is that all the time you've known him?" Morag interrupted.

Doris waved away her skepticism, "It's enough.

Anyway, I've got to know Duke, as a friend," she hastened to add, "and he's been through a lot. We both know that." She waited to see if Morag would protest and, when she didn't, continued, "I don't want to see him getting hurt again, and I know the two of you are trying to see if you can work things out. I'm right, aren't I?"

From the way Morag stumbled over her words as she tried to reply, Doris wasn't in much doubt that what Duke had told her was right, so she took pity on her, as she still hadn't managed to get any coherent words out.

"Don't turn yourself inside out," Doris said with a smile and reached out to grab a hand, which was waving around a little. "It's good to know I'm right. Still, I couldn't help but notice your reaction when Duke waved to you earlier. You know when I mean?"

Morag nodded and, this time, managed to find her voice. "He waved with his…hook."

Doris couldn't help but notice the hesitation in her companion's voice. "Yes. Is that a problem?"

"Are all Americans as blunt as you?" Morag instead asked.

Shrugging, Doris replied, "Probably, but in my case, at least, it's because I care about my friends and won't allow anyone to hurt them."

"I care about Duke too!" Morag hurried to say, now leaning forward herself in her urgency. "I do! Really!" She took hold of Doris by the arm and her grip was so strong, so earnest, that Doris at least could believe that about her.

Gently, she eased Morag's fingers from her arm and massaged the spot, allowing the blood to flow once more. "I believe you," she hurried to assure the woman, who had now edged her way along the bench until they were thigh to thigh. "That being the case, you'll pardon me for being this blunt Yank, but I think you have some work to do. I noticed you flinching when you saw that hook waving at you tonight. It's a part of *him* now, and if there's going to be a future for the two of you, and I think there could be a good one, then you need to get used to it. If you can't, then don't give him false hope." Having voiced her major concern, Doris settled back and waited for the response.

Fortunately, it wasn't raining, and the evening was pleasant with only the odd gust of wind to send a shiver down her spine as Doris witnessed Morag's face as it went through a multitude of emotions before she became able to give her reply. Before she could talk, the moon decided to make a brief appearance. Doris decided she should ignore the tears now running down Morag's face, at least until she knew their cause.

When she spoke, Doris had to lean in so she could hear, as not only had Morag moved back along the bench, but she was speaking barely above a whisper.

"You're right, I know you're right," Morag began, taking a handkerchief from out of her sleeve to wipe her tears away and dab her eyes. "It was such a shock to see him standing there the other night. Then we got talking, and for that night, it was like the war had never happened! We just talked and talked about anything and everything." Morag paused, and under the moonlight, Doris could just make out a frown upon her face. "No," she started up again, looking Doris in the eye, "that's not quite right. We didn't talk about the war, about what had happened to him."

"Why do you think that was?" Doris asked.

At least Morag didn't try to shrug the question off.

"I don't know. Perhaps because for the first time since my parents effectively disowned me and I ended up here, I was happy."

Doris asked the question she'd been dying to find out the answer to. "Does the hook, the loss of his hand, really make so much of a difference to you? He's still the same man."

At those words, Morag actually shuddered and Doris got annoyed with her again. "Oh for crying out loud!" She grabbed Morag's hands and pulled her to her feet. "Nothing can change what's happened. He's not going to wake up in the morning having grown a new hand! So my first question is do you love him? Don't think about it, just answer!" she told her.

"Yes!" Morag snapped back immediately, taken by surprise and then, upon realizing what she'd said, began looking around, her eyes open as wide as a deer's caught in car headlights.

Surmising that Morag was searching for Duke, and grateful that he wasn't visible in the reception, Doris hurried on. Knowing the woman was currently acting and speaking on instinct at this moment, she asked, "Can you get used to his disability?"

This time, Morag took a few tense minutes to answer, and Doris knew everything could hinge upon what she said. She allowed her the time. When she looked up, there were more tears, yet a smile was also on her face. Unexpectedly, Morag squeezed Doris's hands and, taking to her heels, pulled her towards the hotel. "Let's find out!"

Allowing herself to be towed along, Doris found herself back inside the hotel within seconds. "Duke! Duke!" Morag was calling, causing all and sundry to stare before the man in question appeared from around a corner.

When he saw what the cause of the commotion was, he hurried over. "Morag?"

Letting go of Doris's hand, Morag flung herself upon the startled man. Arms wrapped around his neck, she kissed him soundly on the lips, eyes closed in ecstasy, ignoring the mixed expressions of both disapproval and support from those present.

"I'd better get back to work," she told him, pulling back from his startled yet very happy face. "But first, we need to talk."

Just before he found himself led back towards the restaurant, Duke was able to quickly say to Doris, "What did you do?"

Though she didn't have time to answer, Doris didn't particularly care, as what she saw before the pair were out of sight did more than mere words could have done to set her mind to rest.

Morag was holding Duke's left hand, his hook, as she led him off.

Chapter Twenty-Two

After a superb meal of lamb and fresh shallots, which Duke, who was in an extremely good mood, kept trying to convince her were the favorite snack of the rare Albino Haggis, Doris and Ceiwen strolled back to the castle. It was a cloudy night, though when the moon made an appearance, it lighted up their way nicely, and the pair were happy enough to simply walk in companiable silence.

Though Morag hadn't been able to leave her duties to join them at their meal, she'd made many passes around them, and during most, Doris had been very pleased to catch her letting a hand trail along Duke's shoulders. Duke, not unexpectedly, had made his excuses to stay behind, promising he'd see them both at breakfast the next morning this time, and Doris had been too happy for him to engage in some good-natured teasing. Both she and Ceiwen had wished the pair a goodnight and a pleasant evening as they left, though Morag had surprised Doris by kissing her on the cheek and enveloping her in what could only be described as a bear-hug. "I'll be seeing you before you leave," she'd told her as she let Doris go.

Coming up to the castle and the guard post, an inhuman wailing burst forth. Doris and Ceiwen both turned their eyes to the sky, though it was currently clouded over. "Not a sausage," he muttered.

"Not that we'd be able to spot anything until it was on top of us anyway," Doris told Ceiwen, taking him by the arm and hurrying him along to the castle and its air raid shelters.

"Best get to the shelters, miss, sir," the private on guard advised them both after quickly checking their documentation and waving them through.

Ceiwen put on his best concerned-officer routine as he told the man and his companion, "Don't take any chances. Likely it's a false alarm, but get your heads under cover if bombs do begin to fall. Understood?"

Both men allowed the relief they felt at being given permission to seek shelter show in their voices, as they both barked an enthusiastic, "Yes, sir!" at the pair's departing backs.

No sooner had they made it as far as the courtyard than they became aware of a roaring sound approaching from the east, getting louder by the second. Both stopped and looked up once more.

"Do you recognize that sound?" Ceiwen asked, savvy enough to ask the pilot about the sound of what they both knew to be aero engines.

Doris shook her head. "Difficult to tell. Being honest, I've not heard a German engine," she admitted. "It asks the question though, why would an air raid alarm go off for one of ours?"

Ceiwen looked down at Doris. "Good point. Come on, I think the nearest shelter's this way." He pointed towards a corner.

Before they could break into a run, Doris spotted someone coming towards them. The sight made her come to a sudden stop and she felt her blood freeze in her veins. Totally out of step with the situation, she heard the sound of a drum.

Not wishing to take her eyes off the apparition, she squeezed the arm of Ceiwen, who also appeared to have become rooted to the spot. "Are you seeing this?"

"I'm not sure what I'm seeing, or hearing," Ceiwen replied, though it took him a few tries to get the words out.

"It..." She tried again. "It hasn't got a...head!" she eventually managed to get out.

"The drums are getting louder," Ceiwen said, leaning towards Doris. "What the hell's going on?"

Before either could say another word, the roaring of the engines above them grew suddenly louder and a huge shadow zoomed over the castle, nearly knocking them both off their feet as it cleared the roofs and zoomed off. Judging by the sound from the engines, it was banking around for another run.

"Bloody hell! Run, Rob!" Doris yelled, the situation forcing what they'd witnessed from their minds and causing their bodies to go onto automatic pilot. Both took to their heels, pounding across the remaining courtyard and throwing themselves at the entrance to the shelter. They were not a moment too soon, either, as the roar of the approaching engines was joined by a heavy staccato *thump-thump* sound and cannon shells kicked up the stones mere feet behind them, showering them both with shards which stung their clothes and the backs of their heads.

"What the bloody hell are you two playing at?" a voice in the dim light of the shelter shouted. "Shut that bloody door!"

Raising a hand to the back of her head, Doris closed the door nearly shut.

"I said close that door!" came the voice again, now joined by the shape of a large person approaching them. As it reached where they stood, the body came to a stumbling halt. "Ah, sorry, sir. Meant no disrespect, only I'm the shelter marshal and, well, I'm in charge here."

Ceiwen approached the man and, taking him by surprise, reached out and took his hand. Shaking it, he told him, "Quite right too, Corporal. Please don't apologize for doing your job." Glancing over his shoulder, he asked Doris, "Has it gone?"

Doris had her head through the crack in the door. "I can't hear anything, so I think it must have." Just then, the all-clear sounded and Doris pushed the door farther open before turning back to announce, "That's as official as it gets, I'd say."

Doris and Ceiwen stood to one side to allow everyone to file out. No sooner than they were left alone, there came the pounding of army boots and Ceiwen's escort appeared. Sergeant Lewis didn't look very happy.

"Sir." He snapped off a smart salute and then, as if he couldn't keep the words in any longer, "I do wish you would tell us when you're going outside the castle. We are supposed to be your escort. Sir," he added, in case he'd gone too far.

Doris could almost imagine the multiple replies going through Ceiwen's mind and, partly to give her heart a little time to take its rhythm back to normal after their close call, leant against the wall of the shelter to see what he'd come up with.

After a few strategic coughs to give him some thinking time, Ceiwen settled for, "So noted, Sergeant. I shall consider myself admonished."

The sergeant appeared skeptical, but he had little

choice other than to accept Ceiwen at his word. "Thank you, sir. Normal time in the morning?"

"Normal time, Sergeant." Ceiwen nodded. "Dismissed."

The sergeant and his men, who didn't look in a great mood either, considering they'd likely been on standby all evening since Lewis had found Ceiwen missing again, about-turned and trotted off.

Once they were out of earshot, Doris remarked, "Nicely done!"

"Thank you," he replied.

"Good thing he didn't spot these," she informed him, sweeping a hand over the ground around them, which was pockmarked with small craters and gashes where the cannon shells had impacted.

****

Next morning, the three were making their way from the officer's mess towards their vehicles and waiting escort. By unspoken agreement, neither Doris nor Ceiwen had talked about the headless apparition they'd witnessed the previous night. That would come, but not yet.

Ceiwen pointed at the waiting group. "Going by Lewis's stance, I'd say he's still not happy with us, especially me. Mind you, I can't blame him. We are stopping him from doing his job," he added, edging a little behind Duke.

"I don't blame him," Doris mumbled. "Especially after what happened when we got back."

Duke glanced across at her. "Why're you…Ah, still no sign of Taxi," he stated.

Doris kicked a stone into the gutter. "No."

A few steps closer, Duke came to an abrupt halt,

holding up a hand to stop his companions. "Hold on. What do you mean? What did happen after you got back? Doris, have you been causing more trouble?"

If Doris hadn't been annoyed before, she was now. "I don't cause trouble everywhere, you know!" As they happened to be near the air raid shelter, she grabbed him by the arm and towed him over. "Look down," she instructed him. "What do you think caused these?" She pointed to the almost perfectly straight rows of impressions in the courtyard, which ran a good fifty-odd yards and halfway up the wall next to the shelter. "I'll give you a hint—it wasn't industrious moles!"

Duke bent down and poked one or two of the holes with his hook, before looking up at Doris and Ceiwen. "Exactly what did I miss?"

"You heard the air raid siren?" Doris asked. "Well, some Jerry pilot decided to strafe the castle."

Standing bolt upright so quickly Doris thought he might snap a vertebra, Duke seemed to be checking the area, perhaps for other damage, before turning back to the pair. "Well, looks like I came close to losing another General Ceiwen."

The Ceiwen present looked affronted, before letting out a chuckle. He shook his head. "Well, it's good to know someone would have missed me."

Duke jerked his hook over his shoulder. "Is that why Lewis looks particularly annoyed with us?"

"Probably." Doris shrugged, and they started off.

"In that case, do me a favor, the both of you? Let's have a by-the-books day, okay?"

Ceiwen and Doris exchanged looks, before Doris replied for them both, "We can manage that."

"Good, thank you," Duke replied, letting out a sigh

of relief. "Now, if you'd both go and take a seat in the Humber, I'll go and smooth things over with Lewis." He'd taken a couple of steps before he stopped and turned his head, opened his mouth and then, likely thinking better of it, closed it and made his way over to where the escort were waiting at the lorry.

Opening the rear door for Ceiwen, then taking her seat behind the wheel, Doris asked, "Do you think he was going to suggest that attack last night was aimed at you?"

Ceiwen burst out in laughter before his mind caught up with what she'd said, cutting off the sound abruptly. "That's not a nice thought."

Doris observed the man for a few seconds whilst she mulled over what she'd just suggested and Ceiwen's reply. "No, I suppose it isn't," she agreed. Glancing back over to where the attack had been, she shook her head and gave her now slightly ashen-faced companion an encouraging smile. "Ignore me. If it was, it was very amateur, haphazard even. Fancy sending over one aircraft to conduct a strafing attack on the castle. He'd never have been able to identify you in the dark, not even if he'd tried a daylight attack, and if he had, I wouldn't have given much for his chances of getting back."

Further discussion was interrupted by a rear door opening to admit a distracted-looking Duke.

"What's wrong?" Ceiwen asked, watching as the man fumbled with the lock of his briefcase.

"Hold the end please," Duke asked, instead of supplying an answer and offered him the bottom of the case to hold.

Doris, watching with mounting curiosity, couldn't help exclaiming, "What the hell's that?" as Duke pulled out a pistol.

He didn't bother to look up. Instead, he tucked the weapon under his left arm and pulled the toggle back, checking inside the chamber, before releasing it. There followed a low click and then he returned it to his briefcase, which he then took back from Ceiwen. "Thanks," he said and tucked the case in beside him.

"You've got a gun," Doris leant over the back of the seat and tapped a finger against the holster he wore. "Why do you need another gun?" She noticed he cradled his hook as she asked, though he did answer.

"I'm not a good shot with my revolver." He was the one tapping his holster this time. "It's too heavy for my right hand. The luger's lighter, and I can handle and reload it easier."

"Why a German pistol? If you don't mind my asking," Ceiwen said.

"I picked it up in France in 1940." Duke looked away and ran his hand through his hair before, with definite hesitation in his voice informed them, "Since I...obtained it, it's become a bit of a lucky charm. It's saved my life on more than one occasion. Maybe I'll tell you about some of those, one day," he added.

Doris raised a hand and coughed. "Forgive me for pointing it out, but..." She waggled her left hand.

Duke looked at her and actually grinned. "I don't think I can blame it for being no good against a Stuka, do you?"

"Quite right," Doris grinned back. "Now, perhaps you'll tell us why you're checking it now?"

When he didn't reply straight away, Doris knew the conversation she'd had with Ceiwen just now may have been nearer the mark than she'd thought. Obviously the air attack last night had been nothing other than a coincidence, though. "Go on," Doris gently prodded.

"Very well," he began. "Perhaps we've been a little more successful in convincing the Nazis that Ceiwen's up here and hard at work than we needed."

"Meaning?" Ceiwen wanted to know.

"Meaning…I think we need to be a bit more on our guard."

Doris turned fully around in her seat, holding out an eager hand. "In that case, where's my pistol?"

Chapter Twenty-Three

"I'm sorry, miss." The guard stood beside the entrance to David's Tower, though he didn't sound particularly sorry at all, and from the way the hand near the trigger guard of his rifle was twitching, he was itching for an argument, if not to actually shoot someone.

In spite of this, Doris had never been one to be put off something, once her mind was set. After a tiring day driving Ceiwen and Duke left, right, and center—she was tempted to ask to look at Duke's itinerary, as she was certain there were easier routes he could pick—she'd skipped tea to widen her search for the missing Taxi. Before that evening, she'd concentrated upon the area in which she'd found him, though with no luck. Now, she found herself before this less-than-helpful single guard, and she wanted to look inside the ruined tower. If she were a lone cat, it would make a perfect place to hide!

"But all I want to do is to take a quick peek inside, shout his name a few times," she pleaded. It seemed the natural tone of voice to use, as the chap before her looked like he could burst out of his uniform at any moment. What was it about some army units, she pondered? Where most of their men were, well, of normal build, there were always more than a sizeable percentage who made you question if their parents were gorillas! "I'm sure you know I'm looking for my cat?" she decided to add, as he may have been one of the few in the castle who weren't aware.

"I'm a dog man, meself," he informed her, before making a horrid sound in the back of his throat and spitting out something disgusting to the side.

Fighting away the impulse to let out a loud, "Yuck!" Doris instead grimaced, rapidly replacing the expression with a sweet smile. Perhaps flattery would get her somewhere.

"That must be nice. Did you have one before the war started?" she asked. Trying to butter him up couldn't help.

Before replying, the man quickly looked around and, seeing no one else in sight, pulled a dog-end of a cigarette from behind his ear, lit it, and took a long drag. "We did, but dad drowned it when it lost a fight." To Doris's wide-eyed look of horror, the man merely shrugged. "That's life."

It took Doris a few seconds to recover her composure. Then she tried again. "Please, I only want a minute or two. I won't be any bother, and then I'll be gone."

After another long pull, he again shook his head. "More'n me life's worth."

Doris tried to look around him, only he kept moving into her line of sight.

"Look 'ere. I've got me orders and that's it," he stated.

Her curiosity had now been piqued and Doris found herself asking, "What are you guarding, then?"

The man's mouth opened and closed a couple of times before sound finally came out, "That's none of your business, so stop being nosy."

Playing a hunch, Doris asked, "You don't know why you're here, do you?"

He leant down until his head was on a level with Doris's, the smell of cheap tobacco almost overwhelming her, and she found herself taking a small step back.

"Please?" Doris tried.

The pair became locked in a staring contest which ended with the sentry blinking and rubbing his head furiously. He stamped out the remains of his cigarette before looking around once more. Lowering his voice, he told her, "If it'll stop you annoying me, you can stick your 'ead inside the tower and have a yell. Final offer."

Before he had the chance to change his mind, Doris slapped him on the back, told him, "Deal!" and was stepping past him before he knew it.

Quickly, he strode past Doris, stopping her before she could actually enter the tower. Eyeing up her new acquaintance, she took in a deep breath and shouted, "Taxi! Taxi!" at the top of her lungs.

They both waited in silence for a couple of minutes and when there was no answering cry, the sentry gave her something which could be taken for a sympathetic smile. "Sorry," he told her, shrugging, before adding, "Look, now I can see 'ow important this moggy is, I'll keep me ear to the ground."

Though disappointed, Doris held out her hand and immediately gritted her teeth as the following handshake nearly broke all the bones in her hand. "Thank you…" she said through clenched teeth.

"Wilson, but call me Frank," he announced, with a wide grin which displayed a number of missing teeth.

"Frank. Good to meet you. I'm Doris," she added,

beginning to turn and resume her search elsewhere, only to turn back. In doing so, she missed the way his eyes went momentarily blank upon hearing her name. "Frank, answer this Yank a question—are you Scottish? I'm not good with all your accents, but you sound like some of the locals to me."

Drawing himself up to his not-inconsiderable full height, he beat his free fist to his chest, saying, "And proud of it. I'm from Leith." To Doris's puzzled expression, he added "That's at the very north of the city, right on the coast."

Though this still didn't mean much to Doris, it at least answered her question. So, working on the assumption that even if she was about to make a fool of herself, she was very unlikely to run into this soldier again once her time on this duty was up, she cleared her throat and dived in, "So, you're a local?" Frank duly nodded. "Have you ever," she then lowered her voice, so he had to lean in to hear, "heard this place, the castle, is haunted?"

Somewhat to her surprise, Frank didn't burst out laughing. Instead, he took a step back and regarded her with surprisingly shrewd eyes, as if daring her to fall about laughing and telling him she was joking. When she didn't, he once again took a look around, presumably to make certain they still weren't being overheard, before nodding his head and saying, "Oh aye, it's haunted all right. Why? What did you see?"

As he didn't seem to be playing with her, Doris told him what she'd seen, though she left out the fact Ceiwen was with her. "It was just after the air raid warning siren went off. I was about to hurry across the courtyard to get to the nearest shelter when I heard this drumming sound." As his eyebrows failed to react in surprise, she carried on. "Then, I became aware of this well, thing…shadow…apparition…whatever…before me. It was quite clear, though it did shimmer a little. It appeared to be wearing an old—very old—type of British army uniform, and it was playing a drum. Only…"

When Doris couldn't find the words, Frank supplied them: "Only, he had no head."

His words were surprisingly soft and comforted Doris somewhat that perhaps she wasn't crazy or seeing things.

"Yes! Exactly that!"

"Lass, you've been honored. The Headless Drummer Boy is famous, yet legend says he's never seen unless it's to warn of an attack on the castle."

All Doris could think of to say in reply was, "I should have told him he was a bit late last night."

****

The next day had been a mixture of boredom—the visits had all been to more units hidden away and sending signals out to real and fictitious units—and frustration. Tea had been traditional and not very filling, one of egg and chips, and Doris was sorely tempted to slip out to The Young Chevalier for something else later. Together with the lack of success in tracking down Taxi, it was a rather morose figure that Lance Corporal Albert Miller stumbled across.

"Hello, stranger," he greeted her, plonking himself down on the steps to her billet. "You look like you've lost a quid and found a tanner!"

Doris canted her head to the side. "You know, if you'd said that to me a few years ago, before I came over, I wouldn't have had a clue what you were on about."

"And now?" he asked, offering her a cigarette, then taking one for himself and putting the packet away after she'd shaken her head.

"I feel like I haven't even found a nickel," she told him, running her fingers through her hair.

Albert took a long pull on his cigarette. "Well, I haven't got a clue how much a nickel is, but I get your meaning. I assume there's still no sign of Taxi?"

She shook her head before saying, "I know I only had him for a few days, but I really grew to love the little guy."

They sat in companionable silence for a short while, until eventually Albert felt he had to point something out. "You have considered that Taxi probably didn't have a good or easy life before you found him?"

"I have," Doris replied, her face now a picture of misery.

"Well, I'd hope therefore that he could take care of himself. You know, he is a bit of a street-cat."

Doris, considering what he'd told her before, reluctantly agreed, "I suppose, only that doesn't explain why I found him inside a rubbish bag."

Albert took another pull from his cigarette. "Maybe someone found him up to something they didn't like? Not everyone likes cats."

"I know, I know," Doris told him, fighting to keep her temper from fraying.

Standing back up, Albert mashed the remains of his cigarette into the ground before straightening his cap. "I've got to be off. Oh, I thought you should know—by my reckoning, you've now got half the castle looking out for your Taxi." When Doris looked up in surprise at this statement, he elaborated. "You're out all day, so you don't get to hear what goes on. If you're outside, every now and then, you'll hear a great shout of 'Taxi!' I'd love to know what anyone outside the walls must think. Probably that we've all gone mad! Well, see you around, Doris."

****

Hands thrust deep into her trouser pockets, Doris wandered around the castle not really knowing what to do with herself. No longer in the mood to go out to the Young Chevalier—partially as she suspected Sergeant Lewis to be staking out the exit from the castle and she wasn't in the mood for an argument—she meandered around, occasionally shouting out for her lost cat though even she could hear her voice no longer held the same level of expectation as when he'd first gone missing. This wasn't a happy thought, seeing as it had only been a few days, but it only served to make her feel even more morose.

She'd just about decided to have an early night when she heard her name being called out.

"Doris! Hey, Doris! Wait up!"

Pausing on the steps to her accommodation, she turned to see Duke trotting over towards her and waving his good hand her way. Tucked under his other arm, he appeared to be gripping a couple of film tins.

When he reached her, she pointed at the cans. "Are those the Pathé films you confiscated?"

He nodded. "Just finished editing. Care to see the results?" he asked.

"Why not?" Doris replied, trying to dredge up some enthusiasm for her friend's sake.

Duke wasn't a fool, but he also knew by now when not to push Doris. She was definitely one of those people who did not react well to being advised to cheer up. Instead, he offered her his arm. "Come on, then, let's go to the projector room."

Ten minutes later, the two of them were in a blacked-out room that Duke described as smaller than the dining room of his parents but bigger than his favorite pen. When Doris didn't call him out for being awkward, he told her to give him a few minutes and picked up the phone. "Mess manager, please," she heard him say and then, a few seconds later, "Hello? Major Newton-Baxtor here. Could you send someone down with two pints of Guinness? We're in the projection room. Five minutes? Perfect. Thank you." He ended the call to see that Doris's eyes had met his. "I take it you're not adverse?"

She shook her head. "I think that'll be just what the doctor ordered."

Once their drinks had been delivered, Doris smacked her lips in anticipation before taking a long pull on her pint of black gold. "Ah, that I really needed," she told him, settling back into an armchair with a sigh of satisfaction.

"Glad to be of help," Duke told her, "though why you love this…drink, so much, is beyond me." As if to illustrate his meaning, he took the merest sip, trying, and failing, to hide a grimace of distaste.

"If you don't want it…" Doris left the question open-ended, though pointing at her glass, which was already half empty.

Getting up from his seat, he took his pint and set it down on the table where the projector was set up. "That's all right, I'll force myself."

"Spoilsport," Doris muttered, getting up to turn off the lights. "Ready?" she asked.

After the films had finished, Doris got up, turned the lights back on, and waited until Duke had put the films away and joined her.

"Well, what do you think?" he asked. "Anything spring to your attention?"

Doris opened her mouth to reply, then thought better of it and took a sip from the remains of her drink. From the way her companion was leaning towards her, there was obviously something about what she'd just seen which had importance, perhaps something which was not meant to be obvious. After giving herself a good amount of thinking time, Doris couldn't put her finger upon what Duke had done to the film. Giving up, she stared at Duke, who had what could only be described as a smug expression on his face. "Go on, then. Tell me what you've done, how clever you are."

Duke didn't trouble to contradict her. "So you didn't notice anything…strange? The whole things looked…natural? What did you see?"

"Well," Doris mused, thinking back on what she'd just seen, "there was our general giving his speech, quite clear and pretty much as I remember."

"And?"

"And there were some good shots of him talking to the mechanics next to the Mustang."

"And?" Duke repeated.

"And," Doris parroted, beginning to feel a little annoyed, "that's it. Lots of background shots of the station with people getting along with their work. Nothing out of the ordinary, I guess."

"Excellent!" Duke clapped his hands together.

Doris finished her pint and plonked the empty glass down upon the table with a satisfying thud. "Come on then, Major. What did I miss?"

Duke wagged a finger at her. "No need for name-calling. I do hope you'll forgive me. I've used you as a guinea pig. You see," he hastened to forestall the protest he saw was about to burst from her, "you're one of the most perceptive people I've ever known, and I knew that if you didn't spot anything untoward, and I saw how closely you were watching the films, then I've done a good job."

"And what exactly is it that you've done? If you can tell me, that is," she added.

"Let me put it this way. What did you notice *wasn't* there?"

Doris opened her mouth, about to ask him what he meant and then changed her mind when it struck her what he was leading her on to. "The half-tracks!" She snapped her fingers. "That's what you mean, isn't it? What happened to the flying half-tracks?"

"Believe it or not, they're still there," Duke told her. Settling back into his seat and crossing his arms.

"No they're not," Doris replied unhesitatingly.

"Yes, they are," he reiterated. "Only, when the film is seen at normal speed, you can't see them."

"What do you…" she began to say, before snapping her fingers again, "Stop me if I'm wrong, but have you left a few random frames in place? And, unless you run the film frame by frame, you won't be able to see them! Won't the Pathé people be angry when they see all those shots missing?" Doris then asked.

Duke shook his head, "I doubt it and, to be honest, I couldn't care less. Even the most jumped-up director couldn't expect to be allowed to show anything like that at the cinema."

"What happens to the films next? I mean, there's obviously a point behind all you've done."

"The point is, the Germans will get hold of this film, there's no doubt about that. After all, it's going to be copied and shown across the country. At some point, a copy will make its way across the channel, which is exactly what we want, and the Germans will examine it, with typical Teutonic thoroughness, in great detail, frame by frame."

"Which is when they'll see the half-tracks at the airfield," Doris supplied.

"Exactly! They'll see just what we want them to see. And the conclusion they'll come to?" he asked.

Doris tapped a finger against her teeth while she gave the question some thought. "Well, why would a load of vehicles be this far north? There has to be a purpose. You wouldn't leave them there for no good reason."

"Good. You're getting there," he said, with approval.

"You're going to owe me another pint, my friend," Doris informed him before saying, "The thing which springs to mind is they're there to be put to a good use, and the nearest enemy territory to that airfield is Norway."

"Spot on! You're quite correct. There's no other reason for them to be up here."

"How long do you expect it to be before the Germans see the films, then?" Doris asked.

"Oh, a few days, I should imagine," Duke said. "I'll give the Pathé chaps the films back in the morning, and I know how keen they are to get them out there, so I don't think I'm being unrealistic."

"What do you think they, the Germans, will do? You know, once they've seen them," Doris asked.

"I should imagine they'll be very keen to get some photographs of the airfields around here."

Doris frowned. "That's going to be difficult, though. We've got air superiority and pretty much anything the Germans send over here these days gets shot out of the sky."

"And you know this how?" Duke wanted to know, frowning.

Doris shrugged her shoulders. "I speak with a lot of pilots in my job."

"Hmm." Duke shook his head. "You're right, but let's keep that between us. Anyway, the obvious plan—and, again, keep this to yourself—is to allow a few recce planes to get through. Not many, but enough so they'll get the confirmation of a build-up of equipment that will, together with all the radio chatter and signal intercepts, allow them to piece together the puzzle as we want them to."

Doris didn't speak for a minute or two, and when she did, she only said one word, "Sneaky."

Duke cocked his head in acknowledgement. "We try."

Getting to her feet, Doris picked up her empty glass and waved it under his nose, "Right, you can buy me that pint now."

Chapter Twenty-Four

Private Douglas, now fully recovered from his bouts of air sickness, was one of the last to leave the Other Ranks Mess the next morning. Normally a man with a healthy appetite, he'd been unable to keep anything down since the flight back from Belfast until he'd sat down that morning. Now, with a reminder from the rest of the squad to, "Hurry up!" ringing in his ears, he crammed down a last slice of fried bread, followed it down with the last of his cup of tea, and grabbing his kit hurried towards the door.

Coming up the steps, he was busy securing his belt so wasn't paying full attention to where he was going, and so didn't see the arm which pushed him backwards, crashing him into a heap at the door of the mess. As blackness overtook him, he became aware of a wetness spreading under his trousers. He was just able to mumble, "Great. I've wet myself too!" before succumbing to unconsciousness.

****

"Major-General Edmund Hakewill-Smith," Doris read from the document Duke was holding.

Flicking the piece of paper away from prying eyes a few seconds too late, Duke turned around to an unexpected sight. "Do you need a hand down?"

Doris thought quickly before replying, "Sure, only don't nip my fingers off," she told him, holding out her hand and laying it upon his hook.

"I'll try not to." He smiled, as Doris slid down off the roof of the Humber. "You know," he began before turning his head to sneeze.

"Bless you," Doris said. "Where did that come from?" she asked as she tipped her head back. "It's a lovely morning, not a breath in the air."

After a couple of sniffles, Duke was able to say, "No idea. Funny thing, same happened yesterday morning. After a few minutes, I was fine. Bloody annoying, actually! Anyway, if you wanted to know who we were seeing today, you only had to ask. I'd have told you in the car when we set off anyway."

Doris chuckled. "I was curious as to what had you so engrossed."

Somewhat to her surprise, Duke opened her door. "Get behind the wheel, Third Officer, and start driving, I'll fill you in on the way. It's already nearly nine and we should have been away a good twenty minutes ago."

"Sorry about that," Doris told him as he slammed the door shut behind her. "I thought I saw a flash of grey tail and I had to see if it was Taxi."

"And what did all your scurrying around reveal?" Ceiwen enquired once Duke had settled himself in, having also witnessed the way Doris had shot off.

Doris turned away, lest the two men see her blush. "A squirrel…don't laugh!" she quickly added, trying to spare her blushes, turning around to lean over the rear of the seat. What she was presented with, were two men who seemed to be in perfect control of their emotions and not the least in danger of laughing.

"We wouldn't laugh, Doris," Duke informed her, crossing his heart with his good hand. "We, and by we, I believe I should encompass the entire castle, know how much this moggy…Taxi, sorry, means to you."

"Even if he does make you sneeze," Doris put in.

"Even if he makes me sneeze," Duke agreed. "After the last few days, I'd almost be glad to feel like that again, just so you could have the little chap back."

Doris frowned at his words, blessed him when he sneezed once more, and then gunned the engine and enquired, "Where to today, then?"

Duke leaned over the seat with a grunt. "Should really have done this outside," he muttered, before putting a map before Doris's eyes. "Target for today is Dundee."

Whipping the map out of his hands, Doris scanned it for a few minutes before returning it to its owner. "Right, better get down to South Queensferry and catch the ferry. You know, the sooner they build a bridge across the Leith, the better!" she informed them.

"When do you think we'll get there?" Duke asked, glancing at his wristwatch.

As they left the castle, the lorry and its escort close behind, Doris enquired, "What time did you say we'd be there?"

"I didn't," Duke replied. "It's like a spot check. After all, it is one of the real units this general is in charge of."

As they drove through Edinburgh towards the ferry, Doris listened with great interest as Duke gave her an outline as to what training the 52nd Division were involved in. She learned what long experience with the military would have engrained within her—that the unit's personnel preferred to be called by its full title of "The 52nd Lowland Infantry Division." When she pointed out that this was a bit of a mouthful, Ceiwen interjected that if she wished to discuss this with a member of the unit, then he'd be happy to drive her to the nearest doctor as soon as it was safe. Her immediate reaction of stating that it would have been the other person who'd need a doctor, was shot down by both her companions because, as they rightly pointed out, and she had to admit, these were battle-hardened soldiers who would be likely to act first and think later. She'd quickly agreed.

"You need to remember that these men have been training since May of 1942," Duke elaborated. "They're hungry for battle, and the smallest thing is likely to set them off. Forget all this tosh about the British soldier being a gentleman. That went out of the window in the trenches of the Western Front in the last war. Their officers know they could do with an operation, and over the last few weeks, some carefully chosen officers have been dropping hints about them being made ready to invade Norway. I believe Norwegian dictionaries and phrase books have even been distributed, with some being *carelessly,* shall we say, left lying around various Scottish cities and towns."

"And they don't know that all they're doing, especially now, is all part of this huge deception plan?"

"I'm not totally certain," Duke replied, "though I'd give you good odds that only Ceiwen and one or two others would be in the know."

Doris stopped talking and asking questions then. She wasn't going to admit it, but all the talk about the troops they were about to meet had slightly unnerved her. Perhaps it had been the realization of what soldiers were expected to do, or to become—killers. In all the time she'd spent in this country, she'd never actually come across troops who were expected to fight the enemy man to man. In fact, the signals chaps back at the castle and whom she'd met during this assignment were the closest she'd got to fighting troops until now, and it didn't look like her experiences with them were going to stand her in good stead. Glancing behind, she wondered how Frank was getting along on his new assignment.

Not until the short ferry journey across the river had been negotiated and they were well out of the city did Doris ask what they were going to be doing.

"We'll be watching a couple of exercises, showing Ceiwen's face—Ceiwen licked a finger and slicked down an eyebrow at this—before moving down to look at a unit that's simulating an artillery shoot."

"Sounds thrilling," Doris mumbled, settling in to enjoy the rest of the drive.

****

"Private Wilson!" Sergeant Lewis shouted, as Doris's new friend Frank struggled to line up exactly as the sergeant wanted. "I know you're only a signaler, and this isn't your normal job, but you volunteered to take Private Douglas's place this morning. Don't make me speak to your commander and tell him you don't know your left from your right. Now, line up and smarten up! The general's about to inspect us, and you will not, I repeat *not*, let me down!"

Once Lewis had marched past her to take up his position for when the commander of the 52nd arrived, Doris shot Frank a smile and a cheery wave, hoping to cheer him up. Okay, even she could see that he wasn't the best at drill, but his heart was in the right place. How many other people would not only carry an unconscious colleague so he could get medical help, but would also volunteer his services to take the man's place in their escort for the day. His commanding officer had, when Duke had spoken to him about his proposal, informed Duke that it was the man's day off and if he wanted to spend it on a long and uncomfortable journey bouncing up and down in the back of a lorry, then he wouldn't object.

From the slight shrug of his shoulders that Doris noticed as he caught her eye, it looked like the escort commander's words had simply slipped off his shoulders, like water off a duck's back. She liked that, and hoped she'd have the opportunity to tell him so.

"He's a strange one, that Wilson chap," Duke whispered in her ear, making her jump.

"Christ! Don't creep up on a girl like that," Doris scolded him, turning around and aiming a whack at Duke's shoulder, only for him to turn away at the last moment and her fist connected with his hook. "Oww!" she cried, tucking her fist under her armpit. "Bloody hell, that's got some weight behind it!"

At these words, Duke held up his arm and scrutinized it, as if he'd never seen it before. "You know," he decided, bringing it down on the roof of the Humber, where it made a resounding clash, "I never thought about it before."

It was now Doris's turn to scrutinize him and, fighting the urge to hit him once more, decided that he was playing with her. She shook her head and blew on her sore hand. "Yes, you have, and I'm sorry."

Glancing around, Duke made sure no one was looking their way before smiling, as it didn't do for an officer to look overly friendly. "Let's say, I've got used to it, but I wouldn't recommend giving it a try."

Smiling at the humor Duke displayed, even though it was only for her benefit, Doris remembered what had started the back-and-forth banter. "Anyway, I don't know what you mean. I met Frank Wilson the other evening when I was out looking for Taxi." She shrugged. "He seems nice enough. Don't think he's ever going to win any intellectual contests, but still, I don't think he means any harm. It was good of him to step in, too."

"Good, but strange," Duke agreed, with a shake of his head.

The two of them watched as Frank, now finally in line with the rest of the escort, snapped to attention as Lewis issued the order. Both generals strode into view, passed down the short line of men with barely a second glance, causing Doris to sigh in annoyance and mutter, "What a waste of time," as, with perfect timing, they walked past her.

Major General Hakewill-Smith was a very imposing fellow who, for someone who appeared to be approaching fifty years old, appeared to have the drive and vigor of a much younger man, judging from the way he all but leapt up onto the upturned tea chest he was using as a platform from which to address the assembled men.

As Doris found all public speeches boring in the extreme, she tuned out everything he said except for his last few lines.

"And, remember, it's a live-firing exercise today, so keep your heads down and make sure you don't drift out of the marked sectors. You're not going up any mountains today, but we'll be back into that phase of your training again shortly, so I'm not losing anyone to an accident today. Good luck."

With those words, he stepped down and accepted a salute and then a handshake from Ceiwen. The two of them shared a few words before Hakewill-Smith strode off to start the exercise. Ceiwen joined Duke and Doris and, together, the three followed the real general towards the tent he was using for a headquarters. Inside it they found themselves in the semi-darkness. The flaps which could be opened to let in light were closed, and the overwhelming sensation was one of noise also, considering the limited amount of space, the sheer number of people present was awesome. Doris almost regretted that it took a nod from Ceiwen to permit her entry. She'd rather be outside, even though it had just started to drizzle with rain.

With nowhere obvious to sit, she stuck close to Duke, who was right on Ceiwen's shoulder. All credit to the man, despite her teasing him about his lack of acting skills, he was holding his nerve and delivering a fine performance. From what Doris could tell, he was nodding in all the right places and showing due deference to the division's commander as he led him to peruse various maps which were laid over flimsy-looking wooden tables, even pointing things marked out and getting smiles in reply.

"He's doing well," she leaned in and whispered into Duke's ear.

"Very well," he told her back. "Still, we'd best be making a move." He looked at his watch, Doris noting with interest that the numbers were luminous. "Not only do we need to get to our next unit, but I'd rather not take a risk with hanging around any longer. There's always the chance we'll run into someone who knew the real

Ceiwen, and he'll be out of his depth sooner rather than later, the longer he talks to General Hakewill-Smith."

"Won't the real general be annoyed if we leave now? I thought we were supposed to hang around for a number of exercises," Doris pointed out.

"What can I say? I hadn't expected to be enclosed inside a tent. I can't control the situation, and Ceiwen will—and you know it too—make a mistake if we take any more time."

Doris looked up in time to notice that Ceiwen laughed a few beats after everyone else at something Hakewill-Smith said. "Do it."

Duke tapped Ceiwen on the elbow and, when he turned, gave the man a single nod. Instantly understanding, Ceiwen said something to Hakewill-Smith, who briefly shook his hand before turning his attention back to directing the exercise.

Ten minutes later, they were all back at their transport, with Sergeant Lewis once again berating Frank Wilson for some infraction.

Doris felt Ceiwen grip her arm. "Don't interfere, Doris. Lewis won't thank you, and neither will this Wilson fellow. The sergeant seems a good man, so trust that he must have his reasons."

As Doris opened the door for her companions, she looked up as their escort thundered past to take up their positions in the lorry. She waited until Frank was coming up level with her and threw him a wide smile of encouragement. Much to her disbelief, he didn't return it, instead, the eyes which looked back at her seemed to be on fire, and Doris felt a chill race down her spine. Had she been mistaken about his friendliness? Was something going on of which she was not yet aware?

Chapter Twenty-Five

"I thought you said they were simulating an artillery shoot?" Doris shouted, trying to time her words between the roar of the guns.

"That's what we'd agreed!" Duke yelled back.

Deciding further attempts at conversation would be an exercise in futility, Doris merely nodded and waited until each of the six twenty-five-pound field guns ranged before her had fired their allocation of ammunition. An artillery sergeant was waving his hands at the group, and both Doris and Ceiwen took this as the signal it was safe for them to remove their hands from over their ears. Hoping the ringing in her ears would soon die away, she tapped Duke on the shoulder, knowing the noise would have been much worse for him to endure than for her, being able to cover only one ear effectively.

"Are you all right?"

After a moment, Duke nodded his head, though he told her, "I've had worse. Give me a minute or two."

Joined now by the captain in charge of the troop, the man had noticed Duke's trouble. "How are you feeling, sir?"

After saying much the same thing to the young man as he'd already told Doris, Duke added, "You took us by surprise, otherwise I'd have been prepared. You do know," he began, glancing around to make sure only the four of them could hear what he was going to say, "that we weren't actually expecting a real shoot?"

The captain appeared to be blushing, though in the gathering twilight it was difficult to tell for certain. "I do. Only…" He didn't seem to want to finish his explanation.

"Pray continue, young man," Ceiwen ordered, in his best general voice.

"Only my sergeant saw the paperwork I'd filled in, to place the six guns on our strength, and assumed I wanted it to be sent in. Next thing I know, the guns turned up along with the crews to serve them, and with a supply of ammunition, both live and practice."

"Which did you just fire off?" Doris wanted to know.

After yet another double-take at the unfamiliar uniform, the captain, like most people, decided to answer her question. "Live, though that's the last of it."

Duke placed a comradely arm around the captain's shoulder. The poor man looked like he'd prefer the ground to open up and swallow him. Instead, he had more questions to answer.

"If I understand it correctly, instead of about half a dozen men, and an excess of radio equipment, you've now got a fully trained battery of guns and the crews to go with them. You see my problem, Captain?"

By now, the captain looked distinctly unhappy and also more than a little uncomfortable, as the arm Duke had slung around his shoulders was the one with a hook for his hand. The captain was probably a nice man and good at his job, Doris thought, but he was in charge of this small unit whose purpose, Duke had filled them in on the way, was merely to play tape recordings of artillery shoots in the background, as they sent radio messages back and forth, whilst slipping in the odd remark about the effectiveness of the shells they were using against the same kind of terrain they expected to find when they were deployed. The idea being to let the Germans come to the conclusion that terrain they were training for was Norway. Scripts had been prepared in which mention was to be made about the difficulty of loading using the cold-weather mittens they'd been issued with, to further the illusion. Now, because of a sergeant who'd been too efficient, a fictitious unit had been turned into a real one.

Realizing the situation he was in, the captain did the only thing possible. "I'll sort it out, sir. Though I'm not sure how to go about sending the guns back, to be honest," he admitted.

Duke removed his arm, much to the man's obvious relief. "Good chap, that's exactly what I wanted you to say. Leave this with me. I've a little more, ah, clout with these things, with the people we need to speak with. You just take your sergeant to one side and make him aware, without revealing exactly why you'll be losing the guns, that he should leave the running of the unit to you and he should take care of the men."

Obviously relieved that the mess he was in would be resolved, the captain snapped to attention and saluted the major. "Thank you, sir. I'd very much appreciate it."

Ceiwen stepped in, seeing the man needed something to take his mind off the current situation. "Take me to your radio tent and let me see what you're actually doing. I'd be very interested to listen in."

As the two walked ahead, Doris fell into step with Duke, "Nicely done. I was wondering how you were going to sort out this sticky little problem."

"You didn't think he'd be able to sort it out himself?" Duke asked.

She nodded. "Probably. Only, knowing the army, they'd likely have deployed for real by the time it all got sorted. As we both know, you can get things fixed a lot quicker. I suspect with one or two phone calls when we get back to Edinburgh tonight."

Duke held open a tent flap for her. "Perhaps three."

****

As things turned out, Doris and Ceiwen didn't see anything of Duke for an hour or so after they got back to the castle. The pair were seated in the officer's mess where Doris was trying to convince her companion to treat her to some of his old showbiz act, only for him to, quite rightly as she'd just admitted, refuse on the grounds that he would, at the very least, raise the odd eyebrow.

"What are you two talking about?" Duke enquired, taking a seat.

Keeping his voice down, Ceiwen leaned across to tell him, "Only Doris trying to get me in trouble again."

"You don't know how lucky you are, sir," she also said in as quiet a voice as she could, "that I can't tell you what I'm thinking right now."

Further conversation was forestalled by the arrival of the same steward Doris had previously met. "General, Major, Third Officer, would anyone like something to drink?" he asked.

Doris opened her mouth, only for Duke to shake his head, knowing she'd been about to tell the steward to address her by her first name. A brief look up into the man's eyes and Doris changed what she was going to say to, "A pint of Guinness, if you've got some, please."

"That we do," he replied and shortly he left to bring

in two pints of bitter and Doris's beloved black gold. As he left, he ducked down and whispered into her ear, "Sorry, still no sign."

After a reasonable meal of trout and vegetables, which Doris had to be persuaded to eat as the fish had made her think about Taxi once more, they tucked in to a serving of Spotted Dick for pudding. Once done, they all pushed their chairs back and, with a nod to Percy by Doris, made their way back outside.

"What's on the agenda for this evening, then, Duke?" Doris asked, turning her head away so she didn't belch in her friends' faces.

"I've got to give the film back to the Pathé chaps," Duke announced.

"You're going down The Chevalier?" Ceiwen asked, immediately interested. "Mind if I tag along?"

Surprisingly, it was Doris who had to let him down. "I take it you haven't noticed that Sergeant Lewis has begun to have a couple of your escort follow you around?"

Initially puzzled by what she meant, Ceiwen looked around and indeed standing as unobtrusively as it was possible for two heavily armed soldiers, were two of their escorts. To her surprise, one of them was Frank Wilson.

The sight of him reminded Doris of the strange look she believed he'd given her back at the artillery camp. She took it upon herself to get to the bottom of things and, fixing a determined expression on her face, she strode over. "Hello, Frank. Bit surprised to see you still on duty. Don't they need you back?"

It was immediately apparent to Doris that she hadn't being imagining things. Though his expression didn't display any anger towards her, so she could have read him wrong, there also wasn't any of the friendliness he'd displayed when she'd been looking for Taxi. When he spoke, his eyes looked anywhere but at her, something Doris didn't fail to notice.

"Douglas is still in the hospital and my boss is happy for me to help out," he told her.

"Seriously," she persisted, "you don't have other duties? You can't be on guard every evening, and you must be here to do something other than fill in for a bodyguard."

"Nothing I can tell you about…Doris," he added. The accompanying smile sent a shudder down her spine.

His belated attempt at reverting back to the man she thought she'd met didn't fool her, and she took a precautionary half-step back, though the precaution was likely completely unnecessary, since one of their original escort was a mere couple of feet away from them and there were plenty of people milling around.

"Fine, be like that," she told Frank. She turned to face the other guard and asked, "I assume you're here to dissuade Ceiwen from anymore nighttime excursions?"

The man nodded. "Afraid so, ma'am. If you wouldn't mind letting Ceiwen know, we'd appreciate it. It'd make our night easier."

Doris decided to ask, "What would happen if he decided to go for a walk?"

Before he answered, the man looked over Doris's shoulder to where both Ceiwen and Duke were watching proceedings with interest. "Well, we can't stop him from going anywhere—he is a General after all—but if he did go outside the castle grounds, we are under orders to follow him."

"Everywhere?" Doris wanted to know.

"Um, everywhere," the man reluctantly confirmed.

****

"Exactly how hacked off was he?" Duke asked, as they approached The Young Chevalier.

"Very!" Doris grinned, though more because Duke had taken out a comb and whipped it through his hair, than at the sullen face Ceiwen had pulled upon being advised that it was easier for everyone if he stayed in the castle that evening. "I left him muttering about spending the evening in the mess. I don't envy the stewards much as, castle or not, I doubt they have the same quality of whiskey as this place does," Doris declared, bobbing her head as they came up to the entrance. "Major's first," she said, opening the door and bowing, sweeping her hat near to the ground with a flourish an Elizabethan gentleman would have been proud of. Once they were inside, Doris glanced around before asking, "When and where are you meeting the film guys?"

"In about ten minutes," he answered whilst looking at his wristwatch, "and in the lounge bar."

Doris offered him her arm. "Come on. So long as Morag won't kill me, let me buy you a drink whilst we wait."

Duke observed his companion as she took a long, somewhat loud slurp from her Guinness. "I've been watching you," he began, though could get no further before having to swallow as Doris had raised both eyebrows. "In a positive way, of course," he hastened to amend, taking a sip of his whiskey.

"Go on," Doris told him. "I'm intrigued to see where this is going."

"I'm curious, does anything faze you? From what

I've witnessed, I'd have to say that the loss of Taxi is what's upset you the most. Why is that?"

Instead of answering right away, Doris sat back in the rounded lounge seat she occupied, and steepled her hands before her face, looking over the top of her fingers at the good major. Her expression could only be described as serious. "I'll answer you honestly, why not?" she shrugged. "You'd be wrong to think nothing fazes me." She leaned in and lowered her voice, forcing Duke to shuffle closer. "I lost my first husband in the Spanish Civil War and thought I'd never love again. Then, I found my Walter. I never set out to fall in love when I came over here, but there you go, you never know when it'll happen. He's a newspaper man, local to where we live, with flat feet, so he can only serve in the Home Guard. Everything's nice and safe, I thought, he's not going to go and get himself killed for somebody else's ideology. Then he goes and saves a mate when a grenade practice goes wrong."

At those words, Duke clutched his hook, his face draining of blood. "Bloody hell! Is he…"

Doris managed a small laugh. "No, he's okay…now. He took some shrapnel, and had a nasty head wound, but seems fully recovered now. He even got decorated for what he did," she added.

Noting the pride in her voice when she told him this, Duke sat back, took a sip of his drink and stated, "Quite right too." He raised his glass, sensing Doris needed a break. "To Walter!"

"Walter!" Doris echoed, and promptly downed a good couple of inches of her Guinness. She placed her glass down. "So, as you can tell, things do get to me but, in this instance, you're right. I miss him, Taxi, that is."

As they'd both settled back in their seats, both were now speaking at a normal volume, and both now believed they knew the other a little better now.

"We'll find him, I'm certain of it!" Duke told her firmly.

Doris was saved the trouble of replying as Duke suddenly got to his feet. Turning in her seat, Doris saw the Pathé chaps had entered the bar. She settled back to enjoy what she was sure would be an entertaining show. Doris didn't have anything against either man, in fact she felt a little sorry for them, as they didn't know they were being used to help the deception plan. Mind you, if they were as patriotic as most British people seemed to be, and if they'd have been given the option, she was certain both would readily have agreed to help. Only this was war, so she also understood why chances could not be taken.

Greeting the fellows, Duke shook their hands. "Mr. Tilbury, Mr. Jenkins, please, take a seat. Can I get either of you a drink?"

Taking a seat, Bowler Hat Man, now correctly known as Tilbury, shook his head, whilst the younger one, Bert Jenkins, mimicked the gesture, though there was disappointment written all over his face. Clearly the man had been hoping for a pint to wet his whistle.

"No, thank you, Major, but appreciate the offer."

From the curious way he was looking at Duke, it was clear the man was wondering how he knew his name. Then a smile came to his lips, and he shook his head.

Ignoring her initial decision to remain quiet, Doris had to enquire, "What's so amusing, Mr. Tilbury?"

"Hmm?" From the way he turned his head, Doris would have sworn he hadn't noticed her presence before she spoke. Annoyed, she repeated her question. "Oh, a ridiculous thought just passed through my mind."

"Which was?" she asked.

"Well, I don't recall giving the Major here our names, yet we spoke previously on the telephone about the return of the film." He waved a hand at the cans of film at Duke's feet.

"And?" Doris was getting annoyed with him for not getting to the point.

"Well, he obviously got them from reception. How else?" he declared.

"How else, indeed?" Doris echoed, glancing at Duke from the corner of her eye. She recognized the twinkle in his eye and decided to let him take over. "Major?"

Firstly, Duke reach down and placed the film cans upon the table, nudging their glasses slightly out of the way. With a nonchalant shrug of his shoulders whilst scratching an ear with his hook, a gesture Doris was certain was calculated to unnerve the man (and of which she wholeheartedly approved), he left a hand upon the top can and told Tilbury, "I've not spoken with reception about either of you," he assured him. "There was no need when I could go straight through to your room."

Oh, to be able to read a mind, Doris thought. From where she sat, Doris had a great view of the range of emotions which flitted across the man's face before finally settling upon, much to her satisfaction, what looked like a mixture of terror and admiration, though more terror. After a few seconds, whilst his mouth was busy doing an impression of a goldfish, he recovered enough to ask, "Well...that's as...can I now take possession of my film?"

Looking down at the cans upon which his good hand

rested, Duke reacted as if he'd only just remembered them. He pushed them slightly towards the man who, in a hasty rush, grabbed them up and cradled them upon his lap.

"They're all yours. Thank you for your cooperation," he informed the men, with a small smile.

"Don't remember being asked," Tilbury muttered, getting to his feet, Jenkins matching his superior.

"When do you expect that to be in the cinemas?" Doris asked.

"Couple of days," Jenkins answered immediately, earning himself a reproachful glare from his boss.

"Yes," he answered. "My bosses are eager for this to be shown as soon as possible. Ceiwen's always big news."

"Excellent!" Duke answered.

"If there's nothing else?" Tilbury asked.

Duke shook his head before telling them, "No. Again, my thanks and the best of luck, gentlemen."

Very quickly, both Pathé men made a swift exit from the bar, leaving Doris and Duke alone to their drinks.

Doris picked up her glass, drained the rest of it in one, and held out her hand for Duke's glass so she could get them both a refill. "Come on, then, how did you get their names? If you really didn't call reception…MI5! I'm right, aren't I?"

Handing her his now empty glass, Duke chuckled and shook his head. "I asked Morag."

Doris looked into his eyes, trying to make up her mind whether to believe him or not. With his recently renewed relationship with Morag and, of course, the fact she worked in the hotel, it was very probable but, so far as Duke was concerned, there were always other possibilities.

Chapter Twenty-Six

"Penny! Is that you?" Doris shouted down the telephone line. Now she'd finally been connected, she was wondering if it had been worth the effort.

After spending a rather pleasant and amusing evening at the Chevalier, Duke had insisted upon escorting her back home rather than spending some extra time with Morag. Morag had been fine with this, and indeed, they only left when the bar shut, having spent the time with the fiery Scottish lady at the same table they'd occupied with the Pathé men. Doris had suggested she should let the two have some time together, only for Morag to press her back into her seat and tell her she would stay, as she'd been the one who'd made her see sense regarding her relationship with Duke and, so far as she was concerned, they were now best friends! Doris wasn't sure she'd go that far, but, thinking it would be good to have a friend at the other end of this small island, she didn't make a protest.

Pressing the receiver against her ear as hard as she could, Dori could just make out her best friend's voice, though it sounded as if it were through a rabbit hole. "Doris! About time you called. We were starting to think you'd forgotten us!"

"As if," Doris shouted, hoping she wasn't disturbing anyone.

Glancing around at her surroundings, Doris could

only wonder at the vagaries of rank in the armed forces. Ceiwen's room wasn't much larger than hers and, setting aside the fact that he wasn't a real general, it was still amazing how much effort went into making someone of his rank comfortable. Not only was there a sofa—it had seen better times, but a sofa was a sofa—his room had running water and a telephone! When she'd mentioned to Duke that she'd like to call up her friends down south, he'd told her to leave it to him. As soon as they got back to the castle, he asked her to give him a few minutes and to wait in her room but he'd be right back. Sure enough, he was soon escorting her up to Ceiwen's room. The man had been rather gracious in giving up his room so she could have her privacy, informing her to come and find him in the mess once she'd finished, leaving her his room key so she could lock up.

"How've you all been? Anyone missing me?" she asked.

"If you're asking where Walter is, he's on guard tonight. Sorry, hon, no one knew you were going to call."

"Oh!" Doris felt her heart plummet. No matter how she'd been looking forward to speaking to her friends, it was Walter with whom she really wanted to reconnect. She still considered herself a newlywed, and there had been certain *suggestions* she'd wanted to tell her husband about what she'd do with him once she got back. She'd been looking forward to a little naughty talk. They had a very lively love life, one which—and she was still surprised about this—their landlady hadn't complained about yet, and she was missing their intimacy while away from him now. "Well, tell him I called, and that I love him, very, very much."

"Which reminds me. Ruth expected you to call and

wanted me to let you know she knows how much you miss him."

For a few seconds, all Doris could hear from the other end of the line was a cacophony of laughter. She waited for it to die down before saying, "Very funny," though she was glad none of them could see how red her cheeks had gone. "Just for that, I won't be bringing you back a haggis." Into the silence she now had, Doris told them what she'd prepared for this moment: "It's one of those rare albino ones you all told us about."

"You're having me on," Penny eventually managed to say.

"No way! It's kind of cute, in a strange lopsided manner. Though how exactly it evolved as it did, I don't know."

"You can stop now," Penny told her.

"How it doesn't go around and around in circles, I'll never figure out," Doris informed Penny, really beginning to get into her stride now. "I thought at first it must give a bit of a hop every now and then, maybe a skip in there too, but I've never been able to catch it. Still, it seems to turn around fine."

"It does?" Penny seemed bemused by what she was hearing.

Doris didn't give her the chance to interrupt. "As for all that hair, I don't suppose you know how to tell which end is which, do you? Which reminds me…do these things ever go to the toilet? I've been watching for that too, you know, as a way to tell which end is which. Both ends seem to have eyes! What's that all about?" When she didn't get a reply, she tapped the receiver against the side of her head. "Hello? Anyone there?"

"Doris? It's Jane. What did you say? Poor Penny's

on the floor, she won't stop laughing!"

"Ha! Serves her right," Doris said.

"All I can get out of her is one word—haggis," Jane replied.

Very glad they couldn't see her wide grin, Doris allowed herself to laugh out loud. "Well, after what you lot told me about the wildlife up here, I thought I'd get a little of my own back."

"Let me guess. You brought up the subject." Not for nothing was Jane her commander.

Though she couldn't see, Doris nodded. "Right in the middle of a restaurant full of what seemed to be the local rich people."

Now Jane also laughed. "Sounds perfect!"

"Are you happy with yourselves?" Doris asked.

"Very!" This was both Jane and Penny, who'd recovered enough to get her voice back. "Are you doing all right?" Jane asked, suddenly serious. "Not had any trouble?"

Quickly, Doris mulled over whether to tell Jane about Taxi, but decided that, with Duck, she and her animals were already responsible for causing enough of a nuisance and until she knew if the Taxi situation would resolve itself to her satisfaction, there was no point.

"Nothing springs to mind, Jane. I've been a credit to the ATA!"

"Hmm, well, if you say so. I'm sure if you did, we'd hear about it sooner or later. I can only say, 'Keep up the good work.' "

"Hey!" Doris remembered, "There is something you can do for me. Keep an eye out for a Pathé newsreel coming out in the next few days. It'll be about a General Ceiwen's—that's pronounced Kine-Wen—visit up here.

I'd love to hear what you think about it."

"Any particular reason?" Jane asked.

"You'll know when you see it," Doris told her enigmatically.

"All right," Jane replied, before asking, "When will you be back? Still the 15th?"

"At the moment, yes," Doris confirmed, before saying, "I miss you guys."

"Miss you too, Doris," Jane and Penny both said.

Sniffing, as she could tell that if she were to speak to her friends for much longer she'd likely begin to cry, Doris decided she'd be best off if she ended the call now. It had been so very nice speaking with the two of them, but it made her feel homesick.

"I'd better go now, girls, though I'll see you soon. Love you all and, safe flying!"

****

"Are you always here?" Doris asked as she entered the officer's mess bar.

Percy Snodgrass tipped his head a little in greeting, glancing furtively around as he did so, "A very good evening to you, Doris."

Touched that the young man had remembered her instruction to use her first name, Doris smiled in return. Looking around, she spotted Ceiwen at the same table as Duke, each nursing a glass of what was probably whiskey. From the expression on Duke's face after he'd just taken a sip, what was on offer wasn't up to the standard at the hotel.

"Afraid I've had no success with Taxi," Percy told her, shaking his head.

She patted him on the shoulder for his honesty and thoughtfulness, telling him, "I appreciate your trying, very much." Deciding that though the room was full of a few stuffy male officers, she couldn't see a single female, she should show real thanks, and to reinforce what she'd told the man at breakfast the other day, she went up on tiptoes and quickly pecked Percy on the cheek. "Don't work too hard."

The young man couldn't have been kissed very much, as he'd rapidly gone beetroot red and it took him a few false starts before he was able to find his voice. "What can I get you?"

Though it was tempting to ask for another pint of the black gold, Doris, remembering that she'd be driving tomorrow and that she'd be best to have a clear head, asked him for a lemonade, if they had it. Percy told her he'd rustle one up from somewhere, and with a smile of thanks, she strode over to where her companions were seated.

Sitting down in a free seat, Doris handed Ceiwen back his door key. "Thank you."

"Did it go well?" Duke asked.

Doris nodded, "Very. I'd almost forgotten how much fun we have when we're together. I also managed to get my own back about the haggis. Thanks, Percy," she said to the young steward as he set a bubbling glass of lemonade before her.

"I'm not sure I want to ask what you said," Duke told her. "Though I hope you told them that you'd been a credit to the ATA."

"I did! Mind you, I'm not sure if Jane believes me. She said she'd soon hear otherwise if I hadn't."

"Well, if you don't mind my saying, I'd be happy to vouch for you once we get back down," Duke informed her.

"Same here," Ceiwen added. "She doesn't have to know I'm not a real general."

"That means a lot, thanks, guys!" Doris smiled, raising her glass in salute. After taking a tentative sip of what turned out to be a superb lemonade, she suspected Percy had whisked it up especially for her, and if so, she'd like to know where he'd got the ingredients. She asked Duke, "So, where are we off to tomorrow?"

"We're going to the other side of the Firth of Forth," Duke informed them and then, when both his companions appeared not to be any wiser, picked up his briefcase, opened it, and handed them each a stiff piece of paper.

"What's this?" Ceiwen asked, beating Doris to the question by a mere half second.

"Your passes. The whole of that area has been declared a Protected Area, and you won't be able to get within ten miles without one of those so, keep them close. They're only valid for tomorrow."

"And we're going there to do what?" Doris persisted.

"You'll love it!" Duke told her, beaming.

After a few moments, Doris leaned towards Ceiwen and asked, "Is it me, or does he look like a shark about to devour us when he smiles like that?"

Instead of speaking, Duke raised his glass in salute, draining it before placing it back on the table and, after looking at his watch, standing up. "Well, I'm off to bed."

After consulting her own watch, Doris did the same, though it did seem a bit of a shame not to take her time over the lemonade. Still, if she was going to put her plan into action, she'd better do so before she changed her mind.

"Me too. Coming, General?" She asked, her voice polite and at just the right volume for everyone else in the room to hear. Displaying deference would do no one any harm.

As they left the mess, Doris heard what sounded like a rumble of thunder. Stopping just inside the door, she asked the other two, "Strange, it didn't seem like it was going to rain when I came in." She was about to step outside when there came a louder, much more thunderous rumble and, the next second, right where she'd have been had she not stopped, a number of roof slates smashed to the ground!

Chapter Twenty-Seven

In spite of the day having been pleasant, quite warm actually, Doris was discovering that spending the night in the back of her Humber, with a window wound all the way down, was…cold. Very cold, and she was regretting leaving a blanket on her bed.

It had been Duke's sneezing which had sparked the idea in her mind. There was no reason why she'd be right, but also no reason why she'd be wrong. Taxi had to be spending the night somewhere so, why not the Humber? Duke liked the fresh air and seemed to have his rear window open more often than not and, she had to admit, she'd sometimes forgotten to wind it back up when they arrived home at the castle. As he sat on the left side of the rear seat, she knew it can't have been easy for him to open the window with his hook, so she understood why he'd often not wind it back up. So, after they'd last arrived back, she'd hung back and done as careful an inspection as she could of the interior, telling them that she was going to give the car a quick clean.

It hadn't taken her long to find some grey hairs wedged into the door frame where the window ran, and as these did not match the hair color of either of her male companions, she was pretty certain she could be right. Of course, it could still be that bloody squirrel, she mused, idly wondering if the mess cooks would make squirrel pie. Still, it was the best lead she'd had, so she'd decided her best bet would be to spend at least one night bedding down in the Humber. With her days up in Scotland getting few, she was running out of options. Doris desperately didn't want to leave without Taxi, and even though she'd only had him for a few days, she could feel a tug of her heartstrings whenever she thought of his furry little face. If she never found him, she knew she'd always be thinking of what could have been. She didn't know what Jane would think about it, but Doris had been planning on outfitting him with a set of kitty-sized flying goggles and taking him with her on any twin-engined assignments. She was sure she could persuade one of the ground crew back at Hamble to knock her up a basket for when she had to travel back.

With this happy thought whirling around her mind, Doris gradually fell asleep.

It was a happy trick of Doris's that, when she needed to be, she could allow herself to be awakened by the smallest thing, all she had to do was fix that reason in her mind a few minutes before she finally closed her eyes and...*Wham*!

Jerking awake, Doris sat bolt upright and found herself staring into the wide-open-in-surprise eyes of what was unmistakably Taxi! Blinking furiously, she saw that the cat was balancing on the open sill of the window, his tail lashing back and forth in annoyance at finding someone occupying what Doris now knew to be one of his sleeping places.

Slowly, so as not to scare him off, she pushed aside the blanket and sat up. "Hello there," she said, keeping her voice low and steady. "What've you been up to?"

"Meow!" he replied, and Doris chose to take that as cat for, "This and that."

"I've missed you, you know," Doris went on, before telling him, "I wish you hadn't shot off. I've grown very accustomed to your fuzzy little face."

This time, she got what sounded more like a "Mrow?" including the question mark at the end. She took this to mean he'd missed her too.

Drawing her legs up beneath her bottom, she edged nearer the window, Taxi watching her every movement, though to Doris's eyes, he showed no signs of disappearing. She patted the blanket beside her. "Want to come in out of the cold?"

After he'd canted his head left and right a few times, Taxi appeared to have decided that this was a good idea. He extended a front paw, and she saw his bottom wiggle from side to side and recognized the movement as a precursor to pouncing, so she moved a little back to give him more room.

In the moment he chose to spring, a pair of burly arms came out of nowhere, grabbing the cat roughly by the middle. Momentarily stunned, the few seconds Doris wasted were enough to give the catnapper a vital head start. It didn't help things that Doris had to stop to untangle her legs before she could jump out of the car. Unfortunately, in her haste, she hadn't pulled on her shoes and small, sharp stones rapidly dug through her socks as she ran in the direction she believed the man had gone. Spurred on by worry, panic, and anger that her dear moggy might be about to be hurt, or worse, she did her best to ignore the now intense pain her feet were causing her. As she rounded a corner, she became aware that she was slowing down and the pounding of what she recognized as army boots was now receding into the darkness. Finally, after turning another corner, the sound of the running steps had ceased. Panting, she leaned against a wall and listened as hard as she could.

Eventually, she had to accept it; she'd lost them. Not caring for where she was, nor for whatever the time was, she threw back her head and screamed her frustration at the top of her voice!

****

"There you are!" Duke shouted, approaching the Humber the next morning. As he got closer, he realized that his assumption Doris was leaning nonchalantly against the wall by the car was completely wrong. At the sound of his voice, her head had jerked up and the face staring back at him was of someone in total despair. "My god!" he exclaimed, rushing forward and grabbing her by the shoulders.

"Duke?" Doris's voice came out monotone, as if she wasn't aware she was even speaking, and the eyes which stared back at him held no focus.

"Is something wrong, sir?" Unnoticed by either, Sergeant Lewis had appeared at their side.

Duke glanced at the man from out of the corner of his eye and instructed, "Just keep everyone away, Sergeant. Give us some space," he ordered, turning his attention back to Doris, though he did nod his thanks at Ceiwen as the man also approached, veering off to go and stand next to Lewis.

Taking her hand in his hook, which she didn't seem aware of, he opened the back door of the Humber and fed her inside, closing the door behind her. He shot around the other side and sat down next to her, noticing that her window was open, but he decided against leaning over her to close it. This time her held her hand in his real one, stroking it a little clumsily with his thumb, trying to soothe her. After a minute, the action seemed to break through wherever she'd drifted off to.

"Thanks, Duke," Doris told him, extracting her hand from his. "I'm fine."

Not only the tone of her voice but the fact that she hadn't looked at him upon saying the words were enough for him to know she was lying; she knew it too. With a deep sigh, Doris turned her head to look at the still open window and told him what had happened.

"You know," he began, "you're sometimes too brave for your own good."

Doris chuckled, though with her dry throat, it came out as more of a croak. "Not the first time I've been told that."

"You could have been injured, attacked, killed!" he informed her, all of which had gone through Doris's mind as she'd hobbled back to the car, too tired and disheartened to go back to her room.

"I wanted to be back here," she told him. "In case he managed to break free. I wanted to be here for him," she repeated.

Duke watched her carefully, this was a side of Doris few people saw, the vulnerable side, and he could see there was a battle going on inside her. All of a sudden, she threw her head back and roared her frustration. Taken by surprise, Duke threw himself back against the door, which flew open and he tumbled backwards onto the ground.

Quicker than he'd have thought possible, Doris scrambled across the seat and was by his side to offer him a hand to his feet. "Sorry about that," she mumbled, as he took her hand and got up.

Brushing his trousers down, he nodded before

saying, "That's all right. How are you now? It sounded like you needed that."

Eyes flashing, Doris replied, "Oh, I did, I really did. Just you wait until I get my hands on the bugger who took him!"

After a quick glance around, Ceiwen, Sergeant Lewis and his men were still milling around, all doing their best to appear not like they were trying to listen in. Duke shook his head. "Probably not the best of ideas. I don't suppose you noticed anything about the one who took him?"

It took a while before Doris replied, "I can't be sure," she began, "it was only a fleeting glance in the moonlight, but I think he had a tattoo on his left forearm, a flash or a lightning bolt, against a wobbly circle, or at least that's what it looked like to me. It was too dark to tell for sure, though I'd bet good money on it being one of the signalers, as I can't see it being one of our escorts, and I don't know of anyone else who'd be in the castle." She gave it further thought. "Actually, as I was looking at him and he was face on to me, let's make it his right arm."

"That's not something I'd go around saying out loud," Duke warned her.

Doris thumped the roof of the Humber in frustration. "I was so close!" she cried in exasperation before settling down on the back seat once more.

Someone behind them cleared his throat and both of them looked up to see Ceiwen and Lewis loitering near them. "Sorry to ask, sir," Lewis said, "but what's happening about today? Are we still moving out?"

"Doris," Ceiwen said, "I can't help but notice your feet—are you hurt?" he asked, pointing at where her sock-clad feet were dangling off the bench seat.

"Hmm? Oh!" Doris hoisted up first one and then the other foot, holding each up so she could inspect any damage.

Seeing her struggling to look, Ceiwen volunteered, "May I?" then took first her left and then, after a moment, her right foot. "Well, I don't know how, but I'd say your left one has some spot of blood on the sole but as for your right one, you've holes in your sock and I can see some pockmarks in your sole and a few minor cuts." He stood up, brushed his hands together, and told Duke, "They're not too bad, but I would recommend the medics take a look at them."

"I'm fine," Doris insisted, though from the looks on all three men's faces, none believed her. "All right," she reluctantly said, "I'm not quite all right, though I'm sure there's nothing wrong a few bits of sticking plaster can't fix." When no one said anything, she tried again, "Look, give me half an hour to get fixed up and I'll be ready to go."

As Sergeant Lewis was present, Duke had to ask Ceiwen, "It's up to you, General. We've no fixed time to keep to."

Ceiwen made his decision. "Go and get fixed up, Doris. We'll be waiting."

Without thinking what she was doing, Doris jumped up and out of the car, kissed Ceiwen on the cheek, told them all, "I'll be back before you know it!" and shot off, leaving a very red-faced general.

Chapter Twenty-Eight

Doris suppressed a yawn of epic proportions, for the umpteenth time that day, and she glanced at her watch. It was only just past two-thirty in the afternoon. She idly wondered how it would look if she curled up on the back seat of her Humber and took a catnap... Ouch! Scolding herself for the very poor choice of words, Doris pinched her cheek, willing herself to stay awake. The view didn't help, either, being simply that of another small tent city. Honestly, though she wasn't sleeping in one, if she never saw another, it'd be too soon. Heaven help Walter if he suggested they go camping!

She'd been left to kick her heels for the past hour with no one for company. Duke had suggested that one of the guards remain with her, though more for company than for her protection, he'd hastened to amend when she'd shot him a look which could have shot down a squadron of Messerschmitts! Frank Wilson had swiftly put up his hand, only for Doris to immediately put her foot down—metaphorically, as they hurt much more than she'd let on to the medic who'd patched her up—and tell Sergeant Lewis that she didn't need a nursemaid, thank you very much!

She'd been closely watching Frank's face, for what exactly, she didn't know, but his face had been a mask, almost like someone had set it in stone, giving nothing away. Only when they'd finally accepted her wishes did she notice that Frank was taking the opportunity to rub his right arm. There was something about him, besides being about a head taller than anyone else, which was bothering her, and she couldn't put her finger on what it was. Only when the guard had marched off in their usual protective formation around the two officers and disappeared from sight, had it hit her. Frank Wilson was the only member of the guard to have his sleeves down. Something about that simple fact bothered her. She knew enough about senior NCOs that if there was one thing they hated, it was a lack of uniformity. Which begged two questions—one being, why was Frank still part of the guard? Upon thinking this, Doris immediately scolded herself and vowed to go and see how Private Douglas was feeling when she got back that evening, as obviously he couldn't be up to returning to duty yet. As for the second question, well, she was certain there was a reason why he was allowed to be dressed differently than the other members of the guard. She'd have to see if she could get the reason out of Lewis later. Now that was a thought to keep her awake!

Perhaps a short stroll would help clear her head. Taking advantage of her civilian status and trying not to think what Jane would say if she could see her, Doris unbuttoned her jacket and carried it over her arm. After a moment, she also took off her hat. She wouldn't go too far, since she didn't know when her companions would be back and it wouldn't look good for her not to be within sight once they returned, so she glanced around until she spied a bit of slightly higher ground which might allow her to have a view of the Firth.

Not being familiar with the word, she'd asked Duke on the way there what the difference was between an estuary, which it looked like to her on her map, and a firth. Doris was smart, worldly wise, but she wasn't a fan of jargon, and when Duke began to go on about salinity levels and the relationship between firths and fjords, she'd told him to forget it, as it wasn't that important.

Taking a swig from her water bottle, Doris rested her feet as best as she could. The medic had done a good job, and though she hadn't needed any stitches, he had been clear in telling her what he thought of her idea of going back on driving duty immediately. For this, she'd immediately liked him and so had felt bad about not taking his advice, though she had promised him she'd do her best not to be too hard on them. He still hadn't been pleased, but he'd softened a little when she'd told him she hoped that, if she ever had to go into battle, he'd be the kind of person she'd like to know was waiting to patch her up.

Resisting the urge to unlace and take off her shoes, Doris settled back and made herself as comfortable as she could on the reasonably dry ground. Before her, the firth—Doris had decided she might as well call it what everyone else called it—seemed reasonably busy with ships of all sizes and types going back and forth, both military and civilian. Watching the sight was slightly hypnotic, and after only about ten or fifteen minutes, she could feel her eyes getting heavy again. After she'd got back to the Humber last night, she'd slumped across the rear seat but had been too miserable to get more than the odd snatch of sleep. She was paying for it now, and so, knowing she'd need to have her wits about her to drive back to the castle safely. The Humber was not the easiest of cars to drive, as she was discovering. She pinched herself again, and when that didn't help too much, she drew back her arm and slapped her own face, too hard.

"Need a helping hand, luv?" some corporal asked, laughing as he sauntered past.

"If I were feeling up to it, I'd make you laugh on the other side of your face," she muttered. The man kept going, shaking his head from side to side at his own joke, not knowing how lucky he was.

Getting to her feet, she wiped the tears which had sprung to her eyes, hoping her cheek wasn't too red. When she'd cleared her vision, she gasped. The next vessel to come into view was a tug, and behind it, linked by a towrope, was what she believed to be a destroyer, listing perilously towards her shoreline, its decks almost awash. "Bloody hell!" she cried, as she took the sight in.

As the obviously damaged vessel cleared a freighter going the other way, Doris was treated, if that was the word, to a full view. Behind the destroyer, another tug was tasked with keeping the small flotilla straight. As her thoughts turned to the ship's crew, she passed her gaze over the stricken vessel. Though no expert, she surmised that for it to be listing so, it must have taken severe underwater damage. There were two small gun turrets forward, towards the bow, and only one appeared to have guns present. She shuddered, not caring to dwell upon what could have happened and what would likely have become of its crew when it did. She may have been a pilot, but she had learned enough to know that destroyers were very lightly armored compared to, say, a battleship. As the ship moved along, she could clearly see gaping holes in the second funnel, and much of the hull, right until you got to the rear turret, was blackened. A severe fire must have raged, and she mentally complimented the ship's crew on not only putting out the fire but getting the ship back home as well. Not many small warships with the amount of punishment as this one had taken were able to accomplish that feat! She bowed her head until it passed, in a gesture of silent honor to the vessel and her brave crew.

"That was quite a sight, wasn't it?" a voice by her side stated.

"Why were you hanging back?" Doris asked. "I noticed you approaching about a minute ago."

"I could tell how the sight was affecting you," Duke said. "You looked like you needed a…moment."

Doris raised an eyebrow, but didn't say anything more until the destroyer and her tugs had disappeared behind an island beneath the Forth Rail Bridge. "Very perceptive of you, but thanks. That was quite a sight."

Duke raised his hook so it was before his face and waved it back and forth before his face. Then he split the hooks to hang the briefcase on. Raising his arm, he waggled it back and forth a little, telling Doris, "I've been practicing this. First time it's not fallen off, the briefcase, I mean," he told her, smiling. He offered her his free arm. "If you're ready? We've finished here."

"Thank God for that!" Doris exclaimed. "I was in danger of dropping off there a few times. Promise me this—next time, take me with you? I'll try to get some sleep the night before, next time."

"Speaking of," Duke said as they approached the Humber, where Ceiwen and the escort were waiting, "how are the feet feeling? Honest answer."

As he'd phrased the question so, she replied, "Sore, but probably better than they should be."

Duke nodded in agreement. "I've walked the grounds of the castle enough since we've been here to know that you got away with it. I'm simply so surprised you didn't cut your feet to ribbons."

"Next time, I'll sleep with my shoes on."

Duke pulled up a little short of the party waiting for them and planted himself before her. "Wait! You're going to wait in the Humber again? Tonight?"

"I'll be careful," she told him. "I do learn from my mistakes, you know."

****

"Sorry we couldn't bring you along with us earlier," Duke told Doris. "We did ask, as I know you don't like being left out, only the colonel in charge was…shall we put it, he was rather anti-women."

"And you didn't want me to cause a scene," Doris stated, unable to keep a tone of annoyance from her voice. "I've told you I can keep my temper!" she snapped, slightly lessening the weight of her statement.

Upon which Duke promptly soothed her wounded pride. "I had full confidence in your ability to keep your tongue in check," he informed her from the back seat of the Humber. I didn't have the same confidence in the fool we had to deal with."

Ceiwen snorted with laughter. "Honestly, Doris, Duke did you a favor. Even my acting skills were pushed to breaking point. I don't think I've ever come across such a pompous ass in my life!"

Feeling mollified, Doris happily slapped the steering wheel.

"Ceiwen's got a point. If ever there was a case against the old-boys public school system, that chap would be a prime example. Oh, take the next left, please," he told Doris, having consulted the map on his lap.

"Yes, sir!" Doris treated him to a deference of rank, to show him her appreciation of him thinking about her feelings. "I can observe the next meeting?" she asked.

"Shouldn't be a problem," Duke told her. "The captain in charge of the small unit is a good friend of mine."

Doris raised an eyebrow at this news. "Is he…in the know?"

"Sharp right coming up and then you've a bumpy mud and grass track for about half a mile, so be careful. To answer your question yes, he's another that knows, as do all his team."

"And how many's that?" Doris asked.

"Only about a dozen. It's just as well he likes camping though. The poor bugger has been stuck up here for the best part of a month and is likely to be here for another couple at least. You saw all the cargo we loaded in Lewis's lorry? We're taking the opportunity of bringing them some rations, and a few treats."

"Why treats?" Ceiwen asked, proving that he was listening.

"Simple," Duke began. "Part of their orders were, once they were set up, they were not allowed to leave camp. Everything would be brought in to them once a week, by trusted personnel, who would give a password which would change daily."

"I hate to ask, "Doris said, swallowing so she could speak, "but what happens if someone gives the wrong password?"

As Duke hesitated slightly before replying, Doris knew she wouldn't like the reply; she was right.

"Captain Bright and his men have strict orders that if, and only if, the wrong password is given and they believe they are under a genuine risk of being infiltrated, they can shoot to kill."

"Bloody hell!" Doris and Ceiwen said at the same time, and with identical shakes of the head.

"Bloody hell, indeed," Duke agreed. "However," he added, "this is war, and remember what we're trying to do."

"You trust him and his men to make the right decision, if it came to that?" Doris asked.

"I trust him, yes. As for his men? Well, I don't know them personally, so I'd have to say I couldn't tell you for sure. Hopefully, they'll never have to act upon the orders."

It was a pensive threesome which approached the small copse of trees Duke pointed them towards. As they came to a stop, the lorry right behind them, a man-shaped bush detached itself from the tree line and pointed at them a piece of wood which was definitely not a part of a tree any longer.

"Password!" a man's voice demanded.

Winding down the back window, Duke stuck his head out, not appearing at all fazed by the rifle whose muzzle was only about a foot from his face. "Sphinx 859."

"958 Cleopatra," the man replied, then shouldered his rifle. "Major Newton-Baxtor, sir. Good to see you again," he told them, before going back to where he'd been standing.

Next moment, he pulled upon a rope which had been tucked away behind a tree trunk, which drew aside a net which had been so expertly camouflaged with leaves, bracken and bark that it had been invisible to the naked eye, even from only five feet away. This opened up a space just large enough to allow them and their escorting lorry to pass through. As soon as the lorry had passed, the net drew back across and Duke instructed Doris to come to a stop.

"Okay, stop here, please, Doris. We can get out now."

Though it was only just past three in the afternoon, Doris had to allow her eyes a minute or two to acclimatize to the gloom she now found herself in. As her eyesight got used to the low light, she could make out more detail. Directly before her was one of the larger military tents she was now used to, undoubtedly where all the work was done, and surrounding it, a collection of smaller tents where she presumed the men all slept. Barely a few yards behind and to their side, more camouflage nets had been strung up, essentially surrounding the camp and hiding it from prying eyes.

"General!"

Striding out of the tent, hurriedly placing his hat upon his head, was an officer. This was Captain Bright, Doris assumed. Though it was difficult to be certain, in spite of now being under cover for a few minutes—details were a lot harder to make out than under normal circumstances—she could at least tell that this chap was on a level with her height, and even in her limited experience this made him unusual. The wide smile he turned upon their group as he saluted Ceiwen spoke volumes of an excess of personality though. His exuberant "Duke!" and the way he pumped her friend's hand up and down confirmed her assessment. When Duke introduced her, she made certain to release his hand virtually as soon as she'd shaken it, lest she pull a muscle.

"Come in, come in," he said, shucking aside the flap on the larger tent and ushering them inside.

Leaving their escort outside, whilst some of the captain's men started to unload their supplies from the lorry, Doris brought up the rear. No sooner had she entered than Bright let the flap drop closed. Reaching above his head without looking, he turned on a gas light and the inside of the tent was bathed in a low light, which was enough to see in, barely.

"Captain," Duke started, "why don't you fill us in?"

"I'll be delighted. General, Doris, if you'd follow me." He led them towards a radio set in a corner of the tent, where sat a man with the single pips of a second lieutenant on his shoulders. "Jeff, if you're ready, go ahead." The captain held a finger up against his lips, though they all knew to be quiet.

For the next few minutes, the three listened in silent fascination as the young man before them spoke quickly yet clearly into his microphone. Though she didn't follow very much of what he was saying, her eyebrows did shoot up when she heard him say, in clear English, that all Norwegian speakers were instructed to report to HQ in Edinburgh. She caught Duke smiling when he heard this.

"All correct, sir?" the man asked, after placing his microphone down and turning off the radio set.

Bright patted him on the shoulder. "Exactly as planned. Well done." He waited for Jeff to leave the tent before asking Ceiwen, "Everything satisfactory, sir?"

Doris was watching the pair closely, so when Duke gave a barely perceptible nod, Ceiwen enthusiastically replied, "Very, thank you, Captain. Please pass on my congratulations to your lieutenant and your men on a job very well done. Tell me, before we go, is there anything we can do to make things a little easier for you whilst you're here? Apart from telling you for how long you're likely to have to stay, that is."

The captain let out a little chuckle and shook his head. "Well, that was going to be my first question sir, but as you've answered it…"

"Come on, Paul, think, there must be something you need?" Duke asked his friend.

From the way he hesitated, Doris would have bet the man would have gone red, if the light were good enough to see clearly by.

"Perhaps some more toilet paper? Some more books."

Duke clapped the man on his shoulder. "Leave it with me. Right, I'm sorry it's only been a flying visit, but I have to get Ceiwen back to base."

At this, Ceiwen held out his hand. "Keep up the good work, Captain. I'll see to it personally that you get what you want within the next couple of days."

"Thank you, sir," the captain replied and went to hold up the tent flap for them again.

Sergeant Lewis came up. "All the supplies are unloaded, sir."

Ceiwen gave a nod. "Good. Mount up, Sergeant, and we'll be on the way."

With another round of goodbyes, they reversed from the camouflaged site and were on their way back to Edinburgh.

Doris waited until they were back on the main road before saying, "Is anyone going to tell me exactly what we just saw? I mean, what was with that Norwegian speakers thing? Surely that's not something which should have gone out over the radio?"

"You picked that up? Great!" Duke said, clapping his hands.

"Well, yeah! He did say the words out loud," Doris told him.

"He was supposed to!"

"Because…"she began to say, before changing her mind, "because it was another part of the false trail you're sowing!"

"Bingo!" Duke glanced at his watch. "In about an hour, another camp will send out a coded message telling Captain Bright's unit off for their indiscretion…"

"And because it was sent under a cypher, will make the Germans think that the earlier message has genuine weight!" Doris finished. "Sneaky!"

"We do our best," Duke replied.

Doris smiled to herself, happy to be part of a job well done, and maybe, just maybe, bringing the end of the war a tiny bit closer.

Chapter Twenty-Nine

Arriving back at Edinburgh Castle, Doris parked in her normal space, whilst their escort's lorry came to a halt just behind her. Now they were back at their temporary home, Doris allowed her attention to focus once more upon the whereabouts of Taxi. Days were getting fewer, and she was finding it very difficult to hide her anxiety. Both Duke and Ceiwen were well attuned to this, and before she could get out of the Humber, they were beside her door.

Opening it, Duke stepped aside. "We need to have a word with you."

Doris didn't trouble to keep the note of suspicion from her voice. "Really. What about?"

"We assume you're planning upon spending another night here," Ceiwen stated, waving a hand towards the back seat.

More than a little wary, Doris replied, "Might be. Why?"

"Because we don't think it's a very good idea."

"No, we certainly don't," Ceiwen added, nodding vigorously.

A likely argument was nipped in the bud by the unexpected arrival of Sergeant Lewis. Once they arrived back at Edinburgh Castle, Duke usually informed the escort of the time to be ready to leave tomorrow, then dismissed them and they were free for the rest of the day.

Perhaps it had been because Duke had been fixed upon confronting Doris about her plans, but that hadn't happened this time, and the sergeant took it upon himself to interrupt with his usual snappy salute.

"Sir," was all he was able to get out before Duke whirled around.

"Ah, yes, Sergeant. Sorry, I nearly forgot. Eight in the morning for you and your men. Dismissed," he added, before turning back to where Doris, fists balled on her hips, appeared ready for a fight.

The sergeant had other ideas. "Begging your pardon, sir, but me and the boys heard what happened last night—castle grapevine, sir—and, sorry, miss," he addressed Doris, "we agree with the major. It's too dangerous for you to stay in the car overnight again. We reckon you were lucky. Whoever took Taxi was spooked by your chasing them, but we don't think that'd happen a second time."

Faced with opposition from all sides, Doris stood there, thinking things over. Nobody disturbed her. All knew full well that though she was nominally under the command of the major and the general, she was also not in the forces and, being who she was, would likely go ahead and do whatever the hell she wanted, no matter how reasonably anyone argued. It was, after a few tense minutes, much to everyone's surprise and relief that Doris's fists relaxed and she leant back against the Humber.

"Much as I hate to admit it, Sergeant, you're right…and you don't know how hard that is to say." She shot a sideways glance at Duke, who looked very much like he'd like nothing better than to say that he did! Wisely, he kept his mouth shut. "So, suggestions? We all know I'm not going to let this drop!"

Before either officer could speak, Lewis offered an unexpected option. "All of the boys have volunteered to take your place in the car tonight, miss."

Doris leant around the mountain at where the escort were trying to appear nonchalant a few yards away, trying to appear like they weren't listening, whilst it being patently obvious they were. If she had to bet, she'd give good odds on not everyone having *volunteered*.

Lewis swiveled his head to see what Doris was looking at and coughed, shifting a little from foot to foot. "Well, I say *everyone* volunteered, there was one person I couldn't persuade."

It wasn't hard to tell who was the odd one out. Standing with his back to them and slightly apart from the rest, Frank Wilson kept glancing around before turning back, hoping no one had seen his face. When he did it again, his eyes met Doris's and his left hand shot out to cover his right forearm in a now familiar gesture. Quickly, she turned back to face her companions, hoping Wilson hadn't caught her watching him.

She made a decision. "Sergeant, could you dismiss your men? There's something I need to speak about with you, out of certain people's ears."

Lewis waited a moment, just to see if Doris was going to elaborate, and when she didn't, he turned and barked, "Right, you lot! Eight of the clock tomorrow morning, back here. Go and get some scram and don't have too much fun tonight. I don't want anyone spending a night in the cells!" He waited until they'd disappeared from sight, no doubt relieved they wouldn't have to spend an uncomfortable night curled up on the back seat of the Humber. "Right, what was it you wanted to say?"

he asked, at a more normal volume.

Doris noted that both Duke and Ceiwen also were looking at her curiously so, not wishing to take any chances, she took a quick walk around both vehicles and then, once she was satisfied that no one else was within earshot, cleared her throat and said what was on her mind. "Isn't anyone else curious about Frank Wilson? Why's his boss so ready to let him work with us? Surely there are better things for him to do? He is a Signaler."

After a moment, Lewis deferred to Duke. "Sir? I hate to put it this way, but he's with us by your leave."

It was interesting to see the major wrong-footed, Doris thought, and she could well imagine the cogs of the man's mind clicking round and round. Eventually, he did something she hadn't expected—he asked Ceiwen for his opinion. Perhaps it was for show, but it was still a welcome display that he was coming to respect the job the man was doing.

"General, what do you think? Can we do without Wilson?"

Ceiwen recovered admirably from the shock of the unexpected question. "Without wishing to risk fate, we've done well so far, and I'm sure we could do without Wilson for the last couple of days." He turned to Lewis and asked, "Which reminds me. Sergeant, how is Private Douglas? Will the doctors release him in time to fly back down south with us?"

Impressed that Ceiwen had remembered their injured man's name, and that it might save her time in looking for Taxi, she listened attentively to Lewis's reply.

"Like a caged lion, sir! I reckon if the M.O. doesn't release him, he'll take matters into his own hands."

"Excellent!" Ceiwen replied, before saying to Duke, "In that case, I believe we can do without Wilson. Do you agree, Major?"

"Yes, sir. Lewis," Duke addressed the sergeant, "before you do anything else tonight, make Wilson aware we won't need his services anymore."

"Yes, sir!" Lewis replied enthusiastically.

"Now, Doris," Duke turned back to her, "you wanted to talk to us in private. It wasn't only why Wilson was still with us."

Doris shook her head. "No, sir, it wasn't," she confirmed. Doris took a deep breath, "You know I mentioned that I thought the person who took Taxi had a tattoo on his forearm?"

"I remember," Duke said. "Go on. I'm beginning to follow where you're going."

"Lewis, why did Wilson have his sleeves down? Don't you army types like everyone to look alike?"

Sergeant Lewis nodded, "He told me he had a nasty rash which the doctor had given him cream for, and that he needed to keep it covered."

Doris raised an eyebrow. "And, you didn't check?" When Lewis didn't reply straight away, she prodded him.

"It's, er…" Lewis took his cap off and ran a hand through his hair before replacing it, "a little embarrassing. I'm a bit squeamish."

Fortunately, Duke voiced what everyone else was probably thinking. "You'll pardon me for saying this, Sergeant, but…" He ran out of words and resorted to waving his hands in Ceiwen's direction.

In the gathering twilight, Doris could swear Lewis's cheeks were turning red, and resolved to save the man a little further embarrassment. "Well, I don't believe him. I think he's covering up a guilty tattoo."

Quicker than everyone else in putting two and two together, Duke snapped his fingers. "You believe Wilson took your cat? But, why?"

Doris shrugged. "I haven't worked that out yet, but yes, I think it's him."

"If you're right," Duke began, "what do you want to do? Also, and I hate to bring this up, Doris, what if Taxi's not alive?"

Grimacing, Doris couldn't suppress a shiver. "I'd rather not think about that possibility. As for what I want to do? I haven't changed my mind."

****

"How am I supposed to catch him in the act now?" Doris muttered to herself, slamming the door to her room.

It had taken all through tea, not that she could remember what it was she'd eaten, for Duke and Ceiwen to talk her around. She still couldn't believe Duke would be sleeping in the Humber, pretending to be her! Of course, with a cast of two, Lewis was out because of his sheer size—it would look like there was a bear trying to wear her Air Transport Auxiliary jacket, even if he could have laid down on the back seat—and Ceiwen because he was supposed to be the general and so was also out. No matter how she'd try to put it, the two had shot down her argument. None of this had done anything to improve her mood.

Now, back in her room, she flopped down on her bed and, for want of anything else being available, proceeded to thump the life out of her mattress. After a minute, she stopped, knowing it wasn't doing any good and got to her feet. Before she knew it, she was pacing the room instead, until she realized the futility of this too. Kicking off her shoes, she picked up her book from beside her bed, frowning at the dust cover, before her fuzzy brain remembered that she'd changed the dust cover and it actually was Miss Marple's *The Moving Finger* and not *Death on the Nile*.

She glanced at her watch—just after eight-thirty—and flopped her head back onto the pillow in frustration. Hanging around the mess for a few hours after finishing her meal and scanning her way through the newspapers since her mind hadn't been interested in actually reading the content, had wasted some time before bed, but it hadn't been enough to make her tired enough to go to sleep. Leaving the mess, she'd then spent a few hours walking around and shouting for Taxi, forcing herself not to go back to the Humber. Duke had forbidden her to go anywhere near it, threatening her with putting her on a train back to Hamble if she did.

Sighing deeply, she found her page and was dismayed to find she was barely halfway through the book! She knew why. Since Taxi's disappearance, she'd spent so much energy each night in searching for him that she was exhausted by the time she went to bed and asleep before her head touched the pillow.

Careful not to break the spine, a pet hate of both hers and Betty's, she began to read. When she realized she'd read the same page three times—Jerry had asked Mr. Symmington for his permission to pursue Megan, even though she'd just turned down his marriage proposal—she shut the book and laid it upon her chest. It was no good. Even the delights of Miss Marple weren't enough to distract her.

It was then, as she was aimlessly casting her eyes around her room, that she spotted it. Halfway under the door, was a folded piece of paper. Forcing herself not to throw the book aside, she rolled onto the floor and grabbed the paper. Opening it, she gasped and felt her blood run cold.

Be next to the one o'clock gun at nine pm, or the cat gets it.

Chapter Thirty

Flinging open the door, Doris earnestly looked both ways down the corridor and when this revealed no one, she clutched the note tightly in her hand and took the stairs three at a time, jumping the last four to land on her hands and knees. Ignoring the pain which shot from her left knee to her thigh, she kicked the entrance door open and stood gaping outside. By now, night had fallen and, to her frustration, all was quiet outside. Holding her breath, Doris strained her ears, hoping to hear…she wasn't entirely sure what. Either way, by the time she had to take a breath, the only sound she could hear was the occasional vehicle from outside the castle grounds but nothing suspicious from inside, like the sound of running feet.

"Nothing! What the hell?" Doris swore, and kicked a stone before turning and going back upstairs.

Slamming her bedroom door, Doris was so frustrated she didn't notice the large person in khaki doing his best to squeeze himself into the shadow of the landing above. Once the door closed, this person crept down the stairs, taking great care not to make a squeak on the polished stone and, after making certain they weren't observed, left the building and disappeared.

Inside her room, Doris looked at her watch, swore, and hurriedly retied her shoelaces. Dragging on her jacket, she cast her eyes around her room. What to bring with her? There wasn't much time to waste, not if she was going to make it to this gun. She had a fair idea where it was, but just to be sure, she picked up the map of the castle Duke had given her when they'd arrived. Quickly, she found where she was, then traced a route to the one o'clock gun, figuring it would take her about five minutes at a quick jog.

With another look at her watch, ten to nine, she stuffed the map in her trouser pocket, grabbed her overnight bag, hoping it wouldn't be needed, and once more hare out of her room. Then she burst back in, obtained and tucked under her free arm the cardboard box from the top of her wardrobe, which had contained Taxi's salmon, before rushing out, not bothering to lock the door.

By the time she got to the steps leading up to the gun, she was sweating, though not too out of breath to remember to slow her pace before coming to a stop at the base of the steps. Wishing her heart would quiet down, she did her best to tell if there was anyone above her. For a moment, she wished Duke or even Ceiwen could be there with her, but just as quickly she dismissed the notion. Even if she'd have run off to get Duke as soon as she found the note, there wouldn't have been enough time to get to the Humber, explain things to him, and then make it here in time. Who knows what the person who had Taxi—she hoped this wasn't someone playing a silly joke on her—would have done if she'd turned up with someone else in tow?

No, this was the only option. She had to obey the instructions and arrive alone. The only thing that mattered at that moment was seeing if Taxi was alive and, if he was, finding a way to keep him like that. With a wry smile, two thoughts ran simultaneously through her mind: she remembered Jane's orders not to bring the uniform into disrepute and wondered what on earth Walter would say if he could see what she was about to do. Sighing, she placed one foot before the other and climbed the steps, knowing there was no point in worrying about things beyond her control. She stayed from putting her left foot down onto the step that would bring her head into view of the gun. Was that the sound of a footstep she could hear behind her? Looking behind, there was nothing there. Shrugging, she put it down to her imagination and, with a deep breath, placed her foot down and put her head into the firing line.

As soon as she stepped out onto the plateau, a dark shape detached itself from beside the gun. At the same time, she heard the welcome yet plaintive yowl of what she knew to be Taxi.

Fighting down the urge to rush forward, she tightened her grip on her overnight pack, settling it more comfortably in her hand, and shuffled the cardboard box back into place.

"That's far enough!" barked a male voice, one she recognized, as she came within about ten feet of what was plainly a rather large man.

Hoping her voice wouldn't embarrass her, Doris jutted out her chin. "I thought I recognized that tattoo." Though she was pointing at the arm in question, which Wilson subconsciously rubbed, Doris's eyes were drawn to a sack at the man's feet. It was being held down by one of his large feet, as it did its best to squirm away, accompanied by the sound of an angry cat. "If you've hurt Taxi…"

"You'll do what?" Wilson sneered, snatching up the

sack and going over to the railings. He dangled it over the drop. "That little blighter scratched the hell out of my leg! I think I should drop him right now!"

Putting the cardboard box down, Doris held up her free hand, hoping to pacify the man. "All right, I'm here. You going to tell me what this is all about? Getting some kind of hold over me won't make it any easier for you to kill Ceiwen."

"Kill Ceiwen?" he threw his head back and, showing complete disdain for what Doris thought was going to be a quiet blackmail attempt, laughed his head off. "Why do you think I've bothered about that old fool?"

"Well, I don't know," Doris muttered, sounding a little confused.

"True, though I've got the option of killing him, or rather I've been told the Germans would like him dead, if I get the chance, but I don't care about him. No, lass," he shook his head, "this is all about you."

Feeling a little silly, Doris prodded a finger at her chest. "Me? But, I'd never met you before a few days ago. What could you possibly have against me?"

Still dangling the sack nonchalantly over the rails, Wilson shook his head. "Me? I don't have anything against you, but my old boss? Oh, believe me, he hates your guts, Yank."

Thoroughly confused, Doris could only shake her head and ask, "You're going to have to be clearer. Who exactly is your boss, and what did I do to him?"

To her utmost relief, Wilson heaved the wriggling sack back over the rails and went to lean against the gun. "Does the name Harold Verdon ring any bells?"

Automatically, Doris opened her mouth to deny knowing the name and then snapped it shut as a repressed memory resurfaced. Her eyebrows shot up and Wilson nodded in satisfaction.

"I see you remember him."

As there was obviously no point in denying it, Doris told him, "I remember him. How's the swine doing? And what's he to you?"

"How's he doing?" Wilson roared, causing Doris to take an involuntary step back in surprise. "How's he doing? You shot his bloody balls off! How do you think he's doing?"

"Probably not having as good a time as he once did," Doris automatically replied, before adding, "Mind you, last I heard, he was locked up, so I don't suppose it matters much."

"You've quite a mouth on you," Wilson said, shaking his head. "Especially for someone who doesn't have long to live."

A sound from behind her nearly made her turn her head. Whatever was causing it could be either help or hindrance, though either way she didn't let on to Wilson she was aware of it. If whatever was causing it was on Wilson's side, well, she could barely be in a worse state, and if they were on her side, she didn't see how they could help her in time.

Perhaps she could keep him talking? Play for time? "So you're also one of that lunatic Moseley's men," she stated.

"Watch your mouth!" he told her. "Yes, I'm proud to support Moseley, and as for what you did? I couldn't believe it when Verdon's letter got to me!"

"So Verdon sent a letter to you? Telling you to kill me?" Doris was playing for time and hoped the man wasn't clever enough to work that out. "How the hell did he know I was coming up here, let alone that you'd be in a position to kill me?"

For some reason, the man actually proceeded to fill her in. Doris couldn't help but think it was like something from an Agatha Christie novel.

"Oh, he didn't. The man's angry, he hates your guts, and he's got plenty of time on his hands, so he sent a letter to everyone he used to work with. Mine came from my mum, and quite a tale it told." Wilson then turned his back, reached into his jacket with his free hand, and when he turned back, he was pointing a revolver at her.

"Whoa!" Doris managed to get out, the box dropping from under her arm. Time could be running out—she had to try and keep Wilson talking, as each second could be her last, and she'd read enough books to believe that the longer you could keep the villain talking, the more chance you had to making it out alive. "At least tell me how come you're not in prison? Didn't they throw the lot of you inside when war broke out?" As soon as she'd finished speaking, she cursed her voice and hoped it running away with itself wouldn't hasten her death.

"You do like the sound of your voice, don't you?" Wilson told her, echoing her own thoughts. "I don't suppose it's going to make much difference. You're right, I was in prison, but they let me out when I convinced them I wasn't a danger to anyone. When I couldn't get a decent job, I decided to join up. Got hold of some false papers and joined up." He sneered at her, whilst casually waving the revolver around. "Guess I got lucky, eh?"

Sensing time was drawing short and praying that her sixth sense was right in demanding she turn around to seek out the source of the noise she'd heard once again, and a possible rescue was at hand, she stepped nearer her assailant.

"That's close enough," he told her, levelling the revolver at her once more when she was barely an arm's length away.

Taking a deep breath and hoping her voice would be calmer than she felt inside, she said words which could have come straight out of a cheap pulp novel. "You're never going to get away with this!"

Perhaps it was the absolute ridiculousness of this statement, but Wilson suddenly barked out loud with laughter.

Drawing up all her reserves of courage, Doris spun around and brought her flight bag around in a wide circle. Using the momentum, she aimed it square at Wilson's outstretched arm. By some miracle, her aim was true and the impact sent the revolver flying out of his hand, to clatter away and be lost in the darkness. The moon was pale that night, and though it provided enough light with which to see and talk, there was no way the gun would be found by any way other than luck.

Roaring in pain and anger, Wilson clutched his hand. Taking her chance, Doris snatched for the sack and actually managed to grab hold of it. She was in the act of turning to make a run for it and had managed to turn her back, when she felt a rough hand fasten around the wrist in which she held her bag. The grip tightened until she yelped in pain and was forced to let go of it.

"You little bitch!" Wilson growled, dragging her close. "You've broken my hand!"

Not troubling to reply, as she knew she could need all the breath in her body, Doris struggled to free herself, only causing Wilson to tighten his grip. Not knowing if the sack was tied closed and hating that she was forced to do so, Doris threw the sack containing Taxi as far as she could behind her. If they both survived this, she'd make it up to him, only right now her one thought was to get Taxi as far away from them as she could.

His broken hand hanging limply by his side and his face twisted in pain and anger, Wilson made the mistake of letting go of her wrist, probably to get a better grip. Seizing what might be her one chance, only later wondering why she didn't make a run for it, Doris seized hold of his broken hand, brought it up to her mouth and bit down, hard. Wilson twisted, turned, trying to make a grab for her neck with his good hand but every time he came near, Doris bit down even more and his good hand flailed away in pain.

With an effort, Wilson ripped his hand free, immediately letting out his loudest scream yet. In his haste to free himself, he left a good-sized chunk from the side of the hand behind, clamped between Doris's teeth. Spitting the flesh out, Doris tried not to think of what she'd just had to do. Instead, she wiped her mouth on her sleeve and turned to run—too late.

Despite being injured, Wilson was still much, much bigger and stronger than Doris, and in an act of desperation he launched himself at her, hitting her in the lower back. Both of them crashed to the ground, with Wilson half on top of Doris, whilst she was flat on the rough ground. Worst, both of her arms were pinned beneath her body and the weight of the man prevented her from getting them free. The thought flashed through her mind that this was it, she was about to die, and she'd now never spend the many years of happiness with her

Walter that she was so looking forward to. She felt the pressure of an arm across the back of her neck.

All of a sudden, there was what could only be described as an unearthly yell, and she found herself free of Wilson's weight. Doris rolled over, opened her eyes, and turned her head to the side. What she saw would have taken her breath away, if she'd had any left.

"Get off her now!" ordered a harsh voice which, nevertheless, sounded familiar. The next second, the same voice, this time much kinder sounding, asked, "You all right?"

Standing over a now trembling Wilson was her steward friend from the officer's mess, and he was, with a very steady hand, pointing Wilson's revolver at him.

"Percy? Hell, am I glad to see you!"

Chapter Thirty-One

They must have been making more noise than Doris thought. No sooner had she spoken her relief to Percy than the sounds of multiple army boots could be heard thundering up the steps. Next thing they knew, they were surrounded by eight soldiers, all in full kit, including steel helmets, and brandishing rifles at all three of them.

Recovering her wits, Doris scrambled to place her body between Percy and the newcomers, whilst making certain Percy could keep his revolver covering Wilson. She held her hands up before her. "Hold on! Hold on! Nobody shoot!"

A man who bore corporal's stripes on his upper arm pushed his way through the men until he stood before Doris, who was trying to place her arms in front of every rifle muzzle all at the same time. The man must have had a degree of common sense as, within seconds, he ordered, "At ease, men. All except you, Barnes, and you, Owens, with me!"

The corporal, who Doris assumed was the guard commander, led the way until he and his two men were to one side of Percy, from where he could get a clear view of the situation. Doris, assuming none of the soldiers was about to shoot her, quickly stepped back until she was opposite them. "Lower the gun, please, Percy," she asked, trying and hoping her voice sounded calmer than it did inside her head.

Percy, with a quick glance at Doris, who nodded her confirmation, did as she asked, though he didn't move an inch. As he was built like a stick, this was rather brave of him, because Doris wouldn't have been surprised if Wilson had tried to make a run for it. One look at the man though was enough to convince Doris he was broken; literally.

The corporal, after ordering his two men to cover Wilson, whom he ordered to stay where he was, addressed a question to Doris. "Would you like to tell me what happened here?"

Doris straightened up. "Certainly, corporal, but firstly, there's a revolver somewhere around here that you need to find."

"Right here!" Percy announced, holding the weapon in question up in the air. "I found it when I followed you up here."

"In that case," Doris said, smiling now that Wilson's gun couldn't fall into the wrong hands, "I threw a sack in that direction." She pointed over Wilson's head. "I need to find it. My cat's inside."

Pretty much at any other time or place, this would have been a strange thing to say or hear but, Doris wasn't the hardest of people not to know about. The corporal snapped his fingers and said, "Doris...Air Transport Auxiliary pilot! Yes, I've heard all about this...Taxi, isn't it?" Upon getting a nod of confirmation, he then detailed two of his men to go and look in the direction she'd pointed.

"Hey! I need a doctor!" Wilson shouted from his position still on the floor.

Making certain he wouldn't get in the line of sight of his men, who were pointing their rifles at Wilson, the corporal ignored the demand and kneeled down, being joined by Doris. "Short version?"

"Short version," Doris repeated. "This bastard kidnapped my cat because he wanted to kill me."

This obtained a startled look before the man recovered. "Perhaps a little more detail." Wilson moaned in pain, only to be told to, "Shut up!"

"You know him?" Doris couldn't help but ask.

"I know him, all right," he confirmed. "Caused nothing but trouble since he got here. Unless there was something in it for him, he wasn't interested in helping out. Shame we can't use things like this to clear minefields!"

Perhaps it was the relief of unexpectedly finding herself alive, but Doris couldn't stop the burst of laughter which escaped her. "I'll have to tell my friends that," she told him.

Before she could elaborate, a male voice she recognized boomed out, "Make way! Coming through!" and next second, she found herself being dragged up by her shoulders and found herself face to face with a very relieved-looking Duke. Close behind him was Ceiwen.

The sight of the pair seemed to deflate the remaining tension in Doris's body, especially as it coincided with the return of one of the men who'd been sent off to hunt for the sack. In his arms he cradled Taxi, who was looking around with interest at what was going on, appearing none the worse for wear from his ordeal.

"I believe this chap is yours, miss," the man said to Doris.

Taking her furry friend in her arms, Doris cuddled him into her neck, kissed the top of his head, and then tucked him securely down her jacket. With one hand scratching the cat's head, she looked up at the soldier who'd found him. "Thank you so much! Could I ask you another quick favor? Somewhere over there is a cardboard box. It's got half a salmon in it. Can you find it, please? I don't think I'll be very popular if that's left around to stink up the place."

The man briefly glanced at his guard commander for permission, then trotted off. Doris returned her attention to where Duke seemed to be about to pull a muscle from not being able to speak, but before he could get a word out, Doris wanted to know, "How did you get here? I didn't hear anyone being told to go and get you."

"I saw the guard, here, run past the Humber and decided, from my excessive experience of your good self, that something was going on and you were going to be at the center of whatever it was. Which is?"

Seeing that she had the attention of the guard commander as well as both Duke and Ceiwen, Doris did as the corporal asked and elaborated a little. "Wilson here is one of Moseley's men, and about three months ago, his old boss made the mistake of trying to blackmail one of my best mates."

"So she shot him!" Wilson broke in. "She shot his balls off!"

Everyone present, including the two who were supposed to be keeping their guns on Wilson before they remembered their duties, turned to gape at Doris, who felt compelled to say, "In self-defense, and it wasn't like I was aiming…there. Anyway, his boss sent out letters, urging his old mates to kill me. Wilson here, or whatever his name is, as that's not his real one," she added, making certain Duke heard, "got one and decided the best way to get me alone was to kidnap my cat."

Everyone once again looked at the moaning man on the ground.

"Is that why you're here? At this time of night?" Ceiwen asked.

Remembering who he was supposed to be, Doris said, "Yes, General. He pushed this note," she took it out of her pocket and handed it to the guard commander, "under my door to lure me here."

"And you didn't think of letting us know?" From his tone, Doris knew the corporal was annoyed, and it was likely the combined effect of everything turning out right and the presence of two high-ranking officers which prevented him from shouting at her. In his place, Doris thought, she'd feel the same.

Hoping to mollify the man somewhat, Doris smiled at him. "Sorry, but by the time I found the note, there wasn't time. The same reason I didn't come and find you, Major," Doris added to Duke.

"One last question for now, and then we'll take care of the prisoner," the corporal said. "How did he end up with," he leaned in a little closed to take a look at Wilson's injuries before pulling back and giving a little shake, "what looks like a broken hand, and a sizeable chunk missing from it?"

Doris closed her eyes, unable to help giving a slight shudder at the memory of the fight, eventually opening her eyes to find looks of compassion and understanding in those present. Undoubtedly, most had guessed at least part of what had happened, but Doris knew she'd have to tell it sooner or later and, amongst the support of everyone there, sooner would be best. "When he pulled the revolver on me, I could only think of keeping him talking, hoping an opportunity to do something would present itself. It did, so I whacked him with my overnight bag." She nudged the bag, which was at her feet, with a toe. "It broke his hand and caused him to lose hold of the gun. Then we had a tussle and I found his hand in my mouth, so I bit him."

Duke turned to Percy and held out a hand. After a moment to work out what he meant, Percy placed Wilson's revolver into the palm. Duke immediately unloaded it and handed both the gun and the ammunition to the guard commander, who swiftly pocketed both.

"I've seen you," Duke said, "in the officer's mess. You're Steward Snodgrass, right?"

"Right, sir!" Percy replied, with a nod of his head. "How did you know?"

"I never forget a face, Snodgrass, nor a name. Particularly one like yours," he added smiling to lighten his words. "What were you doing here?"

"Looking for Taxi," Percy immediately replied. "I've got to know and respect Doris here since she arrived, and there's a lot of us who know how much she's missed Taxi since he went missing. We've been looking when we can too."

"And tonight?" the guard commander asked, following where Duke was leading.

"I was out, looking around, when Doris sped past without noticing me. So, after giving it a quick thought, I decided to follow her. I'd got halfway up the steps when I heard voices and decided to listen in first. As soon as I realized what was happening, I knew I didn't have time to come and find you either, Corporal, and so I crept up the rest of the steps and kept to the shadows as I tried to work out if I could help Doris."

"How did you get the gun?" Duke asked.

Percy shrugged. "It slid to a stop against my foot. I suppose that's what happened when Doris knocked it out of his hand."

When nobody else spoke, Doris took it upon herself to say, "Well, I for one am very happy you were here. You probably saved my life."

When Percy replied, she guessed he was glad it was dark, as she could nearly hear the embarrassment in his voice. "It looked like you were doing okay all by yourself."

The corporal coughed to get their attention. "Right, let's get back to the guardroom. You two, pick up Wilson. Barnes, run back and get the medics to meet us there. Then go and make the lieutenant aware of what's happening. We'll be right behind you, so get moving."

"One second, please," Doris asked the corporal. "I need to ask Wilson a question." When the corporal motioned for his men to turn Wilson to face her, Doris nearly took a step back before swallowing and speaking before she lost her nerve. "Let me get this right. You were only pretending to be friendly to me the first time we met?"

Big as he was, the men either side of him nearly matched the prisoner for size and were in a damned better physical state than Wilson. Together, they prompted Wilson, with a little judicious use of an elbow or two, to reply, "'Course I was. Once I knew it was you, why carry on?"

"And you were sure it was me?"

Wilson attempted to laugh, only for it to come out as more of a snort. "With that accent and uniform? Who else could it be? My boss gave me a very good description, and I doubt there are two nosey Yanks in your crowd. Wish I'd got rid of that bloody cat, though," he muttered. "Can't stand the bloody things."

Doris took an involuntary step towards him, only to feel Duke's firm hand on her shoulder, "Leave it," he told her and, with a deep breath, Doris regained control and stepped away.

"Barnes, why are you still here? Get a move on, man!" the corporal ordered.

Once the man had scarpered off, the corporal looked at Doris. "We'll need to get a statement from you, Miss, er, Doris."

Before Doris could speak, Ceiwen suggested, "Major, if you wouldn't mind going with the corporal, I'll escort Doris back to her room, and we'll meet you all at the guardroom. Satisfactory, Third Officer? Corporal?"

Seeing that the man had given Doris the time she needed to help sort out her head, Doris spoke up. "That's most kind of you, General." Knowing the man couldn't argue, she then told the corporal, "We'll see you shortly, Corporal."

****

The walk back to Doris's room was accomplished in silence, though she was very aware of Ceiwen keeping a very close eye on her as they walked. She was quite impressed by his ability to walk a reasonably straight line without looking where he was going; she was also grateful.

All the way there, Taxi made no move to escape from within her jacket, seemingly content to lie against her chest and purr. Only when she pushed open her door did he raise his head, as if to check he'd been taken to somewhere he knew, somewhere he felt safe.

"Where do you want this?" Ceiwen immediately asked, now holding out the cardboard box containing the remnants of the cat's salmon. "It's quite, what's the word, pungent!"

Doris closed the door behind him, only then saying, "It stinks, that's the expression you were looking for."

Ceiwen let out a chuckle. "It certainly is! So…"

"On top of the wardrobe will do," Doris told him.

"Do you mind if I open the window a little?" he asked. "Only a little. We don't want the chap to escape again," he added.

"Hold on, please," she asked, sitting down on the bed. "Right, if you'd open the window as wide as it will go."

Ceiwen raised an eyebrow. "You're sure? Aren't you afraid he'll do another runner?"

When Doris looked up, he could see she was struggling to keep her emotions in check. "Very. I was thinking all the way back here that no matter how I feel, no matter how much I want him to stay, and I really do want him to stay, he has to want to stay. It has to be his decision."

Looking rather apprehensive, Ceiwen nevertheless stepped away from the now open window. "How, exactly, are you going to do that?"

Before replying, Doris kissed the top of Taxi's head, only then looking up. "By opening my jacket. If he jumps out, it's not to be."

Ceiwen went and looked out the window. "Forgive me for pointing this out, but it's rather high. Wouldn't it be better, and safer, just to open the door?"

Frowning, Doris got to her feet, keeping her jacket buttoned up, and looked out. "Ah, I'd forgotten."

"And, I must point out, a lot of people around here have spent a lot of time searching for him. Won't it really, really annoy them if you do this and he does run off? Had you thought of that?"

Doris went to the door, opened it, and only then said, "I have, but I have to do it."

"How, er, confident are you that he'll stay?"

"Fifty-fifty." She shrugged.

"Is that it? They're not good odds," Ceiwen pointed out.

"I know." Doris also shrugged. "But I've still got to do it."

Ceiwen sighed and came to stand beside her, He lightly ruffled the cat's head. "Come on, then, let's get it over with."

Without saying another word, Doris took a deep breath and unbuttoned her jacket. Taxi raised his head from where it had been resting under her jaw, took a look in the direction of the door and opened his mouth to yawn before settling back in place and continuing to purr.

"Leave the door, please," Doris asked Ceiwen, who'd made to close it. Still with her jacket open, she sat back down on her bed and gently placed Taxi upon her pillow. Again, he opened his eyes, but this time, as he continued purring, he waited for Doris to stroke his flank a few times before settling back down. "I'm just going to give him a quick look, make sure Wilson didn't hurt him," she informed Ceiwen.

During the few minutes it took Doris to check him over, Taxi allowed her to gently pull and prod him, but he didn't make a move to leave his comfy bed.

"I think you can close the door now," Doris said, looking up, a wide smile on her lips.

Chapter Thirty-Two

"You took your time," Duke muttered in Doris's ear as she and Ceiwen finally walked into the guardroom.

"Sue me," Doris happily told him, before holding out her hand to the lieutenant who was the guard commander that week, then taking the seat before his desk.

"And you must be Doris Johnson," he said, rising slightly from his seat to shake her hand. "How's Taxi? No ill effects, I hope?"

Doris shook her head, unable as yet to wipe the smile from her face. "Thank heavens, no, the little chap seems none the worse for wear. I left him asleep on my bed, tucking into a bit of salmon."

At this news, the man pulled a piece of paper towards him, licked the end of his pencil, and, after tracing down the list upon it, found what he was looking for and scored right through it. "I guess the case of the missing salmon from the officer's mess is now solved." He smiled at Doris before shoving the paper back into its place.

"I've no idea what that means," she announced, face deadpan, before asking, "Right, I'm here. I've got my cat back, and you've got the person who took him. What do you need from me?"

After skimming through the incident report before him, the lieutenant moved it and a pen towards Doris.

"Not very much, actually. Wilson—he still won't tell us his real name, but that's not too important right now—has confessed to everything. He found Taxi on the day he ran away and kept him hidden in the attic of his barracks, knowing full well who he was and that everyone was looking for him. You, er, did a very good job getting nearly the whole castle involved with your search. Well done! Everything you told my corporal happened exactly as you described, including Snodgrass's part. I'll be putting him in for a commendation, I believe you'll be pleased to know. There is one part of this affair which does worry me. He mentioned that this Verdon character has written to all his old cronies about you specifically, with the request to kill you."

Doris shrugged, trying to appear nonchalant, even though hearing the words said out loud once more was a little unnerving. "I know, but there's not much I can do about it."

"No, but I can help there," Duke announced.

The lieutenant appeared to be surprised by this statement. Even though Doris didn't have any cast-iron proof of who Duke really worked for, it was likely the lieutenant would have had no dealings with the major before and so would be completely in the dark. "Major? Pardon me for asking, but how can you help?"

Duke treated the man to a smile which would have sent a shiver down the spine of a man a hundred years dead, and Doris would have sworn the temperature in what was already a cold office went down several degrees.

"You leave that to me, Lieutenant. Now, Doris, if you could read the report and, assuming you're happy with it, sign it, we can leave the lieutenant to his duties."

Two minutes later, Doris signed and pushed the report back across the desk. "Just one thing, please. Has Wilson been seen by the medics?"

"Yes," the lieutenant replied. "They confirmed he does have a broken hand, which they can fix, though they can only stitch up the wound you made. He's going to end up with little use of that hand, in their initial diagnosis."

Doris got to her feet, smoothed down her jacket, and shook the man's hand once more. Finally, she went over and gave Percy, who'd been standing beside the corporal, a hug before grinning and saying, "Good! Major, Sir." The three of them, Ceiwen having silently observed proceedings from beside the door, left quietly as she said, "Let's go to the mess for a drink. I've a nasty taste in my mouth I need to get rid of."

****

Soon, the three were sat in the officer's mess, all three nursing whiskeys. Doris had tried to explain it wasn't her drink of choice, but they'd run out of Guinness and she was too tired to think of anything else.

Once the first toast had been made to the safe return of Taxi, Doris glanced around to make certain they couldn't be overheard. "There's something I need to tell you, something which isn't in the report I signed. Wilson couldn't stop talking—I think that's got a lot to do with why I'm still alive, if I'm being honest," she said, "and he did mention that the general is also a target for the Nazis." Duke and Ceiwen's eyes went wide with surprise.

Duke was quick to put the pieces together. "You're saying that not only does this Verdon want to have you killed, but he also wants Ceiwen dead?"

Ceiwen asked, "But why would he want to kill him…um, me?"

Duke didn't have to think hard. "My guess? It's not personal, but he probably thinks he'd be doing Germany a favor. It's well known, amongst certain factions, that Ceiwen is one of our generals that Hitler fears. At this stage of the war, though, it wouldn't make much of a difference if he was dead."

"He is dead," Doris pointed out, before saying, "Sorry," to their Ceiwen, being careful with her words, just in case.

"Well," Duke began, settling back into his seat and taking a sip from his drink, "we knew there was a chance Germany would make an attempt on your life, and I don't suppose we can entirely discount the possibility that they are behind it." He got to his feet and, because he knew he was being watched now, said, "Sir, I have a few phone calls to make. I'll see you in the morning. Doris…" He tipped his head to both and then strode out of the mess.

"That was a turn-up," Ceiwen said, finishing his drink.

"It always sounds silly, but how are you feeling?" Doris asked him.

He held up his empty glass. "In need of a refill."

Doris got to her feet and took his glass. "Your wish is my command. Same again?" A few minutes later, Doris was back and placed the refreshed glass before him.

"You could have called over a steward," he pointed out.

Doris shook her head. "Not my style. Now, how are

you feeling, General?"

"I'll say this—I'll be glad when this engagement's over. Still, and I hope this isn't tempting fate, at least it's a bunch of amateurs who're after me. Mind if I change the subject?" he said and then asked, before Doris could say anything, "Those tiles which just missed you? Do you reckon Wilson was behind that?"

After a moment's thinking time, Doris shrugged. "Probably not that I could prove."

Ceiwen took a sip. "Do you think there's any point in mentioning it?"

"Probably not. What with his confession and the report I signed, plus Percy as a witness, I don't think he'll be seeing the free light of day for a long while. Now," she said, getting to her feet and draining her glass, "if you'll excuse me, General, I must get back to my cat. We've some time to make up." She leant in so no one else had a chance to hear her. "Don't let the Drummer Boy spook you!"

His reply caused all the heads in the mess to turn his way and then swivel towards Doris, not that she cared. "I'll get you for that, Third Officer Johnson!"

****

News that Taxi had been recovered safe and sound seemed to have spread like wildfire around the castle. No sooner had she cleaned up Taxi's newspaper and changed, there was a knock on her door. Opening it, she was delighted to find it was Percy, and even better, he came bearing gifts!

"It's well-chopped ham," he explained, handing over a package wrapped in grease-proof paper, "courtesy of the chef. He says that if you need more, just let me know and he'll make up another."

Taking the package, Doris opened the wardrobe and placed it on the top shelf before setting out the chair for him. "Please thank him for me."

"I will," he told her, sitting down. He reached out a hand, placing his fingers beneath Taxi's nose. Taxi had woken up at the knock on the door and was looking at the visitor with interest. Sniffing his fingers, the cat quickly began purring before getting to his feet, stretching, and then bounding over to land upon Percy's lap. Taxi leant up, stretching his neck, and Percy, taking the hint, lowered his head so Taxi could rub his nose against the human's. Wisely, Percy didn't say a thing, though his open mouth spoke volumes!

After a few more nose rubs, Taxi curled around and settled down on his lap, though he kept his eyes open and looked alternately at Doris and Percy, all the time purring whilst kneading away with his paws on Percy's lap.

"I'm glad he's not using his claws," Percy told Doris.

There was another knock on the door.

"I'll get it," Doris said. "Rachel! How nice to see you, come in, come in! Do you know Percy?" she asked.

"No," she merely replied, obviously distracted by the sight of Taxi looking up at her. She knelt down and began to stroke Taxi down the full length of his back, which merely made him turn up the volume on his purr. "So this is Taxi. My, but aren't you a handsome tabby!" Taxi's head seemed to nod in agreement.

Doris shook her head at the love her two visitors were showering upon the cat, not that she blamed them, as he was a very handsome cat. "I forget, neither of you have actually seen him before, have you."

"No," they replied in unison, as both were very

distracted in showering the cat with adoration. For his part, Taxi was lapping up every moment, though he soon began to yawn and, in an instant, had jumped back onto the bed and snuggled against Doris's hip.

There was another knock at the door, so Rachel opened it and had the shock of her life when she found Duke standing there. "Sir! Um, what can I do for you, sir?"

Before replying, Duke took a look around the room. "Good evening, young lady," he said. "Snodgrass," he nodded at where the young man had got to his feet. Duke held out his hand to him where, after a moment's hesitation, it was shaken. "I haven't had the chance to say thank you. What you did was very brave, and I won't forget it."

Percy seemed a little taken aback, though he recovered enough to say, "Glad I could help, sir."

"Now, it's late, and I'm going to ignore your presence in what is supposed to be an officer's accommodation block. This young lady has had a difficult night, and if I'm going to trust my life to her driving tomorrow morning, then I'd prefer it if she gets some sleep."

Both Rachel and Percy nodded and, with a last stroke of a now-fast-asleep Taxi each, made their way to the door. As Percy went to leave, Duke asked him whilst holding up a large piece of paper, "One moment. Stick this paper on the outside door, will you? I don't want any more well-intentioned visitors tonight."

Once the two had left, Duke turned back to speak to Doris, only to find she had lain back on the bed, her feet tucked up, with Taxi snuggled up against her chest. Smiling, Duke took up a blanket from the bottom of the bed and pulled it around the sleeping pair.

"Sweet dreams," he told them, before shutting the door and sneezing.

"Bless you!" Doris muttered, before drawing Taxi closer. Soon, the only sound to be heard was that of their synchronized snoring.

Chapter Thirty-Three

"Everything all right with Taxi?" Ceiwen asked from the back seat of the Humber. "Little chap slept fine?"

Smiling to herself, Doris told them, "*We* slept the sleep of the dead, and I for one haven't felt so rested in days."

Duke tapped her on the shoulder. "Very happy to hear. Mind you, we drive on the left-hand side in this country." His finger pointed at a large group of oncoming lorries.

"Oh hell," Doris muttered, as she jerked the wheel to bring them back onto the correct side of the road. Behind them, somebody in their escort was leaning on the lorry's horn.

"I never noticed," Ceiwen stated. "Mind you, it does explain why our escort were making such a racket."

"You could have told me a bit sooner," Doris complained. "How long have I been on the wrong side of the road?"

"During the time you were telling us about Taxi," Duke informed her.

"Oh good, so, not that long then," Doris said, though not troubling to keep the relief from her voice.

"But long enough," Duke told her. "For all our sakes, let's keep the subject of Taxi from conversation for the rest of the drive. Agreed?"

Knowing he was right and more shaken up than she'd care to admit, Doris firmed up her grip on the steering wheel, determined to be more professional. "No arguments here. Sorry about that, guys," she apologized.

They continued on their way generally north until they pulled over about two hours later through a pair of open ornate wrought iron gates. After a bumpy ten-minute drive on a gravel track which slowly wound its way down, they came into view of a large, turreted manor house on the edge of a lake which disappeared out of view behind some hills in the distance. A few more minutes and Doris pulled up before the imposing wooden front door.

"Oh, I wish you could have warned me about that track," Doris moaned, getting out of the Humber and placing her hands upon her lower back. She did her best to stretch out the kinks she'd accumulated in the short last part of their journey. "I'm used to being sore from my flights, but wow, that track's something else!"

Wincing, she opened the rear door and watched as her two companions exited with much the same moans and groans as she'd made. "Thank you, Doris," Ceiwen managed to say.

There was a squeal of brakes as the lorry came to a rest a short way behind them, having had to take it much slower down the track. Even so, the effort to lessen the suffering of the escort inside didn't seem to have been worth it, judging by the loud complaints coming from both the cab and the body. None of the men who gingerly clambered out looked at all happy, with only Lewis appearing near his normal self, though after looking closer at the man, Doris believed this was more by a force of will than anything else.

"So," groaned Doris one final time, "why are we here again? I think all those bumps have muddled my brain."

Duke glanced around, though who he thought was about to overhear them was beyond Doris. The front door of the slightly spooky gothic mansion remained closed, and the escort was taking longer to form up than Lewis liked, going on how much shouting he was doing.

"I'll be quick. The lord of the manor," he waved his hand behind his back, "has been on the books of MI5 since before the war as a known Nazi sympathizer."

"So why's he not in prison?" Doris not unnaturally asked.

"I can't go into that."

"You *are* MI5! I knew it!" Doris let a grin split her face.

Duke frowned. "I did not say that, and this is not the time or place. May I continue? Thank you. Now, as to why he's not in prison. It was deemed that he would be of more use to us by leaving him here. Also he's in a wheelchair, result of some wound from the Boer War, I believe. He rarely leaves this place, and when he does, he's tailed everywhere. He does nothing and communicates with no one without our knowledge. He's having a few old army chums from the Great War around, so we wrangled an invite to the lunchtime buffet. It seems he's never seen a female pilot before. Yes," he added, at her look of incredulity, "even after all this time. We're going to let *slip* a few, shall we say, half-secrets, a few sweeteners to help the ruse."

"How will you know if it worked?" Doris asked.

"Well, we haven't been able to find it, but we know he's got a transmitter somewhere in this place. Believe me, I'd love to search it, only look at the size of it—it'd take way too much time. He's a toff, and not one of the smart ones, and we've done this before. If we're right, he'll wait just long enough to see us out of the gates before he's on his radio."

"How will that help? There's no way we'll get back to the castle in time to listen in," Doris said.

Duke strode up to the lorry and patted the canvas side. "We've got a receiver in the back. We'll go just far enough down the road so we're well out of sight, and then we'll pull over."

Any further explanation was rendered moot as they all became aware of loud footsteps the other side of the door.

Duke just had time to say, "Follow my lead," before the door opened.

At that moment, the door opened and the person silhouetted in the door greeted them. "Duke?"

****

A small glass of sherry in her left hand, her ATA cap under her right arm—she wasn't going to trust it to the maid of a strange house—Doris stood before a window in the library at the back of the house, where the midday gathering was being held, and openly observed Duke. This was a man who was barely keeping himself reined in; she didn't blame him.

In the relatively short time she'd known the man, she couldn't recall him being lost for words. Seeing Morag in the open door had been totally unexpected, and before he'd had the chance to any anything, the lord of the manor had appeared by her side, forcing him to go into full ADC mode. Brief introductions were made, which were cut short as the heavens chose that moment to open and the visitors were ushered inside. Well, not everyone was. Before the door was closed, there occurred a difference of opinions between Sergeant Lewis and the manor's elderly butler, who initially refused to let any of Ceiwen's escort inside. Eventually, with Duke's reluctant intervention, it was agreed that Lewis and two of his men would station themselves around the house, whilst the rest would station themselves at the front and rear entrances and patrol around the house.

Her thoughts were interrupted by Ceiwen approaching her, accompanied by a man in a wheelchair, the lord of the manor she presumed, with a visibly agitated Duke bringing up the rear. Wheeling the chair was the source of his agitation.

"Third Officer Doris Johnson," Ceiwen began the introductions, "of His Majesty's Air Transport Auxiliary, may I present your host, Lord Gordon St. Crail."

Not at all certain what the protocol was for meeting a lord, and taking into account all she knew about the man's odious political leanings, Doris contented herself with tipping her head the minutest bit possible towards the man. Obviously unaware the young lady he was being introduced to knew all about him, the lord, who must have been eighty if he were a day, held up a hand nigh on covered with liver spots. Trying to keep most of her repulsion from her face, Doris shook it, letting go as soon as the man made to move it towards his lips. There was only so far she was prepared to go for someone else's King and Country.

"Your lordship," she said, surreptitiously wiping her hand on her trousers before placing it behind her back.

It seemed the lord required little, if any, encouragement, as before anyone else could say a thing, the man had leaned forward and launched into a discourse on the history of the ATA, including many things Doris was only vaguely aware of. His audience all did their best to feign keen interest, but Doris was finding it harder and harder to keep from yawning. Morag, who appeared to have recovered from her shock at finding her boyfriend on the step, had taken the opportunity to slip behind the wheelchair to stand next to Duke as soon as Lord St. Crail opened his mouth. If she'd been hoping to have a quiet word with him, she was thwarted. Lord St. Crail's voice was low, very low, barely above a whisper, and once he'd begun to speak, everyone else in the room had gone quiet and seemed to be hanging upon his every word. Nazi spy or not, he had the ability to captivate and hold a room's attention; even Doris found herself involuntarily leaning in so as to not miss a word.

Unfortunately, for Doris, there came a point where he stopped talking, his eyes staring up at her from behind the pince-nez upon his nose. Belatedly, she realized he must have asked her a question and was waiting upon her reply. Blinking, she replayed his last few words. But came up blank. Behind the man, Duke caught her eye. Slowly, he mouthed the words, she thought, *How long*. Hoping she'd understood him right, she quickly looked down and told Lord St. Crail, "Around two years, though I've been flying for much longer than that."

"And where do you come from, my dear?" he then asked.

Fighting the urge to inform the man she wasn't his *dear*, Doris managed to not quite grit her teeth when she told him, "New York, and," she hoped to cut off his next question, "I don't miss it all that much. I'm very much at home in Great Britain." She silently congratulated herself on not restricting herself to saying England. In spite of the eerie way in which everyone in the room was still silent, she didn't wish to risk antagonizing a room full of probably proud Scots. She'd gathered enough from her time up north to know that to be called English was tantamount to a capital offense. Glancing around the room, she saw nothing untoward. Most of the people seemed to be simply waiting for the lord to stop talking, with some even openly yawning and looking at their watches. Perhaps it was a tradition that when the lord of the manor speaks, everyone else must be quiet?

When she didn't elaborate, the man nodded and turned his head up to address Morag. "I think we've taken up enough of this young lady's time. Take me out to the rear garden, please. I'd like some fresh air."

With a final nod from the man and a shrug of her shoulders as Morag trundled him past Duke, the conversation in the room restarted. Doris felt her shoulders sag in relief. It had been only a short conversation, mostly from his side, but she had no wish to talk to the man again, if it could be at all helped. Wheelchair bound he might be, but his aura was still present in the room. She decided it would not be a good idea to underestimate the man.

Taking advantage of being left alone with Ceiwen, she looked around, making certain no one would overhear, and sidled closer, "What's Morag doing here?"

Ceiwen shook his head. "I haven't a clue. Duke's been distracted since she opened the door," he added, once more surprising her. "I must admit, both that and her wheeling him around is…disturbing."

Just then, Duke appeared at their side and announced, in a slightly louder voice than he'd normally use, "Sir. I need to talk to you a moment, please? And you, Third Officer."

"Lead on, Major," Ceiwen informed him.

Shortly after, the three were let into a billiard room by a servant, with all three waiting for the door to close before anyone spoke. Ceiwen opened his mouth, but before he could speak, Duke held a finger to his lips. Before their astonished eyes, he then proceeded to perform what could only be a quick search for hidden listening devices. Obviously he didn't have the time to perform as deep a search as he'd have liked, but all the same, he looked under the billiard table, in its pockets, checked each cue to see if it unscrewed, hopped up on the table to look under the single light present in the room, upturned the two chairs, and even went so far as to rap at the wooden paneling. Finally, he nodded. "That'll have to do."

"I can guess what you want to talk about, Duke," Doris said. "Have you been able to speak with Morag?"

Before answering, Duke turned to the table, delved into one of the pockets to retrieve a red ball, which he then sent careening around the cushions. Even before he spoke, this would have been enough of an answer for either of his companions. "No. What's she doing here? I had no idea she knew this man!" He then proceeded to roll the same ball back and forth, up and down the table.

As he did so, Doris used the opportunity to ask a question which had occurred to her, after what Duke had just said. "If you had known, would you still have come? I mean, I don't know what your plan is, but would it have affected it?"

Now he had a dilemma to think about, Duke let the ball gently roll to a halt, as he stopped to regard Doris and what she'd said. Eventually and with a sad shake of his head, Duke replied, "No, I wouldn't. I still need to know what she's doing here, though."

Before anyone could say anything else, the door of the room burst open, admitting the woman they were all discussing, who slammed it shut behind her.

She hurried over to Duke and, ignoring the other two, took hold of his good hand and told him, her face a mask of anxiety, "I haven't got much time. We need to talk."

Chapter Thirty-Four

"Are you hurt? Are they holding you against your will?"

As the pair were right next to her, Doris couldn't help but bear witness to everything which happened, and it was touching to hear the concern lacing Duke's voice as he burst forth with the first questions which entered his mind. Judging by the expression upon Morag's face at hearing him, maybe he'd jumped the gun a little.

"What? No, hold on, maybe I should have made myself clearer," Morag replied.

Instead of answering, Duke shot to the door, yanked it open and stepped boldly out into the corridor. "No one," he mumbled as he came back in, shutting the door considerably less violently than how he'd gone through it. "What's going on, Morag? From what you just said, I thought we'd walked into a kidnapping!" When Morag didn't immediately dismiss his suggestion, Duke was before her straight away, once more asking, "Well, what is going on then? From how you came in the room and what you said, you can't deny why I'd come to that conclusion."

"He's right," Doris felt compelled to add. If she wasn't going to try and make the conversation private, then Doris would assume it was safe to participate.

"Yes," Ceiwen added, obviously having come to the same conclusion. "What on earth's the matter?"

From the startled expression upon her face, Morag had just realized how she'd come across. She took a deep breath. "I've not been kidnapped…"

"In that case, what are you doing here?" Duke asked.

Morag smiled. "I could see you were shocked to see me."

"Considering what you said when you came into the room, don't you think you'd better hurry up a little with the explanation?" Doris said, not worrying about upsetting Morag. If there was a reason to hurry, all this prevarication wasn't doing any good.

Instead of being annoyed, as most people would be, Morag instead leaned over and gave Doris a quick kiss on the cheek before straightening up. "I knew I was right to like you. We're going to have a real drink, real soon!"

Doris smiled in return, but said, "Morag, focus!"

"Right, sorry." She faced Duke once more. "Here…" She ducked a hand inside her blouse and handed him a piece of paper. "Do you read German?"

Raising an eyebrow, as this was an unexpected question, Duke took the paper without actually answering. Carefully, he examined it from all angles before unfolding it, taking care not to unfold it farther than how it naturally fell.

Aware of whom he was purporting to be, Ceiwen couldn't stop himself from asking, "Well? What does it say?"

"Where did you get this?" Duke asked Morag, ignoring Ceiwen.

"I was clearing up in Lord St. Crail's office when I got here earlier this morning—he fired his last assistant a month ago, apparently—and I found that under his desk. Well, pretty much everyone around here is aware of his political leanings, and curiosity got the better of me." She shrugged. "Unfortunately, I don't speak German, and I knew you'd be here today."

"Does he know it's gone?" Duke immediately asked.

Morag shook her head. "He hasn't been near his office all day, too busy fussing around, making sure everything's all just so." Duke looked back at the paper before refolding it and handing it back to her. "Well?"

Making certain to catch everyone's eye before he spoke, Duke told them, "It's German, all right, and it came through two days ago. I'd say it's the beginning of a longer message, probably only the first page. It instructs St. Crail to meet with Ceiwen, try to ingratiate himself with the general. That's all we've got."

"Did you know about this?" Doris asked, mindful of what Duke had told them earlier about this man.

Duke shook his head. "When I phoned the office last night, they told me a message had come in, but they hadn't decoded it yet. This is probably it."

"I don't suppose there's a way you could phone them, or contact them to find out what the rest of it says?" Doris asked.

"You really do have a head for this stuff," Duke murmured. He looked surprised when he looked at Doris to find her grinning back at him. He coughed before saying, "I wouldn't trust any of the telephones here."

"What about the radio in the lorry?" Doris asked.

"No good." Duke shook his head. "Range is too short."

"Excuse me?" Morag interrupted. "Radio? What's going on here?"

Duke briefly studied his girlfriend before eventually

telling her, "Not now. I'll tell you, but now's not the time. Look, we've got to be quick. What are you doing here? Surely you're not being this man's maid!"

Morag shook her head, "Never!" she replied, her tone of voice making it clear she was as firm as could be. "My parents were friends with his daughter and are up here on business. St. Crail found out about that somehow and insisted they come along today. Anyway, they couldn't think of a way to refuse, and I got talked into accompanying them. Well, you've seen how forceful a character he is, and when he asked if I'd do a tidy up, I found myself obeying. Rather annoying. By the way, they're delighted we're back together and would love to see you, if you've the time, that is. I know you're due to go back…"

Duke quickly shushed her. "Please, don't say anything more on that."

Moray had opened her mouth, undoubtedly to protest, but then simply nodded her head as she realized why Duke had acted as he had.

"Right," Duke announced, "we all need to be getting back. I expect ears are twitching, considering how long we've been gone. Morag, did anyone see you coming in?"

She shook her head. "There were two men at the far end of the corridor who look much more like bodyguards than guests to me. Anyhow, they were too busy talking to each other to see me slip in."

"Leave them to me," Ceiwen volunteered. "May as well use the rank for a bit of intimidation, eh!"

Duke smiled appreciatively. "Thanks, good idea. Doris, would you accompany Morag? I'd feel better if she wasn't alone when she puts that back. I'd go, but," he shrugged, "where the good general here is, I must be."

Making as much noise as possible, Ceiwen strode out of the billiard room, announcing in a very loud voice to the large men Morag had mentioned, "You there! First, a whisky for me and my ADC, and you," Ceiwen made sure to point at the other man, his friend having already disappeared, "take me to his lordship. I wish to thank him for having us." When the man made no move, Ceiwen, who'd reached him by now, rapped the man on the chest with an outstretched finger—to Doris's immense pride, as she and Morag were peeking out from the barely open billiard room door. "Move along there, man! We haven't got all day."

Perhaps it was shock at being addressed in such a manner by someone who was about a foot smaller, but the man nodded and, with a wave of his hand, indicated that Ceiwen and Duke should follow him.

Doris gave it a few seconds before telling Morag, "Let's go!"

Once the door had been closed ever so quietly behind them, Morag whispered back, "Follow me." She led the way in the opposite direction, turning this way and that, leaving Doris with the impression they were in a bricks-and-mortar maze. Only once or twice did she get a fleeting glimpse of a window before Morag turned a corner and they were presented with a sturdy, dark wooden door. Upon it was a brass plate proclaiming, *Private*, in bold script. Morag grasped the matching brass handle and turned it downwards; nothing happened. The same thing happened the next two times. "Hell's teeth! It's locked!" she hissed at Doris, who'd already guessed the problem.

"Go and keep watch," Doris instructed her friend.

"Leave this to me." As Morag swiftly went to take up a station at the turning, Doris took a small leather case from her inside pocket and selected a short, thin metal tool. Seeing Morag had stopped to stare, Doris smacked her bottom, "Go on!"

No sooner had Morag taken up a station than Doris caught her eye and waved her back. With a quick wipe of the surfaces she'd touched, Doris made a *ta-da* gesture. "Make it quick. I'll be lookout."

As the office door shut behind her, Doris took up her station. After a minute, she was already looking at her watch. Another thirty seconds later, she thought she could hear footsteps approaching and her anxiety began to peak. "Come on, come on!" she urged under her breath. The steps were getting closer, and Doris began to consider her options. Feigning being drunk was obviously out of order, she was Ceiwen's driver, after all, plus there simply hadn't been time to get drunk. Maybe she should fall back on the usual excuse when you're found somewhere you should not be, and pretend she was looking for the powder room…

Whilst looking at her watch, she'd been a little surprised to find that they'd been at the manor for nearly an hour and a half! It certainly didn't seem like it. Quickly pulling her handkerchief from her pocket as she went, she dashed to the office door. Opening it, she was about to hiss at Morag to open it, but Morag had been about to open the door herself and couldn't stop a painful squeal from issuing from her lips as her wrist was twisted.

A voice saying, "Did you hear something?" came from somewhere too close for comfort.

In her haste to not be found where they were, Doris

grabbed Morag by her injured wrist, the girl gaining much credit for not letting out more than a whimper. With Morag in tow, she hurried away from the office, after making sure it was closed behind them. They managed to turn the corner and were halfway down the corridor when a shoe appeared around the next corner.

Stopping in her tracks, Doris turned her back on those approaching and cradled Morag's wrist in her hands, saying, "I thought you knew the way to the kitchen?"

"What are you two doing here?" asked a man whose parents may well have included a gorilla on one side.

Following the adage that attack was the best form of defense, Doris immediately half-turned her head and with her most concerned expression upon her face, "Thank God! Maybe you can show us where the kitchen is? My friend's hurt her wrist."

Perhaps it was the number of words all in one go which threw the pair off their stride, but when nothing but an "Um," came from either of the men's lips, Doris pressed her mental advantage. "Come on. Do either of you know, or not? My friend is in pain, and I want to put her wrist under a cold tap." Now she had the pair thoroughly confused, Doris grabbed one with her free hand and turned him around. "Is it this way?"

His companion, perhaps the one using the shared brain cell that day, mumbled, "Follow me."

Though he didn't sound entirely sure of what was going on, Doris fell into step behind him, pulling Morag in beside her even though the corridor was barely wide enough for them to walk side by side. With her eyes, she hoped she managed to convey that Morag should play along and follow Doris's lead. Either she jarred the girl's wrist, or Morag wasn't a bad actress, but she let out a small moan of pain at exactly the moment the leading chap turned his head to speak. This was enough for him to change his mind and, in a very short time, they all found themselves in the kitchen.

When it looked like the men intended to stay with them, Doris gathered her courage once more. "A little privacy, gentlemen, please?" she asked, thanking small mercies that the kitchen had been empty when they'd arrived.

For a few moments, it looked like they were going to object, but something must have made them have second thoughts, and the one with the brain cell merely told them, "Don't wander around the manor again." With this warning, they left them alone.

Moving in so she could whisper without fear of being overheard, Doris said, "Let's give them a minute," before stepping back and saying in her normal voice, "Come on, let's have a look at that wrist." Before Morag could object, Doris had thrust the injured wrist under the cold tap. Judging by her squeak, it was a very cold tap.

Under cover of the running water, Morag asked, "What about the door? It's not locked."

Doris nodded, unable to keep the worried expression from her face. "I know, there wasn't time. We'll just have to trust to luck."

Chapter Thirty-Five

After taking as long as they thought they could get away with holding Morag's wrist under the cold tap—too long, so far the girl in question was concerned, as she was getting worried that Doris would freeze her arm off—Doris passed Morag a tea towel so she could dry herself. As she went to catch it, she had to twist her arm, and as her fingers closed around it, she let out a yelp, dropping it to the floor.

Doris was by her side in an instant. "Oh hell, that didn't sound good."

"You think?" Morag, cradling her wrist once more, didn't bother keeping the annoyance out of her voice.

"Let me take a look," she asked and, reluctantly, Morag held out her arm.

"Exactly how much medical training do you have?" she asked, as Doris nodded away.

With perfect timing, the American looked up to say, "Not much," at the exact moment she caused her friend to wince in pain. "Ah," she began, before pressing in the same place and getting the same reaction. "I think I may have twisted your wrist." She looked around before going to get a clean tea towel. "Come on, I don't really feel like asking anyone where the medical kit is. I'll wrap your wrist up in this." She turned back to the same place she'd got the towel from and resurfaced with some string. "This'll do to tie it up with until you can get it dressed properly."

As they left the kitchen, they ran into the same two goons. "What took you so long?" the same one who'd done most of the talking last time asked. By way of an answer, Morag lifted her injured arm up before his eyes, causing the man to take a step back. "Er, right," he stumbled, finally moving out of the way. "Better let you two get back to the party," he suggested, moving out of their way.

Whether he was waiting for them or not, Duke appeared before them as they walked down the corridor towards the library. "Where have you two been?" he began, before spotting Morag's wrist. "What on earth happened to you?"

"This?" she held up her wrist. "I had a little…accident. Doris fixed me up," she supplied, managing a grin and nearly causing her friend to break into laughter. "Don't worry," she quickly told Duke, as he looked quite worried, "it's only twisted."

"We think," Doris added.

"And…that?" Duke couldn't help but ask.

The two girls looked at each other before Doris suggested, "I had to make do with what I had to hand."

"You don't think there's a proper medical kit around here somewhere?" Duke asked.

Morag gripped his hook, shaking her head. "I don't think that'd be a good idea."

Doris leaned in so she could quickly tell him, "We were almost caught."

Catching on, he nodded and stepped out of the way so the girls could enter the library before him, with Morag cradling her bad arm to her body, doing her best to hide it from easy view. Her parents must have been waiting for her, as no sooner was she fully in than a couple Doris thought had to be them detached themselves from a group of people and descended upon Morag, with her father exclaiming, "What the hell happened to you?" Before Doris could begin to explain, Morag was whisked off.

She didn't have the chance to go after them, as Duke took her by the elbow and pulled her back into the hall. "Don't say a word, just listen. This is what I need you to do."

No sooner had the pair re-entered the library than they accosted by Ceiwen, their host close behind him. He had just enough time to say, "We were just about to send out a search party, Third Officer."

Propelled by hands whose face she didn't get the chance to see, Lord St. Crail leant forward in his wheelchair and, with speed which took her by surprise such that she didn't get a chance to move, grabbed one of Doris's hands. "Yes, one of my servants has just told me what happened." He glanced around. "Your friend, Morag, she's all right?"

Resisting the urge to pull her hand from his sweaty one, though she wouldn't resist too long, Doris gave what she hoped would be interpreted as a grateful squeeze. "She will be. A twisted wrist, that's all, but I feel so guilty!"

She must have put the right amount of culpability into her voice, as the man squeezed back and Doris had to resist the impulse to look down to check sweat wasn't running out from where their hands were joined. "Surely it was an accident. Please, tell me what happened?"

The man certainly had something in his voice, Doris thought, finally freeing her hand and flexing her fingers.

"It's silly," she got in straight away. "I was looking for the toilet, to freshen up, and I got lost. I didn't realize your house was so big, your lordship." There was no harm in buttering up the man's ego. "When she found me, I turned, but slipped, and grabbed the first thing to hand to stop myself from falling."

"Which was Morag's wrist," he filled in, exactly as Doris hoped.

"Exactly!" Doris added a delighted clap, though the action embarrassed her. Still, if he bought her story, it would be worth it. "And in all the excitement, I still haven't found it!"

The man fixed Doris with a steady gaze, which Doris matched. Finally, he nodded, "I'll get someone to show you the way," he told her. "We wouldn't want you to get lost, again, would we?"

"Oh, would you?" Doris said playing her part to the hilt, before half-turning her head to glance back at where both Ceiwen and Duke were stood a step or two behind her. "The general's told me we really should be getting back. We're leaving around first light on Monday morning, so we can't…"

As expected, Doris felt a hand grip her shoulder.

"Doris!" Duke used his best authoritative voice, adding a shake of his head.

Ducking her head so St. Crail couldn't see her eyes, she adopted a sufficiently suppliant posture and with a half-mumbled, "Sorry, I shouldn't have said that," stepped back until she was behind her companions.

****

Standing beside the open back door of the Humber, Doris watched as Ceiwen, with Duke standing by his side, said the formal goodbyes to St. Crail. This seemed to involve much bobbing of heads by everyone and multiple handshakes. Doris was just relieved she'd had time to…relieve herself, before they left. Finally, Ceiwen, with Duke close behind and the lord being wheeled at Ceiwen's side, approached the Humber, and Doris did her best to stand to attention, one hand upon the open door. If she was being truthful, so long as she never had to touch the odious man ever again, she'd play the part of a dutiful chauffeur to the hilt.

"Sir!" she nearly barked as Ceiwen ducked into the car, shutting the door behind him. She noticed St. Crail reaching out a hand towards her, and she quickly skipped out of his reach to go around to the other side of the Humber so she could open the door for Duke.

"Thank you, Johnson," Duke said, making sure the lord heard, as he clambered in.

This time, she didn't wait for Lewis and his men to board their lorry before starting up the big Humber, allowing her ears a moment to savor what she always thought of as a growl. As the rear window nearest St. Crail was open, the man having banged upon it with his stick, Doris had to wait to be given the go-ahead to pull away.

Her ears perked up when she heard her name. "I hope it won't be long before we see you again, Third Officer Johnson."

Hoping a neutral, "Your lordship," would suffice, she put the Humber into gear and gently let out the clutch. As she hoped, the slight forward movement was enough to make the man roll his wheelchair backwards.

Glancing out her window, Doris quickly waved to Morag and her parents, who stood just outside the front door. Morag waved her tea-toweled arm in the air, proving that at least the bodge-job she'd done with the string was holding together. She mouthed *hotel*, and Doris nodded in understanding.

No one spoke as they bounced their way back up the drive, all being too busy making certain their teeth didn't clash together, having learned their lesson from the drive down. Duke waited until they were almost five miles down the main, beautifully paved (in Doris's humble opinion) road before tapping her on the shoulder and told her to turn off at the next layby. A few minutes later, the two vehicles pulled over and they all piled out of the Humber and were waiting as the lorry came to a stop behind them.

Duke banged his hand against the body of the lorry. "Get the radio working, lads!"

Working on the assumption that as she'd signed the Official Secrets Act, and taking into consideration all she'd learned and been a part of lately, Doris took up position behind the open rear of the lorry and watched with much interest as a couple of lads from the escort busied themselves with some rather interesting radios. Being a pilot, she was used to various instruments, including radios, but these looked quite different from what she'd used. Curiosity got the better of her, so she took a step closer, only to feel a heavy but gentle hand fall upon her shoulder. She looked up into the serious face of Sergeant Lewis.

"Sorry, Doris"—at least he was now using her first name—"but I can't allow you any closer. Top secret, you understand."

Doris nodded her understanding. "No problem." She stepped an extra few paces back, earning her a nod and smile of thanks from the hulking man.

"Cup of tea?" one of Lewis's men asked her, holding up a flask and a metal cup.

Doris shrugged. "Well, it's not going to be coffee, but if it's hot and wet, yes, please." She accepted the cup and held it out. "Fill me up, please." After her cup had been filled, she remembered, "I've been meaning to ask. Will Private Douglas be fit enough to come back with us on Monday?"

Sergeant Lewis must have overheard. After he'd helped Duke up into the back of the lorry—his hook didn't give him very much traction and Lewis had been around enough to be able to give what help was needed without making the man feel like he'd asked for any—he came up to the pair. "He was discharged this morning, but we decided we could get by without him for this trip. He'll be back on duty tomorrow. Nothing seems to be permanently hurt, other than his pride."

Doris blew into her cup. "And is it true that Wilson was the one who knocked him down?"

Hefting the Thompson submachine gun he was carrying so it sat a little less awkwardly, Lewis accepted a cup of tea with a single nod before replying, "It's true. He's lucky he's not facing a charge of murder! Mind you, now he's banged up, and taking into account the number of charges he's facing, he's singing like a canary. With a little luck, you shouldn't be in any danger from his whole lot, shortly."

Umming a reply which could have been taken either way, Doris took a swig from her cup, shoving down the automatic shiver which tea seemed to elicit from her. "I won't put a hex on it by totally agreeing with you, Sergeant," she eventually said. "Though I shall be silently hopeful. I know I can't say anything about what we're doing up here, but I may have a word with the Major and see if I can at least tell my boss about my almost being shot. More heads are better than one, as the saying doesn't quite go," she finished with a chuckle.

"I don't see too much of a problem with that," Duke's voice piped up.

Looking up, they could see the man's head poking out from the tarpaulin covering the rear of the lorry.

"Sorry, Major, didn't mean to disturb you, sir," Lewis said.

Duke glanced down at the man. "Nothing's happened so far, so don't worry. And Doris," he went on, fixing his gaze upon her, "I didn't mean to listen in, but I meant what I just said. When we get back to Hamble, we'll speak with your boss. Okay?"

Doris gave the man a thumbs-up, at exactly the same time a raised voice from inside the lorry barked out, "Major!" and his head disappeared back inside.

Knowing when she shouldn't be in the way, Doris looked up at Lewis. "I'll leave you all to your duties. I'll be in the Humber, if you need me."

"Anything happened?" Ceiwen asked her from the back seat, as soon as Doris climbed back into her position behind the wheel.

Shaking her head, Doris held out her cup. "Care for a tea? I've only had a little."

Holding out a hand, Ceiwen accepted the cup. "Gladly, thank you, Doris."

"I really can't see how you Brits can love that stuff." She shook her head.

After finishing off half the cup in one go, Ceiwen cradled the warm cup in both hands. "There are many of us Brits who'd say the same about coffee, you know."

"Touché," Doris replied.

"Any idea how long we're likely to be here?" he asked.

Doris shook her head and, reaching into her jacket pocket, pulled out a book. "No idea, so whilst you enjoy your tea, Miss Marple and I shall get back to some serious sleuthing." Matching words to action, Doris quickly found her place, only for fate to decide, with perfect timing, to get in the way.

"We've got him!"

The loud cry was easily heard inside the Humber and Doris put the book carefully away, lest Betty have her guts for garters when she got back. Even so, she was close behind Ceiwen, who'd leapt out of the back seat and was running towards the rear of the lorry. When Doris joined him, Duke had already flung the tarpaulin aside and his men could be seen closing the radio and the rest of the electronic gadgets down. The major was scribbling furiously into a notebook. When he paused in his writing, he glanced up and saw the pair silently, yet eagerly waiting upon him. Obviously not wanting to lose his train of thought, he rewarded the pair with a big grin, and then was back to his writing.

Playing the part of the general, Ceiwen made a point of calling Lewis and his men back from their patrol. Once they were assembled, he told them, "I wanted to inform you all that today's mission has been a complete success. Though you don't know it, you are all integral to both today's and the ongoing success of our operation. You have both my and the Major's thanks."

Sergeant Lewis stood to attention, almost bursting with pride at the unexpected words. "On behalf of the men, thank you, sir." He saluted and then requested,

"Permission to dismiss the men back to their posts, sir?"

Ceiwen returned the salute. "Carry on, Sergeant."

Doris once more stood to one side and, feeling much more relaxed than she had been for most of the day, watched the chaps in the lorry finish packing everything into its travelling crates, while she reflected that, everything considered, it had been a good day.

Chapter Thirty-Six

Taxi greeted Doris's arrival back in their room by raising his head from his position on her pillow, yawning, and going right back to sleep. "I've missed you too, little guy," she told him, ruffling his ears. She sniffed the air, then wished she hadn't. Glancing towards the corner where she'd laid out some newspaper for him, it was as she expected. "I'm not surprised you're sleeping. If I were responsible for that mess, I'd keep my head down too."

Before cleaning up, Doris opened the window a crack, just enough to allow a gust of fresh air to flow into the room; Taxi started to snore. "It's all right for some," she chuckled, holding the wrapped-up newspaper. "Hold down the fort, I'll be back in a tick," she said. When she opened the door, Doris had to take a hasty step backwards as right before her were three unexpected guests. "Albert! What the hell?"

Lance Corporal Albert Miller quickly dropped the hand he'd been about to knock upon her door with and bumped back into his companions.

"Careful," Rachel Carter told him, stepping to one side and onto the toe of Doris's steward friend, Percy Snodgrass.

"Glad these things have a decent toe-cap," he muttered.

Now the door was open, Albert had his mouth open

to speak, only to snap it shut and wrap his hands around his nose, "What the hell's that smell?"

Without thinking, Doris held up the screwed-up newspaper. "Sorry about that. Taxi had to go."

Her visitors took another step back, all three now wafting their hands before their faces.

"I'm sure that should be against the Geneva Convention," Percy muttered, before gallantly holding out a hand. "Give that here. You've visitors, so I'll get rid of it." Doris handed it over without a second thought, and he darted back down the steps straight away.

"Don't forget to wash your hands before you come back!" Rachel shouted after his departing back.

"Come in, come in," Doris invited the pair left, leaving the door open behind them to air her room a little more. "It's lovely to see you both. What can I do for you?"

Waiting whilst the pair settled themselves upon her bed, with Rachel scooping up Taxi and settling the unprotesting cat onto her lap, Doris took up the chair. She noticed that other than cracking open one eye to see who was handling him, Taxi didn't appear to have any inclination to do anything, let alone make a run out the door.

"Good boy," she couldn't resist telling him, as she reached forward and ruffled his ears.

"You are," Rachel agreed, bobbing down and planting a kiss on his furry head. "We came to see that this young man was in good health after his ordeal, didn't we," she informed Doris.

"And, to bring you this," Albert said, holding up a square-ish object covered in newspaper.

"Um..." Doris accepted the object, holding it up

before her face and turning it this way and that. "Thank you?"

"Open it!" Rachel urged, her hands gently squirming Taxi's ears, which the cat obviously loved, judging by the loud purr he was treating them to.

Carefully, as the newspaper had at least one other use it could be put to, Doris unwrapped the present. "That's wonderful! It's just what I need!" she exclaimed, turning it back and forth, a grin of delight upon her face.

"We knew you'd need something to carry him around in," Albert told her, just as the sound of running boots up the steps outside announced the return of Percy, who slouched against the doorway to get his breath back.

"A lot of the lads chipped in," Albert told her. "We all feel, well, bloody awful that one of our own was the catnapper."

"Catnapper?" Doris said, trying the word out for size. "I don't think I've heard of that word before."

Albert went a little red around the ears. "No idea if it's a real word." He shrugged. "But it seems to fit. Anyway, as you already know, his release is the talk of the castle and we wanted to do something for him, and for you. Do you like it?"

Doris placed the object down before her, looking up so the three could see her face and know she was sincere. "I do. It's just what I need. You're right, I was wondering how I was going to get him home safely." She glanced down at the roughly two feet by one plywood box. "Plenty of air holes, the straw's a good idea, and the carrying handle appears nice and sturdy. I do like the signatures it's covered with. Whose idea was that?"

Albert, somewhat sheepishly, held up a hand. "Blame me," he said. "There wasn't enough to do for everyone who wanted to chip in so it seemed a good way for everyone to show their support. Plus, this way, you'll never forget us!"

"Something tells me I won't be forgetting my adventures up here anytime soon," she told them with a smile.

Taxi added punctuation by farting loudly, before settling further into Rachel's lap and cranking up his contented purr a few notches.

****

Once her visitors had said their goodbyes, Doris took Rachel's place on her bed and gave Taxi a loving squeeze. "You know," she began, "I've no idea how I'm going to explain you to Ruth. She has a dog, you know, a real sweety called Bobby. Not to mention, there's Duck. He's a duck," she told him, staring into the eyes he'd deemed to open. "That one," she mused, "may be more of a problem. He's got a bit of an…attitude." She'd paused while seeking the right word and eventually settled upon the best she could do. "Okay, he's got a foul temper, pun implied," she added, "so I may have to try and keep the pair of you apart for a while."

A rap on the door made her jerk her head upwards, to find herself looking up into the inquisitive gaze of Duke and Ceiwen, who both stood in the open doorway. She'd forgotten to close it after her guests left.

"Sounds like you're going to have an interesting time, once you get back," Ceiwen said, grinning from ear to ear.

"And that's quite a menagerie you're collecting," Duke mentioned. "Duck. Really?"

Doris shrugged. "Why not? Donald's been taken."

"Donald?" Duke asked, with a shake of her head.

"He's a cartoon character," Ceiwen informed him and then, when the man appeared no clearer to understanding, added, "Never mind. You wouldn't understand unless you've seen it"

Duke only shook his head once more. "Sorry, I expect I'm being a bit dim, but I never used to go to the pictures much, even before the war."

"That's okay," Doris quickly began. "Suffice to say, Duck's a wild duck, though I'm sure my friends would tell you he's actually a psychopath. I seem to be the only one he'll tolerate," she ended with a shrug. "Bobby's my landlady's cocker spaniel—and our airfield's air raid warning system."

At her urging, the pair came into her room, Duke taking the chair she'd been sitting on whilst Ceiwen leant against the desk. "Would you care to elaborate?" Ceiwen asked, mirroring what everyone who came into the room seemed to do, by leaning forward to give Taxi a stroke.

Doris didn't trouble keeping the pride from her voice as she brought forth the memory of when her doggy friend had probably saved multiple lives. "You can choose to believe it or not, but he turned up one day barking his head off. There was nothing to be seen, no alarm had gone off, yet he got the attention of everyone on the airfield and, because everyone was on alert, when we heard the sound of an unknown engine, we all dived into the slit trenches or air raid shelters. Because of him, no one was hurt—well, my friend Betty had a bit of a concussion, but nothing serious."

Duke whistled. "That's quite a story," he said, with Ceiwen nodding enthusiastically in agreement.

"And every word of it is true," Doris firmly informed him.

"I have no doubt," Duke agreed. "Well, I wish you, and your landlady, luck."

"Was there something I can do for you both?" Doris asked, now the issue of her short and furries had been put to bed. "I thought we'd finished for the day."

"You hared off before I could tell you about tomorrow," Duke said.

"Sorry about that," Doris told him. "I wanted to see how Taxi was. So tell me, what's happening? Where're we off to?"

"Hold on," Ceiwen told them, getting to his feet. "Let me close the door."

Duke nodded his thanks and waited for Ceiwen to settle back against the desk before saying, "As you know, tomorrow will be our last day here before we fly back down on Monday, so we're all going to be very busy and it'll be a five o'clock start. We're firstly going to pay a visit to Linlithgow Palace. Captain McSwain's unit has a very important part to play in this operation, and not only do we want to make sure he knows to keep his mouth shut about the real general," Duke told her, not troubling to soften his words, "but there are going to be visiting brass from some genuine units present. They'll be closely guarded, so they don't go anywhere they shouldn't or see anything, either."

"Why are they going to be there, then?" Doris not unreasonably asked.

"We're going to arrange some swapping of unit badges. That kind of thing goes down well. I'm pretty sure that when they get back to their units, more than a few will get left around the towns and villages where they're based."

"I like it!" Doris announced. "We're free for the

night, then?"

Duke nodded. "You are, but I wouldn't recommend going into the city, if you don't mind my advice this once. As I said, it's going to be busy tomorrow. Once we finish at the castle, we'll be coming straight back here. The lads and I will be packing everything away. We aim to be back just after midday, and I'll need you to go to Turnhouse and prep your Anson. I'd like to take off around eight in the morning. So, as you can see, it'll be best if we all have a restful evening."

Doris jumped to her feet. "In that case," she clapped her hands together, "I'll wish you gentlemen a good night. I've a cat to feed, and then Miss Marple and I shall settle in for a restful evening."

Chapter Thirty-Seven

Despite most everyone, including the usually stoic Sergeant Lewis, seeming to be taking part in a yawning contest when they'd met up in the early Sunday morning gloom, by the time they arrived at Linlithgow Palace everyone was wide awake.

"Do you think they'll have anything for breakfast we could snaffle, sir?" Lewis asked of Duke as he formed the escort up. At the mention of breakfast, every one of his men, including the now-fit-again Douglas, turned their attention to the officer. Doris would swear she could hear more than one stomach rumble, including her own.

Duke waited until they were formed up before telling them, "Gentlemen. Once again, my thanks for all you've done and, in case I don't get the chance to say so later, both my and the general's best wishes to you all for the rest of the war. May you all come through the testing times ahead, safely and in one piece. General Ceiwen has left instructions behind the bar in the other ranks mess. Tonight, you will not pay for your drinks." He waited with a smile for the resultant cheer to die down. "Don't go overboard. Believe me," and here his voice took on a sharp *don't mess with me* tone, "if any one of you is unable to perform their duties tomorrow morning, I'll have you up on a charge so fast your feet won't touch the floor. Do we understand each other?"

A shouted chorus of, "Yes sir!" answered his question.

Doris waited until they were joined by Ceiwen and on their way towards the entrance of the ruined palace, with the escort a few yards either side of the three and all doing their best to display nothing but the upmost professionalism, before she leant in and tapped Duke on the arm. "Seriously, I agree with Lewis. Do you think they'll have anything to eat? That muck the mess calls tea that they gave us was not only cold, but hardly filling."

"I'll make sure of it," Ceiwen got in first. "I'm hungry too."

As it turned out, not only did Captain McSwain show no signs of letting on that Ceiwen wasn't the real general, he seemed to be going out of his way to show due deference to the man's rank. Once he'd been made aware, it took only ten minutes for hot rolls filled with bacon to appear, accompanied by mugs of steaming hot tea. Though she was curious, Doris didn't trouble with asking where they'd managed to get hold of so much bacon. Knowing how resourceful—she chose the word carefully even though she didn't say anything out loud—soldiers could be, she decided she didn't want to know and simply joined with everyone else in enjoying the unexpected bounty.

A couple of privates trotted out to pick up the empty mugs, whilst Lewis detailed one of his men to dispose of the bacon butty wrappings.

The captain came up, stamped to attention before Duke, saluted, and asked, "Was breakfast satisfactory, Major?"

"Very, thank you, Captain. Thank your cooks from

me, please."

As the man detailed one of his men to pass on Duke's request, Doris took the opportunity to say to Ceiwen, "I don't know about you, but I'll be glad to get this one over with. All this false politeness is muddling my head."

After the impromptu though nevertheless welcome breakfast, proceedings moved swiftly along. Whether the good captain had the officers from the real units locked away in some side room ready to be released upon the world, Doris never found out. All she knew was that no sooner had everything been cleared away than she seemed to be surrounded by around a dozen officers, all of whom were clutching multiple cap and uniform badges.

As if some unspoken alarm had gone off, Ceiwen was suddenly engulfed by officers of every rank, all trying to be the first to be seen and to speak with Ceiwen. From behind them appeared a dozen or so men all with cameras slung around their necks. In an instant, she was transported back to her time at the Girl Scouts Jamborees. The whole scene appeared to be an organized melee. Ceiwen had certainly grown into his part lately, as he didn't seem fazed by any of it, happily smiling as his picture was taken wearing various regimental caps and shaking hands as he accepted badges. She couldn't see him putting a foot wrong.

"It's going well, isn't it?" Duke had appeared by her side and was watching the proceedings with what could only be a satisfied smile upon his face. He had his arms crossed and was absently rubbing his hook between his real thumb and a finger.

Doris nodded, though there was something about the

scene which wasn't sitting right with her, and she was trying to put her finger upon it. "Looks like it," she absently agreed. "You're not going to miss all those different regiments in the pictures, are you?"

"Definitely not. It's just what we want!"

"Uh huh." Doris watched as a very young officer got over-excited and tossed his cap into the air after Ceiwen had handed it back to him. The man was roundly scolded by a captain, immediately making himself scarce.

Suddenly, it hit Doris what had been niggling at her since she'd first noticed the photographers. "Duke, the photographers. Isn't it a bit, well, dangerous, to have someone from *The Daily Post* and," she squinted at the name stenciled on the bag hanging from another man's shoulder, "even the *Times*, here? Surely they shouldn't know about this place?"

Grinning, Duke told her, "Don't be fooled by the names, none of the chaps taking pictures are from the real newspapers, they're all army and know not to have anything in the background of the pictures which could give a clue where they were taken, so there's no danger of compromising this place. The officers all seem to be enjoying themselves, so I doubt if any will notice anything out of the ordinary."

"Don't you need articles to go with the pictures?" Doris asked, beginning to understand what Duke had arranged.

Duke nodded. "Already written."

"And, I presume, none of these officers know this is all a set-up?"

"No. Not only don't they need to know, but it makes this scenario natural. Don't you agree?"

Doris could only shake her head, though she was

trying to keep a smile from her face at the same time. "Couldn't agree more. So," she asked, "I assume as soon as all the pictures are taken, everything will be whisked down to London to make tomorrow's newspaper?" A couple of the photographers spotted her at that moment and swung their cameras her way, getting a few shots off before she was able to turn her back.

"Exactly!"

They both ducked as another cap flew their way.

"You're very good at this," Doris told him, hoping none of the photographers would be silly enough to sneak up on her whilst her back was turned. She didn't want to cause any more trouble this late in the assignment.

Duke bent to retrieve the cap and headed back into the melee, as Ceiwen looked like he was about to be engulfed in good will.

****

It was good to see her Anson again, and even though Doris wanted to be back at the castle so she could wash away the grime and dust before a last night out at The Young Chevalier, she forced herself to be slow and methodical as she checked over the plane. Occasionally, she'd stroke the wings, ignoring the strange looks she received as she muttered endearments, feeling stupidly guilty at leaving it unused for so long. Once she was satisfied, she locked it up once more, jumped back into the Humber, and sped off as fast as she could, back to the castle.

On the way back from the photo call, Duke had discussed the rest of the day's plans, letting both Doris and Ceiwen know their visits were over. Once they got back to Edinburgh, the escort would be dismissed, apart from Sergeant Lewis and two other ranks, who he'd detail to accompany them into the city later that evening. Duke wanted to see Morag before they flew back the next day, and Doris was almost as keen to see her as he was.

Waved quickly through the gates—being one of the few women on-site had its advantages, though the men on duty did check her pass, fully aware that it was more than their lives were worth not to perform their duties correctly—Doris still took care to park the Humber and lock it before running along to her quarters. As she went, it seemed almost everyone she passed asked how Taxi was. Doris contented herself with waving and smiling, as she didn't trust her voice not to crack if she tried to answer them. She was realizing how much she was going to miss the city and, perhaps a little to her surprise, Scotland—it was one beautiful little country. Maybe she and Walter could come back once the war was over. The thought brought her mind back to her friend Mary's manor house, and she wondered how the friends she'd made earlier that year were getting along. Her heart ached for the wounded it now contained in its wartime role as a military hospital.

Without realizing it, she found herself at the door to her room. From within, she could hear Taxi meowing his head off and taking a quick look at her watch, she saw why. It was nearly six 'o'clock! Where had the time gone? Fishing her key out of her pocket, she opened the door and immediately dropped it to the floor, as Taxi launched himself into her arms, nuzzled his head under her chin, and proceeded to purr.

"Yes, I love you too," she told him, juggling his bottom so she wouldn't be in danger of dropping him, "and I know food's late."

At hearing the magic word *food*, Taxi bumped his forehead against her nose, planted all four feet against her chest, and launched off. Performing a half somersault, he landed on the floor beside the saucer Doris used as his food dish. Looking over his shoulder up at his owner, Taxi let forth with one more loud meow and then stared down at his empty saucer.

"I can take a hint," she told him. Opening her wardrobe, she reached up for the sealed tin containing Taxi's ham and liberally sprinkled most of its contents upon the saucer. "Eat up! You can have the rest for breakfast in the morning." Doris reached down to run her hand along the length of Taxi's spine, marveling at the amazing transformation he'd made from the scruffy bundle of fur she'd saved into the luxuriously, shiny coat he now sported. She picked up the hairbrush she used on him each night and turned it this way and that. "Let's not tell my husband we're sharing this brush, eh? At least not until I've managed to get another."

Taxi glanced up, possibly eyeing the brush, before returning to his meal.

"We're agreed then. You know," Doris said, kicking off her shoes and pulling her socks off, "I don't know how I'm going to explain you to both Walter and Ruth, but you're going to love them! Now, if you'll excuse me, I'm off for a quick shower, and as the water's been cold most often, it'll be a quick one. Don't wolf your food!" she told him, receiving a meaty belch in reply.

****

"Am I late?" Doris asked, as she met up with Duke, Ceiwen, Sergeant Lewis, and two of his men, beside the guardroom.

"Only a couple of minutes," Duke replied.

Doris glanced around the small company, remarking, "I see we all took the trouble to spruce up our uniforms. Looking good, Sergeant," she praised Lewis.

"Thank you, ma'am…Third Officer…Doris," he stammered.

Perhaps the chap wasn't used to praise, she thought, as the man did his best to hide behind his two men. No easy task, as he towered over both.

"Just Doris," she told him again, taking pity, and he nodded back in agreement, his shoulders seeming to relax a little.

"Well, shall we go?" Duke suggested, quickly falling into step besides Ceiwen, playing the part of the dedicated Aide-de-Camp to the last.

At first, Doris thought their escort was unarmed, not an unreasonable assumption, she thought, seeing as they were merely going from the castle a quite short distance. This thought she quickly dismissed, remembering the mission they were taking part in, and took a closer look. Neither the sergeant nor his privates were carrying either rifles or submachine guns, but each did have a holster secured around his waist. It would be a safe assumption that none were empty. Glancing at Duke and Ceiwen, strolling along besides her, both also had holsters, and Duke had his ubiquitous briefcase, so he had his Luger to hand too. So, all in all, they were quite a well-armed party.

Soon enough they came to The Young Chevalier and filed inside. Waiting for them in the reception was Morag. The young lady held up a hand to gain their attention and Doris felt her stomach lurch. Her other one, the one she'd grabbed the other day, was heavily bandaged.

Beating Duke to her side, Doris took her good hand in hers. "I am so, so sorry! What did I do?"

Morag raised the arm, a small smile upon her lips. "This? It's nothing. Only a sprain."

Once Morag had assured her again that she wasn't in pain, Doris stepped back, and Duke held out his arm. Doris was very pleased to see Morag had no hesitation in taking his hook. Leaning forward, she pressed her lips to his, albeit briefly, as after all they had an audience.

"I'm so pleased you could make it tonight," Morag said, as she led the way towards the bar.

"We'll be over in the corner, sir, if you need us," Lewis told Ceiwen, who took out his wallet and handed them a five-pound note, causing the man to begin to protest.

Ceiwen waved an arm at the man. "Spend what you want. We've dragged you away from your fellows and you've missed your dinner, so order what you all want from the menu. I promise to not keep you out too long. Now, off you go."

If Lewis was embarrassed at Ceiwen's generosity, his two mates had no such reservations, and as Doris took a seat she saw one of them raise his finger to gain the attention of the barman.

"That was very generous of you, sir," Doris said to Ceiwen as they all settled in.

Ceiwen shrugged. "I'm sure I could claim it back, if it comes to it." Turning to Morag, he asked, "You're certain you'll be all right, my dear?"

"Positive," she assured him. "Now, will everyone stop fussing? Right here, please," she told a girl who'd appeared bearing a tray with four large whiskys and a bottle of the golden nectar. "Your health." She raised her glass for the toast. Once everyone had knocked back their glasses and Duke had refilled them, she asked, "So, what's next?"

By silent agreement, Duke spoke for them all. "Unfortunately for me, we have to fly back down south tomorrow morning."

"I had a feeling you were going to say something like that," Morag said, shaking her head sadly.

"Our job's finished," Duke informed her.

Before he could continue, Morag asked, the need in her voice plain to hear, "But when will I see you again? We've only just got back together and I, well, I don't want to lose you again, not now I've persuaded you to give me a second chance!"

Not letting go of his girlfriend's hand, Duke sent a silent plea Doris's way.

Doris immediately understood. Placing a light hand upon Ceiwen's sleeve, "Why don't we leave these lovebirds alone, General?"

Ceiwen knocked back his second drink, then got to his feet. "Well, short and sweet, as they say. Morag Blessed," he began, taking the hand she offered, which he raised to his lips to place the briefest of kisses upon it before presenting it back to Duke, "my ADC is truly blessed to have you by his side. I hope we meet again, in happier times."

Doris felt no need to show such restraint and leant down to give her new friend a huge hug. "Here's the phone number where I live," she said, pressing a piece of paper into her hand and squeezing it shut. "Don't worry if someone called Ruth answers. She's my landlady, but also one of my best friends."

Leaving the pair deep in conversation, Doris and Ceiwen made their way towards the bar where Lewis and his men were standing, identical expressions of disappointment upon their faces. Each held a half empty pint of beer.

Ceiwen took it upon himself to speak. "Gentlemen. I'm sorry, but I must bring the evening to an early end. Did you order anything to eat?" he asked, receiving a nod from each. Ceiwen called over the barman. "Please inform the kitchen that the meals these gentlemen ordered will not be required and we do not require a refund."

Having settled that matter, he stepped back and waited. After a second, the men took his hint and drained their glasses. "Ready, sir," Lewis informed Ceiwen. Then he held out a shovel of a hand in which must have been the change from the note Ceiwen had given him earlier.

Ceiwen shook his head. "Wouldn't hear of it. Put it behind the bar for me when you get there later."

Fighting and failing to keep his eyebrows from rocketing up towards his hairline, Lewis managed to stammer his thanks.

Once they were outside, Doris thought of a great way to end her last evening in Edinburgh, which she believed would also go down well with her companions. "General, if memory serves, there's a very good fish 'n' chips shop near. What do you think about a fish shop supper?"

This suggestion immediately got everyone's attention. "Excellent notion!" Ceiwen agreed. "Lead on!"

As they approached the fish shop, Doris spied a

telephone box. "Sir, would you mind ordering me just fish 'n' chips? I'm going to quickly phone home."

Checking she had some change, Doris hurried into the box. She couldn't be long, but it'd be lovely to speak to Betty again, and they'd all be very happy to know she would be back as planned, the next day.

Chapter Thirty-Eight

Having lured Taxi into his new cat box by the expedient of laying a tray of ham therein, Doris was exiting her accommodation block and on the way to their transport when she heard running footsteps behind her. Quickly placing Taxi onto the ground at her feet, she turned, arms raised in defense before her face, to find it was only the friends she'd made hurrying up to her. She let her hands drop to her side.

"I was about to ask what the hands bit was all about," Albert Miller said, "but I'm guessing you're still thinking about that piece of scum, Wilson."

Doris shrugged. "Sorry. But quite right." She glanced at her farewell committee, breaking into a smile at the sight of Percy and Rachel holding hands. "Well, well, is love in the air?"

Rachel blushed, though she didn't let go of the steward's hand. "Maybe," she shyly said, not meeting Doris's eye.

Percy did let go, but only to bob down and put his fingers into the box so he could give Taxi a fuss. "If it is, it's all this chap's fault," he announced, being rewarded with a deep purr for his words.

"What are you two doing here?" Doris asked as he straightened up. "Shouldn't you be at work?"

"Special permission to say goodbye to a couple of new friends," Rachel informed her. "Let's just say the two of you breathed new life into this place. It's quite special, to say you live in a castle, but it doesn't stop the work getting boring at times."

"Very true," Albert put in. "I doubt if anyone would want to have the experiences you've had, but you have to admit, it was a bit exciting."

Doris moved to pick up Taxi, only for Albert to beat her to it, whilst Percy quickly took the case from her hand, leaving her with just her overnight bag.

"We've got this," Albert told her. "Come on, we'd better get going." He glanced at his watch. "What time are you leaving?"

"About half six," Doris told him, looking at her own. "Which means we'd better get a move on, or I'll be late."

When Doris and her entourage arrived at the Humber, waiting for them was what seemed to be half the castle's garrison, all of whom wanted to shake her hand and ruffle Taxi's head.

"Honestly, does no one work around here?" she shouted over the mild-mannered ruckus which broke out.

"You seem to have quite the send-off, Doris," Duke remarked, having pushed his way through the throng to reach her side.

Though she wasn't, really, Doris shrugged and said, "Sorry."

"As we're a little tight for time…" he muttered, clambering up onto the driver's side step of the lorry. Banging his hand upon the cab roof for attention, he shouted, "Thank you all for coming. Now, you have five minutes only, and then we have to be on our way!"

A few minutes later, and as her arms were beginning to tire, Albert appeared at her side. He held out his arms. "Here, let me take him for you. We've put your stuff into the Humber."

Duke held up his arm, his hook tapping his watch. "Doris! In the car, now!"

Doris laid a hand upon her friend's shoulder, telling him, "Come on," before cupping her hands around her mouth to say loudly to the crowd, "Sorry folks! Thanks for coming, and keep safe!"

Waiting for them at the Humber were Percy and Rachel. As Albert carefully placed Taxi's box in the passenger seat's foot well, its occupant having taken all the noise and fuss in his stride so well that he was curled up for a post-goodbye snooze, Doris embraced the other two.

"Thank you, both. I hope we meet again one day." She turned to Albert and pulled him in for a huge hug, telling him, "Thank you. Thank you for saving my life."

Once he'd been released, he shook his head. "I wouldn't go that far. Wilson was quite a mess, you know. You didn't need my help."

"Let's agree to disagree," she told him. "I won't forget you, Albert Miller."

"Nor I you," he told her.

There was a loud, pointed cough, and Doris looked up. "Oops, duty calls," she said, hurrying around to open the door for Ceiwen, "Sorry, sir."

"Thank you, Doris," Ceiwen said, with a knowing wink.

Rachel hurried up to Doris as she got behind the wheel. "Hold on! Here," she pressed three large packets of sandwiches and three large thermoses into her hands. "These are for your journey. They're better than anything you'll get from the mess at Turnhouse!"

Placing the packages upon the seat beside her, Doris

turned to give her friend a final hug. "Thank you! That's so thoughtful."

"I've never seen anything like that," Duke remarked from the rear seat, once they were finally on their way. "I was beginning to wonder at one point if we'd ever get away!"

"It wasn't like I planned it," Doris countered.

"You misunderstand," he began. "I'm simply amazed."

"Speaking of amazing," Doris said. "I notice you're not sneezing. Whilst I think about it, I haven't seen you sneezing or your eyes streaming lately when you've been around Taxi. What gives? Have you discovered some miracle cure? Or you're suddenly not allergic to cats after all?"

"Now you mention it…" Ceiwen joined in.

Duke fished in his pocket, bringing out a small brown paper bag. "There's no trick, no miracle." He put a couple of fingers into the bag and held up a bit of white fluff. "Cotton wool up the nose stops me sneezing, and after a little experimentation, smearing petroleum jelly under my nose seems to help with my eyes. Don't ask me why, it just does."

"Well, I can't say anything but 'well done, you.' And, on behalf of Taxi and me, thank you for your efforts. I can't imagine any of that's comfortable."

As if his nose were reading her mind, Duke sneezed, explosively and with much waving of his arm. A tiny ball of white shot past Doris's left ear and hit the dashboard before dropping to the floor.

"It's not totally effective," he sniffed, rapidly blowing and wiping his nose, before stuffing a fresh piece up his nostril.

Doris quickly glanced back. "And I appreciate it all the more…now I've had that demonstration."

****

Once they arrived at Turnhouse and Doris was satisfied nothing had gone wrong with the plane overnight, Duke supervised Lewis and his men in loading up the Anson, whilst Ceiwen continued his general role by standing back and watching. Doris did a check once they'd finished and was happy to see that they'd done a good job of spreading the load evenly, so the aircraft's center of balance wouldn't be affected.

"You've done that before," she clapped Lewis upon the elbow.

"A few times," he told her. "Where do you want this little chap?" he asked, pointing at Taxi's box, which Doris was holding, having already stowed her own luggage.

"Here," she held out the box to Lewis and clambered into the aircraft. Turning around, she held out her arms, and once it was once more safely in her grip, turned again and made her way into the cockpit. "I think you should have the best seat in the place, barring mine of course," she told Taxi. For the next few minutes, she double- and triple-checked that his box was thoroughly secured into the co-pilot's seat by the harness meant to hold a person in place there. Facing forward, he wouldn't get much of a view. There were wooden bars across the front, but they were quite thick. "Sorry you can't see much," she told him. Looking around to make sure no one was around, she quickly undid the latch holding the lid on and lifted Taxi out, tucking him under one arm. The expression he turned upon her was one of affront. "Sorry. I want to check that the paper doesn't need changing before we set off."

"I see I'm relegated to the rear."

Doris looked behind her, Taxi protesting when she accidentally brushed his head against the seat back, and she found Ceiwen standing there, observing what was going on. She turned back, more carefully this time, and placed Taxi into his box again, dipping into her pocket to feed him a few scraps of ham before locking down the lid. "Sorry, needs must and Duke should have someone to talk to during the flight. You saw what he's going through for Taxi and me," she said, passing him two pairs of headphones. "Could you put his on his seat, please? Thanks."

"Of course, Mrs. Johnson," he acceded, staying in character and disappearing back through the bulkhead.

Once she was satisfied Taxi was secure, Doris made her way back down the aircraft and out onto the hard standing. Waiting there was Sergeant Lewis and his escort, and Doris was just in time to hear Duke saying, "Sergeant, you and your men have been exemplary in your duties and I shall be saying so in the report I'll be sending in to your commanding officer." He turned to look at Doris who, assuming he wanted to know if she was ready to take off, gave him a thumbs-up gesture. "Thank you. Dismissed!"

"Squad! Squad, attention!" Lewis shouted. As his men snapped to attention, he saluted Duke, who returned the salute. "Squad! Squad, dismiss!" The escort did a half turn to their right and then made off towards the waiting lorry and Humber. Lewis made a beeline for Doris, holding out his hand as he came to a stop before her. "Doris," he began, looking down at her, a smile gracing his features, "it's been an experience and a pleasure to be around you. God speed, ma'am," and he quickly bent down and surprised the heck out of her by kissing her quickly on the left cheek. Not giving her the time to recover or reply, he turned on his heel and made his way towards the Humber, hopping into the passenger seat. The last she heard of his voice was him shouting out—undoubtedly in response to the cacophony of wolf-whistles the kiss had elicited—"That will do!" at the top of his voice.

"You really know how to get a reaction out of people," Duke told her, as he strode past her to settle in the Anson.

Following him, Doris shut and secured the door behind her, remarking, as she passed Duke settling himself in, "Don't choke on the cotton wool."

****

Doris took the opportunity during the refueling stop at RAF East Moor to clean both Taxi's box and the unhappy cat himself. The faces on the visiting aircraft flight's ground crew when she appeared with a yowling cat box in hand and asked to be pointed towards the nearest tap, were priceless. Only Duke's scowling face and the way he stood next to the refueling bowser clacking his hook together prevented unwarranted comments. It also likely hurried up the refueling process, with the added benefit of making sure the now-empty thermoses were refilled with hot tea.

By the time Doris and a rather soggy and very ratty-looking—not to mention loudly complaining—Taxi rejoined them, the refueling crew had finished and made themselves scarce. Doris took in the scene at once, noting a chuckling Ceiwen visible through the Anson's windows and Duke standing cradling his hook in the doorway.

"I see you're amusing yourself," she told him, as she passed Taxi's box up to him, getting a sneeze in return. "Bless you."

Securing the door, Doris took Taxi back, allowing Duke to remove his cotton wool, wipe his nose, and replace his anti-cat devices. "Thanks," he was eventually able to say.

"Strap in and plug in," she advised, patting him on the shoulder, adding, "Thanks again," knowing he'd realize she was referring to what he was putting up with for her.

The sandwiches were, as Rachel promised, quite delicious. "Best ham-and-cheese sandwich I've had in ages!" Doris declared over the intercom.

"I quite agree," Ceiwen was the first to answer. "In fact, I'm going to put my head down for a while. How long until we land, please, Doris?"

"Maybe an hour or so, "Doris replied.

Around ten minutes later, Duke appeared in the bulkhead behind Doris's pilot seat and tapped her on the shoulder.

"What's wrong?" she immediately asked, quickly glancing around. All she could see was a quietly snoozing Ceiwen, his headset nestling on his lap.

"Nothing's wrong," he assured her. "It just struck me that I hadn't thanked you."

"For what?" Doris enquired, honestly perplexed.

"Whatever it was you said to Morag when the two of you were outside the Chevalier that evening. It changed everything."

Doris took a swig from her thermos, and though she didn't grimace too much, she still couldn't resist saying,

"Still not as good as coffee. Sorry, you'll need to explain a bit more."

Duke shook his head when she offered him her thermos. "What I mean is, before you talked, and I wasn't sure you'd both come back into the hotel in one piece at the time, she was still holding back, as if she wasn't sure about committing to us."

"And then?"

"And when she came back in, she held my hook and told me she loved me. Before then, she couldn't even bear to look at it. What did you say?"

Doris shrugged as she reached across with her right hand to squeeze and stroke the paw Taxi had stretched through the bars of his box. "Nothing much. I just persuaded her to admit to herself how she really felt and that some things shouldn't matter. She already knew this. She just needed to be able to say it out loud."

"Well," Duke said, stretching, "we're in your debt, Doris."

"Send me an invite, and I'll happily dance at your wedding!" she told him.

He squeezed her shoulder. "I'd be delighted." Glancing outside before retaking his seat, something in the distance off the port wing caught his eye. There it was again! He had no doubt that was the glint of sunlight off metal… "Doris, I don't suppose you know if there's any traffic in the area?"

Turning her head, Doris stared in the same direction Duke was looking. "I wouldn't know. Here…" She reached under her seat and passed him a pair of binoculars. "Take a closer look."

For the next minute or so, Duke kept the binoculars trained on what had to be an aircraft, before saying, "I'm no expert in aircraft, but I'd swear that plane is on an intercept course with us."

"Keep an eye on it," Doris told him. "I'm going to change course by ten degrees. Let me know if it follows."

After a few moments, Duke took the binoculars from his eyes. "Definitely following us."

"Can you make out what it is? I'll be surprised if it's German, to be honest."

He put the binoculars back to his eyes. "I think…yes, I think it's a B17."

"Around here? Well, we're around Northampton, so I suppose it could be. Only I wouldn't expect to see one stooging around at this time of day, especially on its own. Around midday, they'd be somewhere over Europe. You can't see any others?"

Duke looked around, quickly, yet taking enough time to be methodical, before saying, "No, looks like he's on his own. Here," he handed her the binoculars, "take them and tell me what you can see. How far off do you think they are?"

"Hmm, well, maybe a few miles off now, and it's definitely a B17. Hold on," she told him, taking the binoculars away from her eyes to check they were still flying straight and level before taking another look. "I don't believe it! It's a B17 all right, but it's got German markings!"

Chapter Thirty-Nine

By now, the stranger was close enough there was no need for binoculars. Stowing them back under her seat, Doris set her jaw. "I've a bad feeling about this. Duke, wake Ceiwen up and get strapped in tight, both of you."

"What are you going to do?" Duke asked, not moving yet.

"You see the German markings?"

Duke nodded, not wasting words.

"I've heard rumors the Nazis were using our aircraft when they've been forced down. Well, this is obviously one of those. The question is, what are they up to? I'm going to try a few gentle changes of course, to see if we really are what they're homing in on."

Disappearing behind her, Duke went and woke up their companion, which was confirmed when she heard Ceiwen's voice come over her headphones. "Doris, Duke just told me what's happening. Can we outrun them?"

Not doubting herself and not wanting to give her friends false hope, Doris informed them, "Unlikely. Assuming that thing is fully serviceable, they're at least a hundred miles an hour faster than us."

The changes Doris made did not make any difference, just as she'd expected, as the B17 continued on its inexorable course. All too soon, the black-crossed aircraft was off Doris's port beam and she could easily see into the other aircraft's cockpit across the hundred or so yards of space there was between them.

"There's a sight you don't see every day," she mumbled, nearly jumping as she felt a hand upon her shoulder.

"Ignore me," Duke told her and, quick as you like, he unstrapped Taxi's box and disappeared into the rear fuselage. Very shortly afterwards, he sat down in the vacated co-pilot's seat. "Don't worry, he's strapped in, and Ceiwen's taking care of him. What's happening? What's he doing?"

Both of them looked across, to see the man in the co-pilot's seat of the B17 clearly jabbing his finger down.

"What the hell?" Duke exclaimed.

As if to emphasize what they were seeing, the radio in their ears crackled into life and they heard a voice in heavily accented English say, "Anson, you will stay on this course and land in a field on my direction in five minutes. Fail to follow my instructions, and we will destroy you."

"That's interesting," Doris remarked after a few seconds.

"You definitely can't outrun them?" Ceiwen asked.

"No chance," Doris confirmed. She looked around, not bothering to hide the action from the crew of the B17, a number of whom she could now see watching them, as she knew it was what they would do in her place. "Let's see what happens. You all trust me?" she asked.

"Of course," Duke told her.

"With my life," Ceiwen added.

"Thanks," Doris replied. Gently, she moved the control yoke a little to the right and they began to slip off course. The response from the B17 cam instantly, as a stream of machinegun fire hissed across their nose, forcing Doris to return to the previous course.

The radio sprang back to life. "That is your only warning, Third Officer Johnson," advised the same voice.

Both Doris and Duke looked across and now, ominously, they could see the upper turret and side-fuselage machineguns trained upon her.

"I guess we know St Crail's radio message got through," Duke said, his mouth set in a grim straight line.

In response, Doris grabbed the microphone. "In for a penny…Mayday! Mayday! This is Lost Child. Am under attack by German Marked B17! I repeat, May…"

She got no further, as this time when their enemy opened fire, they felt bullets strike home somewhere in the rear fuselage.

"Bugger!" Doris swore dropping the microphone into her lap, her head swiveling round to see if she could see where they were hit. "I can't see anything. Duke, do you have anything? You all right in the back?" she shouted.

"I'm not sure," Duke admitted.

"We've a few new holes back here, but we're both in one piece," Ceiwen reported, causing them both to look back through the bulkhead. Ceiwen looked a little pale, and though they couldn't hear him, Taxi's mouth was opening and closing in distress.

"Johnson," the Germanic voice came into their ears once more, "do not test me. There is no escape. Continue your course."

Doris covered her microphone. "Now they've gone too far. They've upset my cat!"

"Do you think anyone heard you?" Duke asked.

She shrugged her shoulders. "We can only hope."

"Johnson," the voice came into their ears once more. "Keep on course and lower your undercarriage. You will be met by German parachutists."

"What are you going to do?" Duke asked, keeping an eye on the B17.

Doris waved a hand towards the B17, wanting them to see her at least pretend to acknowledge the instruction. "Can you see that bank of clouds to your right? About half a mile away."

Duke tried to make it appear like he wasn't looking anywhere but at the B17. "Just. What are you thinking?"

"I think it's now or never. We've been slowly descending for a while. We're only a few thousand feet above the ground now, and I'd like a little space to maneuver with. Make sure you're both strapped in tight," she told them. "We're going to make a run for it."

Giving them ten seconds, Doris counted under her teeth and then threw the throttles fully forward and pulled up and to her right, angling the nose towards the clouds. The Nazi pilot had obviously been expecting some kind of move, though. Nearly as quickly, he pulled the bomber up and onto their tail. Though the B17 was faster than the Anson, Doris had a head start and accelerated to full speed more quickly. Seconds later, they were in the cloud. Not waiting for anything to happen, Doris pulled a hard left-hand turn, hoping the Nazi would expect her to keep to her course. No sooner had she completed her turn than the B17 flashed past their tail. Someone must have seen them, though, as fire blazed from the tail gunner, fortunately missing them this time.

"Christ!" Duke shouted, gripping the edge of his seat.

Betting that the B17 would turn as tightly as possible in order to catch them, Doris glanced at her artificial horizon indicator and kept her turn going, trying to keep inside the cloud bank and, mostly, succeeding. "Bugger," she said again, quickly turning back into the bank. She was always surprised that it was darker inside a cloud than it looked from the outside. "Fluffy and white, my foot," she muttered, as they were once more enveloped. Tracer fire flashed past their nose and around and over them.

"They can't see us," Duke announced. "I think they're firing blind. How long do you think you can keep this up?"

"Not long," Doris told him through gritted teeth. "We're running out of space, and he may not be able to see us, but I can see him," she pointed a finger to her left, where a blurry grey, cigar-shaped mass could be seen. No sooner had she spoken, than fire erupted from the bomber's side-mounted machinegun, swiftly joined by the upper turret. Doris had already begun to climb the Anson as she'd spoken, so most of their fire missed. Some rounds did hit home beneath their feet. "I think they've hit the undercarriage," she muttered, knowing there was nothing she could do about it right then.

Continuing the climb, they broke through the upper levels of the cloud, finding themselves in bright blue sky and brilliant sunshine.

"They're closing in!" Ceiwen warned.

"Can we make it back to the clouds?" Duke asked.

Glancing behind, Doris grimaced. "I doubt it. They've got between us, and I can't see anywhere else to try to hide." Looking around, Doris made a decision. "Hold on!" and without further warning, pushed the yoke down hard, rolling the aircraft as it went, flashing underneath the closing B17 which was unable to match her violent maneuver.

As they went past, she saw Duke push open his window panel and point his luger—which she hadn't even noticed he'd had on him—out the window and open fire on their enemy as the two aircraft passed. "Bastard!" Duke shouted, as he emptied the magazine.

"Didn't expect that to work," Doris announced, as they entered the cloud bank once more.

"Great flying!" Duke told her. "Can you keep it up?"

"No bloody idea," Doris said, "but I'd rather go on trying than surrender to this scum."

"Well said!" Ceiwen hollered.

Weaving left and right, Doris grimaced with the effort of gripping the controls and maneuvering harder than she'd ever done in her life. Something caught her attention—light reflecting off metal somewhere to her right. She banked a little towards the sight and was elated to find that she'd been mistaken as the light reflected off more than one thing, and this high up she believed it could only be one thing. "Where's the B17?" she shouted.

"Turning in behind us," Duke reported.

"Right, let's see if we're lucky today," Doris said, setting course for the closing aircraft, of which she was in doubt as to what they were now. "Help me, Duke! Place your hand over mine, and push!" she instructed him. Together, they pushed the throttle levers as far forward as they would go, the combination of their hands straining to keep them in place.

"Where are we going?" he asked.

"Straight ahead," Doris told him. "Aircraft, and I'm gambling they're ours. Is he still coming, General?"

After a moment, the reply came, "He's now behind us, and closing."

"Spitfires!" Doris announced. "Those are Spits, I'm certain!"

As soon as the words were out of her mouth, the radio burst to life: "Lost Child! Lost Child, this is Pimpernel section. I see you. Break left, break left!"

Now clearly visible, four Spitfires flashed past as Doris, removing her hand from the throttles, banked as she'd been instructed. A second later, the leading pair opened fire, their cannon clearly audible as they passed. The crew of the Anson took great delight as German language flooded their earphones. Continuing her turn, Doris banked the aircraft, and very shortly they all were witness to the spectacular yet frightening conclusion of the action. Perhaps it was the adrenalin still coursing through their veins, but none of the occupants of the Anson were able to tear their eyes from what followed.

Faced with the sudden appearance of four heavily armed, top-of-the-line fighters, the B17 tried to make for the same cloud bank in which Doris had so successfully hidden. Things were very different now though, and the Spitfire pilots knew the B17's vulnerable spot. In line-astern formation, they flew straight towards the bomber's nose. As the three watched, cannon shells smashed into the bomber, the fighters pressing home their attack, not heeding the stream of return fire, which soon slackened off, a surefire sign that their attack was hitting home.

Under their gaze, smoke began to pour from two of

the B17's engines, and they could see pieces of aluminum being torn off the aircraft, clearly staggering under the punishment it was receiving. Not letting up, the Spitfires turned tightly and came in for another attack. As they opened fire once more, three parachutes were seen to tumble from the bomb bay. With a sickening lurch in her stomach, Doris saw only two of them opened. Enemy or not, it wasn't a fate she'd wish on anyone.

Even as she watched, the B17 suddenly lurched, the nose pitched down, and it began a slow dive towards the ground.

"Get out, get out," Doris could hear her voice saying, not even thinking about the fact that a bare few minutes ago the same aircraft she was witnessing in its death throes had been trying to kill her. Nobody was listening, though, and before their eyes, the B17 nosed into the ground and exploded in a ball of flame.

Doris had to force herself not to let go of the control yoke in relief, as the threat to their lives was extinguished. She was forced to concentrate as the radio came back to life, "Lost Child, this is Pimpernel. Is everyone okay? Your kite looks like a sieve!"

Clearing her throat, Doris took up her microphone. "Pimpernel, this is Lost Child. Thank you, yes, we're all right. Very glad you were around."

"Lost Child, Pimpernel. we were out on patrol, glad to have been of assistance. Can you make it to your base? Do you need an escort?"

Doris tested her controls, making certain nothing had been hit in the battle which affected her control of the Anson, and was very satisfied to find everything seemed to respond.

Duke, who'd been listening in, asked, "What about the undercarriage?"

"I'd rather carry on for Hamble. Landing there's going to be the same as anywhere. I reckon it'll take about forty-odd minutes."

"You okay with that, General?" Duke asked.

"After what she's just done for us? She can do what she wants!" came back the reply.

"In that case," Duke said, "let's go home."

"Pimpernel, this is Lost Child. Thank you for everything. We're going to carry on for home. No escort necessary."

The reply came straight away. "Lost Child, Pimpernel here. Understood. I'm detaching two of my section to escort you, no argument. We're going to stay here and wait so the two chaps who bailed out don't get away, make sure the army can pick them up."

Doris exchanged glances with Duke before replying, "Agreed, Pimpernel. Thanks again. Out."

Quickly enough, two of the Spitfires formed up, one on each wing, about fifty yards away. Doris and Duke waved at both of them, receiving the same back, before settling onto a course for Hamble.

Ceiwen came over the intercom. "After everything that's just happened, I hate to add to our woes, but some help back here would be appreciated. Taxi's been sick!"

Chapter Forty

Flight Captain Jain Howell stood on the steps of the ops hut. She'd spent most of the day since around midday either sitting on the steps or standing upon them, waiting, listening for the familiar sound of a pair of cheetah engines.

"Have a cuppa," said the voice of her number two. "If you're not going to eat, then at least have something to drink. You do remember Mavis knows how to make a decent cup of tea now?"

Accepting the cup, she brought it to her lips, much experience making her cautious in spite of Penny's words. Looking up, she smacked her lips. "Thanks! That was just what I needed."

Glancing at her watch, Penny asked, "Is she late?"

Jane shook her head. "No idea. I was a bit surprised when Betty told us they were going to be flying in to us. Which reminds me...any problems with the general's escort?"

It was Penny's turn to laugh. "They've been no trouble at all. They've all de-camped into the mess and are lounging around drinking tea and sleeping." The telephone chose that moment to ring. "I'll get it," Penny informed Jane, hurrying inside.

"If that's Mavis ringing to complain about them, tell her they're her problem!"

"Jane! Get in here!" Penny shouted, urgency

dripping from her voice.

"What's wrong?" Jane asked as she dashed to her side.

Penny replaced the receiver, then told Jane, "That was ops. Firecracker's five minutes out , but Doris isn't certain the undercarriage is locked down. Then, they said something about being attacked by a B17."

Jane looked incredulous. "I beg your pardon?"

"That's what they told me." Penny shrugged.

Not dwelling on what she'd been told, no matter how unbelievable, Jane instructed Penny, "Get the crash wagon out, have the medics on standby, then meet me on the flight line." Without waiting to repeat herself, Jane ran out the door.

****

"How many turns was that again?" Duke asked.

Doris wiped the sweat from her forehead before saying, her expression grim, "A hundred and thirty eight."

"Which is…"

"Six short of what it should take," Doris finished, settling back into her seat and readjusting her harness.

"Do you think it'll hold?" Duke was putting words to the question on both their minds.

Before replying, Doris looked up and through the front cockpit window. "We'll find out shortly. I can see Hamble's runway. Gentlemen, make sure you're well strapped in, and General, please keep an eye on Taxi for me." She then called up, "Pimpernel Three, Pimpernel Three. Thanks for the escort home."

"Lost Child, Pimpernel Three replying. Received and understood. God speed!" the Spitfire pilot replied before both escort planes waggled their wings, banked sharply, and were gone.

"Bye, little friends," Doris said in parting before settling in for what could be a very dicey landing. "Everyone ready?" she shouted, loud enough not to need the intercom. Both Duke and Ceiwen shouted their readiness back to her.

Doris lined up the Anson and steadied her breathing as much as she could to begin her final descent, trying to ignore the fire and medical wagons waiting by the runway. "Hopefully, I won't be needing you today, boys," she muttered right before the wheels hit the runway. Though slightly more bumpy than she'd have liked, the undercarriage held. Braking somewhat gingerly, even though the end of the runway and its notorious ditch were rapidly approaching, Doris was still able to turn in time and, letting out a breath she hadn't known she'd been holding, taxied up to the flight line hut before braking to a stop. Outside, one of the ground crew hurried to place chocks under the wheels.

As Doris went through her post-flight checks, Duke threw off his harness and planted a huge kiss on top of Doris's head. "Brilliant flying! I'm going to ask for you to be transferred to my staff!"

Flopping back against her seat, Doris looked up at the beaming man. "No thanks, you lead too boring a life for my liking."

After a few seconds, they both burst into laughter born from the relief of a disaster avoided. Ceiwen joined them, laughing as well before also kissing Doris.

"Taxi! He's all right?" Doris demanded when she got her breath back.

Ceiwen nodded. "Believe it or not, he's fast asleep."

The celebratory mood was broken as the Anson's

door was jerked open. Jane stuck her head through the opening. "Anyone hurt?"

"Jane!" Doris shouted in delight, and with little ceremony, pushed past Duke and Ceiwen and leapt through the door, enveloping her friend in a fierce bear hug.

"I've missed you too, you crazy Yank," Jane replied, returning the hug with interest. "But what have you done to my nice shiny new plane!"

The touching moment was interrupted by a squeal of brakes as Ceiwen's new escort made an appearance and tumbled out of their lorry.

Duke jumped past her. "Leave this lot to me," he told the pair.

"Don't forget Taxi," Ceiwen said, appearing in the doorway, the cat's box in his arms.

Doris held out her arms to accept the box, placing it carefully at her feet, as Jane asked, "Taxi?"

Ceiwen stepped out of the aircraft and, patting Doris on the shoulder as he passed, went over to join Duke and the escort now standing to attention.

Opening the top of the box, Doris lifted out and introduced Jane to her cat. "This is Taxi, Isn't he sweet?"

Jane never had the chance to reply as, no sooner had Doris made the introductions than there was a grinding of metal and the Anson's battle-damaged undercarriage collapsed, bringing the battered plane crashing to the ground.

As Jane looked upon the wreck of her once pristine aircraft, her mouth open, Penny skidded to a halt. "Doris? What the…?"

Taxi hanging limply in her arms, Doris turned to survey the wonderful plane which had brought them safely through so much. Taking a few steps forward, she reached out to stroke the now bent fuselage. "Good girl."

****

"I'm sorry, Duke," Jane said, "I wasn't thinking. If I'd thought before phoning Betty, perhaps we wouldn't have been attacked."

"This is really good tea!" Duke announced.

After the poor Anson had been unloaded, everyone, except the escort who were waiting outside, had congregated in the ops hut to enjoy a welcome cuppa.

Looking up from where he was sat, Duke looked relaxed and calm as anything "Perhaps it wasn't the smartest thing you've ever done, but I think it forced the Germans' hand. I've just finished talking to the military police unit who picked up those two German airmen. Well, when they were threatened with being shot as spies, they couldn't stop talking. I won't bore you with every detail, but suffice to say, they've been after Ceiwen for a while, and when they intercepted your call, they scrambled to put together that mission."

Doris thought for a second. "Looking back on it, I suppose it did have a hint of desperation about it."

"It nearly worked, though," Duke pointed out.

"Nearly wasn't good enough for them," Doris said.

Duke raised his cup and both Doris and a listening-in Ceiwen raised their teacups as he proposed a toast: "To 'not nearly'!"

Jane came out of her office to join them, with Penny close behind. "Major, your escort say they're ready to go."

With an exaggerated groan, Duke heaved himself out of his seat. "If we must, we must," he answered. "General, are you ready?" he asked.

Ceiwen faced Doris. "Third Officer Johnson..." He held out his hand. "I think I can say, unequivocally, that you saved our lives today. I won't forget you."

Playing her role one last time, Doris stood to proper military attention for the first time in her life and shook the man's hand. "General, it's been my pleasure. All the best of luck, sir."

Ceiwen nodded, then, quick as you like, he came up and whispered into Doris's ear, "If you don't tell anyone about the headless drummer boy, I won't either." With Doris slightly flummoxed by this, he nodded at both Jane and Penny, opened the door, and left the hut. Doris shook her head to clear it of an unwanted memory.

"I'd better go keep an eye on him," Duke said with a smile.

"What's going to happen to...Rob, now that this is over?" she hastily asked Duke, ignoring the curious glances from her friends.

He briefly looked over at where Jane and Penny were openly watching the two. "I can't explain here but, and I know you believe me, he'll be well rewarded. Mind you, how I'm going to explain some of his expenses is beyond me! Now, you're sure I can't tempt you to come and work for me?"

Doris shook the man's hand. "Sorry, no chance. This place would fall apart without me."

Laughing, Duke said goodbye to Jane and Penny, and he too left the hut.

With everything finally over, Doris allowed her body to relax, safe once more amongst her best friends. That was when Jane looked over and told her, "Oh, I almost forgot, Betty wants a word with you, something about the case of *The Moving Finger*."

The color drained from Doris's face and she buried her face in her hands. "I'm in so much trouble."

Afterword

The idea for this book came after I'd watched one of my Lady Wife's favorite WW2 movies, *I Was Monty's Double*. You may not have heard of this one, as it's a little obscure. Nevertheless, it's an excellent account of the smokescreen the British Military created to convince the Germans that General Montgomery was anywhere but where he could be involved in preparations for the invasion. I won't spoil the movie for you, though I will give you a wee snippet—the actor playing General Montgomery was the same man who pretended to be him during the real deception. If you think he's not the greatest actor, don't let that put you off, please!

To support the proposed invasion of northern France, the Allies also decided to implement a comprehensive deception campaign, under the cover name of Bodyguard. Bodyguard's aim was to deceive Hitler and his senior military commanders on the location and timing of Allied actions. Bodyguard became the overall cover name for a series of deception operations designed to deliberately deceive the German Armed Forces High Command as to the real intentions and objectives of Allied operations throughout 1944. Under Bodyguard, Operation Fortitude was specifically designed to support the invasion of Normandy.

Fortitude consisted of two main operations. Fortitude-North was designed to convince the Germans that the Allied invasion in 1944 would come through Norway and Sweden. Fortitude-South was developed to convince the Germans that the main invasion of France would be the Pas de Calais while other potential invasion sites, including Normandy, were merely diversions.

For Fortitude-North to be successful, the impression had to be given that a real invasion force, of the size of a typical Allied Army, existed. It needed to be created, there being no 'real' forces available. Due to Scotland's location, German aerial reconnaissance of the Norway invasion force was very difficult. Therefore, the Allies placed heavy reliance upon the German intercept operations (known as the Y-service) and Special Means spies to receive and deliver the message. Special Means specifically meant the use of German spies who were caught early in the war and convinced to work as double agents, their cooperation usually obtained by threatening to shoot them as spies. If they didn't cooperate, their role and identity was taken over by British intelligence.

General Ceiwen is based upon a Colonel R. M. Macleod, who really was based at Edinburgh Castle, which was also the headquarters for the fictitious Fourth Army. The colonel had previously served as a military attaché in Berlin and so was well known to the Germans, hence why I chose to base my fictitious officer on this gentleman. Macleod's duties included assembling numerous officers and radio operators in order to give the impression of the volume of signal and radio traffic expected from an army. Scripted communications were used to create a believable picture for the German Abwehr (counter-intelligence service). Wireless operators and officers were kept in the same units so that if their voices were heard, they would become associated with that unit. All of which became part of my story.

These transmissions began on the 22nd March 1944, and by 6th April, the network was fully active. The German receiving and direction-finding equipment was highly efficient and it was only a matter of time until the headquarters of the Fourth Army would be identified. Coincidence or not, Edinburgh Castle was strafed by a German fighter only three days after transmitting was begun. In this, the Fourth Army's only combat encounter, no one was hurt.

To further reinforce the impression of a real army being built up, real shipping was brought into the Firth of Forth. Though the Royal Air Force kept a Combat Air Patrol above these ships, every now and then, they would allow a German reconnaissance flight to photograph the shipping. There was indeed a scenario where a call went out for Norwegian speakers, closely followed by a retraction telling off the unit which sent it out, for its indiscretion, much in the way I have used in the story. Sorry, it was too good to leave out, once I found out about it.

Something which was an important part of Fortitude North but which I could not include, was the diplomatic pressure both real and imaginary which was put upon Sweden (which had managed to remain essentially neutral). A German spy in Stockholm was fed social gossip and newspaper stories, all tied up with hinting that Sweden could become part of the allied war effort, either willingly or not. The Swedish stock market was even manipulated to raise the price of Norwegian securities to make investors suspect an imminent invasion.

Fortitude-North was a complete success, as it tied up 27 German divisions for the defense of both Norway and Denmark. All this was accomplished by 28 officers and 334 men of other ranks, simulating an army of 100,000 men. It doesn't take much imagination to know what damage those 27 divisions could have inflicted upon the lightly armed assault troops on and just after D-Day.

Countless lives were saved by this skillfully executed plan.

As for the German B17. Too far-fetched, you may believe. Well, you'd be wrong. The Germans did repair B17s forced down in occupied Europe. They also flew B24 Liberators, British Spitfires, and many other types. A special unit, KG300, was formed by the Germans for the purpose of using these aircraft. There are documented cases of lone B17s trying to join up with returning formations, only to be turned away as they were wearing the wrong insignia. I took this one step further. Incidentally, the Allies did the same with German planes.

The above is only an introduction to what lengths the Allies went to in order to minimize the casualties on D-Day. It doesn't bear thinking what the beaches could have been like without these efforts, most of which were unknown to the public both at the time and for years to follow.

Now, what about the ghost of the headless drummer boy? Surely I've made that up! Sorry to disappoint you. He was first seen (and heard) in 1650 before Oliver Cromwell's attack on the castle, and subsequent sightings are said to have indicated the castle was in danger.

I would dearly love to have included elements of colluding Nazi spies, but they would not have been local and therefore too unbelievable. That being said, who knows what the future holds for the Ladies of the Air Transport Auxiliary Mystery Club!

A word about the author…

Mick is a hopeless romantic who was born in England and spent fifteen years roaming around the world in the pay of the late HM Queen Elisabeth II in the Royal Air Force, before putting down roots and realising how much he missed the travel. This, he's replaced somewhat with his writing, including reviewing books and supporting fellow saga and romance authors in promoting their novels.

He's the proud keeper of two Romanian Were-Cats bent on world domination, is mad on the music of the Beach Boys, and enjoys the theatre and humouring his Manchester United-supporting wife. (Please don't mention this last to her!)

Thank you for purchasing
this publication of The Wild Rose Press, Inc.

For questions or more information
contact us at
info@thewildrosepress.com.

The Wild Rose Press, Inc.
www.thewildrosepress.com

Milton Keynes UK
Ingram Content Group UK Ltd.
UKHW020953160924
448404UK00013B/645

9 781509 258628